MORALLY CORRUPT

VERONICA LANCET

For every girl who has "lightly" stalked their crush.
I hope he calls you "my wife" now ;)

CONTENT WARNINGS

Attempted rape
blood & gore
bullying
cannibalism
CSA (not detailed, recounted)
death
Desecration of a corpse
drug addiction (main character)
Exhibitionism
guns
graphic violence
graphic sexual situations
Kidnapping
murder
prostitution
suicide
Sex clubs
rape
serious injury
Sociopathy
torture

1

BIANCA

"You can start."

I nod to the prostitute as I take a seat. The chair is parallel to the bed, and this angle allows for perfect visibility. Raising my gun just a little so they can see I'm not kidding, I lean back and make myself comfortable.

The woman drops to her knees, her hands trembling as they struggle with the fastening of the man's pants. I roll my eyes at her obvious anxiousness and spare a glance at my watch. Vlad will not like this.

"Faster!" I snap, thinking I'd already wasted enough time with the threats. If she keeps this up, I'll have a furious Vlad on my hands, and all for nothing.

"Y-y-yes," she stammers and finally takes his dick out. Surprisingly, he's hard. Then again, given his age, he probably took something to help him out. I motion for her to continue.

She lowers her head, and opening her mouth, she takes him in. I narrow my eyes, trying to look at her technique. I'm busy observing when the door bursts open.

"B, what's taking so long?" Vlad groans as he enters the room, locking the door behind him. He takes one look at the bed, then his eyes find me before shaking his head.

"He was having a tête-à-tête with a prostitute," I shrug, pointing toward the mid-coitus couple.

"So?" He arches an eyebrow, hand on dagger as he playfully rotates it in the air. "What are you waiting for?" he asks, exasperated. I knew I should have been more succinct in my threats to get the action going faster. Vlad is not the patient type.

"Don't you see?" I stand up, coming around the bed and pointing toward the huddled figures. "This is my opportunity to learn from a professional. Miss . . ." I look at her.

"Abigail," she breathes out, her lip trembling.

"Thank you. Miss Abigail here was just about to demonstrate the act of fellatio."

We'd been ordered to assassinate the CEO of an oil company — Mr. Horace Bentham. I don't know if it had been luck or fate, but I'd got to him just as he was about to dip his wick in Miss Abigail. Now, I am not one to miss an opportunity when it's staring me in the face. Mr. Bentham would be dead, but only after I've assuaged my curiosity.

"A blowjob, you mean." Vlad rolls his eyes at me, swinging his knife around and making sure the guests understand the unspoken threat.

"Same thing." I wave my hand dismissively, and I take my seat once more. "Come, watch! You might learn a thing or two, as well."

"I'm fine," he replies drily. "You have ten minutes. No more. We need to hand in the proof that he's dead." He takes two steps and positions himself next to the windowsill.

I frown.

"Ten minutes? Is that how long sex lasts? I thought it was longer." I try to think back to all the magazines I'd read, but I realize none of them gave an explicit duration.

"B," he groans, bringing his hand up to massage his temples. "I don't know how long sex lasts, but we are on a mission. He should have been dead half an hour ago. You're taking a risk."

"Pretty please?" I bat my lashes at him, watching mild annoyance turn to defeat in one . . . two . . . Yes!

"Fine. But you owe me."

"Of course!" I beam. I know the rules. It's always quid pro quo with Vlad. We've been partners for three years now, and while our at his face and I can see he's invested in this. Great! Another one of his science experiments.

I settle back in my chair, and we both watch as Abigail keeps on fucking herself on a dead man's cock. Time goes by, and nothing happens.

"Let's finish this and go." I get up to leave, already miffed with Vlad.

He doesn't seem to hear me, as he tilts his head to the right, his eyes focused on Abigail.

"Vlad!" I snap my fingers in front of him, but he just swipes my hand aside. He raises his eyes to look at me, a bored expression on his face.

"Fucking hell!" I curse, snatching my gun from his hand. "One thing I asked. Just one. And you had to ruin it."

"But how often do you get to see someone fuck a corpse?" He asks me, looking so innocent. I narrow my eyes at him.

"You're sick," I mutter under my breath. While I am not quite normal myself, I'm certainly nowhere near Vlad's level of fucked up. That is a competition I will always lose, as much as it pains me to admit.

Grabbing onto his jacket, I pull him to his feet, ready to end this. He seems to have other ideas, though, as he wraps his hand around my arm, pushing me out of the way.

My mouth drops open, my eyes wide as I look at him incredulously. Did he just push me? It's instinctive as my fist shoots out, nabbing his cheek. Head to the side, he checks his jaw for any damage, before slowly turning toward me, his eyes glinting with excitement.

"You want it rough, little goddess?" he says a second before he delivers an uppercut straight to my gut. I don't even get to wince in pain as I get ready to parry his next hit, all the while landing others of my own.

Fists flying, we're messing around at this point.

Then it all stops.

Vlad's got one hand wrapped around my throat, and with the other, he throws his dagger so it lodges straight in between

Abigail's eyes as she was about to make her escape. Releasing me, he goes to check on both bodies.

I massage my neck, stretching a little.

"This is on you," I add when he turns his face at the blood pooling on the carpet. "We could have done it so much cleaner." I shake my head.

"If it wasn't for your brilliant idea to watch them fuck, maybe we wouldn't be here, would we?"

"Hey!" I exclaim, outraged.

"Let's call it a draw," he sighs. "You wanted to learn about sex and I . . . well, I wanted to learn about sex after death. I'd say we both got what we wanted."

"No, I did not." I cross my arms, pissed at how everything had turned out. "You ruined a perfectly good chance! How am I supposed to get good at it now?" The more I think about this failed attempt, the angrier I get. Next time, I'm making sure Vlad is as far away as possible from me when I try anything similar.

"I don't know, practice? Should be like fighting. Practice makes best," he says with a shrug, setting about decapitating Bentham. We need to show proof that the man is dead.

"But I can't do that." I frown. He's right that practice makes best, but it wouldn't work for me in this scenario. "There's only one man I want, and I need to be the best at sex so I can blow his mind. Then he'll fall madly in love with me, and we'll live happily ever after." My soliloquy finished; I breathe out a dreamy smile.

"I don't know, B. Figure something out. Seduce him in disguise if you must, but stop compromising our missions. This isn't the first time you've been absentminded because of that wimp."

For once, I overlook his insult as I latch onto his previous words. Seduce him in disguise? Get him to fuck me? My mind is slowly working, putting together all the variables, when suddenly a big smile stretches across my face.

"You're a genius!" I jump up and down in excitement. I dash to his side and give him a big kiss on the cheek. "That's exactly what I'll do!" Why didn't I think of this before? It's simply the best solution.

***

"This is you trying to make it up to me, isn't it?" I arch an eyebrow at Vlad as he's pretending to check out the wigs.

"Who? Me?" He feigns innocence, passing me a white-haired one. I put it on and then look in the mirror.

"It makes me look old," I scowl, turning my attention to the other colors.

"Might be in your favor. He might not be into the whole snatching the cradle thing you got going on."

"I'm not that young." I say, even though, objectively, I might be too young for him. But he doesn't need to know my age. I put the wig back and browse the other colors. I can't seem to decide what I want to go for.

Vlad passes me another one, and I'm about to refuse, given his obviously questionable tastes, when I notice the color.

Pink.

I snatch it out of his hands, putting it on immediately. A short, straight bob cut, the wig has a pink, almost magenta hue to it. The bangs end just above my eyebrows. As I study all the angles, I get another idea.

"I should get some contacts too." If my goal is to eventually blow Theo's mind as myself, then I need to make myself as unrecognizable as possible.

Vlad grunts, already preoccupied with something else. I snicker at him and go to the checkout. It takes us a few hours of navigating different shops before my disguise is finally coming together.

"Don't you have someone else you can bring along? Like a girlfriend?" I hear Vlad mutter under his breath as I'm trying on a dress in the changing room.

"You know I don't." I pull aside the curtain to address him. "The last girlfriend I had decided to betray me after I pulled on her ponytails." Thinking of that incident has me fuming. I'd just wanted her hair tie — it was a pleasant color.

"And how long ago was that?" Vlad asks sarcastically, and I punch him.

"Shut it!" Yeah, it was during kindergarten, so what? I've had plenty of opportunities to make girlfriends, but it's too much effort. Why should I waste my time with another human being when there's only one person deserving of my full attention?

"That looks good," he suddenly mentions when he gets a better look at what I'm wearing. I'd chosen an incredibly short, skin-tight purple dress. "I've seen hookers wear that," he continues, and my face falls.

"Gee, thanks," I reply drily. Now I see why he's perpetually single — he simply has a way with compliments.

"Why? That's what you want, no? Hookers dress to attract." He shrugs.

I pause, digesting his words. He's not wrong. I may need to pull out the big guns, and by that I mean put all my assets on display.

"Fine. I'll take this." I pull the curtain deep in thought. I need to make this the perfect outfit to attract Theo's attention. Vlad is right in that regard. I need to make Theo salivate at the sight of me.

We spend the rest of the day going from shop to shop, buying more things until my outfit is done.

The last stop is at a beauty salon. Vlad checks out though, saying his duty is done. Seeing how restless he's become; I take pity on him and release him from best friend duty. I'm almost offended at his sigh of relief when he leaves, but then I remember he's not used to people, anyway. I must have worn him down.

Good!

The lady at the beauty salon is nice enough to explain what she's doing, and I pay careful attention so I can emulate the steps. I'd told her I wanted to become someone unrecognizable, and she'd complied.

Heavy contouring, highlight, bold eyeshadow and red lipstick. All that paired with the pink wig and the new green contacts will ensure I'm unrecognizable.

Now there's only one thing left to do — create the circumstances of our meetings.

For the past three years, I've been keeping tabs on him, venturing out to see him now and then — the reality is just much sweeter than pictures. I know exactly what he's been up to, and who he's been meeting. And I'd made sure there were no women. I mean, not that hard in the first place, since he doesn't seem to have a particular interest in dating.

Which brings me to my current dilemma. I've put in so much effort to tempt him, but I still need an opportunity to work my charm on him.

I dial my go-to P.I. and I tell him to pay careful attention to where Theo goes.

One way or another, he's mine.

2
BIANCA

You could say I'm not the most patient person. Especially when it concerns Theo. That I've lasted so long is a testament to my sheer willpower and a realization that our meet-cute must be perfect.

It's been a few weeks now that I've been working on an approach to get to Theo with my new disguise. For a while, I'd thought it was hopeless. Maybe his lack of interest in dating coupled with my interference by eliminating all women from his proximity had made it impossible to approach him.

But then my P.I got back to me with an update. Theo's new position in the mayor's office meant he was spending a lot of time socializing with his peers at an exclusive club in the city — The Palace.

I'd done my research. The Palace wasn't just any club. It catered to the elite, and it provided both entertainment and . . . relief of a certain type. When I heard that, I was sure this was my moment.

It had taken me quite some time to infiltrate The Palace by becoming a server. You'd think it would be easy enough to score such a job, but I'd had to be vetted by three people (two of which I'd bribed) before I was officially hired. Like an excellent employee, I'd showed up every night for my shift, hoping to catch sight of Theo.

One week passed, then two weeks, and all I was getting was less sleep and more untoward remarks. The number of people I'd had to refrain from killing had been too high for my liking.

And so I find myself, once again, prancing around with a fake smile on my face, coked up from sniffing that damned powder, and ready to murder someone.

"Darlin' do me a favor and wipe this table down, will you?" an old man calls out to me. I have to grit my teeth at the appellation. I'm no one's darling, and I'd love to show Mr. Geezer at table two just how much I appreciate being cat-called. I've already suffered one attempted sexual assault for one night, and the only reason that man isn't dead is because I had to hurry inside and clock in. This job is too strict on working times.

I swallow a retort and start cleaning his table, trying to ignore the way he's leering at me, his gaze too focused on my cleavage.

Fucking hell!

I'm mentally debating whether or not I should shoot him when a group of people make their way inside and toward the VIP wing. I turn my head to study the newcomers and that's when I see him.

Theo.

My Theo.

He's here.

I strengthen my spine, my eyes following his movements as he heads toward the back of the club. Absentmindedly, I drop the cleaning rag on the floor, my feet leading me toward one thing — him.

I quickly check with the girls working the VIP wing, and I resort to buying one of them out of her shift. Nevertheless, it's not long before I'm in the same space as him . . . so close I can practically smell him.

I close my eyes and inhale, a smile spreading on my lips. This is it. My chance.

Theo and his entourage settle down at one table and drinks are served. They seem to be deep in conversation, and as I see other girls walking around suggestively, I prepare myself.

This is it! I must make an impression.

So many times I've imagined this moment, and now that it's here, I don't even know what to do first.

Lap dance?

No, too common. There are already a few girls around doing that.

No, I have to make my entrance with a bang.

Determined to give my best, I school my features into a seductive smile, and I start walking.

Boobs out — check.

Hips swaying — check.

Biting my lips seductively — check.

And now .. eye contact — check.

His eyes flicker over my body and he doesn't look away. I advance slowly, and in the reddish light of the club, Theo looks even more attractive.

When I'm almost next to him, I notice his dilated pupils, the way his mouth is slightly agape.

How I wish I could kiss that mouth.

The way his eyes are roving over my body tells me he likes what he sees. I decide to be brazen, and as I hold his gaze, I slowly lower myself to my knees, placing one cheek on his thigh.

Some men are watching intently, while others are busy with their own entertainment.

But I tune it all out. I focus on the handsome man in front of me and I relish the proximity. This is the first time I've touched him in the flesh and I find my senses are getting numb, almost as if his mere touch is getting me drunk.

A shiver goes down my spine as I trace the contours of his muscles. Surprisingly, Theo is seriously packing. You would have never expected that behind his boring gray suits there would be a wall of muscle.

"You know the rules, handsome?" I turn to him, licking my lips suggestively. He's holding himself still, watching me intently.

"Look, but don't touch?" His voice is just like him — all male. There is a roughness to it that just serves to turn me on even more.

"This one, you can touch." I say, mesmerized by him. I keep

touching him, my hand creeping higher and higher. I watch as his Adam's apple bobs up and down in anticipation.

"And what else?" He breathes out, almost as if he'd run a marathon. This might be my first attempt at seduction, but I can tell that I have him.

His hand comes up, his palm settling on my cheek. I lean into him, savoring the feel of his skin next to mine. His thumb slowly caresses my lips, smearing some red lipstick. I don't even think as I open my mouth and suck, my tongue gliding over his digit.

"You can do whatever you want to me." He has no idea just how much I mean those words.

My hands continue to roam over his thighs, going higher and reaching the growing bulge in his pants — the proof that he does, indeed, want me.

A little nervous, but mostly intoxicated by desire, I work on the zipper of his trousers. It might seem I'm going a little too slow, but I'm trying extremely hard to mask the sweat accumulating in my palms, and the fact that I have no idea what I'm doing.

I keep eye contact as I lower the fly and take him in hand. The moment I wrap my fingers around his cock, I let out a loud moan.

God, he's certainly not disappointing!

His clothes are definitely a camouflage for the man underneath, his generous size exciting and scaring me at the same time.

It might hurt.

I push that thought aside and I focus on the present.

Moving my hand up and down, I become more familiar with him. The warm flesh is beckoning, and I don't even think as I dip my head low and take him in my mouth. I lick the entire length before focusing on the head, sucking him, my tongue playing with the underside — just as I'd seen the hooker do. Going by his reaction, I'm doing it well enough.

His head is thrown back, his mouth slightly parted, and his hooded eyes are watching me. Spurred by his expression, I take more of him inside, struggling to accommodate his size. I gag when the head hits the back of my throat, but he seems to enjoy this, so I will myself to relax.

Theo seems lost to sensation, his hands resting on top of

my head and controlling my movements. The moment I slow down my ministrations, he takes over, lowering me over his length and fucking my mouth repeatedly. My eyes tear up as he holds me down, my lips at the base of his cock. His chest rumbles with a groan, and hot liquid shoots down my throat. I'm so fucking turned on right now, and the taste of him lingering on my tongue is making me grow even wetter. I'm two seconds away from grinding on his leg, so I lean back, still keeping my eyes on him. Now, I need to make a memorable exit.

Slowly, I lick my lips clean and give him a wink before standing up to leave.

His voice seems pained as he asks.

"Your name. What's your name?" My back is to him, so he doesn't see the slow tug of my lips, satisfaction settling deep into my core.

"Pink," I drawl, "my name is Pink." I don't look back as I head directly to the staff area.

My heart is beating loudly in my chest, my panties soaked. I did it. I fucking did it. And oh, was it everything I had thought it would be and more?

I prop myself against the lockers, trying to catch my breath, my mind slowly replaying every moment — every touch and every sound. God . . . My hand sneaks under the waistband of my panties, my fingers on my clit, seeking that relief. I turn my head to the side, stifling a moan as I bite into my shoulder. I hold on to the memory of his cock in my mouth, his cum on my tongue — a few strokes and I come, the orgasm so intense, I stagger off my feet.

Damn!

"Pink!" Someone yells from the door and reality crashes down on me, dissipating my previous high.

"Yes?" I respond, glad to see my voice sounds unaffected.

"The manager wants to see you." One girl peeks her head inside, looking at me with a scowl.

I nod and follow her.

I've had limited interactions with the manager, and of all the times he decides to call on me, he does it now? He should be grateful I don't have a gun attached to my thigh, or he'd . . .

"Pink." He stands up from his seat, his expression contrite. I almost roll my eyes, but I still need the job — especially now. He narrows his eyes at me before shaking his head.

"I've been made aware of what you just did," he starts, as if he can't watch the camera feed from behind his desk. There's CCTV all throughout the club. He probably jacks off to it, the pervert.

"Oh?" I raise my eyebrows, pretending to be oblivious to what he's referring to.

"You can't just perform sexual acts in the club. That's why we provide special rooms." He scowls at me.

"I'm so sorry," I say immediately, and I school my features to look guilty — and apologetic.

He looks me up and down for a second. I hope he won't get any ideas. I really don't want to kill him and lose my job.

"This is your first warning. Don't do it again. Next time, make them book a room." He waves his hand dismissively and I know I got off easy. Those rooms cost a fortune, so it's no wonder he doesn't want to lose potential clients.

I nod and quietly make my way out, heading back to the VIP wing and hoping Theo might still be there.

To my great disappointment, he's not.

Damn it!

***

Trudging my way to the club, I have to make a conscious effort to keep my eyes open. After last night, I'd barely slept a wink. Still, I have to be here on the off chance that Theo shows up. A quick glance at my watch and I realize I'm late.

Shit!

I increase my pace, hurrying to clock in before the absence is put on my record. Almost dashing through the club hallways, I greet the night manager and go to the lockers to change. As soon as I have my outfit on, I decide to head straight to the VIP lounge. If he's at the club, then he's most likely to be there.

The club is sectioned in two parts, one room for the regular people and another for the ones requiring more privacy. There is a dark tunnel connecting both of them, and only select people are allowed in — those with access to the entire club. Before I switch places with another girl working the VIP side, I have to be sure Theo is present. One night there and I'd realized that the girls were expected to be propositioned. I don't want to risk injuring anyone if I get pissed — especially someone important.

Being late also means there's less traffic in the tunnel at this time. I pause for a second to catch my breath and to compose myself. I still have to look my best.

I pat my dress down, making sure to emphasize the contour of my breasts. I'd seen the way Theo had looked at my cleavage, so I'd put on an extra-padded bra today. I'm trying to adjust one boob, when suddenly someone pulls on my arm.

I'm thrust against the wall, and my fight instincts kick in.

He didn't!

I feel a fiery breath on skin, skimming the curve of my neck and toward my ear.

"I've been looking for you, Barbie girl." His voice sends a shiver down my back, and I know instinctively who it is.

Theo!

"Is that so?" I ask breathlessly. The moment I confirm his identity, my body does a one-eighty. Goosebumps cover my skin, and the increasing arousal I'm feeling has me crossing my legs to find some relief.

His hand moves up, trailing feather-like touches up my arm before dipping between my breasts. My breath hitches as he stops, and anticipation builds.

"We have unfinished business," he continues, his voice so suave — palpable sin. I don't trust myself anymore, and my hands grip onto his biceps for support.

Oh la la, more muscle.

"Do we?" God, I must sound like an idiot, but it's his fault. How can I be coherent when the object of my desire is within reach — close enough to touch?

"You're such a fucking tease," he rasps, his face moving closer, "you think you can strut into the room, blow me until I see stars and then simply disappear?"

"I thought men enjoyed the chase." His hand is moving down, tantalizingly close to the spot that needs him the most.

"Oh, I do. I spent hours last night imagining all the ways I'd fuck you when I caught you." A whimper escapes my lips, and I feel myself growing wetter by the second. "Tell me, Barbie girl," his lips are hovering right above my flesh, "how do you like to get fucked?" His tongue sneaks out to lick right below my ear. When I feel the warm contact on my neck, I sigh, closing my eyes. My whole body contracts, my fingers digging into his arms. His chuckle brings me down to earth. "One touch of my lips and you came," he says, amused. I'm breathing hard, trying to gather my wits.

"I see you, Barbie girl. You want it rough," his teeth nibble at my earlobe "hard and fast in a body-bruising way. You want me to fuck you like the dirty little girl you are." Theo skims his fingers up my thigh, tracing the material of my panties.

"Please," I moan, overwhelmed by the sensory overload.

"Please what, Barbie girl?"

"Please fuck me." I want to tell him how much I want him, how I might die if I don't feel him inside of me right this second, but words seem to fail me.

"Your wish is my command." I feel his smile against my neck, and in no time, he rips the fishnets off my body, pushing my panties to the side. His hand sneaks between my lips, and I almost die from the sensation.

"So wet," he murmurs, his tone dripping with satisfaction as he grazes over my clit, inserting one digit inside of me, "and so tight."

"Only for you." Only ever for you. He's the first and only man I'd allow to touch me like that.

"Is that so?" He removes his finger and I'm suddenly left bereft. I whimper at the loss, but watch as he brings it to his mouth, licking off my juices.

Fuck! I'm in trouble.

It all happens so fast I can barely register it. In one swoop, he has me backed further into the wall, my legs wrapped around his waist. His hard length comes into contact with my center, and I let out a loud moan.

I need this like I need my next breath, and with shaky fingers I try to unbutton his pants.

"In a hurry, are we?" He breathes against my face. I can only nod, and his hands replace mine, taking his cock out and stroking it along the wet seam of my pussy.

"Fuck!" I cry out, knowing it's just a matter of seconds now.

He fumbles to put on a condom and before I know it, he's pushing against me.

"So fucking tight," he rasps in my ear, and I turn my head to the side, hoping he won't see the tears in my eyes.

It burns!

Shit! I should have expected the pain given his size.

His hands are on my ass, hauling me over his length until he's fully embedded inside of me. He groans low in his throat, his forehead resting on mine. I lock my legs behind his back, holding him to me, hoping the pain will subside.

"You're wrecking me, Barbie girl," he says before his mouth seeks mine. My first kiss, and it's not gentle or tentative. No, it's a full-on parrying of tongues and mashing of mouths. I revel in the sensation of having him inside of me, of finally becoming one.

Because he is mine. He just doesn't know it yet.

He pulls back, withdrawing almost all the way before thrusting in again. His tongue is emulating the movements of his cock and I no longer care about pain, or anything really. It's just us — me and him.

His fingers dig into my ass, his movements gaining momentum. He thrusts into me like a madman, the tip of his cock hitting deep inside and making me gasp.

"Goddamn it." His grunts are huskier and one hand travels up to my neck, grabbing me in a painful hold and twisting my head around so I'm looking straight into his eyes. "You're a witch, Pink. You've bewitched me," he murmurs before kissing me harder. His mouth trails down my neck until he reaches my tits. Tugging my dress down, he pops one nipple into his mouth, suckling.

God!

His teeth scrape my breasts as he licks and laps at me. Just as he moves to the other breast, my hands find their way into his hair, urging him on, drawing him closer.

Theo picks up speed, his cock moving in and out of me before he suddenly stills, his entire body taut with tension.

"Witch," he whispers again as he comes. I wrap my arms around him, holding onto him as he rides his pleasure.

Breathing hard, he raises his head from the crook of my neck, his forehead full of perspiration.

"Shit!" he curses. "You didn't come, did you?" My first intention is to lie and say that I did, so I open my mouth to do that, but the words get stuck into my throat as his fingers deftly work my clit. He's still inside of me, and that fullness coupled with the tingles from my clit has me coming in no time.

"Good," he praises, "good girl."

My lips stretch into a smile as he helps me down, withdrawing from me completely. One glance down has me panicking though, as I spot some blood at the base of the condom.

I immediately get on my knees, quickly removing the rubber and taking his length in my mouth.

"Just like that." His hand comes over my hair, brushing it aside. "Clean that cock real nice, my dirty little girl."

And I do. Because that's all I ever want to be.

His dirty little girl.

3

THEO

"**H**er body had bruises everywhere, and the forensic pathologist suggested she was likely beaten to death."

I nod, my fingers playing absentmindedly with a pencil. This debriefing is taking longer than I expected, considering I know all the information presented.

The mayor had personally sent me to oversee this case within the NYPD, since the murder was that of a high-profile individual. Even knowing what's at stake, my mind simply can't focus on what's being said.

All I can think of is Pink.

The way she'd come for me. The noises she'd made when I'd fucked her tight little pussy. I almost groan out loud at the memory of her clenching around my cock, her fingers pulling at my hair as I'd sucked a nipple in my mouth. The way I know for sure I'm returning for more.

I shift a little, feeling the blood rushing down to my lower region the more I picture her.

Maybe it's all the pent-up lust from years of abstinence.

When I was younger, I balked at the pressure to be with someone like that. All my peers were going to prostitutes, availing themselves of their services. It was expected of me, too, but I could never go through with it. It was too impersonal...too transactional.

But Pink . . . no one's ever gotten my attention like Pink did.

Yes, this might be transactional too, but the attraction between us is palpable, pulsating in the air. Just being in the same room as her makes my senses prickle with awareness. She exudes such raw sexuality that I want to consume her whole. And I will.

"Mr. Hastings is here as a liaison to the mayor's office." The presenter's words wake me from my reverie, and I quickly close my eyes and take a deep breath. "Why don't you introduce yourself, Mr. Hastings?"

I stand up, putting on my best professional expression.

"Thank you," I say before continuing. "I am Theodore Hastings. I graduated from Quantico some years ago, but I've been off field work for a year now." I give some background information about my credentials before I launch into the importance of the case at hand.

"Romina Lastra, nee Agosti, isn't just any murder victim. Unofficially, her father, Rocco Agosti, is part of the Italian mafia. Our sources have identified several illegal businesses related to the Agosti name. Her husband is touted to be a mobster as well, but we haven't had many reports linking Valentino Lastra to any illegal activity." I take a deep breath. "It's all unofficial, of course, but we're talking about faction disputes here. And since right now the most probable culprit is her husband . . ." I let the words hang, and they seem to catch my meaning.

"We need to be careful in our investigation," one man notes, and I nod.

"Yes. The last thing we want now is to involuntarily cause a mob war. Knowing what's at stake, I want everyone to focus on this investigation." I turn to address the forensic team. "I'm not saying this to create any bias, rather I want you all to carefully examine the evidence and make sure you are as thorough as possible."

I go through a few more details before dismissing the meeting. When everyone's left the room, I take out my phone and see a few missed calls from Marcel. Worried it might be something urgent, I dial his number right away.

I'd met Marcel a couple of years ago by chance. We used to live in the same apartment building and I would often see him at the gym. He always kept to himself, and I'd noticed him shutting down every single attempt at flirtation with the opposite sex.

This one time, a girl had intruded too far into his personal space and touched him. I don't know exactly what had happened in that moment, but it was like watching someone flip a switch. Marcel had collapsed on the floor, his eyes wide and unblinking. He'd been unresponsive, so I'd immediately called an ambulance, going with him to the hospital.

He'd had a panic attack.

That day I'd learned of his aversion to touch and that it seemed to be directly connected to some trauma. I'd never pried, however, seeing how private of a person he was. But from our initial conversation at the hospital, where he'd thanked me for my involvement, a comfortable friendship had arisen.

The first year, we'd interacted mostly as neighbors, but slowly he'd become a little more comfortable talking to me.

"Marcel?" I ask when he answers the phone. "Is there something wrong?" Given his taciturn and aloof nature, it's exceedingly rare for him to be the one to initiate a call — let alone more.

"No." He pauses. "I was driving by the station and wanted to see if you're done with your meeting."

"Just finished."

"Great. I'm in the parking lot," he says, and he hangs up. Odd.

After I gather all my materials, I make my way to his car, getting in the passenger's seat.

"Kind of you to drop by," I add drily after I fasten my seat belt.

"I was in the area." He shrugs. Starting the car, he drives toward our apartment building. "How was the meeting? Any updates on the perpetrator?" He asks, quite possibly the most words he's ever said at once.

"Not really. The husband's still the primary suspect, although I want to revisit the evidence," I say almost absentmindedly.

"Do you even have other suspects?"

I turn to look at him. His expression is somber, his eyes on the road.

"You know I can't say that," I add jokingly, a little curious about his sudden interest in the case.

"Right," Marcel says, although his tone doesn't seem too convincing.

"Are you done with finals?" I change the subject. He's in his first year of law school, even though I can't imagine how that works for him, with his anti-social tendencies.

"Yeah." That's all he says, and shaking my head, I drop it. I know I'm not likely to get more from him.

We get to the apartment building and we each go our separate ways.

The moment I open the door, I am assaulted by my little roommates, all crowding at my feet and meowing loudly.

"There, there, did you miss me that much?" Dropping my briefcase, I stoop down to take them into my arms. It's not that easy to juggle four cats in my arms, but our daily routine is already established, so they know not to squirm.

I take them with me to the couch, and I make sure to equally pet each one. One shelter I volunteer at seems to always have too many cats and too little funds. Somehow, I always end up adopting the cats that have nowhere to go. I'd told myself I would stop, especially since they are awfully competitive about my attention and can get quite mean. But last time, when I'd seen an injured white kitten on the verge of being booted, I couldn't find it in me to say no — especially since it reminded me of my childhood cat, Spot.

Taking out some cat food, I lay it on the floor and watch, amused as they fight over who eats first.

Thinking of taking a shower, I head to the bathroom. Seeing the house so empty, so bare, I'm struck by how bleak my life is. What do I even do? I wake up, go to work, then back home and sleep again. It's all a never-ending cycle, a self-imposed routine that I'd drilled into my skull for years now. Maybe my encounter with Pink did more than awaken my dead libido. Maybe I'm finally allowing myself to consider what it would be like to have a warm body to wake up to in the morning, someone to share happiness and concerns.

Not for the first time, I have to wonder what I'm doing with my life. Is it even worth it? This revenge I set out to deliver more than a decade ago?

What will happen when I'm done? The wind will still howl through the hallway and the rooms will still be empty.

I have to admit there is a side of me that yearns for a partnership, for family and for kids . . . but there's also the other side of me that vowed to see justice made. And somehow, they don't seem to be mutually compatible.

I can't ever, in good faith, invite danger into my home, knowingly put my wife and kids at risk.

***

The following day, I head to the mayor's office for a short meeting on Romina's case. I'm ushered inside by his secretary, but I'm surprised to see he is not alone. Martin Ashby, renowned billionaire and the financial force behind the mayor, casually turns to me.

"Hastings, long time no see," he exclaims, rising to his feet to shake my hand. I'd run into Martin quite a few times since working with the mayor. You could say he knows everyone who is anyone in the city, and I get the feeling a lot of them owe him favors.

I don't exactly know how the mayor and Martin met, or the extent of their relationship, but it is unusual to see them together in his office. Such meetings are better relegated for more private quarters.

"Mr. Ashby." I incline my head. He motions me to the settee and the mayor hands me a drink.

"I was just asking Justin to join me on the golf course this weekend. Why don't you come too?" Martin adds, nodding toward the mayor.

"If I am free." I attempt a smile. Golf is boring. Golf with these people would be even more boring.

"Come on, Hastings. It's a miracle I bumped into you. It's been what . . . a year? Yeah, one or two years since I saw you last. Don't tell me you're purposefully avoiding me." His tone is joking, but I can see the underlying threat. Martin enjoys keeping tabs on everyone, and that seems to include me too.

"I'll make an effort," I amend, hoping this answer is better.

"You should drop by my house sometime, meet my daughter. You're single, right?" he continues and I maintain my expression.

"Indeed," I answer, gritting my teeth. I don't like where this is going.

"Marvelous. I think you'd like my daughter. Meek little thing, and very sheltered. She'd make the perfect housewife." He praises her attributes, and I have to stifle the urge to roll my eyes. Has anyone told him we're not in the fifties anymore?

"Yes," he continues, looking me up and down. "I think you two would suit just nice."

"And how old is your daughter?" I try to shift the conversation a little, not wanting him to proclaim me his son-in-law in the next second.

He pauses, narrowing his eyes as if trying to remember. "She just turned nineteen. Ripe for the plucking." He raises an eyebrow at me suggestively and I nearly gag. Nineteen? That's way too young for me — there's almost a decade standing between us.

I force a smile and try to steer the conversation in a different direction. The last thing I want is for Martin to offer me his barely legal daughter. But then, looking at his sleazy ass, I guess it's to be expected he'd try to pimp out his own child. I suddenly feel sorry for the girl and for whatever awaits her.

4

BIANCA

Sucking my cheeks in, I apply more contour, wanting my cheekbones to be more defined — and my age hidden. Pouting, I angle my face in the mirror so I can check if it's blended well. When I'm finally satisfied, I put on red lipstick and it's done. I hurry outside and hail a cab toward The Palace.

Hard to believe it's been almost a year since I first saw Theo at the club. That time in which I met with Theo weekly, sometimes even more often. I've gotten so used to having him close that the thought of it ending terrifies me.

No! Never!

Who am I kidding? I'm becoming greedier. Once a week is no longer enough. Just like my coke addiction got out of control, so did my yearning for him. I want him with a passion so strong, I'd kill anyone who dared interfere. I long for him and even sleep eludes me when he's not around — ok, maybe the coke has something to do with that too. That doesn't change the fact that I need more.

I want to own him.

As soon as I am at the club, I head directly to our usual room, hoping I'll be early enough to compose myself and look the embodiment of cool chic. I punch in the code, and I'm extremely surprised to see him already inside. I take a deep breath and I put on my most seductive smile.

"Theo?" I purr, my voice an octave lower than normal. He half-turns, his eyes eating me up. He casually makes his way toward me, grasping my chin between his thumbs.

"Now, what did we agree on, Barbie girl?" His eyes are fixed on my mouth, and I immediately know what he wants.

In no time, I take off my cardigan to reveal the lace lingerie I'd worn just for him. Then I drop to my knees.

"Sir." I bat my lashes at him, and he regales me with a smirk. There's something different about him today, some type of coiling tension. His thumb swipes across my mouth, smearing the red lipstick.

"You have quite a mouth on you, dirty girl. Why don't you put it to better use?" I tilt my head, looking at him with feigned innocence. It only spurs him further as he unzips himself, thrusting his cock in my mouth. I quickly accommodate him, sucking and lapping at him like I'd learned in the past year.

"Enough," he commands, and I immediately obey. "On the table. Ass in the air."

The lingerie I'd worn comprises a bralette that reaches my midriff and a thong that connects with a garter. Knowing how good my body looks in it, I give him a spectacle as I crawl on all fours toward the table, wiggling my ass in the air the entire time. I prop myself on the table and look back slightly. His eyes are watching me intently, and a shiver goes down my back.

Whenever we are in the same room, there's this sizzling electricity in the air, and even the hair on my arms stands up. But when he looks at me like that . . . like he wants to eat me alive, I feel like combusting from a mix of desire and arousal — and if it goes unfulfilled for much longer, I will.

He comes behind me, securing a blindfold over my eyes. His fingers trail down my spine and toward my butt. When he reaches my thong, he slowly slips it off my legs, leaving me bare for his view.

"Sir?" I ask when nothing happens. Then, suddenly, his mouth is on my pussy. I gasp as I feel his tongue probing deeper, stroking me inside. My entire body shudders, and I grip the edge of the table to hold myself still.

"You like that, don't you?" He breathes against me, the warm air of his breath mixing with my wetness and making me squirm.

"Please, sir," I say, wanting him to put me out of my misery. Two fingers join his mouth, and he works them in and out of me while his mouth is on my clit, sucking and nibbling. I clench around his digits, the orgasm hitting me so hard I see black before my eyes. Flat on the table, I almost pass out from the intensity of the pleasure.

Theo rises, his hands once again on my butt and massaging my cheeks. Taking some wetness from my pussy, he spreads it higher, towards my other hole.

"Tell me, Barbie girl, have you ever been fucked here?" he asks, the tip of his finger pushing in ever so slightly. My breath hitches, and excitement builds anew.

"No," I whisper, barely able to let out a sound.

"What was that my dirty little girl? I didn't hear you." His fingers go even deeper before retreating.

"No, never," I say with more conviction.

"And you'll let me be the first?" he asks, still playing with me. He might not know it, but he has all my firsts.

"Will I be your first too?" I don't know what prompts me to voice this, especially since I know he doesn't like it when I speak back to him in the bedroom. The moment the question is out of my mouth, though, I take a deep breath, awaiting my punishment.

A deep chuckle permeates the air.

"Would you like that, Barbie girl? Would you like to be my first?"

"Yes." I don't even think as I say this. The thought of Theo touching someone else physically pains me.

He doesn't answer. Instead, his palm comes down on my ass, the slap loud, the pain making me flinch.

"You know why I'm doing this, don't you?" he asks just as he slaps my ass again.

"Yes, sir," I meekly respond.

"Good." He hums his approval, continuing to dole out the punishment. Slap after slap, my ass must be red by now. I almost tear up from the pain, but I've had worse, so I steel myself.

Then he stops.

"You are, Barbie girl. You're the first," he says, amused. "Does that please you?"

"Yes. Yes, sir." My tone is entirely too enthusiastic as I reply.

"Enough that you'll let me fuck your ass?" His hand comes down on the battered cheeks again, but this time he's tenderly caressing them.

"Yes."

He leaves my side for a second, before returning and pouring some type of oil on my back. He spreads it around and massages it into my skin. Going lower, he pours even more liquid between my ass cheeks. His finger moves in and out of my hole, lathering the entire area with the lubricant.

I'm only getting used to the unfamiliar sensation when his finger is replaced by the head of his cock. He pushes in slowly, the pressure almost too much. I hold on to the table as he inches his way inside of me. After the initial burn, the pain gives way to a pleasant fullness. I wiggle my butt around, and his cock slips inside even more.

"That's it, Barbie girl. If you could see the way your ass is eating up my cock," he grunts, his breathing irregular.

"More. Please, sir." At my words, Theo grips my hips and pushes all the way inside, the feeling of him there so abundant, I can't help but release a whimper. He's balls-deep in my ass, and the thought of it feels me with giddiness.

And I'm his first.

"Oh," I moan as he retreats, only to surge forward once more.

Mine. Yes, he's mine.

At first, his thrusts are slow and tentative, but once he sees he's not hurting me in any way, he increases his speed.

And oh, God!

The pressure gives way to pleasure, and my entire body is tingling with the nearing of an orgasm.

Just as I'm about to reach that height, he pulls out, flipping me on my back and removing the blindfold. In no time, his cock is back in my ass, his hands on my tits.

"That's it, Barbie girl. I want you to see who's fucking you," he rasps as he increases the speed of his thrusts, his fingers playing with my puckered nipples.

The combined sensations are too much, and my mouth forms a silent 'o' as I keep myself from screaming out.

One hand still on my breast, the other moves lower and he circles my clit at the perfect time. Overwhelmed by the intensity of the orgasm, my eyes roll in the back of my head, my body convulsing and tightening over his cock.

"Fuck yeah," Theo grunts, pulling out and discarding the condom on the floor before taking himself in hand and coming all over my stomach. "Damn it, Pink, a man needs health insurance with you." He gives me a lopsided smile before collapsing next to me on the table.

"Health insurance or a body bag?" I ask before I can think it through.

Great with the morbid humor, B!

Theo doesn't reply for a second before bursting into laughter. "You're one of a kind, Barbie girl."

***

Once back in the cab, I pull at my wig, my frustration increasing by the moment. It always happens when I have to leave Theo, knowing full-well I'd like nothing more than to attach myself to his hip.

Before I head home, I do a quick detour to my spare apartment to shed my disguise and make sure I look presentable. Even though I always do my best to avoid my father, it's best to not raise suspicions — not that he'd think I'm capable of such increased mental capacity, me being a woman and all that.

When I finally reach home, I tiptoe around the grand hall, aiming to head directly to my room. To my great dismay — and annoyance — my father is at home.

"Bianca," he calls my name as he struts in, his face sporting a perpetual scowl.

I square my shoulders and look down.

"Yes?" My voice is soft and submissive.

"Andrew told me you won't be home this weekend. What's that about?" He narrows his eyes at me, and I curse Drew for a moment.

"I have a competition for college." I keep my explanation short, knowing he doesn't really care. He scoffs at my words, not because I'm going to the competition, but because he's still pissed at me for attending college.

"Don't do anything to embarrass me." He stops next to me, and I make myself look meeker.

"Of course, Father."

"Good," he huffs out, leaving.

I take a deep breath, thankful the meeting went well. All my plans are contingent on keeping both my identities separate.

The following day, I leave early, heading straight to Penn Station to take the train. It takes an hour and a half to get to Philadelphia, where I'm supposed to meet with Vlad at the Rittenhouse Hotel. Before leaving the station, though, I go to a restroom and change my clothes, donning my Artemis disguise — leather pants, a leather jacket on top of a black shirt, and a long red wig. I holster two guns in the waistband of the pants and hide two daggers in my boots. With everything in place, I put on a pair of sunglasses and swing the backpack on, exiting the station.

The hotel is a short walk from the station, so I swiftly check in under an assumed name and head to the room. Not surprisingly, Vlad isn't here yet.

I do a quick scan about the room, familiarizing myself with the layout. Like many others, this mission involves some fake seduction on my part, luring the victim to the room, and then doing the killing. Whenever we have such missions, Vlad takes the role of coordinator while I become the bait. I roll my eyes at the designations, although I have to begrudgingly admit that he is the brains behind our missions. Alas, at least I get the kill.

It's proven to be a point of contention many times — who gets the kill? We have many games we play to establish who will be the one to pull the trigger, or in his case, the knife. We're both incredibly competitive people so the games can become ... intense.

My phone rings and I see a text from Vlad. He's running late.

Cursing under my breath, I decide to head to the bar for some refreshments. I have enough time until our victim, a business executive, is set to arrive at the hotel. Before I leave the room, I take out a key and open the small locket I carry around my neck; I sprinkle a little white powder on it. I bring the tip of the key to my nose and inhale, needing my daily dose of energy. Making sure there's no white residue, I leave the room.

I'm in the hallway, waiting for the elevator when I hear some disturbance. I tip my glasses lower on my nose, trying to see who's causing the commotion.

A burly man in his thirties is dragging a girl around by her hair, all the while cursing her out. Her features are drawn in pain, and she seems resigned to whatever he has in store for her.

They move to pass by me, and maybe it's my boredom, but I put my foot forward to trip the man. He sees it just in time, though, and stops.

"What the fuck, bitch?" He shifts toward me, and the girl yelps in pain.

"Didn't your mother teach you how to treat a lady?" I raise an eyebrow at him, my eyes moving over the girl's figure and noting the various bruises.

He throws his head back and laughs. At this point, I grow annoyed, so I just wait for him to dig his grave even more.

"Lady? This?" He smirks arrogantly and shoves the girl to the floor. He turns his attention to me, looking me up and down. "You don't look like a lady to me, either." He drawls and I have to roll my eyes.

"Really?" I ask drily, begging him to make a move.

"Right, you're one of those biker chicks, aren't you? The ones that like it rough." His smile grows as he lifts one hand to touch me. It doesn't get that far. I catch his hand mid-air, and I bend it at an odd angle, hearing a couple bones break.

He yelps in pain, and a smile tugs at my lips at the sound, not unlike the one the girl made.

"What the fuck!" He tries to jab me with the other arm, so I lift my foot and I kick him in the chest — hard. He falls down next to the girl. I'm about to give him some more of his own medicine when the girl covers him with her body.

"Leave him alone!" she cries, and I stop, flabbergasted.

"You . . . You're defending him?" I ask, almost in disbelief.

"He's my husband," she replies, cooing all over the mother-fucker's body.

"Who beats you."

"You don't know anything!" she says accusatorily, helping him to his feet and moving out of reach. He's shooting daggers at me, but I guess he's not much of a tough guy now with a broken wrist.

I let this one slide, since the girl's chosen her own fate. She could have asked, and I would have gladly killed him for her.

I shrug, putting it out of my mind. Her loss.

The elevator doors open, and I go to the ground floor. I plop myself at the bar and order a dirty martini.

One drink shouldn't be too bad, right?

I sip the drink slowly, when I see a group of people come in. All are dressed in formal suits, and given that it's still noon, I'm a little intrigued.

Is my businessman early?

I shift a little so I can have a full view of the new arrivals. It's . . . five people. No, I count six. And one of them is . . . my eyes widen and I quickly push my glasses up my nose.

Theo!

What is he doing here? I lower my head, keeping my focus on my drink. He wouldn't recognize me, I'm certain of it. Vlad's told me that unless you're specifically looking for them, the similarities aren't that glaring. Especially since I'm not wearing any makeup right now, and I have long red hair.

As I try to convince myself that he won't recognize me, I can't help it as I sneak a few glances toward his entourage. They just sat down on the couches in the dining area, still within my field of vision.

Half an hour later, and another martini down, I'm still staring. God, he is handsome! Especially there, in his element, looking all cocky and self-assured. I almost get wet just thinking about those big hands of his on my body, him pounding into me.

A sigh escapes me, and the bartender regards me a little suspiciously.

"Another one," I say, pointing to my drink.

"But . . ." He looks as if he might argue, but shaking his head, he prepares me another martini.

I bring the glass to my lips just as Theo and the men with him stand up, shaking hands. It's at that moment that a loud noise permeates the air.

My semi-dulled senses are suddenly on alert, looking toward the direction of the noise.

Shots.

I hop off the chair, my focus on Theo and him alone. Everyone is panicking, some people falling to the floor. The entrance doors open wide to show at least four heavily armed men coming inside.

Fuck!

I spare a glance at Theo and the position of his body tells me he's about to do something stupid. In a few steps I'm on him, tackling him to the ground.

"Stay still," I hiss, trying to mask my voice. He frowns at me, but nods.

"I see four," he remarks.

"Five," I whisper, noting another one in the back.

I take out the guns from the waistline of my pants, and I hand him one. He should know how to use one, given his background.

He eyes the weapon suspiciously before taking it. The men with him are all on the floor, shriveled up with fear. For a second, I'm curious what the meeting was all about, but seeing that we have more pressing matters at hand, I decide to look into that later.

"You take those, I'll take the ones on the right." I point in two directions, and he nods.

Pointing my gun toward the armed men, I shoot.

Maybe I drank too much.

It takes me twice as many shots to kill the man, mostly because my eyesight is a little fuzzy.

Fuck!

I blink twice, trying to get a hold of myself, when a bullet whizzes past me and embeds itself in the man aiming at me. I turn slightly to see Theo give me a small signal to keep my head in the game. If this weren't such a life and death situation, I would have swooned. My Theo just saved me.

I stifle the smile making its way on my face, and I straighten myself.

"How many more?" I ask, my back hitting his as we scour for the other men.

"I got two," he says.

"Same. So, one?" He shakes his head slightly.

"I think so."

People are still on the ground, shaking, and Theo tries his best to assure them they're in safe hands and that he is police.

We move around, guns pointed, backs glued to each other. Then another man opens fire. I see him just in time to push Theo out of the way and shoot. The bullet finds its way between his eyes and he drops dead.

"Nice," Theo praises.

We scout the area anew, and no other gunmen are present. I realize I need to make myself scarce. I take the stairs a few floors up before taking the elevator to the top where my room is.

To my surprise, Vlad is already there. I frown. When did he arrive?

"Did you enjoy your little break?" he asks drily, flinging a new set of clothes in my direction, together with a blonde wig. "You were reckless. Again." He rolls his eyes at me and comes closer, sniffing me. "And drunk."

"I only had a couple," I add.

"A couple too many when we had a mission." He shakes his head. "You don't have to worry about that, at least. I took care of it."

"What do you mean? Did you steal my kill?" I'm incensed, and my fingers tighten over my gun.

"Didn't you have two of those?" he asks in that bored manner of his. My eyes widen. Shit!

"They're untraceable," I respond, but he's not having it.

"Doesn't matter. Reckless. I should kill that suit of yours one of these days, maybe then your productivity will increase."

"Don't you dare!" I burst out, my voice louder than I'd intended. "Never threaten Theo again, or you'll have an enemy out of me."

"Another one?" He snorts. "Bring it on, *malyshka*. I wonder, between the two of us, who would win? I'll even let you sober up," he adds, amused.

"Sure," I answer sarcastically, taking the clothes and heading to the bathroom.

Thing is, I don't know who would win. Unless he loses his mind, my bet would be on Vlad, not that I'd ever tell him that.

***

Mission accomplished by Vlad, I get to return home early. We'd slipped out of the hotel while the police were investigating the area, barely escaping the scrutiny, since Theo was apparently seeking a red-head with sick aim. I smile to myself, satisfied that even in my disguise, I'd managed to show Theo my abilities, and we'd even fought side by side.

I sigh just thinking about it. How it would feel to be myself with Theo, for us to be a team — us against the world. The sad thing is that I know that will never happen. Knowing his obsession with justice, I'm well-aware he would never accept a vigilante like me. Hell, who am I even kidding, a killer like me?

I'm lost in my thoughts when my father once again calls out to me. What is it with him these days? Usually, we interact every other week.

"Bianca." He purses his lips, looking down at me. I really want to roll my eyes at him, but instead I just stretch my lips in a sweet smile.

"Yes, Father?"

"We're having important guests next Sunday. Be sure to be present and on your best behavior."

"Of course, Father," I agree immediately, although inside I'm fuming at his audacity to order me around. If only I had a knife right now, I'd stab and stab, and for once, I'd enjoy the blood messily spurting around.

"Good. Dress conservatively. These are important men, and they don't . . ." He looks at me as if I disgust him, "like when women are too forward. Make sure you know your place." He turns on his feet and leaves.

If looks could kill, he'd be on the floor right now. They don't like women who are too forward? My lip curls in disdain. Fucking pussies. They're just afraid to be put in their place by a woman.

Oh, how sweet it would be to make them eat their words and show them exactly what a woman can do. I guess I am a hypocrite though, since I'm holding so hard onto my meek girl image just so I can one day appeal to Theo.

5

THEO

"**Y**ou're sure he was the target?" Putting the phone on speaker, I head to the mirror to arrange my tie.

"Yeah. We found detailed plans at their hideout. They'd been following him for a while." My friend from the Philly force recounts how they'd ransacked the place and what they'd found.

"At least you can close the case," I add drily.

"True. Thanks for the effort. If it weren't for you and that woman, more people would have gotten hurt."

I grunt something and hang up.

No one had been able to identify the mysterious woman from the scene of the shooting. Even her gun was untraceable — black market. But she'd been one hell of a markswoman, even drunk. A smile tugs at the corner of my lips as I remember smelling the alcohol on her breath.

The police had concluded that the target had been an electronics company CEO. He'd recently laid off half of his workforce due to some financial difficulties, but the workers were under the impression that it was a case of embezzlement and poor management rather than just a poor turnover. While the shooters are dead now, the investigators found enough evidence to prove that it was indeed a case of syphoning funds and the CEO is now under arrest and pending trial.

I spare a glance at the clock on the wall and sigh in relief. I still have time.

After being hounded by Martin one too many times, I'd finally accepted his lunch invitation. From what I'd gathered from the mayor, Martin likes to host monthly Sunday lunches with different influential men.

The only reason I'm looking forward to this event is because Martin's connections might help me advance my own plans.

As soon as I reach his house, I am greeted by a footman who leads me to the drawing room — very old-fashioned. Then again, Martin's entire persona is the epitome of old money, and his imposing mansion is just what you'd expect of him.

"You are a little early, Mr. Hastings," the footman comments. "The other guests have not yet arrived, and Mr. Ashby is still busy. He has instructed me, however, to show you to the drawing room, where his daughter will keep you company."

I struggle to keep a straight face at his words, mostly because I can recognize this for the ploy it is. Martin's daughter must be what, twenty by now? It's not as if he hasn't tried to orchestrate an introduction before. It seems it's finally worked out for him.

"Thank you," I reply with a tight smile.

As we walk toward the room, a sweet piano melody resounds in the house. The footman shows me to the door and takes his leave.

A little curious, yet mostly apprehensive, I push through the double doors and enter the room. Inundated by light, the room has ceiling-high windows that face the back of the house, the green lawn stretching into a forest in the distance. I follow the rays of the sun as they bathe a white piano that is situated in the middle of the room.

A girl, no, a woman, is seated at the piano, eyes closed, her hands gliding over the keys and emitting the most melodious sound I'd ever heard. I don't think she hears me come in. There's a tranquility to her face, the way it subtly moves to the tune of the song, the small, almost imperceptible movement of her eyes under her closed eyelids.

I stop, and I stare, transfixed.

Her black hair is long, the ends curling inward. It flows down her back almost like an ebony cascade. She's wearing an off-white gown that cups her breasts in a modest fashion before cinching at the waist and flowing downwards. With her pale skin, she almost looks like Snow White.

I shake myself, a little amused by the direction of my thoughts. I'd never thought myself particularly poetic, but the sight of this woman, so immersed in her music as if she's living in her own world, makes me wonder if she's even real. Makes me want to insinuate myself into her world.

I stand there, just watching, for what seems like an eternity. It's only a soft gasp, followed by an "Oh!" that has me alert again. Her eyes snap open and they focus on me. A deep black, I feel myself falling even more.

She might just be the most exquisite woman I've ever seen in my life, her natural beauty so pure and untouched.

"I didn't know there was someone in the room. My apologies." Her voice is just as melodious as the piano music.

"No, I should be the one to apologize. Your music is beautiful." She lowers her eyes slightly, a blush staining her cheeks.

"Thank you," she murmurs, raising up from the piano and coming to stand in front of me.

"You must be one of my father's guests, no?" She gazes up at me, her eyes wide and innocent. She's tiny, her head barely reaching the middle of my chest. Her height, coupled with her slender frame, serves as a friendly reminder that she's almost a decade younger than me — clearly off limits.

"Theodore Hastings," I introduce myself, holding out my hand to her. She gives me a timid smile, hesitantly putting her hand in mine.

"Bianca Ashby."

The contact is brief, but it's enough to mess with my head. She probably has no idea what she does to me, the way my eyes follow the curve of her neck, the swell of her breasts as she invites me to sit down.

I swallow hard, and I try to think of the most disgusting crime scenes I've ever witnessed, hoping the gore will put a damper on my growing erection.

Bianca smiles sweetly at me, but she doesn't attempt to continue the conversation, too shy to even look me directly in the eye.

"Your father told me you're in college?" I try to remember anything Martin might have mentioned about her.

She gives me a soft nod.

"And what are you studying?" God, once again, I feel entirely too old for her.

"Social Studies."

"Really? Why?" I wouldn't have expected that answer from a rich girl. But then, she doesn't look like the typical spoiled little rich girl.

"I want to help people," she says, lowering her gaze as if she's ashamed of her dreams. "I want to make a difference for those less fortunate than me. I know I'm in a position of power and privilege because of my father, so I want to do something to give back to society," she finishes saying this, and I can't help but look at her in awe. She can't be real, can she?

So gorgeous and poised, and she has a big heart too? I swallow hard, the need to touch her is too overwhelming, but I control myself.

"That's a commendable aspiration," I praise, and I'm regaled by one of those beautiful smiles of hers.

Fuck! I'm in trouble.

We don't get to talk much further, as Martin strides in with a few other men. After some brief introductions, we are all ushered to the dining room.

By some luck of fate, Bianca is seated in front of me, so I continue to study her, her beauty something I've never encountered before. And it's not just her looks. There is something about her that pulls me and draws me in.

The conversation flows, and I notice that Bianca continues to smile, but doesn't say much else. Granted, no one seems to address her directly. Even Martin seems to forget the fact that his daughter is sitting at the table, his stories becoming bawdier and teetering on the vulgar side. Bianca maintains her gentle smile, even though I can tell there's a certain tightness to it.

I catch her eye and I give her a reassuring nod, hoping it would comfort her to know she is not forgotten. She blushes and looks down at her plate.

"What about your daughter? She's of age, isn't she?" One of the older men, Anthony Bering, leers at her.

"That she is," Martin smirks.

"Tell me girl, do you have a boyfriend?" He turns his attention wholly on her, and Bianca shifts a little, clearly uncomfortable.

"She's not allowed to," Martin comments, taking a sip of his wine.

"Let her answer. Why isn't she talking?"

Bianca lowers her gaze even more.

"I taught her well, Bering, she knows when to shut up," her father interjects, pride reflected in his gaze.

"She's a meek little thing, isn't she? Perfect for plucking. Probably a virgin too." He can't seem to stop talking, and looking at Martin, he has no intention of putting a stop to this. Bianca's cheeks are burning, and she is trying awfully hard to ignore the comments.

"That's not a way to talk to a lady," I interject, sick of this bawdy talk, especially in Bianca's presence.

"Lady? Tell me, Ashby, how much do you want for her?" Bering chuckles.

"How much are you willing to pay?" Martin raises an eyebrow and I feel my anger rising. Surely, it's just a joke, as much as it is in poor taste.

"I don't know," Bering continues, his eyes roving over Bianca's form. "I don't think she knows how to please a man. Do you, little bird?" He stands up, his fingers on her chin and raising her head up.

Seeing his pudgy little hands on her, I don't even think, I just react. In a matter of seconds, I have him by the collar, my fist plunging into his face. There's outraged gasps around me as Bering falls to the floor.

"I told you that's not a way to treat a lady," I say through gritted teeth. Bering sputters some threatening nonsense, but I don't care.

"Are you okay?" I turn toward Bianca to ask, and she gives me a soft nod, her big, luminous eyes wide as she's looking at me as if I'm her knight in shining armor.

"Let's not get too ahead of ourselves." Martin gets up, coming around to check on Bering. "I'm sure Anthony here only meant well." I frown at his words, and a glance at Bianca tells me I should drop it. I didn't realize her father was so callous to her — his own child. But Martin being Martin . . . It doesn't surprise me. It just makes me feel even worse for her. What is her life even like, having a self-serving narcissist for a father? He clearly doesn't care about her.

"If you'll excuse me," I say rather tersely and take my leave before I do something worse. I already feel bad for leaving Bianca there, an innocent lamb for their slaughter, but I need to realize she's not my concern.

You just met her!

My brain is telling me to drop it, but my heart . . .

Fuck!

I'm almost in the driveway when someone calls out my name. I stop and turn. Bianca is running toward me, her long skirt hampering her movements.

"Mr. Hastings," she says, huffing out a breath as she reaches me.

"Are you okay? What happened?" I immediately ask, my previous thoughts promptly forgotten.

"I wanted to thank you. For what you did in there," she speaks softly, the corner of her mouth raising ever so slightly.

"You don't have to thank me. I did what anyone would have done."

"And yet you were the only one who did." She raises her head to look at me, and we stare at each other for a moment.

I lift my hand and I tug a stray strand of hair behind her ear, marveling at the softness of the texture.

"You shouldn't measure your worth by their words, Bianca."

"Thank you." She gives me another tremulous smile before dashing back toward the house.

I stare at her retreating figure and I know.

I'm in deep trouble.

Fuck!

***

For as long as I've been seeing Pink, we've never exchanged numbers or any personal details. We always scheduled our next meeting in the moment. Which is why I'm here. I will not stand her up, but I need to put a stop to our encounters.

I watch the door of the room open, and Pink struts in, her tits almost spilling out of her top. She drops her jacket to the floor and then she's on me.

"Pink," I say, stopping her hand from reaching for my crotch.

"What?" she pouts at me.

"We need to talk." My tone is different from usual, and I find that I'm not in the mood for any games.

"We can talk . . . and do other things." She smiles, her hand creeping up my thigh.

"No. That's exactly what I want to talk to you about. We can't do this anymore." I grab her hand, trying to put some distance between us.

"What do you mean?" She frowns, tilting her head to the side.

"I'm trying to pursue someone and it wouldn't be right . . ."

"Who?" She cuts me off, her voice holding an edge to it.

I raise an eyebrow at her. We'd agreed on no personal details.

"You don't need to know about it." My voice is impersonal as I say this, but it's better to end things on friendly terms. And going by her reaction, I sense some underlying jealousy.

I stand up and go for the door, but she grabs onto my hand.

"Why? What does she have that I don't?"

"Stop this," I say, disentangling myself from her. There went my attempt at a parting on good terms.

"No. You must tell me. Does she fuck you like I do?" She scowls, and the viciousness of her words leaves me speechless.

Maybe I've given her false hope, but while our chemistry has always been amazing, that's all it's ever been. And I was clear from the beginning.

"Bye, Pink." I turn toward the door once more.

"Tell me!" She raises her voice. "Does she worship your cock like I do?" On her knees, her hands go to my fly. I swat them aside, locking her wrists above her head.

If I must be cruel, then so be it. At least she'll understand that it's over.

"No, but that's just the thing. She's too pure and innocent for that." I push her aside and leave. I can still hear her screams behind me, and I shake my head.

Maybe it is my fault. Maybe I gave her too much attention with our weekly meetings, and she imagined there would be more to our affair. It was just fucking. Savage, out of this world fucking, but it was just fucking.

This woman, though, the one that's been haunting my dreams?

She's my future wife.

6

BIANCA

I'd gone through the worst torment of my life in the last few weeks. So wrecked with worry I'd been that Theo had fallen in love with someone that I could barely sleep. I'd resorted to keeping myself awake by sniffing more and more white powder, all the while checking all surveillance devices I'd placed on his person.

But nothing happened. He never met with anyone.

My paranoia was getting the best of me, and I simply could not focus on anything else but Theo's mystery woman. Who was she? How was she better than me?

Most importantly, how do I kill her?

One late afternoon, I am going through one report that my P.I. had compiled on Theo. So focused I am on what I'm doing that I barely pay any attention to the notice that someone is asking to see me. I absentmindedly think it must be Drew.

Ever since I've become more independent, he'd started stepping back from his duties and had even married last year. Now, he mostly works remotely if I have any assignments for him. He's also the perfect alibi when my father decides to show some interest in what I'm doing.

I head downstairs, and to the drawing room, expecting to see Drew. Instead, I'm more than surprised when it's Theo who is waiting inside the room, his back to the entrance.

46

I carefully step inside, suddenly alert and curious to the reason for his visit.

"Bianca." He turns, offering me half a smile. I reciprocate, putting on my best act.

"Mr. Hastings." I greet him back, still addressing him formally.

"Call me Theo, please," he says, motioning me to the settees.

"Theo." I settle on the couch next to him but still keep an appropriate distance — even if it's killing me. My nostrils are flaring ever so slightly as I take in the scent of him, his nearness, both of which I'd missed so agonizingly much over the last few weeks.

"What brings you here?" I ask, schooling my features to reflect my confusion at his presence when all I want is to jump his bones, tell him to take me right here.

"I wanted to make sure you're ok. After last time . . ." he pauses, "I hope nothing happened after I left." His concern floors me, but then I realize what this is all about.

I'm just a battered woman to him, someone in need of saving. So he's taken it upon himself to make sure I am ok. If I didn't know this was Theo's nature — to save everyone — I might have been hopeful at his inquiry. But as it stands, I can see that I am just another pet project for him.

From reading his file and following his daily life, I'd drawn some conclusions about what makes Theodore Hastings the man he is — his humanity. He simply can't help himself when he sees anyone in trouble, offering to help even if it might be to his disadvantage. He's simply that good, the opposite of me.

But then I realize that this might be to my advantage. Maybe playing the victim is exactly how I can ensnare him.

I look down, and I fidget.

"I'm fine," I say, making sure my voice trembles a little. As expected, he picks up on my distress immediately, and he takes my hands into his. I almost sigh out of pleasure from that contact alone.

"You can tell me if something happened. I don't think I mentioned this last time, but I work with the NYPD." He's clasping my hands, as if to reassure me. I turn my head to the side, a whimper escaping my lips.

"It's nothing I'm not used to," I finally admit, looking at him from the corner of my eyes to gauge his reaction. His eyes widen slightly.

"It's happened before?" he asks as if it's hard for him to hear this, so I just softly nod.

"Goddamn it!" he curses.

"I'm so sorry, Bianca. I'll have a talk with your father." The moment he mentions my father, I vigorously shake my head.

"No. Please. Don't mention it to my father . . ." I keep shaking my head, molding my lips in a thin line to reflect both fear and reluctance.

"But . . ."

"Please, you'll only make it worse." I beg him.

"Then what can I do?"

"You don't have to do anything. It's not your problem."

"I want to," he continues, his expression grim.

"It's fine, really." I stand up, my back to him. Taking a deep breath, I put on the best act of my life.

"You should go, Mr. Hastings."

I don't even turn to see how he might react to this. I just continue what I already started.

"You'll only get me in trouble with my father. He doesn't like me to entertain strange men."

He doesn't speak for a moment, and I have to wonder if I went too far with my rejection.

"I'm sorry you don't feel safe enough to talk to me," he says, his tone defeated.

I don't look back as I leave the room, still debating whether I'm doing the right thing. I'm literally banking on Theo's savior syndrome.

Prove me right, Theo!

The following days turn into weeks and into months. Theo proves to be as relentless as I'd pegged him. Every so often, he would come to check up on me, finding some sort of excuse to question whether I feel unsafe or if anything else happened to me.

He's sweet that way. But even though his visits are quite frequent, it isn't enough anymore. Especially with this mystery woman he'd left Pink for still unknown.

I bite on my pen, trying to figure out what to do next. Sure, I'd appealed to his protective instincts, and he'd taken the bait, coming to see me almost weekly. Still, I need more. I need him to see me in a romantic light.

As I keep on thinking how to turn our relationship around, one of the staff announces that I have a visitor. I go down the stairs a little too fast, deep down hoping it will be Theo.

I'm not disappointed as I see him in the foyer, all dressed up in a suit and flowers in his hand. He looks a little uncertain as his gaze roams around until it settles on me.

"Theo?" I ask, coming to stand on the same level as him.

"B, hi." He gives me a lopsided smile, thrusting the flowers in my direction. "For you."

I frown. "With what occasion?"

"I wanted to talk to you about something, if that's ok," he replies instead, leading me toward the garden.

"What is it?"

During his visits in the last few months, we'd engaged in some small talk and we'd gotten to know each other better. Well, he'd gotten to know Bianca Ashby. I already knew all there was to know about him.

"I know we haven't known each other that long but . . ." He trails off, bringing his hand up to scratch the back of his head.

"I talked to your father, and I asked permission to court you," he blurts out suddenly, and my eyes widen. What? "If you're agreeable, that is," he amends.

"You're asking to date me?" I ask him to clarify, because really, this was the last thing I would have imagined he would say. A spark lights itself within my heart, and I get the urge to smile like a fool — but I know I can't. I need to keep my ruse.

"I know this is rather out of the blue. I've esteemed you for a long time now, but I was trying to give you space to get used to me since I know you've never dated before," he adds, almost apologetic.

"You like me?" I must sound like a broken record, but I need him to spell it out for me so I can throw an inner party and finally plan our future wedding.

"Yes." He nods, and tucking a strand of hair behind my ear, he gives me the most gorgeous smile. I almost swoon, but not quite, since I need to keep up my shy girl image. I lower my head and blush.

"I'd like that very much," I tell him, probably the only honest thing I've ever told him. "You said my father approves?"

"He'd given me permission a few months ago, but it was my prerogative to take it slow. I don't want you to feel pressured in any way to say yes to me . . ."

"No, no," I say, rather quickly. "I'm not pressured. I like you too," I admit, lowering my gaze.

I watch from under my lashes as a wide smile spreads across his face.

"I'm curious," I start, still not looking at him. "Since when have you liked me?"

"Since I first saw you," he answers solemnly and I hold my breath. It can't be, can it?

I wreck my brain for the dates and realize he broke it off with Pink after that disastrous lunch. Is it possible I was the mysterious woman all along? I suddenly want to laugh at the absurdity of it all.

I was jealous of myself.

I school my features, centering my thoughts on the present. I slowly lift my head to gaze at him bashfully.

"I'm glad," I whisper.

Maybe not all is lost.

***

I put in a lot of effort for our first date. After spending hours shopping and watching different tutorials to learn how to comport myself, I feel like I am finally ready.

I'd chosen a black dress that, while modest, still emphasized my curves and drew eyes to my cleavage. Theo needs to be reminded that while I am a sweet, gentle woman, I am still a sexual being and his thoughts should be focused on that. He should yearn for me, but not get me. This is all about building that anticipation that will make him mine in the end.

I slip my feet into a pair of sandals and I head downstairs.

Theo is already waiting for me, looking as sleek as always. Taking advantage of the fact that he has not noticed me yet, I let my gaze roam greedily over his figure. He is so decidedly attractive that I feel myself growing wet just gazing at him. All these months of celibacy haven't done me any good, and I'm one step away from pouncing on him.

He suddenly turns, his eyes roving over my body, the darkening of his irises a good indication that he likes what he sees. By now, I'm quite familiar with Theo's cues, especially his sexual ones. And I know he's one step away from ravishing me, too.

Oh, if only he would . . .

"You look exquisite," he rasps, and I give him a shy smile and a blush.

"Thank you. You too."

He offers me his hand, taking me to a cab and then to our restaurant. I can tell he's put a lot of thought into this. The entire setting is intimate and romantic. We are led to a small alcove, and we both take our seats.

"This is lovely." I add, trying to break the awkward silence. I look up slightly to see Theo staring at me intently. I frown.

"Do I have something on my face?" I ask, afraid I'd smeared some lipstick.

"No." He shakes his head, half-amused, but he doesn't continue.

The server comes around to bring us water and hand us the menu. Theo's eyes narrow as he follows the server's movements. It's only when the server leaves that Theo returns to normal. Odd.

He turns his attention back to me and smiles.

"What are your plans after graduation?" he asks, and I internally smirk. This is what I was waiting for. I'd prepared for this, and I have the perfect answer for anything he might ask.

On the outside, I school my features to convey uncertainty as I start my rehearsed speech.

"I've been thinking about a project . . ." I trail off, "but I don't know if I can do it."

"Of course, you can. What is it?" He reaches across the table to put his hand on top of mine and I soak in the contact, almost moaning at the feel of his skin on mine.

"I want to start a foundation for the less fortunate. I've put together a business plan, but I don't think my father is going to allow me." I lower my gaze as I whisper. "He doesn't like women working." I watch from the corner of my eye as Theo grits his teeth, that statement having the desired effect on him.

"I can talk to him. If you want to do it, you will." He squeezes my hand and I purr in satisfaction.

"Thank you . . . thank you." I return the touch, trying to convey my gratitude.

"None of that. I want you to know I don't hold the same views as your father. While we may know each other in a professional capacity, I don't subscribe to his way of thinking."

"I know. You're a good man," I say and blush. His eyes crinkle at the corners, and he continues.

"What about family? Do you see marriage in your future? Children?" He goes straight to the point, doesn't he? I'd already accounted for that, seeing that Theo is quite traditional in that respect.

"I'd like that. As an only child, I've always wanted a big family. Children . . ." I smile, "I'd like children." The corners of his mouth pull up and I can see he's satisfied with my answer.

The server comes again and places the dishes in front of us. He lingers a little more than necessary in front of me, and I frown. Following the server's line of sight, I see he's a little too entranced by my cleavage. Damn! I wanted to go for classy, not trampy. I'm unsure how to react, since my usual go-to would be to beat the shit out of him, but I can't do that with Theo in front of me.

"Eyes on me, kiddo." Theo suddenly interjects and the waiter flinches. Theo narrows his eyes at his name tag, "Owen," he starts, "I'm not a very forgiving man, especially when it comes to this lady." The threat in his tone was clear and Owen starts shaking his head while mumbling an apology. Theo only raises an eyebrow at him, and Owen immediately scurries back to the staff room.

"You didn't need to be so harsh," I say softly, trying to ease the tension I sense in him.

"You're too naïve, little one. If you knew what he was thinking . . ." He shakes his head. "He needed to know you're off limits."

"I am?" My mouth opens just a fraction, looking at him in wonder.

"You are." He smiles confidently. "When you agreed to date me, you agreed to be mine. And I don't share."

Good. Neither do I.

But I don't voice that. No, I just look away, releasing a soft giggle and pretending to be embarrassed by his words.

We spend the rest of the date discussing various topics, and while I'd prepared an entire list of answers to give him, I find that we do have a lot of things in common, like our stances on politics, religion and social reform.

As the end of the night nears, I instantly get giddy about the thought of him kissing me. The cab drops us at my home and I turn to him, looking expectantly.

"I had a great time," I say, the intensity of his eyes sending a shiver down my back. Yes, this is the moment.

He comes closer, his hand reaching out and caressing my cheek.

"Me too, little one. I'll see you next week." He leans in for the kiss and I close my eyes, my lips ready to meet his.

But they don't.

Because he doesn't kiss my lips.

He barely grazes my forehead.

"Goodnight," he says, and then he's gone.

What? No kiss? Where is my kiss?

I'm left flabbergasted, looking at the spot he's just vacated, and I realize something. Maybe my shy girl pretense is backfiring. At this rate, will he ever touch me?

Shit!

I go straight to my room and I dial Vlad. I know what I have to do; I just need a little something to push him.

"Vlad," I say the moment he picks up, "I need you to hire someone to attack us. I need it to be perfect." I start explaining what I need the attacker to do: scare me enough that I'll need to be consoled. Theo would, of course, save the day, and then he would have to comfort me. Ravaged by anxiety and in his arms, the entire scene would end in my much-desired kiss.

"Slow down," he drawls, "you want me to pay someone to attack you just so your suit can save you? You're crazy."

"I'm not. Think about it! The intensity of the situation will make our endorphins run high, and one thing will lead to another and then . . ."

"Yeah, I got that, but really B? That's your master plan?"

"He kissed my forehead tonight. My forehead." I try to emphasize the gravity of the situation. "What if he doesn't think of me sexually? No, I can't have that happen."

"B," he groans, and I can tell he's going to object more.

"I swear if I don't get any action soon, my lips will wither and fall off. You wouldn't want that, would you?"

"I'm not sure that's biologically possible, but have it your way. I'll find someone. If it backfires, it's on you, but don't say I didn't warn you."

"You're the best," I exclaim and send him a virtual kiss.

My plan will work. All my plans do.

7

THEO

For the millionth time today, I stare at her, my eyes zoning in on her lips.

Fuck! Why did I decide to be such a gentleman?

But then I remind myself that she's never dated before, and I don't want to pressure her to do anything she might not be ready for. Just last time, she confessed that she's never kissed anyone before.

The thought of being her first, in every way possible, fills me with such possessiveness that I never want to let her go. I already have enough trouble letting her go when our dates come to an end.

I want nothing more than to kidnap her and have my way with her.

God!

I groan internally, shocked at the direction of my thoughts. I can't let my baser instincts ruin this for me. I don't want to scare her with my desires, especially when she's barely become comfortable being alone with me outside her house. I need to push everything down, and just focus on the present — on her.

"Have you decided?" I ask when she puts down the menu.

After our first date, I'd tried my best not to overwhelm her, but I just couldn't stay away. I'd dropped by her house the next day and I'd invited her to breakfast. And so a routine had developed. I

55

could not get enough of her. She was like a breath of fresh air with her artless manner and her sunny disposition . And when I looked into those huge, gorgeous eyes of hers, I felt at home.

Especially after a long week at work, these Saturdays together were all I could think of.

"I'll have the omelet," she replies, giving me one of those sweet smiles I've come to crave more than anything.

Who would have thought I would ever find myself in this position? I'd never imagined I would one day consider a future with someone, not with my promise to my parents still fresh in my mind.

But I find that I can't choose one. I'll get my revenge, eventually. But Bianca . . . I want her by my side when that happens.

"I'll have the same," I add.

"I'll quickly go to the restroom before our orders come." She gets up and heads to the back of the restaurant.

I pull up my phone and go through some messages when suddenly a noise gets my attention. People gasping around, I look up to see Bianca slowly approaching, shoulders slumped, gaze alarmed. Behind her is a man ordering directives as he waves a knife around, settling on her neck.

For a second, I stiffen, panic unlike anything I'd experienced before settling deep in my gut. But realizing the seriousness of the matter, I force myself to focus.

I stand, putting my hands up to show I'm unarmed.

"Easy," I start, taking a step forward. "That's my girlfriend you're holding." I catch Bianca's eye and I can see she is terrified but trying to hold it together. "Let her go, please."

"No!" he shouts, the hand holding the knife trembling slightly and digging into her flesh. God, I think I see some red. "It's all your fault! All of you!"

Alarmed at the possibility that he might actually harm her, I take a deep breath and decide to de-escalate.

"Easy. Maybe I can help you. What's your name?"

His eyes move swiftly from side to side, and for a moment I contemplate he might be on narcotics — that would make the situation even more unpredictable.

"Jacob . . ." he mumbles, looking anywhere but at me.

"Jacob, tell me what I can do to help you," I slow my words, trying to make him see me as inoffensive.

"You can't! No one can!" He flails his arm around, his knife now pointing toward me. Seeing that it's no longer at Bianca's throat, I release a relieved sigh.

"Maybe I can. Why don't you tell me about it?" I continue, while signaling to Bianca to make a run for it if she has the chance.

"It's all your fault, fucking elitists. If it weren't for you, I wouldn't have lost my job or ended up on the streets. My wife left me." He sniffles a sob. "She took the kids."

"She made a mistake. You can always turn your life around. Then you can get your wife and kids back," I say and watch the emotions play on his face. Just when I think I've gotten through to him, he tightens his hold on Bianca, placing the knife at her neck again.

"Look, man, there's still a chance to make this right. But if you continue with this . . ." I shake my head. "Then there's no returning, do you get me?" My eyes are fixed on Bianca the whole time, and I think of all the ways I can get her out of harm's way.

"But you don't get me. You don't know what it's like to be me!" His voice is even louder now, and I can tell he's becoming more agitated. Not good.

"Look, why don't you take me instead of her? I work for the police, I'm of more value to you." I hope he'll buy that. He looks at me with an angry expression, but he seems to consider it.

"Fine! But come slowly, or she gets hurt." I do as he says, and he pushes Bianca to the floor just as I am one foot away. Seeing that she's out of his reach, I act. I go straight for the hand that holds the knife, knocking the weapon out and twisting his hand behind his back.

Using my knee, I kick his leg and hold him down on the ground, immobilized. He's thrashing in my hold, but he won't be able to escape anytime soon.

The police soon make their appearance and they take Jacob

into custody. As soon as I am able to, I rush to Bianca's side. She's being treated by the paramedics for her cut.

"Are you ok?" I take her face in my hands, trying to gauge what she's feeling. God, she must have been so scared. "I'm so sorry." I tug her to me and hug her tightly, mad with myself that I put her in danger's way.

"Y-y-yes," she stammers, her small body trembling with residual fear.

"Shh, I got you." I kiss the top of her head, and I stroke her hair. Her hands come around my waist and she holds onto me.

"Thank you," she whispers, burrowing her face deeper in my chest.

When we get back to her house a while later, I feel reluctant leaving her alone, the sight of her so vulnerable, a knife digging in her neck still engraved in my mind.

I hold on to her hand, wanting to feel her warmth, her physical presence.

"You scared me, little one," I admit. She raises her enormous eyes to look at me and my restraint snaps.

Tugging her chin up, I lower my head and brush my lips across hers in the softest caress. She seems surprised, and a sigh escapes her. I part my lips slightly, and she follows my lead, her mouth opening under mine, her tongue probing hesitantly. The first contact sends shivers down my spine, the connection instantaneous.

I growl low in my throat as I deepen the kiss, holding her closer. Her hands brush over my arms, before settling on my face, trailing soft touches all over.

Suddenly, I take a step back, breaking the kiss. I need to put a stop to this before it goes too far — before I scare her with my passion.

Her eyes are glazed with desire, her hair mussed, her mouth oh-so-very well-kissed.

My thumb grazes her swollen lips, and satisfaction fills me to the brim.

She's mine!

"Good night, B," I tell her, turning around and leaving.

God, I really need to learn some self-restraint.

***

After the hostage incident, things change, and not for the better. I can barely stand being apart from her, and I'm afraid my overprotectiveness may stifle her. Wherever she goes, I go. It's as simple as that. I might have even gone a little overboard, as I'd taken advantage of my vacation days to shadow her.

I must have it bad if even work doesn't matter anymore.

Her classes? I'm in the back.

Her internship? I'm waiting around.

Her home? I'm a constant visitor.

Luckily, Martin isn't around all that much or that would have been awkward. But Bianca hasn't said anything. She seems to enjoy my presence as much as I do hers.

It's only after one month that she pulls me aside and tells me she's worried for me.

"Don't get me wrong," she starts, her eyes darting around, "I love having you with me everywhere I go, but I don't think your boss is going to be impressed with your absences."

I purse my lips, realizing where this is going. I'd been entirely too wrapped up in her that my job has come second.

"I know . . ." She puts a hand up to stop me.

"Please don't jeopardize your career because of me. I'm fine, I'm safe, I'm not in danger."

I nod reluctantly.

"I'm sorry I've been crowding you this past month," I apologize, hoping she isn't thinking of breaking up because of my overbearing ways. Because that is simply something that I will not allow.

"You don't have to apologize, Theo. I was just as scared as you, but the danger's already gone." She takes a deep breath, and I brace myself, mentally preparing all the arguments for why she should continue to date me. "I'm just worried they will fire you if you keep this up."

"Don't worry about that. I've never used my vacation days before, so I had plenty." I assure her. "But I hear you. I'll try to be more moderate. But for my peace of mind," I pause, thinking how to say this so she won't think I'm too controlling, "I'd like you to update me often throughout the day." I refrain from saying what I'd actually like — hourly updates. God, what am I turning into?

She gives me a smile. "Deal." On her tiptoes, she jumps up to kiss my cheek.

Damn! And that's exactly what I live for.

8

BIANCA

"You got what you asked for, didn't you? Hastings sure is devoted to you now. A bit too much for my taste, I might add." Vlad lounges in his chair across from me, an amused expression on his face.

After the attack, Theo hadn't left my side — not even for one moment. Not that I'm complaining, if I'm being honest, since it's all I've ever wanted, but it's made doing my job a little hard. I've had to refuse two assignments in that time, and I'd had to limit my coke intake to once a week — if I was lucky. I'd noticed the signs of withdrawal immediately. I'd find myself restless and increasingly irascible.

Even though I'd wished for nothing more than to have Theo tied to me twenty-four seven, it's simply not possible with me leading a double life.

So, I'd had to gently nudge him toward considering his career. He'd been quite receptive, so that issue was easily solved.

"I'm itching to land a kill." I ignore his jibe, taking out my precious baby — my Glock — and cleaning it.

"I might just have something." His smile grows and I have to narrow my eyes at him.

"Really?" I tilt my head, watching him suspiciously. After the last time, I don't think I'll trust him for a while. "You sent a fucking meth-head to attack us, so forgive me for not trusting your judgment." He could have sent anyone, not an unreliable, volcanic meth head that almost slit my throat.

"What are you talking about?" He furrows his brows, leaning forward. "Meth-head? That I sent?" he asks incredulously.

"You don't have to pretend you don't know what I'm talking about." I roll my eyes. "You could have sent someone less unpredictable."

"I didn't send anyone." He purses his lips. "At first I forgot and then Hastings seemed to come around so I didn't think it was necessary anymore."

"Are you fucking kidding me? You didn't send that guy?" Great! Simply great! I could have easily gotten killed because I'd been sure the guy would have never actually harmed me.

Fucking hell!

I don't even think as I lift my gun and shoot, the bullet whizzing past Vlad's ear close enough to draw a droplet of blood.

He doesn't flinch.

Raising an eyebrow at me, he lifts his hand to pick up the blood with his fingers before bringing it to his mouth, licking it off.

"Is that war you're waging right now, little goddess?" He watches me intently, like a big cat on a prowl, ready to jump on its prey at any second.

"You fucking asshole. Do you realize I would have let that motherfucker slit my throat because I thought you hired him?" I stand up, pacing around and trying to calm myself.

Fuck!

"You suddenly care whether you live or die?" He smirks. "That's new."

"Asshole," I mutter under my breath.

He reclines in his chair, making himself more comfortable and seeming entirely unbothered.

"I may not have sent him, but it got you what you wanted, didn't it?" He shrugs.

"That's not the point," I grumble, but the annoyance is wearing off already.

"Just friendly advice. You should lock your suit down fast,

before he finds out he's been awfully deceived. How long have you been dating now? A year? More?"

"It's not that easy," I mumble. Does he think I haven't thought of that? I've been trying to give suggestions now and then, but Theo seems dense to all my attempts. I can't get the man to sleep with me, let alone propose.

I release a big sigh and plop myself back in my seat.

"He won't even go further than kissing. He sees me as this frail woman that he's afraid to offend if he's too forward."

"But isn't that what you wanted? Attract him by seeming inno-cent and shy? He already seems quite taken with you, though," Vlad suggests.

"Enough of that." I wave my hand dismissively, since I've done plenty of thinking on the subject myself, and it always leaves me frustrated. "Tell me about that kill. I need to blow off some steam."

***

More months of sitting around in the hell of sexual frustration, with Theo so close and yet so far. The most we'd done had been a heavy make-out session that had left both of us wanting. Damn him and his fucking misplaced honor. I've even tried to slyly make my way down his pants, but he'd stopped me, saying he doesn't think I'm ready for it.

I. Am. Fucking. Ready.

I am dying, that's how ready I am. It's been what, almost two years since he fucked me as Pink? I can't believe I've made it this long, but my breaking point is nearing.

I may just snap and tear his clothes off, but that would undo years of pretending to be sweet, innocent Bianca.

Fucking hell!

"It says here to add more rose oil," I say to myself as I follow the instructions for the love spell. When the natural cannot yield results, you have to reorient yourself towards the supernatural. Not that I'm a great believer, but at this point, I'm willing to try anything.

If I can't seduce him with my body, I doubt a dozen candles, some rose oil, and an incantation is going to do the job.

But alas, I will try it.

I place the candles in a circle and add some rose oil clock-wise as I recite the verses I'd found on the web.

"So mote it be," I end the chant, closing my eyes and willing it to happen. I imagine Theo on one knee, asking me to marry him, after which, he'd whisk me to bed and make love to me in a thousand ways.

A smile spreads on my face as I imagine it.

The spell done, I await the results.

Days pass, and then weeks, and I'm starting to believe that either magic isn't real, or I must have offended those love fairies somehow.

But just as I feel hopelessness settle deep in my bones, I am regaled with the best of news — from my father, nonetheless.

One afternoon he calls me in his study to inform me that Theo's asked for my hand in marriage and that he will soon propose.

"You'll do better to accept, Bianca. You can't do better than him. He has a bright future ahead of him." My father lists all of Theo's qualities in an attempt to convince me that indeed, he is the best choice of husband.

On the surface, I nod like the obedient daughter that I am, but on the inside, I'm so giddy I high five all the love deities out there for making this happen.

I smile to myself. Now I just have to wait.

9

THEO

Taking a deep breath, I mentally go again over my lines. I need this to be perfect. I've already set up the bedroom. I'd taken to the internet for advice on the perfect proposal, and I'd followed all the advice I could find. From candles, to rose petals, and everything to ensure the atmosphere is as romantic as possible.

Bianca should arrive soon, and as I planned, I'll make her dinner first, and then I'll bring her to the room.

Fuck, I'm too nervous!

We'd talked about our feelings before, but we haven't outrightly exchanged I love you's yet. But tonight is the night. I'll be handing her my heart on a platter.

The oven beeps, and I hurry to remove the tray. I start arranging the plates when the doorbell rings.

The moment I open the door, my jaw almost drops.

She looks like a goddess. My goddess.

She's wearing a dusty pink dress that clings to her body, emphasizing her hips and waist. I swallow hard, the sight of her looking so delicious doing little to calm my nerves.

I open my door wider for her, and she gives me a smile as she walks past me, waving a wine bottle. My eyes follow her around, almost glued to her ass.

"You cooked?" She places the bottle on the table, looking around the kitchen.

"Only for you." I come behind her, hands on her hips, and I lay a kiss on her cheek.

"You have to tell me what the occasion is." She sits daintily on the chair, and I stifle a groan, the sight of her enough to make me hard for days.

"You'll find out." I wink at her and proceed to serve dinner. Opening the bottle of wine, I pour it in our glasses.

"You're finally of age to drink," I add, amused. Sometimes it's easy to forget our age difference, since Bianca has a maturity beyond her years. Maybe I'd been a little reluctant to pursue her in the beginning because I'd thought her too young, but I was just biding my time and fooling myself in the process.

Ours is a matter of eventuality. It had taken me one look at her to know she was mine, a little longer to convince myself to go after her, and a hell of a lot longer to court her. But I know she feels the same as I do. It's in her slight shiver as I touch her, or the light inflection of her voice after I kiss her.

And tonight, she'll know just how much I love her.

We chat about her week. Since graduation, she's been working hard to put together a foundation against homelessness, and her project is picking up speed. I'd told her she could do it, and I made sure to support her at every point. I know how important it is for her to do this well, especially since her father seems to be against her working.

Tipping the glass to my lips, my eyes are on her, taking in her beauty — both inner and outer, and I wonder how I'm so lucky.

Out of everyone else in this world, she's mine and mine alone.

After we're done eating, we wash the dishes together, and I finally get the courage to ask her to the room.

"I have something for you," I tell her, leading her to my bedroom. Before opening the door, I put my hands to her eyes, steering her to the center of the room, so she's standing right in front of the strewn rose petals.

"What's this, Theo?" She giggles softly, and I can't help myself. I lower my lips to her pulse, skimming the sensitive skin toward her ear before whispering.

"Keep your eyes closed."

I move around so I can face her, and taking out the ring box, I prompt her to open her eyes.

When she does, it's to see me on one knee, ring out, in front of a row of roses that spells out *Will You Marry Me?*

She gasps, bringing her hand to her mouth, the corner of her eyes full with unshed tears.

"Bianca Ashby, will you do me the honor of becoming my wife?" I ask officially, and she jumps on me, tackling me to the floor.

"Yes! Yes!" she cries. "A thousand times, yes!" She brings her arms around my neck, holding onto me tight. "I love you, Theo." She whispers in my hair, and I feel my heart stop.

Fuck!

If this isn't true happiness, then I don't know what is.

"I love you too, B. So damn much it hurts," I confess, turning her so I can pepper kisses all over her sweet face. "So much."

Taking the ring out, I slide it up her finger — the perfect fit.

"It's gorgeous, Theo," she says in awe, her mouth slightly agape, her eyes shining with unshed tears. "Thank you."

"Only for you, little one. Only for you."

The candles are bathing the room in light, and her face looks even lovelier. I raise my hand to tuck a stray strand of hair, lingering on her cheek. I'd like nothing more than to throw her on the bed and take her hard and fast. It's not as if I haven't dreamed about that every single night since I met her. But I can't do that. I need to control myself and make her first time special.

But first, I have to make sure she's ready for it. If she's not, then I'll wait for as long as she needs, even if that means I'll be jacking off twice as much.

I move at the same time as she does, and we meet in the middle, our lips slowly caressing each other. I sneak my hand around her waist, bringing her into me and deepening the kiss.

"B . . ." I whisper, breaking apart for a second. "Are you . . ." I trail off, not knowing how to approach this so she doesn't feel pressured.

"Yes, please," she says shyly, backing up just enough so she can slide the zipper of her dress down and slip it down her shoulders. "I want you, Theo. I want all of you." She's now wearing only her bra and her panties, and I groan out loud at the sight. I don't even think as I scoop her in my arms, and take her to the bed, slowly lowering her on to the mattress.

She's unsure as she tries to cover her exposed skin, and I'm once again reminded that this is new to her, and I need to let her set the pace.

I pull my shirt off and throw it on the floor. Her eyes move greedily over my torso and I'm suddenly glad of my gym schedule. I want her to find me as attractive as I find her.

"The pants?" she asks, her tone breathless. I happily oblige her, leaving my boxer briefs on so I don't shock her.

I advance toward her and she licks her lips, looking up at me with that innocent gaze of her.

Fuck!

My cock is straining against the confines of my briefs, and I'm fairly sure she can see just how much I want her. But her eyes seem to focus on my face, as if she's making a conscious effort not to look down.

I take her face between my hands and I proceed to kiss her, nice and slow, enjoying the feel of her — mine for the taking.

Spreading her on the bed and fitting myself on top of her, I proceed to kiss every inch of her skin, wanting to show her just how much I love her, worship her. As I move lower, I snap her bra clasp open and tug it off her. Her hands immediately go to her breasts and she gulps loudly, looking to the side.

"I . . . I've never," she starts, her voice full of embarrassment.

"I know. I'll be gentle, I swear." She nods, turns slightly to look in my eyes.

"I'm on birth control. I . . . I wanted to be prepared," she admits, a blush appearing on her pretty cheeks.

"God, B!" I groan, the idea that she's been looking forward to this as much as me exciting me to no end. "I've always used condoms before, and it was only one other woman," I confess, and her nose scrunches up, a sigh of disappointment escaping her. "Shh, sweet girl." I caress her face. "I wish I waited too. If I knew

I'd find you one day, I swear I wouldn't have touched another woman." I tell her honestly, because when I'm with her, nothing and no one else matters. She's my future, my everything.

She gives me a tremulous smile, her fingers coming to rest on my cheeks and then tracing my lips.

"I'm glad. You're the only one for me, Theo. Always." Her words floor and humble me, so I show her just how much she means to me.

I turn my attention back to her body, trailing wet kisses down her neck and toward her breasts before taking one nipple into my mouth. Her mouth forms an o, but she urges me on. I lick and suck, enjoying the myriad of emotions playing on her face. I need her to be as relaxed as possible, her pleasure my foremost goal. I'm not a small man, and for the first time, I'm afraid it might not be as pleasant for her as I know it will be for me.

I move lower, kissing her stomach before reaching her panties. Hooking my fingers through the band, I tug them down her legs, leaving her bare for my view. She tries to close her legs, but I place a finger on her mound, marveling at the softness of her skin.

"Clean shaven," I murmur, surprised.

"I thought you'd like it," her voice is small as she says this, so I quickly assure her I'd like her any way. That she put effort into this, to please me, makes me even happier.

Settling myself between her legs, I inhale her scent, nuzzling her lips with my mouth before diving in for the first taste. I give her a long lick, and she stiffens against me before relaxing once more. Centering the tip of my tongue over her clit, I circle it in slow motions, making her writhe under me, her hands involuntarily seeking my hair. She clutches at my scalp, and I continue, sucking the nub and nibbling it with my teeth. Her moans permeate the air, and pride swells in my chest.

I'm the one giving her pleasure. I'm the one owning her.

I use my fingers to prepare her, feeling her soft tightness and the way she clenches at my digits. Soon, she crashes, her orgasm making her contract all around my fingers, her soft gasps making my dick even harder.

Fuck! I need to take this slow.

Moving up her body, I give her a languorous kiss, using my hands to push down my briefs.

"I'm told this might hurt a little, sweetheart," I tell her, already feeling bad I'm about to cause her pain. I'd read plenty of articles to prepare for this night, wanting everything to be perfect, and Bianca as ready as possible to prevent any discomfort.

"It's ok. It's you." She gives me one quick kiss on the lips before urging me to proceed. My hands on her ass, I settle in the v of her legs, my cock brushing ever so softly against the wetness of her pussy. A hiss escapes me at the contact, the promise of pleasure to come.

Taking my cock in one hand, I rub it against her pussy, coating it in her juices before I push the tip in. My eyes are on her face, checking for any sign of discomfort, but she's watching me just as intently, her mouth open on an unreleased moan.

I move forward inch by inch, letting her get used to my size. A small crease forms between her brows and I still.

"Does it hurt?" I ask immediately, concerned.

She shakes her head. "It's just new. But I like it." She angles her hips and I slide all the way in. I take a deep breath, now hoping I will last. Her raw heat is almost too much to bear, and I have to stop myself from coming then and there — from one thrust alone.

"God, B. You feel so good," I rasp against her face, my lips seeking hers. I wait until she's ready and when she gives me a nudge, I start moving again. My arms come around her and I hold her tightly to my chest, driving my cock in and out of her. Her breathing picks up, so I quicken my pace, needing her to come all over my cock.

"Theo," she cries, her nails scratching my back and winding tightly around my neck. "Love you."

"Love you, too, sweetheart. So. Damn. Much," I growl in between thrusts. Her mouth is on mine as her walls grip my cock tightly, spasming around me. She lets out a soft moan, and I follow her, spilling myself inside of her. Relishing the feeling of marking her as mine.

We stay like that for a moment before I withdraw, running to the bathroom to get a washcloth. When I return, I spot a few droplets of blood smeared on her thighs and on the sheet — the evidence of her innocence. I clean her carefully, and she gives me the most satisfied purr.

She's mine. She's finally mine.

THREE YEARS LATER

10

BIANCA

It's party time—aka murder time.

I adjust the grip on my rifle and scan the area. I knew I had to be here earlier than the designated time to do a full swipe for potential dangers.

For my spot, I've chosen a small hotel a few blocks from the port where the meeting is about to take place. I'd scouted the area a few days back and calculated the angles and range to be fully prepared for any outcome.

My shooting skills won't beat any distance records, but I can hold my own against any Army-trained sniper. I've been coached by one my entire life. Drew, my bodyguard since I was a little girl, is ex-military. He's also the father I never had, even though my own is very much still alive.

The keyword is *still*. Drew has spent years training me when no one is around to question my activities, and I've taken my lessons seriously.

As I look around the docks and areas where potential shooters might hide, I hit the jackpot. Two men, at twelve o'clock and eight o'clock, are on their stomachs with their gears ready. The position of their rifles tells me they aren't even looking for other targets, but the one set to arrive... now.

Two black cars pull up between the shipping containers. Three people get out from the first one: two nasty-looking men who appear to be bodyguards and then another shorter man in a tailored suit.

That must be Martinez.

I know all about this meeting and its purpose, which is why I'm here. You don't do business with a cartel and expect them to honor their safety assurances. Even I know that.

Just as I know that the man who steps out of the second car hasn't even considered the possibility that this could be a setup.

He is, after all, buying information from the second in command of a fucking cartel. He's dressed in a sleek shirt and fitted pants that emphasize his physique and make my insides burn even now.

Focus, I tell myself.

The second man, Theo, has a briefcase in his hands. He takes a few steps towards Martinez, and words are exchanged. I hear them, but they don't know or need to know that. Theo opens the suitcase to show rows and rows of cash, to which Martinez removes a flash drive from his jacket. It's all about to go down. I quickly turn to the other men and note their tense positions. They're about to shoot.

My finger squeezes the trigger with practiced speed. Once, twice. They drop dead. The shots have alerted the others to the presence of another sniper. The bodyguards are now in shooting position, and I know that the next few seconds are invaluable. Target set and target down. I get one bodyguard and am glad to see Theo seek cover. I don't care about the other bodyguard, but Martinez won't make it alive. He dared to threaten Theo's life, and that makes him a dead man.

I take a few breaths and scan my surroundings. He hides, that motherfucker. Knowing he must have taken refuge behind the car, I take a couple of random shots to draw him out in the open. He must have taken the bait because he runs towards one container to his right, all the while ignoring his bodyguard's warnings. I don't hesitate, putting a bullet right through his skull—a kill shot.

I breathe out, relieved. Screeching car tires alert me to Theo driving away.

Yes, run!

Pulling myself to my knees, I take apart my rifle and store it in the violin case I use as cover.

Quickly, I hurry from the roof and into the staircase where I change into my disguise. I put on the wig, an elegant bob with straight bangs.

I add a pair of spectacles and fake braces. Then I take off my blazer to reveal the high school uniform to one of the schools in the area.

No one will question my guise. In this outfit, I now look completely underage. Taking my violin case, I exit the hotel and hail a cab.

I stop at Chinatown and walk around for a half hour before taking another cab to Midtown, where I've left my car. Once I'm behind the wheel, I quickly shed my disguise and go to my spare apartment to deposit all the materials. Not lingering more than necessary, I then hop in my car once again, going home.

The moment I'm inside the penthouse, a voice greets me.

"Darling?"

"Yes," I answer and turn to see my husband walking towards me with a strange expression on his face.

"What's wrong?" I ask as he takes me into his arms and holds me as if there's no tomorrow.

"Just glad to see you," he whispers in my hair, kissing my forehead, eyes, nose, and finally lips. He looks haggard, as if he's just been through a harrowing experience.

"What?" I manage between kisses.

"I missed you," he rasps out.

"I love you, Theo!" I squeeze him to my chest, knowing exactly what has prompted his display of affection.

"I love you too, dear," he murmurs, taking me to our bedroom and proceeding to make sweet love to me.

I can tell that Theo's shaken up by what happened. He's always been uptight and unyielding with crime and violence. That's why he must never know. My husband must never know the things I do to make sure he's safe.

Never.

"You look amazing." I look in the mirror, adjusting the ribbon at my shirt's neckline. Theo comes from behind, fitting himself to my back and making me shiver. I smile at the interruption and tip my head to kiss him.

"You too." I take in his appearance. He's always been handsome, but he's most attractive when he looks at me with love in his eyes because I know he's *mine*. His short, dark-brown hair has the silkiest texture I've ever felt, and I take every opportunity to run my hands through it. But his eyes made me forget myself all those years ago. Not quite brown, not quite green, they sparkle with warmth and intelligence. He's now dressed for the office, in a dark-blue suit and a white dress shirt.

"When are you coming home?" I ask with a smile on my face.

"After seven. I have a few meetings. Will you be at the foundation all day?"

"Yes, we're having an event in a couple of weeks, so I have to approve all expenditures."

"I'm proud of you." His hands on my hips, he turns me around to give me a breathless kiss.

"Enough of this. You'll be late."

"I'd always be late if it means one more kiss from you," he replies sneakily. I playfully punch him.

"Love you, now go."

"Love you too, sweetie!" He gives me one last glance before grabbing his briefcase and taking off.

Sweetie... Love... I sometimes wonder if he loves *me* or just who I am for him. Could he even love *me* if he knew the real me? The answer is no, and I'm painfully aware of it.

I was sixteen when I first saw him. He'd been fresh out of Quantico, mingling with different prospective employers at one of my father's many banquets. I wasn't supposed to be there, but that hadn't been the first time I'd done something I wasn't supposed to.

That night was the night my obsession with Theo started, and it's never stopped. I remember seeing him in the ballroom, from my hiding place on the veranda. He'd been engaging in conversation with two older men, and he had this severe countenance devoid of any arrogance that just intrigued me.

When he'd turned, and I glimpsed at his face, I saw my future reflected in his eyes. I knew without a doubt that he was mine, and one day, I'd possess him. It hadn't taken me long to find out everything about him and put my plan into motion. It would be another three years before I would officially meet him.

He was just getting his start in the mayor's office and was looking at my father for support, and I was the young daughter of a man he knew and looked up to. Those circumstances had been fortuitous, for I'd had the advantage of my parentage and a wealth of information on his preferences. I'm not ashamed to say that I'd used that information to craft myself into his dream woman.

Innocent, sweet, vulnerable.

Theo had a savior complex. And I just needed to play the damsel in distress. Not that it was too hard with my unyielding father and seemingly restricted upbringing. He'd taken one look at my cowering self and had immediately come to my rescue.

He liked delicate and nurturing women.

I was neither.

But I made myself into one.

Two years of sporadic encounters followed by a year of slow courtship, and I knew I'd won him. Now, three years of marriage later, and my innocent persona has become a second skin. Nurturing, however, that's still hard. It doesn't help that he's been bringing up children for a while now, and I don't know how much longer I can put him off.

I don't see myself as a mother, but more than anything else, I don't want to share him with another being. He's mine, *only* mine. He thinks we've been trying for the past year, but I've been secretly getting the shot. There are just so many things that if my husband found out, he would never forgive me.

With one last glance in the mirror, I pick up my bag and head out.

For the past five years, I've been involved with a foundation for the fight against homelessness that my father founded. Why? I'm sure you've guessed by now. Homelessness is an issue that's very dear to Theo's heart. After his parents died when he was a teenager, he spent some time on the streets to avoid foster homes. Through his intelligence and sheer determination, he finished high school and then put himself through college, getting merit scholarships and working part-time jobs to support himself. In the beginning, he'd wanted to become a lawyer because he'd seen too much injustice in the world.

But Theo isn't a small-scale type of man. He's a visionary. He wants to save everyone, and so he'd gone into law enforcement. Now, he's chief commissioner for NYPD and a trusted friend to the mayor. And I, through my charitable efforts and my connections, am the *perfect* wife for him. An image I intend to keep.

I drop by the foundation and check all the documents. I wasn't exactly lying when I told him I'd be at the foundation; it just wouldn't take the entire day. As director, I have a lot of responsibilities and things to keep up with. I don't enjoy it, and given the size of my trust fund, I shouldn't *even* work. But it makes for an excellent cover when I need to leave the house. I speed through a couple of meetings with the staff and take my leave for the day.

I get in my car and drive to my spare apartment in Midtown. It's a property registered in my late mother's name that I got when I was eighteen. More than an apartment, it's a haven for me and my vices. Since it's almost past midday, the traffic is awful, so it takes awhile for me to reach the apartment.

The place has three bedrooms, but only one of them is functional. I've transformed one bedroom into an armory, and it houses all my priceless possessions: my guns, rifles, knives, and protective gear. It also has tracking technology and listening devices.

The other bedroom is now an enormous closet, and it contains all my disguises. It has a wall-length wardrobe with different outfits and another panel with wigs and complementary accessories that make all the difference when wanting to become someone else. A few mannequins are clothed in disguises that are dear to my heart. In the middle is the one I remember most fondly: a pink bob-cut wig, a tight purple dress that barely covers the butt, fishnets, and a pair of high boots. I close my eyes as I fondly remember my first taste of Theo.

Like all young white-collar workers, he'd taken to frequenting this strip club in East Village. Theo may be the most righteous man I know, but even he can't resist a pair of tits and an inviting smile. That's when I realized that for all his serious demeanor in day-to-day life, he's rough and dominant in the bedroom. He'd fucked me seven ways to Sunday, and I still wanted more. But for all our lengthy affair, I was only a prostitute to him, not Bianca Ashby.

Because Bianca Ashby would never step foot in a strip club, would never be taken roughly, would always be treated like a porcelain doll.

Bianca Ashby wasn't fucked; she was only made love to.

That's probably my biggest regret in how Theo sees me. He's never tried to be anything but sweet and tender in bed. Even when I'd suggested trying something a little spicier, he'd raised an eyebrow and asked jokingly if I'd discovered porn, and that sex in real life isn't like in porn. After that, I hadn't brought it up again, realizing it was a moot point. I was too fragile for him. To be protected at all times, even from other, more non-conventional aspects of desire.

I make my way to the bedroom, looking under the bed for a box that housed another one of my long-term vices. This one I am probably the most ashamed of. I quickly retrieve the box and open it to find countless small packets of white powder. I pocket one and put everything in place. With shaky fingers, I line up some powder on the desk next to the bed, and using a small straw, I inhale two lines. Cleaning my nose of residue powder, I take a seat and open my computer.

A few years ago, I would have denied having an addiction to my dying breath. Now, after enduring withdrawal symptoms several times, I've finally accepted it. I'm an addict.

***

It's funny how it all started. Sadly, I didn't realize how reliant I was on coke until I went through the worst withdrawal symptoms. Until then, I'd told myself that I was taking it because I could and because it gave me single-minded focus when it came to my pursuits. I can still remember the first time I tried it.

I was nineteen and had just found out about the strip club Theo frequented. When I was going to college full time, I would often go the club, hoping to catch him. I'd convinced management to give me a server position. It was finals season, and I was spending all day studying and all night in that damned club. At the end of my first full week, I could barely stand on my feet, and Theo had still not shown up. In one of my breaks, I'd been outside the club, hoping the night's cold air would wake me up. I'd bummed a cigarette off a guy, and he'd commented on my incessant yawning.

"I have just the thing," he'd said and showed a hint of white in his pocket. I'd lifted my eyebrow in question, and he'd motioned to the alley next to the club. Now, I know it's not safe to go with an unknown guy in a dark alley. I mean, it's a poster scenario for assault. But at that point, I was tired and maybe a little curious. I went with him and saw how he lined up the powder on the back of his hand and sniffed. I copied his movements, and it didn't take long for the powder to kick in. It also didn't take long for the asshole to put his hands on me. I mean, really? What did I expect?

"What the fuck?" I spat when his hand had gone to my waist and up.

"Oh, come on, you didn't think that was free?" He smirked.

"How much? I'll pay you."

I shoved his hand away, prepared to give him the cash, but then he replied, "I don't want money. I want," he said, leering at me. His hand went directly to my breast this time, but I expected it. My trained instincts, coupled with the magic powder, kicked in, and I twisted his arm behind his back. Using my foot, I kicked the back of his knees and shoved him to the ground. My other hand went directly to my boot, where I withdrew a small knife. Holding it to his neck, I snickered.

"I told you I would give you cash."

But the more I thought about it, the madder I became. I shoved harder at his tendons with my boot. "You dare touch me?

No one touches me, do you understand?" *No one but my Theo*—the words went unsaid.

I was still holding the knife to his neck and didn't even notice when it dug into his flesh, and blood trickled down.

"Please..." The man almost started wailing, and the sound of him at my mercy gave me a rush. Or maybe it was the drug?

"What was the thing you gave me?"

"C-C-Cocaine," he stammered, and I gave him one last shove.

Moving in front of him, I wiped the knife slowly on his shirt and told him, "Next time a woman says no, it's no." He nodded fervently.

"Run before I change my mind." He'd taken off like a scared rabbit.

Sheathing my knife, I returned to my post at the club, and lo and behold, my night took a turn for the best. Theo was there.

Maybe my love for the magic powder developed because I associated it with my first sexual encounter with Theo. Perhaps that's what I told myself every time I went to that club. Eventually, if I went too many days without it, my hands would shake. For a trained killer, shaking is the worst thing that can happen. After that, it became a necessity, and my addiction solidified.

Could I give it up? Yes, I could. But that would probably mean rehab, which in turn would mean an absence from home and the potential of Theo finding out precisely what I've been up to these past few years.

I let a loud sigh and shake myself from my wandering thoughts. I am looking at my computer screen, waiting for a reply from a weapons supplier I'd contacted on the dark web. He had a new experimental rifle that I've been dying to get my hands on. Problem was? It wasn't strictly legal, and the few shipments that made it to the States had to be delivered personally by an intermediary because of the rarity of the pieces and their price range. This toy would definitely set me back quite a bit.

I have men in New York next week if you're interested

I read the text and take a minute to think about a potential meeting location. I rarely like to use the same place twice for meetups, but this is too short of a notice to scout an area and ensure safety protocols. I'd have to use one hotel I've used in the past. I immediately decide on the Hotel Empire since I know the layout pretty well and have a few exit routes should I require any. I make a call and book room 204 for the next week under one of my fake identities.

Hotel Empire Room 204 14th May 2:00 PM

Okay.

After seeing his reply, I close the connection and put my laptop aside, excitement brimming inside me. In just under a week, I'd have a new toy to play with. It'd been too long since my latest purchase, which I'd used a few days before on those criminals. It's an excellent rifle, but I need something slightly faster to reload since there were a few close calls in that encounter. I have to hope this new one will perform better.

Getting out of the room, I quickly check the time and realize I must have lost track of it since it's a little over three. I go to my armory and pick up the new tracking device I'd recently gotten, along with some new surveillance stuff. I always have something on Theo, but the last one must have gotten lost since I haven't been able to monitor his movements or listen to his phone in a while. Not since before the meeting with Martinez, actually. I shake my head, not wanting to even entertain the thought that he could have found the devices. They must have broken, or maybe he lost them? I just need to install the new ones.

Maybe to some people, it seems wrong that I continuously monitor Theo. Still, knowing his obsession with catching one of the biggest drug lords in America, this is the only way to ensure his safety.

11

THEO

"Look here," Marcel, my trusted friend, points out.

We're looking at a map of the docks and the surrounding area. Marcel is the only one who knows what happened two days ago and why exactly I'd gone to meet Martinez.

However, what is most surprising about that encounter is that Martinez's men had been shot dead by someone. Marcel had spent hours reproaching me that it hadn't been safe to go alone and that he'd warned me. He's right. I had been very naïve about the entire situation. After the shooting had stopped, I'd taken an additional risk in getting the flash drive from Martinez's dead body. I'm not proud of what I'd done, but I'd gone there with every intention of a fair exchange. He'd been the one to bring reinforcements.

But the bigger question remains: *who* shot his men. It had been from a distance, as I could see no one nearby. More importantly, it had targeted Martinez's people only. Grimly, I have to acknowledge that whoever it was probably saved my life.

But why?

Marcel is pointing at probable locations for the shooter given the angle, and one of them happens to be a hotel a few blocks away from the docks.

"You really think this could be it?"

"Yeah, it's this one or the Ukrainian restaurant next to it. It's not too far, but not too close either. From what you described, though, whoever it was knew what they were doing, and they were fast about it."

"Yeah. It was all surreal. I've never been so scared in my life. For a moment, I really didn't think I'd make it."

"I told you it wasn't safe to go alone."

"I know, but I really needed the drive."

"And now you know they wanted to trick you," he admonishes, referring to the fact the drive was empty.

"I just don't get why they would try to kill me. I was only asking for information, and that wasn't even on their cartel."

"Maybe this is bigger than we previously suspected," he says after thinking for a while.

"I don't know. I don't even know where to go from here, except I really want to find the shooter."

"I'll get the security tapes from the hotel and restaurant. It will require we pull in some favors, though. You know it's Russian territory."

"And we'll use that to our advantage. They probably already know about the shooting. It's in their interest to find a rogue sniper, no? On their turf, no less."

"I'll call Vlad. He should be able to get us access to the tapes."

"Great, let me know."

A few hours later, Marcel comes back with the excellent news that Vlad had gotten him access to both locations' feeds. We take a car and head to Brighton Beach to inspect the footage.

Upon arriving, two men meet us. The first one is massive, his bald head covered in tattoos. He isn't precisely friendly looking. The other man is just as tall but leaner. He's dressed in a sleek black suit and has a pair of sunglasses on. As he spots us, he beams.

"Ah, Hastings. Fancy meeting you again and in our area." Vlad flashes me a smile and winks at Marcel.

"Thank you for the footage," I reply, knowing it will be a favor for a favor.

"No worries, you know how this works. Now, let's go in. We

want to catch this shooter of yours too. Not good for the business, you know."

I nod and proceed inside with Marcel and Vlad's massive friend, who seems to always stand behind Vlad in a protective stance. We go to the restaurant first and quickly sift through their limited footage but with no luck. The hotel is a bit trickier since they have more cameras, and as such, we have to be more vigilant. We play the footage for that entire day.

"There's no one suspicious going in. Since it's a sniper, they must have something to carry the equipment," Marcel comments.

"There's no one going in but look here." I point towards the high schooler carrying a violin case. "Would that be big enough for a sniper rifle?"

Vlad laughs.

"Really, Hastings? Your shooter is a schoolgirl?"

"I don't see anyone else as suspicious," I continue. "It could be a disguise."

"A woman, really? Your shooter is a woman?" Vlad keeps shaking his head in disbelief.

"Wait," Marcel suddenly interjects. "This sniper, whoever it was, must have known about the meeting beforehand, and they must have scouted the place to watch the meeting."

"You're right," I agree. "Let's check a few days back; maybe we can find something. Maybe the schoolgirl appears twice?" I add, somehow hoping to prove Vlad wrong.

We rewind five days of footage. It takes us a long time, and Vlad is getting impatient. It's not until I see a familiar dress that I suddenly say, "Stop!"

"What?"

"That... play again." We play the tape again for that specific moment three days before the event at twelve p.m.

"Is that...?" Marcel looks at me with horror in his eyes, and I feel my stomach knotting.

"I think so." I nod, turning my head to study the figure entering the hotel once again. She's wearing a Chanel tweed dress in blue paired with high heels. I'm still not convinced. It can't be.

"I want the same person but leaving," I say, glued to the screen.

We fast forward until she's exiting the hotel, her hair wet and her face uncovered.

"That's..." Marcel whispers.

"My wife," I add, stunned on the spot.

Vlad chuckles and pats me on the back.

"Came to find a shooter, and you find your wife cheating. This has to be the best turn of events of the year."

"No, it can't be... Can I have a copy of this?" The man in charge of the footage looks at Vlad, who nods his approval.

I don't know precisely how we get out of there afterwards, but as we go back to the office, I can't shake the feeling of dread in the pit of my stomach. Because this doesn't just increase my suspicions. It confirms my worst fears. My wife is having an affair.

It started out small, now that I think about it. At the time, it never even crossed my mind to question her actions because I was so sure of her affection. She would work later than usual, and she would make excuses that some projects weren't coming along as she'd thought. Of course, at that time, I'd sympathized with her and done my best to support her through a period of perceived stress. But it wasn't stress, was it? The thing that should have clued me in the most was her reluctance to talk about our future family.

It must have been last year on Valentine's Day when I'd surprised her with a pair of baby shoes and told her my desire to expand our family.

She'd smiled and changed the subject. I approached her with the idea of a baby again when I'd asked her if she'd be willing to stop taking her birth control.

She'd once again tried to dodge the discussion by distracting me with her body. I'd been so aroused that I'd forgotten about the topic immediately.

It wasn't until the third try that she'd relented and told me she'd stop taking her birth control. That had been around six months ago, and a nagging feeling told me she was still taking contraceptives.

This is my wife we're talking about. The woman I'd bonded with over children during our relationship. The woman who'd told me she wanted a house full of children.

This woman, however, doesn't seem to find the idea of having a child particularly appealing.

At the time, I merely put it down to her age. She's in her mid-twenties, whereas I am slowly approaching my mid-thirties. It makes sense in a way that our priorities are different. Still, I cannot help but feel a little cheated since we'd established we'd try to have kids after a few years of marriage.

Then the absences from work happened. Those were the ones that played on my mind most often, and I found my insecurities eating at me. Bianca usually works until six or seven each day, or so she's told me. One month ago, I wanted to surprise her with lunch at the foundation and was told she'd left early. That was odd. I'd called her and asked her where she was. Her answer?

"At work, silly!" She'd giggled and told me she missed me and that she would meet me at home.

I was left dumbfounded at the blatant lie, but I still didn't give up hope. I knew there had to be an explanation for it, and I waited for her to open up. That didn't happen. I'd dropped by her work unannounced a couple more times, and the same lie left her lips.

"I'm at work." When she wasn't. What am I supposed to think? My wife is an attractive woman. With her long, black hair and her pale complexion, she looks like a painting come to life. Her doe-like eyes project her sweetness and innocence, and who wouldn't be drawn to that? It had taken me a full conversation with her to be in her thrall. An entire month to fall in love.

Now, seeing the footage of her exiting that hotel with the wet hair? By itself, it might have been innocuous, but together with the other incidents? I'm almost sure my wife is cheating, and the thought nearly crushes me.

My innocent wife.

Or is she? I'd been her first lover. That, I knew, as she'd been sheltered her entire life. Is she welcoming someone else into her bed? Into her heart? Am I not... enough? Just the thought of another man touching my wife nearly sends me into a violent rage. I tend to contain my emotions to myself, but the mental picture of my wife in bed with another man makes me want to smash something.

Suddenly, I remember that night, sometime at the beginning of our relationship, when she'd gingerly suggested I tie her up and take her from behind. I'd been shocked at her request, given her inexperience. My immediate thought had been that she was under the impression she wasn't pleasing me in bed. I'd asked her where she'd gotten the idea from, and she'd told me from porn. I didn't want my wife to think she was anything less than what I wanted or needed. But I also didn't want her to feel forced to embrace different sexual practices for my sake. I'd tried my best to assure her that our lovemaking was perfect the way it was. After all, one didn't fuck one's wife like a whore. I wanted Bianca to feel my love for her every time I touched her. I never wanted her to feel dirty... used.

But what if it wasn't about pleasing me? What if that's what she actually wants... craves? And for so long, I've denied her that. What if she *wanted* me to be rougher with her? And because I'd ignored her desires for so long, she'd sought it somewhere else?

I'm a mess. All my thoughts are jumbled up, and the moment I get home, I close myself in my study with a bottle of bourbon. Of course, my wife isn't in yet. Paranoia takes hold of me. Is she with her lover? I grip the glass in my hand and quickly empty its contents. I pour another. After a few sips, I hear the front door open and footsteps in the hallway. I pour myself another drink, chug it, and confront my wife.

She's in our bedroom now, wearing only her skirt and her bra, probably just having taken off her shirt.

"Theo." She looks at me and smiles. I cock my head and lean on the doorframe, studying her.

"Theo?" she asks again, her smile trembling a little. I don't answer.

She approaches me and sniffs.

"Did you have anything to drink?" I still don't answer her, looking at her skin for any signs of a lover's possession.

I want to yell at her. *Did you cheat on me?* I want to ask her so many questions, but the alcohol is already taking over. Without a word, I pull her to me and kiss her roughly on the lips. Her mouth quickly opens up under mine, parrying each and every one of my attacks.

"Oh, Theo..." she moans into my mouth, and suddenly, I need to punish her. I jerk her around and push her with her face to the wall.

"Theo?" Her voice is unsure, and if I weren't so drunk, I might have felt bad for treating her like this. But I need to purge any other man from her. My hand sneaks down her legs, and I slowly lift her skirt until it lays in a bundle over her ass. Bianca gasps and thrusts her body towards me, approving of the gesture. In one movement, I tear her stockings and her underwear, and my fingers are inside her. She's enjoying this, based on her noises and the way she's grinding against my fingers. I can't wait anymore. If she wants rough, she'll get rough. I quickly unbuckle my pants, taking my cock out and guiding it inside her in one swift movement. She gasps low in her throat. With one hand, I grasp her hip in a painful hold while with the other, I sneak up her spine and towards her neck. I catch the hair at her nape and tug forcefully while thrusting mercilessly into her at the same time.

"Fuck, Theo, yes!" Her voice only prompts me to go faster, harder, my hands roughing her up painfully. But she enjoys it. My hand goes between her legs, and the moment I touch her clit, she spasms around my cock.

"Shit, Theo, I'm coming." I pull again on her hair and twist her face around so I can kiss her. I keep thrusting and thrusting, feeling my own orgasm nearing. My mind goes blank when I release myself inside her with a groan.

For a moment, we're both silent, breathing hard. I take my cock out of her, putting myself back in my pants. I take a step back and just look at her, as if seeing her for the first time. She glides down the wall to the floor, a satisfied smile on her face.

"That was," she says and then whistles. I just look at her, seeing a stranger.

"Put yourself together." I finally find my voice, sounding gruff even to my ears. "You look like a whore."

With a look of disgust, I leave the room and a confused Bianca on the floor.

The moment I'm out of the room, regret hits me like a bullet in the chest.

What the fuck is wrong with me? I keep repeating the same question again and again. How could I treat her like that? I can't deal with Bianca now. I can't even deal with myself. So, I do what any coward does. I run away. I leave the apartment, take a cab, and end up sleeping the bourbon off in my office.

12

BIANCA

I'm dazed. My body hums with the merciless possession of
Theo's hands. It's almost as if I was Pink again... Almost. But
the look in his eyes as he'd stared down at me makes me
pause.

"You look like a whore," he'd said. In normal circumstances, it
could be construed as dirty talk. But coming from Theo, it's
anything but bedroom talk. He'd meant it as an insult. But why?

On shaky legs, I get up and go to the bathroom. The cum leaks
down my thighs. In any other circumstances, this would have been
hot. Now... it felt sordid.

"Fuck this," I mutter as I divest myself of my torn clothing.
Taking a quick shower, I look for Theo, hoping to talk this out.

Well... he certainly didn't waste any time in leaving.

I'm momentarily angry at him. Fucking me like a whore, in his
own words, then insulting me and finally running away? That isn't
my Theo. What the hell happened to him? Did I do something?

Suddenly, I'm too anxious to function, and with the coke in
my system, I know I'm not going to be sleeping anytime soon.

I fish my phone from my bag and dial Theo. I can't just leave
this as it is. He's never acted like this before. Tapping my foot
anxiously, I wait for him to answer.

"Answer me, damn it!" It keeps ringing and ringing. I close the call and am about to check his tracker, but I suddenly remember I haven't set up a new one yet. Damn.

"Fuck," I curse aloud. I can't deal with this. Not with Theo like this, with no explanation. I try calling again. And again. It's probably ten minutes later of missed calls that he finally answers.

"What?" His voice is muffled, as if he's been sleeping.

"Theo?" I ask softly, not knowing what mood I'd find him in.

"What, Bianca?" he barks.

"Where are you? It's late, and I'm worried."

"Really?" His tone is sarcastic, and I don't like it. Not one bit.

"Theo, did I do something wrong? Please tell me what's going on," My tone takes a pleading note. I have no scruples when it comes to this man. If I have to throw my pride away for him? I'll do it in the blink of an eye. If I have to beg? I'll be on my knees day and night.

Please don't shut me out, I say a mental prayer as I wait for his reply.

A few seconds later, he whispers, "Bianca."

"Please, Theo, come home. We can talk about anything you like here. Please come back."

Another pause.

"I'll be there in a half hour."

"Thank you." He hangs up, and I release a breath I didn't realize I have been holding in.

I go about the kitchen and prepare a relatively easy meal. He'll definitely be hungry if he's been drinking. After I set the table, I take a seat. Staring at the clock on the wall, I wait.

It's like being in a trance. I focus on the clock hands moving with each second, each minute. I'm so absorbed in it that, hearing the front door open startles me. Lifting myself to my feet, I try to put on a smile for his sake.

"Theo," I say, a bit hesitantly. He's standing in the hall, his clothing wrinkled and disheveled, his bloodshot eyes red.

"Bianca... I..." he starts, but then he shakes his head. He takes a few tentative steps and then suddenly closes the distance and throws his arms around me.

"Forgive me." His arms are like a fortress around my body, holding me almost too tightly, but I embrace the possession.

"Please, tell me what's wrong," I whisper, my eyes tearing a little. If there's one weakness I have in this world, it's the man in front of me.

"Shh... It's all my fault. I'm so sorry for treating you like that. It's on me. I took out my frustrations on you." He still doesn't let me go.

"Theo... I didn't mind the sex. But the way you behaved afterward... It was like you couldn't stand the sight of me."

"No." He shakes his head fervently against me. "Never you. I was disgusted with myself. I took you like an animal."

My mouth seeks his jaw, and I pepper kisses all along his face.

"It was new, but... I liked it. We should do it again."

He accepts my kisses, breathing deeply.

"We're okay, no?" I ask again, unable to help myself. Something feels off, and I don't like it one bit.

"Yes, sweet." He finally shifts his head and gives me a kiss on my forehead. "Let's go to bed."

"Okay," I immediately agree, food and everything else forgotten.

He takes my hand and leads me to our room. I take off my robe and watch as he unbuttons his shirt and then takes off his pants. Lifting the cover, he nestles inside and holds his arms out for me. I go willingly, purring when I feel his naked skin against my own.

"I love you, Theo," I whisper as I huddle even closer to his warmth. I want to melt into him, knowing that if we indeed became one, he'd never be able to leave me. He would be *mine*. Utterly and completely *mine*. That's my last thought before falling asleep, but not before I hear him.

"I love you, B, more than anything."

13

THEO

The next morning, we don't talk anymore about what happened last night, about my abysmal behavior, or that I'd gotten shit-faced drunk when I rarely even drink.

Only when I get to work do I think clearly about what happened and my suspicions regarding Bianca's whereabouts. I get progressively pissed at myself for letting my insecurities get the best of me when I don't have any definitive proof she's having an affair. There has to be an explanation for her behavior these past few months, right? I don't want to accuse her of something and break our trust, or worse, see the disappointment in her eyes.

As much as I try to tell myself there has to be an explanation and that she isn't cheating, I can't help but still chew on it even hours later when Marcel comes to talk to me about a case.

He sits in the chair across from me, flipping through some documents. His perfectly put-together looks just emphasize my own wrecked state. He suddenly stops and looks at me pensively.

"Did you ask Bianca about the hotel?" he eventually asks.

"No," I mumble and continue to look at the files in my hand. I don't want to lie to Marcel, but I also don't want to talk to anyone about my and Bianca's problems. It isn't as if I don't trust Marcel. He's been my friend through thick and thin. We'd met at college and had immediately clicked, becoming fast friends. But we rarely talk about women. Marcel's love life is a mystery I'm not ready to crack. He seems too interested in my own, however, as he continues.

"Do you really think she's cheating on you?" I finally raise my eyes to meet his, and he has an incredulous look on his face, as if I'm a fool to even consider it.

"I don't know anymore. I got drunk last night and lashed out at her. Lucky she's a sweetheart, and she forgave me. But damn," I groan.

"I know, man." He threads his hand through his hair and sighs. "Look, I know I'm probably intruding... but I know Bianca, too. She'd never cheat on you."

"I'd never thought she'd cheat either but... there have been some suspicious things."

"Like what?"

"Her lying about where she is, missing work. I don't know what's going on, and she's never even hinted at problems at work or with other friends. I honestly don't know."

"Ask her!"

"Really? That's your best advice? What if she lies again?"

"I still don't think she's cheating. She's not the type."

"I know, and that's what baffles me. What is she hiding?"

"Simple. Get someone to follow her around. See what she's up to."

I sigh. "What if I don't want to find out?"

"That's up to you. I can get you hooked with a man to watch her. I trust him implicitly, and he owes me a favor." When he says that, I can only raise my eyebrows. Marcel has some questionable connections, one of them being the same Vlad who rules over Brighton Beach.

"Who is it?"

"My cousin Rico." He smiles. "He's a hustler. And I told you, he owes me."

"I don't know. I want to meet him first."

"Fair enough, let me give him a call."

Marcel stands, placing the rest of the files on my desk before leaving. I groan. Am I becoming one of those people who have their wives followed? Is this getting out of hand?

Close to the end of the day, as I head towards my car, Marcel gives me a call.

"We're in the back," he says and hangs up. I leave my car and head around to the back to find Marcel in his immaculate suit, standing next to what can only be described as a punk. I take a moment to observe both of them, looking for the similarities that would make them family. Marcel's hair is a sandy blonde with olive skin and amber eyes. Eyes he shares with this Rico. But his cousin is on the fairer side, with light-blond hair and pale skin. Their builds are similar, both of them relatively tall and muscular, but the way they carry themselves and their clothing make all the difference.

Marcel always looks stiff and put together, secretive and mysterious. He never has a hair out of place. The punk is dressed casually, his stance relaxed, and his mouth sports a constant grin. Rico must be in his late teens, early twenties, and the carefree of the youth is reflected in his face.

"This is Rico." Marcel motions to his cousin abruptly, very Marcel-like.

"Nice to meet you." I offer my hand, and he shakes it, giving Marcel the eye. I want to ask him if he's involved in anything illegal. It's just a feeling I got.

"I filled him in on the topic."

"Don't worry, dude, I got you," the punk drawls.

"I'll have Marcel hand you a copy of her usual schedule, but you should really follow her around from the moment she leaves the house."

"Not my first rodeo. I got you." Rico winks before turning his back and getting into a beat-up car. He gives us a hand gesture meant to say goodbye and mockingly addresses Marcel.

"Later, cub!" He takes off.

"You sure you trust him?" I ask Marcel again.

"He's... different. But he can do it, don't worry."

"Good," I say, but I don't know if I mean it. Is any of this good?

"He'll start tomorrow. I told him to call you if there's anything out of the ordinary and not like her regular routine."

"God, I just hope I won't regret this."

"Hey," Marcel starts and puts his hand on my shoulder. The entire gesture is shocking in itself because Marcel always avoids touching others. I look at him and see his consternation.

"It's going to be all right."

I just nod.

14

BIANCA

I'm going about my day as usual when my phone goes off, and *Private Number* appears on the screen. I look around the office, making sure no one is around, and I answer it. Something tells me that whoever is on the other line won't bring any good news.

"Artemis," I answer, using my mercenary code name.

"Little goddess." A chuckle at the end of the line alerts me to the caller's exact identity.

"Berserker," I reply sarcastically, knowing fully well he detests being called by that name.

"Alas, I bring about dire news." He sighs in that dramatic style of his.

"Spill, I can't talk for long."

"Oh, is that wimpy husband of yours around? You wound me."

"Don't force my hand. What is it?"

"That's exactly what I wanted to talk about. Your husband. You'll want to know."

"What is it?"

"Meet me tomorrow at 5. The bar."

"But—" I'm about to answer, but he hangs up on me. Fucker. Ugh... Nothing's going well. What could he have to tell me about my husband? Maybe it's something regarding the incident at the port. Whatever it is, it makes me too anxious.

I go through the motions at work, looking forward to arriving at home and seeing Theo.

We haven't said anything more about what happened last night, and I sincerely hope whatever happened to him isn't related to me or my activities.

Just thinking about the look he'd given me... Chills spread down my body. I could take a bullet, and it wouldn't kill me. But my husband's contempt? That would be the end of me.

When I finally arrive home, the most delicious smell in the world greets me.

"Theo?"

"In the kitchen," he yells. I round the corner to the kitchen to see him in a black shirt and gray sweatpants with an apron on top. He has mittens on his hands, and he's removing a tray from the oven.

"My, my," I start, the corner of my mouth lifting slightly. "What have we here?"

"My apology?" He grins at me and puts the tray on the table.

"And he cooks." I whistle suggestively. "Where can I find a man like that?"

"You have it." He gives me a kiss on the cheek.

"Aren't I lucky?"

"I'm all yours, darling. I come with lasagna too." He smiles and gestures to the food.

"Consider me impressed." I return his kiss and tell him I'll quickly change and join him for dinner.

When I'm back, he's already lit two candles and opened a red wine bottle, pouring it in two glasses.

"Alcohol again?" I raise an eyebrow jokingly, and he smiles sheepishly. "I have to say your apology gets a nine out of ten," I tease after I try a bite of the lasagna.

"Why'd you take one point off?" He frowns at me.

"You didn't get me flowers."

"You're allergic," he counters.

"I don't care; it's all about the gesture."

"But then you would have sneezed."

"Fake flowers." My tongue goes out at him cheekily.

"Should I be cheesy and say you're the most beautiful flower? Would I get the point for that?"

"Ewww, Theo. Too cheesy!" I laugh, and he joins me.

"Fair enough. I had to try."

"You're amazing, you know that?" My face softens as I look at him. I stand and come behind him, winding my arms around his neck.

"Only because it's you." His hand comes up on top of mine, and we stand like that for a moment.

"Okay, that's it. Let's put the dishes in the sink for Martha and let's go watch something."

"Am I forgiven?" His voice is serious now.

"Only if I am, for whatever I did." He shakes his head and purses his lips.

"I told you it was all me."

"Then there's nothing to forgive. Come on, I'll let you choose the show."

"Wow, so magnanimous of you." He follows me into the living room, and we make ourselves comfortable on the floor. It's been a tradition of ours ever since we'd gotten the penthouse. Since the carpets are so incredibly soft, we always end up there and not on the sofa. We browse around for a show, and after a while, he seems to find the courage to ask me something that's clearly been on his mind.

"B... Did you really like it?" He's still looking at the screen and not at me.

"I did." I sigh, and I turn to face him. "Theo, why did you think I wouldn't?"

"B... you're so soft, and you've had such a sheltered upbringing... I didn't think you'd ever..."

"I promise you I enjoyed it. Didn't you?" I throw the question at him.

There's such a duality in Theo, sometimes it's almost too amusing. Knowing how he'd treated Pink and how he'd enjoyed it had made me realize from the beginning that there were some depths to Theo that I just couldn't reach. Not as long as I was Bianca, the pure wife. As Pink, I'd felt it on my own skin how wild and uncontrolled he can be. As Bianca? He'd always held something back. Something animalistic and primal that called to the bloodthirst inside me.

"I did." I put my head on his shoulder and hug his arm. "Tell me something, Theo." I'm feeling daring, especially now that we're opening up to potential sexual adventures.

"What's your darkest sexual fantasy?" Almost as soon as the words are out of my mouth, I feel him stiffen.

"What... what prompted that?"

"Well, if we're going to have an open discussion, why not lay it all out there. What's something you'd really, *really* like to try?"

There's a pause where he almost doesn't breathe.

"To have you at my mercy," he finally says, and it's my turn to frown. That's it?

"You already have me." I try to make light of it.

He gives a tortured laugh.

"You have absolutely no idea what you're saying."

"I'll let you do whatever you want to me," I tell him, hoping he'll give me some specifics.

"Whatever," he repeats almost in wonder. "B... I would destroy you."

I look at him, expecting him to laugh, but he's earnest. My eyes meet his, and I see the truth. He would, in fact, destroy me.

Ah, how I wish he would.

15

BIANCA

I leave for work as usual and stay for a few hours. Then I head to my apartment to get ready for the meeting. I'd barely slept last night. Even after Theo's surprise, I was still anxious about today's meeting. I know Berserker would never contact me if it wasn't something I needed to know. Which makes the anticipation worse?

I get inside my apartment and head for my closet. I put on a pair of leather pants, a black tank top, and a leather jacket with a big bow and arrow on its back. Turning towards the big mirror, I add a long, red wig with big curls and silver contacts. Sheathing a good number of knives in my combat boots, I also add a small gun, just to be sure.

I'd gotten my code name Artemis due to my perfect aim. I've never actually used a bow and arrow, but my reputation for hunting down targets has made sure the name is deserved. Stopping by the bedroom for a dose of magic powder, I then take the elevator and go to the parking lot where my Harley is waiting for me. Whenever I venture into the underground world, I hold onto my Artemis persona, so my disguise always needs to be impeccable. It isn't as if Berserker doesn't know who I am, but the rest of the people do not. And it's better if it stays that way.

After getting on my ride, I speed through the highway and head towards Brooklyn. It doesn't take me too long to reach the club, given that it's still daytime. There are a few outsiders around. I park my Harley and head towards the entrance. A big guy stands outside, but he just nods and opens the door for me.

"The boss is in his office." is all he says.

I nod and enter. On my way to the office, I pass a few tattooed guys who give me odd looks. When I am in front of the door, I knock three times, slowly withdrawing one of the knives from the hiding place.

"Come in."

I enter the room and see him behind his desk, his long legs propped on the table in a relaxed manner.

"Punctual. What else is to be expected from a goddess?" He gives me one of his wicked grins.

"Cut it," I reply and throw the knife an inch from his head. He doesn't flinch. His expression doesn't change. He just watches me. And then he laughs.

"Ahhhh, heavenly love. Of course." He takes his feet off the table and stands, coming around the desk to give me a big hug.

"It's been what... three weeks?"

"Four. But who's counting." I smile and return the hug. "Okay, so spill, what happened."

"Little goddess, so impatient." He shakes his head. He knows that anything Theo related makes me lose control.

"Come on, Vlad. Out with it. You wouldn't have asked me to come if it wasn't serious."

"That's the issue. I don't know how serious." He stops smiling and motions me towards the computer on his desk. He presses a key on it, and a video of me in my Chanel dress from when I'd gone to scout locations for the shooting plays on the screen.

"What's this?"

"This is you being irresponsible. Fucking irresponsible," he says, and I can tell he's disappointed.

"Why do you have this?"

"Because," he starts in an exasperated tone, "Marcel, your husband's dear friend Marcel, asked me for footage in the region related to some shooting. Now, if you'd told me of your plans, I would have known not to give them the footage. But you never ask for help, do you? And now, you're on camera, going inside a seedy hotel a few days before a shooting that resulted in three fucking corpses. Care to tell me what your excuse is? Damn it, B, you're smarter than this."

I'm shocked at his outburst. But more than anything, I'm appalled at what he's saying. I look again at the video and realize that you can tell it *is* me, especially when I'm leaving the hotel. This is bad. He's right. I was careless. Fucking hell. My hands clench at my side.

"Did my husband see this?"

"He did, and he recognized you."

"Fuck," I curse and kick the desk with my foot. "Fuck, Fuck, Fuck!" Shit... was this why he was behaving so oddly? No fucking way. He can't know.

"Did he make the connection?" I ask, and I'm almost afraid to know.

"No... I think I saved your ass, but I threw you under the bus simultaneously."

"Out with it, Vlad. I need to know."

"I might have said it looked like you were having an affair."

My mouth drops open as I stare at him. Affair? Shit. I look back to the video, and I see that my hair was visibly wet when I exited the hotel. I pale. This doesn't look good.

"Did he believe it?"

"I don't know... He looked stricken. I think the seed was planted."

"Fuck. That makes so much sense."

"What?"

"When I got home, probably after he'd seen the footage, he was so drunk. I'd never seen him like that. Then, out of nowhere, he backs me against the wall and fucks the shit out of me. This makes so much sense," I mutter.

I'm pacing now, realizing the reason for his behavior. He'd been jealous. Did he think I'd *ever* cheat on him? I pause to think about it. I'd never let any other man besides him touch me. He couldn't *actually* believe I'd cheat.

"He fucked the shit out of you?" Vlad asks, amused. "I didn't think he had it in him."

"Oh, shut it. What do I do now? I can't have him thinking I'd cheat, but I also can't exactly go tell him, *oh, you know that day, I was just planning to gun down anyone who was a danger to you. Oh, and by the way, I'm a paid killer.* I don't even know which one is worse."

Vlad brings his hand up to rub his chin pensively. "The killer part, definitely. Maybe he's into that cuckold scene. I could give you a hand." I punch his shoulder hard, making him wince and throw up his hands in a sign of peace.

"Stop bad mouthing my husband. I need to think."

"I just don't get it. Why were you so fucking careless?"

"I don't know, okay. It's never happened before." He's silent for a minute, tapping his foot.

"You're using again," he says accusingly, and I give him a sad smile.

"When did I really stop?"

"You should. It's messing with your efficiency. One of these days, you're going to get yourself killed. And you'll have those drugs to thank for that."

"Whatever," I mumble, knowing he's right.

"B," he calls affectionately, "I can help."

"I know... but I don't know if I'm ready."

"One of these days, you'll have to be... I don't like you wasting away because of drugs."

"Says the drug trafficker," I snort.

"Yeah, well, I don't touch that shit."

"Whatever," I say again and try to change the subject. "I'm going to try to sneak my visit to the hotel into a conversation and spin a tale. I really don't want him suspecting anything, especially infidelity."

Vlad shakes his head.

"That husband of yours is going to get himself into trouble one day. You know he's been asking for it ever since he started digging into Jimenez. It's only a matter of time before they hear, and you know what will happen then."

"I'm well aware. Hell, I've been monitoring him ever since we got married, and I've killed every single potential danger. I'll just continue to kill anyone who intends to harm him."

"Until when? How long? You can't keep going like that, B. You're not invincible either. If anything, this video should tell you that you're slipping. And in our world, when you slip, you die."

"I know. Fuck, don't I know it... But he won't give up this crusade of his. He's going after Jimenez regardless of whether I approve or not."

"It's a suicide mission."

"I don't know what I can do. I honestly don't know. He doesn't even tell me that. Everything I know about him that's not on paper is by having him under surveillance. He hides from me just as much as I hide from him."

"Then why don't you try a little truth for a change?" I give a fake laugh.

"The moment he knows who I am... what I am.... is the moment he walks away. I'm sure of it."

"How can you be so sure? You've told me before that you heard he liked innocent women, so you turned yourself into one. But how do you really know he won't accept you for who you are?"

"Because," I say, aggravated at both myself and the situation, "He fucked me once against a wall, and then he was profusely apologizing by cooking and setting up a candlelight dinner. For a fucking quickie against the wall that was a little rougher than the norm. How do you think he'd react to me killing for a living because I enjoy it, not because I need the money? Better yet, how do you think he'd react to knowing he fucked me in the most obscene ways disguised as a hooker before I even met him as Bianca? Oh, and let's not forget the part where I stalked, tracked, and investigated him for years so I could mold myself into his ideal woman?" I'm breathing hard at this point, all my frustrations and worries out in the open.

"Well... when you put it like that, it does sound bad."

"Of course it sounds bad! Even to my ears, it sounds bad, and I did all that. Fuck me now," I say, exasperated.

"But have you thought that maybe if he knew the real you, he'd also show you the real him? Because I'm not convinced of that 'innocent woman' act. You know that men in my culture are often guilty of the Madonna-whore complex. He fits the mold. You also forget I've met the fucker. He's so stiff and proper; I'd never believed him capable of what he did to you as Pink. But he did. That tells me he's hiding something beneath the surface, and it's simmering. Men who hold it in like this... when they explode, it's not pretty."

Biting my nails, I nod. "That's just the thing. For him, Bianca would be the Madonna and Pink the whore. But I don't think he could ever merge the two in his mind."

"You won't know if you don't give him a chance. I'm telling you, B, I just think there's more to the man than we know."

"Ugh... I really didn't need this."

"Now... back to your issue."

"Which one?"

"The coke. How often?"

"Every couple of days," I reply hesitantly.

"Hell, B... it's not okay."

"I know... but I've never had the time to properly wean myself off it."

"You need to do it and soon. It might just get you killed."

"Yeah," I agree.

"Tell your husband you have a trip abroad for your charity or whatever. I'll help you. You know I have the experience."

"When?" I ask, thoughtfully considering his proposition. Just now, I realize how much the drugs have been messing with my mind. Vlad is right. I *am* slipping.

"Next week?"

"I'm meeting an arms dealer on Monday."

"Good. This works. Come to the club on Friday. Say you will be gone for at least a week."

"Vlad... ugh, I don't know. Won't he get suspicious? With the cheating thing and all?"

"You need your wits about you, B, if you want to protect him *and yourself*. I didn't want to tell you this now, but Martinez's death caused quite the commotion among the cartels. There are whispers that Ortega is seeking retribution. And you know who the target will be."

"Then, more than ever, I need to be with Theo."

"I can have my people on him." I shake my head at his words. I can't leave Theo in the care of strangers.

"I can't."

"Damn it, B."

"Look, I can't leave. But I'll do my best to wean myself off on my own."

Vlad sighs in defeat. "Fine. But you call me if you need anything."

"Of course," I agree, and I go for a hug. For all his nagging, Vlad has been a prized friend for an awfully long time. He's probably one of the few people who know the whole truth about me, and I trust him with my life.

"I should probably go."

"Take care. And contact me if anything. I mean it."

"I will." I stand on my tiptoes and kiss his cheek. Then, before I leave, I go to the wall and retrieve my knife.

"Thanks for everything, Berserker." I wink at him, and he groans.

I am a certified sociopath if you couldn't already tell.

You grow up surrounded by wealth and glitz but zero human connection. You act out in a manner that is typical to you, that is normal for you. You lie, cheat, deceive. Until someone comes along and tells you that's not normal. That you're not normal.

That's what happened to me when I was ten.

When I suddenly found out why my father ignored me and why the staff avoided me. I wasn't normal. I was defective. But I was also disruptive.

Evil.

If my father had been religious, he'd have called for an exorcism. But he was just cynical, so he'd shrugged it off and moved on.

It wasn't until Drew was assigned as my bodyguard that someone pointed out my behavior was wrong. Different. He cared enough to get me professional help, even though the prognosis wasn't something to be proud of.

Antisocial Personality Disorder.

Suddenly, there was a reason why I liked violence. Why I didn't value human life. Why I'd spin whatever lie I could to achieve my goals. The shrink told me the cause might be early childhood neglect and abuse. I didn't believe him. After all, I'd never cared whether my father acknowledged me or not. I had my own world.

But as I was growing up, so did my ideas evolve into more complex scenarios. Scenarios that put people at risk and made me into a danger to society. Or so I'd been told.

My father didn't care. Of course, he wouldn't. I didn't care either; I didn't care about society. But Drew cared. Drew had a high sense of morality, and he felt it was his duty to ensure I could control myself.

He'd taken it upon himself to help me channel my rage and bloodthirst into more productive endeavors. He'd taught me how to fight, spar, and shoot. The shooting soothed me. That calmed the rage. It started with pistols. Then, when he discovered I had an inclination for it, he'd taught me how to use sniper rifles. And that's how my love affair with shooting started.

By the time I was sixteen, I was as well trained as any professional. But I also had something most didn't—a disregard for right or wrong. To make sure I kept my urges in check, Drew guided me towards mercenary work. I didn't kill because I needed the money. I killed because I needed to kill.

Besides my comprehensive skill set, I was also blessed with a small frame and quick reflexes that helped me get out of most situations. My penchant for disguises also came in handy, and I always managed to cover my traces thoroughly.

I killed my first target the summer I turned sixteen. It wasn't glamorous or messy. Or anything, really. It was also how I met Vlad, three years my senior and one of the sons of the Pakhan of the Russian Bratva, my contractor. He'd laughed at me when he'd been told I was accompanying him on the mission. We were to kill a Ukrainian official who had a fondness for underage girls and who had gotten on the Bratva's wrong side. Initially, Vlad was supposed to make the killing while I'd serve as a distraction. I didn't care about specifics. I'd gone to a hotel room with the man, and within five minutes, he'd been dead. When Vlad had come in to finish the job, he'd raged at me for stealing his kill.

"I thought you said girls are useless." I'd raised an eyebrow at him and dared him to comment on it. He'd pursed his lips and told me to get out of there.

That was the start of a very rocky partnership. We were paired together on different missions for the whole year, all of which ended in arguments and bickering. For all the disagreements, though, a pleasant camaraderie developed between us. I'd quickly recognized that Vlad, like me, didn't have a moral compass. (Although his sense of humor was more developed than mine.) But we did share something far more critical than any feeling of right and wrong. Loyalty. While we both struggled with human companionship and social interactions, we recognized loyalty for what it was—the ultimate badge of honor.

Although we were branded as monsters by society, we built our own honor system, and we held each other in the highest esteem. We became known as Artemis and the Berserker.

Until it all changed.

It was supposed to be an easy mission. We'd already proven ourselves as a reliable duo. It never occurred to us that we may not return from it alive.

We were sent to accompany a shipment of drugs until it got into the hands of the Bratva. We quickly realized it was all a trap.

"Shut it, *malyshka*, I'm trying to concentrate." He pinched his eyebrows in annoyance at my chatter while flinging the pages of his book. We were sitting around in the back of a truck while the delivery was made.

"You're no fun, Berserker," I replied, knowing he hated being called by that name.

"If you don't stop talking, I'm going to stuff these pages down your throat."

"I'd like to see you try." I flipped him off, and he put the book down, ready to charge me. We always sparred around. Just as he was about to make a grab for me, the truck came to a complete stop, and we were flung about.

"Shit," we both said at the same time, composing ourselves and readying for whatever was happening on the outside. It didn't take long for the shots to fire from all directions.

We looked at each other in confusion. No one had said anything about any danger. Our presence here was supposed to be a mere formality.

Vlad removed his *shashkas* from the back. He always used two, one in each hand. It was strange, but he rarely used guns, preferring the intimate feeling of killing at close range. Whenever he started, however, he went on a killing spree, hence his code name Berserker. It was also why we were the perfect pair. I preferred guns, rarely relying on knives or any other types of weapons. And I always had his back.

"Cover me," he said, and I nodded, removing two Glocks from my holsters and taking my stance. He opened the door to the cargo container with a kick, and we both quickly jumped and sought cover. We assessed the situation and saw that the driver had been killed, as well the other people in the two cars accompanying us.

"How many?" he asked, and I scanned the surroundings.

"I see two up front and three at the cars." I moved a little to the right to get a better view.

"Another one is coming our way." I held my palm to Vlad and counted the seconds with my fingers. Vlad took my signal and charged the man as he came upon us. He crisscrossed his blades at the man's neck, slashing his throat in one motion.

"Take the front, I'll take the back." I nodded and went into the open. I cocked my guns and aimed, killing the two men at the truck's cockpit. From the corner of my eye, I saw Vlad sneaking around the two cars in front, almost upon the other three.

They noticed me, so their attention was occupied. I lifted one of the men I'd killed and used him as a human shield. It wasn't easy as he was a mountain of a man. I was grateful when I saw Vlad throw two knives, each lodging into the men's skulls. The other two seemed disoriented, looking between Vlad and me.

"Now!" Vlad yelled, and I flung the corpse from my side, ducked, then rolled on the ground as shots flew above my head, and took a kill shot as soon as I landed. That was the last man, the other already dead by Vlad's blade.

I took a deep breath and joined Vlad.

"Did you see?" he asked, looking at the carnage before us. I knew what he was referring to. We went to each and every one of the corpses and ripped the sleeves off their shirts.

"It doesn't make sense," I said. We were looking at six individuals with Bratva tattoos. The Bratva tattoo that Vlad sported as well.

"Fuck." He started towards one of the cars. "Get in!" I quickly followed, frowning at his urgency. "What?"

"We need to get back to the quarters. This isn't good." We got into the car, and he already started the engine.

"It's a coup."

"A coup? But who?"

"My stupid ass of a brother, that's who. Fuck! I should have seen it coming. Misha's always been power hungry, but I didn't think he had it in him."

"So, what, he kills the entire family to become Pakhan?"

"Yes. And if we don't get there in time, it will be a blood bath." I'd never seen Vlad so serious. It wasn't until we got to the quarters that I realized why. He didn't care about his father. But his sisters? That was a different matter altogether.

Just as Vlad suspected, his brother had indeed overtaken the quarters. We managed to pull the feed from some of the security cameras and noticed the men had been quickly replaced with people we didn't recognize. One of the cameras we managed to access was from the main hall of the house, and we could see traces of blood everywhere. Not shocking, Dima Kuznetsov, Vlad's father, and the Pakhan of the Bratva lay dead in the middle of the hall.

A demonstration.

Misha, his brother, and the traitor who'd started all this addressed a few people from the center of the room.

We drove fast, but it still took us a while before we got to the quarters. Nestled deep within Brooklyn, the quarters were around Shepherd's Bay. Because we'd been sent to Union Beach, NJ, it was a wonder we managed to make the journey in a half hour. Still, we were a half hour too late.

In fact, the quarters of the Bratva were a couple of old mansions that housed the leading members of the organization and their families and where all-important business was conducted and other less legal means of coercing information out of people.

Vlad didn't even bother to properly park the car as he got out and started towards the gates. Having gotten an idea of what was happening inside, I reached out and stopped him. Instinctively, he flipped my hand off.

"Stop, you moron," I said, "Think about this, you're walking to your death."

That statement made him pause.

"So what? I'll die with honor. Not a traitor."

"You don't need to die if we're smart about this."

"What do you have in mind?" he asked, and I smirked.

"You got yourself a sniper, use it well."

The moment the words were out of my mouth, the corner of his turned up, too. He realized what I was thinking. We spent a few minutes hashing out the plans, and then we went in different directions of the house.

Vlad went through the main gates, ready to greet the carnage made by his brother, while I went towards a broken part of the fence. My goal was to first secure my gear. Having worked for a while now with the Bratva, I had my little office on the premises. Before advancing, though, I made sure my Glocks were fully charged with ammo, then I attached a silencer to each pistol's end.

The key to our plan was the element of surprise that my arrival would cause. Vlad was to only shake things up a little until I got a good shot at Misha.

I managed to sneak through the hole in the fence and then made my way across the lawn, trying to avoid as much attention as possible. Just as I was about to round the corner towards one of the back entrances, a man spotted me. I didn't hesitate as I pulled the trigger for a shot between his eyes. Lowering my gun, I sprinted across and entered the house.

Two more people came across me as I made my way towards my office, both of them now lying in a blood pool. Just as I was about to reach my destination, a bullet whizzed past my shoulder, taking some skin with it. It burned. Oh well, the pain gave me a new purpose. I smiled as I saw the man who'd taken the shot and returned the favor.

I finally opened the door to my office, and with as much speed as I could muster, I assembled my favorite rifle and slung it across my shoulder. Now the more challenging part. To have a full view of the main house's hall, I had to go to the second building's surveillance tower. It would be a challenge to get there unnoticed.

I quickly exited the house and tried to keep out of sight as I ran across the lawn again.

Surprisingly, I reached the second building in record time. Going through yet another back entrance, I had to shoot two more people down before getting to the surveillance tower.

Glad there were no more interruptions inside the room, I locked the door, adding some of the furniture for extra force. Then I took my position and looked through the telescope. I adjusted my view a little, and finally, I could see what was happening in the hall.

Misha was arrogantly pacing the floor. Vlad was being held by two goons. His clothes were full of blood, and so was his face. Not his blood, of that I was confident. Misha seemed to say something, probably gloating about his treachery. I fixated on Misha and waited for him to stand still. His hands flailed around.

"Stop moving!" I muttered to myself.

He moved again to remove one of Vlad's shashkas and hold it

against his throat. I had to hurry. I controlled my breathing and looked for the red dot to coincide with his skull. *Please, move a little to the right*, I whispered to myself.

And he did.

Just as he moved two millimeters to the right, I took my hit, right between his eyes. Kill shot. The moment Misha dropped dead, Vlad wrenched himself free from the men holding him, immediately slaying them. He then stood and looked right at me.

He was a sight, that's to be sure. So bloody and fierce. He was magnificent. If I weren't already in love, I might have differently appreciated the dashing figure he cut all in red.

He winked. I laughed and lowered my rifle. It seems that my best friend was the new Pakhan.

16

THEO

Last night's conversation with Bianca left some lingering thoughts. I'd been shocked when she'd asked me about my darkest sexual fantasies. It had sent me back to a period in my life, before Bianca, when I had indulged in those dark fantasies. It had also made me question whether I was truly satisfied with how things had been with Bianca in the bedroom. Ever since I'd started seriously seeing her, I'd never even entertained the thought of unleashing myself on her.

She'd been so quiet, reserved. So sheltered. Knowing the darkness that had been my life before her, I'd wanted to preserve that innocence against all costs, so our lovemaking had always been tender and restrained. I can picture even now the night I'd taken her virginity. It had been under the covers and in the darkness of the night. She'd been shy and tentative in her explorations, and I'd tried to make her as comfortable as possible. After that, I'd always been as careful as possible with her, not wanting to scare her away with my desires. Looking back now, by treating her with kid gloves, I'd also been denying myself.

Suddenly, thoughts of another woman come to mind, one I'd treated the exact opposite of my wife.

Before Bianca, I hadn't dated, my career goals taking precedence over romance. All my sexual escapades had been relegated to prostitutes, and even those had been rare.

118

I'd met this particular hooker after I'd started joining some of the senior associates in the mayor's office at this strip club named Palace. I'd been watching her the whole night the first time I saw her. But *she* was the one who approached me first.

"You know the rules, handsome?" I was in the VIP section on a couch when she'd come up to me and asked. She was dressed in a purple skintight mini dress that emphasized her curves. She'd had these gorgeous green eyes that seemed to sparkle when she looked at me.

"Look but don't touch?" I'd barely found my words, so mesmerized I'd been by the slope of her breasts and the sway of her hips.

"This one, you can touch." She'd gotten on her knees in front of me, her hands slowly creeping up my thigh.

"And what else?" I'd asked, my right hand caressing her cheek before my thumb slipped behind her lips.

She'd sucked it before saying, "You can do whatever you want to me." Her hands had continued their exploration until they'd reached the growing bulge in my pants. With a languorous pace, she'd opened my trousers and taken me in her hand. Everything had stilled as she'd dropped her head to lick me from base to tip before taking me deep into her throat. My hands had gone to her hair of their own accord, and I'd fucked her mouth like a mad man. After I exploded in her mouth, she'd licked her lips clean and purred. Without a word, she'd stood to leave, but I'd had to get her name.

"Pink," she'd said and walked away.

It wasn't until she was well out of sight that I'd realized she'd just sucked me off in front of everyone. That'd been my first taste of Pink, and I kept coming back for more. For over two years, she'd been my only avenue for physical relief. Then I met Bianca, and I stopped going back to the Palace.

I'm not going to lie and say that my thoughts haven't strayed to Pink once or twice in the past years. She'd been the first woman I'd fucked more than once and on a regular basis. She'd also been the epitome of sexuality wrapped in a delicious package. Few women fucked like Pink did, with such depravity and abandon.

But for all the bliss I'd found inside Pink once upon a time, I'd never exchange what I have now with Bianca. Sex, for the sake of sex, didn't hold a candle for sex with an emotional connection. Even if we lack spiciness in our lovemaking, it's still mind blowing because it's with her.

But it seems that now she's open to trying more. And I can't wait.

"Rico is following her now." Marcel leans against the wall, his nose in a document when he casually informs me about Rico, interrupting me from my reminiscing.

I groan aloud at that. Reality crashes down as I realize that while our sex life may be improving, my wife may also be cheating on me.

"I am curious, though." Marcel comes towards me, dropping the files on the table.

"What?"

"What will you do if she's actually having an affair?" I look at him for a second, considering my reply.

"Will you divorce her?" he continues to probe. I frown at his question, not because it wouldn't be the natural one if one's spouse were having an affair, but because Marcel is the one asking a personal problem. Again.

"I don't know," I reply honestly. Marcel nods and takes a seat, changing topics.

"I got someone willing to give us information about Jimenez. Are you sure you want to proceed? You saw how it all turned out with Martinez. These people are dangerous."

"In my position, I can't really afford to care about the dangers. Not when people are suffering under Jimenez. Not when I know he has undetected sex rings right under the nose of NYPD."

Marcel shakes his head.

"We both know it's not really about your constituents. I'm fairly sure your parents wouldn't want you to disregard your safety." Marcel is close to hitting a nerve, so I just grunt.

We've rarely talked about my parents or my personal connection with Jimenez, and I want to keep it that way. *That* topic belongs to a different arena of my life. One that I'd long left behind.

"What I'm trying to say is that they have connections. Dangerous connections. I'm not talking about people who can ruin your career. I'm talking about people who won't hesitate to put a bullet through your skull. You and everyone you love."

I give him a dry smile. "That's not exactly encouraging."

"No, but you saw how Martinez died. And in their world, that's mercy."

"Sometimes, Marcel, I have the nagging feeling that you know too much of their world."

"You do what you gotta do, right?" He looks away.

"Right..." But I still wonder... He knows my deepest secrets, but do I know his?

It's a little over seven, and I'm just wrapping up my work, ready to go home, when Marcel suddenly appears in my office.

"Rico's got something to tell us," he says before dialing his cousin on his phone and setting it on speaker on the table.

"Yo, cuz." Rico starts, and I can see a nerve twitching in Marcel's eye. He clearly doesn't have any lost love for his cousin.

"I'm with Theo, tell us what you found."

"I got her usual schedule, and it says here she's at the foundation from nine to six with a lunch break at one."

"Yeah, that's her regular schedule," I agree, somehow hoping his next words will confirm that's exactly where she's been between those hours.

"Well... She left work at twelve, then went to an apartment building in Midtown, 67th Street. She was in there until a little over five pm. After that, she left and headed directly to your home."

I am stunned.

Speechless.

I look at Marcel with what must be horror in my eyes because he's the one who hangs up on his cousin, thanking him for his work and telling him to continue watching her.

"I gather you don't know anything about that apartment?"

I just shake my head, still too shocked.

"Can you..." I barely find my voice to ask. "Can you please look into that apartment? Find out who owns it? If there's a... man?"

"On it. It will take a few days, though."

"Yes, don't worry. Take your time."

"I have to warn you, though, as a lawyer," Marcel starts, "You must not let her know you suspect she might be having an affair. Then we won't be able to gather the evidence. In the event of a divorce... You need all types of ammunition you can get."

"I know... I know," I sigh.

"I'm really sorry, Theo. I really thought she was different," Marcel adds, and I give him a sad smile. He's a good friend.

"It's still not certain. There could be another explanation. I'm willing to wait until I see irrevocable proof that she's having an affair. I just don't want to believe she would do that. Now, when I know how much we love each other." What I don't say is that I refuse to believe all her words of love were lies. Yes, there has to be another explanation.

"We will see."

We both leave the building, and during the drive home, I try my best to calm myself. Maybe other people would call me a fool to not believe she might be cheating when there's one piece of evidence after another, all pointing in that direction. But at the same time, if there ever was something that I trust with my life, it would be the depth of Bianca's feelings for me. There's just something between us. This connection I felt within seconds of meeting her. Just being in her presence fills me with so much peace... I just refuse to believe she'd let another man touch her.

When I get home, she's already there. I can see she's showered; her hair is wet, and she's wearing a towel wrapped around her body.

"Theo." She smiles when she sees me, and I do what I always do. I open my arms for her to come. She's a tiny thing, my wife, her head only reaching the middle of my chest. She wraps her arms around my middle and holds tightly. It's now that I notice the differences in our sizes and how easy it would be for me to crush her. My fists clench in the air before I remember and hug her in return.

"Long day at work?" she asks, probably because the stress is written all over my face.

"Too long." I try to make my mouth move in a semblance of a smile, hoping she won't think there's anything off with me.

"Do you like the smell of this shampoo?" she suddenly asks and wrinkles her nose. She's too cute.

I bend towards her to sniff, and I nod.

"Hmm... what is it? I can't put my finger on it."

"Ughh... so a couple days ago... or was it last week?" she starts, and her eyes move to the left as if she's trying to come up with the timeline. "Anyway, doesn't matter. I was about to go for a meeting in Brooklyn, and a pigeon pooped in my hair. So, I had to find somewhere quickly to get rid of that thing. I went to this hotel to quickly shower, and they had the most amazing shampoo I've ever smelled. I don't know what it was but God, Theo... It was *that* good," she moans as she recalls it. "I've been trying to find it ever since, which is the closest I've come. It's a combination of bergamot and orange, I think."

"It's really nice." I manage a smile as I take in the information she's just dumped on me. Surely...

"When was this? The pigeon poop?"

"The pigeon poop." She laughs as if it's the most ridiculous thing, and in a way it is.

"I don't remember exactly, but I was wearing that Chanel dress that you love. A little got on my shoulder too. I think I ruined it when I tried to wash the spot by hand," she complains with a pout.

"Oh no, the blue one?" I ask, trying to confirm what is slowly becoming a vastly different narrative than I would have expected.

"Yeah, that one. The spot I cleaned is a little discolored. I might just take it to a dry cleaner and see if there's anything to be done."

"I can do it for you in the morning when I go to work. There's one next to us."

"Really? Why didn't I ask you before? Must have slipped my

mind. Thank you!" She goes on her tiptoes and gives me a sweet kiss.

"Come eat, I made some pasta!"

I follow her into the kitchen, and we proceed to eat in amiable silence, now and then adding some insights from our work.

I can't believe it. My wife just explained to me the truth about the video. She wasn't meeting any man. She wasn't cheating. The only question is... do I trust her? I have no reason not to. She couldn't have known I suspected anything, and she simply couldn't have known I'd seen the footage from the hotel. Suddenly, I feel ashamed that I'd even contemplated such a thing. The apartment in Midtown must have a clear explanation too, and I'm sure she will tell me.

All in due time.

I can be patient.

———

Later in the night, we're both in bed, flushed and sated, when nagging doubts keep creeping in my brain, so I just blurt out.

"Do you ever regret not experimenting with other men before me?" Now, out of my mouth, the question doesn't sound like it did in my head. It sounds as if I'm criticizing her for being inexperienced when I mean the opposite.

"Theo, what brought this on?" She's half-sitting on my chest, and as she asks, she lifts her head and looks at me with those innocent eyes of hers.

"Never mind," I mumble, trying to get out of this. Her hand comes to my face, and she caresses my jaw.

"I don't, and I never will."

"But haven't you ever thought what it would be like with someone else...?" I don't know why I'm digging my own grave, but I need to know.

"Honestly? No. I didn't even notice other men before I saw you, Theo. I couldn't bear anyone else touching me but you. But why would you ask me this?" Her words, coupled with the sincerity I see reflected in her eyes, mollify my fears.

"Sometimes I'm afraid. I'm scared I might not be enough for you. You're young, vibrant, and beautiful, and I'm..." I don't get to finish as she grabs my face with both hands and stares me in the eyes.

"Don't you dare say anything else. You are the most attractive man in my eyes. Do you really think you're the only man I've ever seen in my life? I've been to so many functions and parties. I've met people. What I haven't met is another man to awaken such a visceral feeling in me. I don't just love you, Theo. You are everything to me. Everything."

I look at her, getting worked up over that declaration, and I feel my chest bursting with love. And just like that, I believe her.

"I love you too, B." I kiss her forehead.

"Good. You better." She giggles. "Although now, it's my turn to ask. Would you have preferred I had more experience? Is that it?"

"Hell, no!" My reply is instantaneous. "I wouldn't change a thing about you, B. I have to admit that knowing I'm the only man you've ever been with does warm my heart, but only because you've chosen *me* to share yourself with. Not anyone else. It makes me feel... special."

"Aww, you say the sweetest things."

"That isn't to say that if you'd been more experienced, I would have loved you any less. I don't want you to even contemplate that."

"Oh." She waves her hand, dismissing the notion. "It would have never happened. I wasn't kidding when I told you that I don't feel even remotely attracted to other men."

"Then, I'm a lucky bastard," I say, wrapping my arms around her and turning so that she's on her back, and I'm settled between her legs.

"I'm the lucky one," she whispers before taking my lips for a kiss while accepting me into her body.

Before I fall asleep, I text Marcel to call off Rico. I will just have to trust my wife.

17

BIANCA

"**I** think I managed to convince him about the hotel," I say over the phone to Vlad.

"I'm curious, what did you come up with?" he asks with a chuckle.

"That I got rained on by pigeon poop and had to take a shower before a meeting?"

"B!" Vlad groans aloud. "Tell me you didn't actually say that?"

"Well..." I bite my nails. "It was along those lines."

"And he actually believed you? I stand corrected, your husband is a wimp."

"Hey! I told you to stop insulting him. I can assure you he is not a wimp."

"Only a wimp would buy that shit because he's afraid to accept the truth. I really don't know why you're so obsessed with the guy."

"If you knew him, you'd be obsessed with him too," I retort, because honestly, in my mind, everyone should be obsessed with Theo.

He is just *that* special.

"Sorry, B, I don't swing that way."

"You don't swing either way, do you?"

"B, don't let out all my secrets, *malyshka.* I need a little

126

mystery. I'll also have you know that leading the Bratva is hard, and my Tinder dates would take offense to me showing up with blood residue on my sleeves after a bout of torture," he whines, and I can already imagine his face.

Truth is, I'd never seen Vlad with a woman, a man, or any other individual. I don't know whether it's his maniacal side that drives them off or merely his disinterest.

But then again, Vlad's never shown any type of feelings other than loyalty. Even his sense of humor is a mask that he started using to avoid scaring people off. It was also why I was the only one who could be partnered up with him, anyone else being too terrified of him.

He'd fought against it at first, saying he didn't need a partner, especially a little girl, but his father had known that he required someone to keep his blood lust in check.

The thing about Vlad is... he seems affable and normal until something sets him off. Then God help anyone in his path. Supposedly, at fifteen, he'd single-handedly offed an entire gang in Harlem, only with his shashkas, and it had taken a sedative to calm him down.

"I've heard some chicks dig the whole blood and gore thing."

"They do only if I'm a sparkling vampire. I keep up with the times, you know. They'd run for the hills if they knew my body count."

"What's your body count?" I ask cheekily.

"I don't kill and tell, B."

"You've probably lost count."

"Yeah... I'm going to plead the fifth on that."

"What kind of assassin are you if you don't have any notches?"

He pauses as if it's a foreign concept. "Do you?"

"Of course. I'm very organized. I would also like to know how many times to ask for forgiveness if Theo finds out."

"Damn, little goddess. Seriously, what did you see in that wimp? You got a suit of all things. Couldn't you at least have gone for a more hands-on profession?"

I sigh... We'd had these conversations before. Vlad's always of the opinion that in our profession, you cannot risk any attachments. He's also never approved of Theo, thinking he was too weak for me.

"Theo has a great capacity for kindness," I say. "He has something I completely lack."

"So, that's it? Just because he's *normal?*" He says normal as if it's the plague. Understandable, though, since we'd both been told we're abnormal our entire lives. We'd both learned to pretend, though.

"No, not just that. I don't know if I ever told you how I met him for the first time. It was at my father's house, and he was hosting a business dinner. As any dutiful daughter, I had to keep up appearances and attend.

"You know how I was with my father's associates. I would always keep my mouth shut and plan their deaths slowly in my head. Well... one of his guests got a little too drunk and insulted me, calling me a doormat, a decoration, and asked how much to buy me."

"Did you kill him?" he suddenly interrupts me.

"A year after, I couldn't risk suspicion."

"Yesss!" I imagine him bumping a fist in the air based on his excited tone.

"Back to the story. He was also getting into my personal space. Theo was the only one who told the man off, defended me, and was on the brink of punching him."

"Oh, so he has some balls?"

"Shut it. He was being kind to someone he didn't know. More importantly, he stood to lose the most, given that he was looking for support from those people."

"Fine, so he's a principled asshole. Still don't know why you bother so much," he mumbles.

"You wouldn't understand. You've never loved someone like I love Theo."

He's quiet for a minute.

"Is it love, though? Are you even capable of love?"

I contemplate his question.

"I don't know. I don't know how regular people love. I only

know that what I feel for him is strong enough that I'd kill anything and anyone attempting to harm him. So, whatever I am capable of feeling is all for him."

"I'm jealous, little goddess." His voice is dreamy. "I wish I could feel... anything, really. The only semblance of feeling I can muster is when I kill, and even then, it's like a high that wears off almost as soon as it starts. Fight for your wimp then, B. You know I'll always have your back."

"I know, Vlad. Same here."

"Now, though, the real reason why I called you."

"You didn't call to ask for the state of my marriage? I'm disappointed."

"As you can see, I'm very invested in your marriage, but that's not why I wanted to talk to you."

"Okay, what is it?"

"The arms dealer you said you were meeting on Monday. I got some intel that it might not be legit."

"What do you mean?"

"Several organizations have been trying to acquire those new weapons from them. All of them have been busts."

"Fuck! I was looking forward to a new rifle."

"I want in on the guy you're meeting, though. There have been rumors of rats that target specific people for these purchases."

"And you think because of my connection to you, it might be someone on the inside?"

"I'm not sure, but I don't want any loose ends. If there's a rat in my midst, I have to exterminate."

"Okay, let's do this then. The meeting is Monday at two p.m., Room 204 at Empire. We can go earlier and set up the room."

"It will be like old times, little goddess."

"Like old times... Sure." I chuckle, knowing fully well that old times means chaos and mayhem.

"I'll pick you up at your apartment."

"Fine. I'll see you then."

"Later." He hangs up.

Talking to Vlad always puts me in a good mood. But now that my marriage isn't on the brink of collapse anymore, I'm in an even better mood. Since tomorrow marks the start of the weekend, and both Theo and I are free, I decided to plan a little something to show him that he's the only object of my affection. Or obsession, I should say.

I smile to myself, mentally planning our weekend escapade.

18

BIANCA

"**A**re you not going to tell me where we're going?" I'm currently driving while Theo is anxiously trying to keep his calm in the seat next to me.

"Come on, babe, just wait until we get there."

"Is it going to be much longer?" I sneak a peek at him, and I see him holding onto the handle.

"Why, Theodore Hastings, if anyone saw you right now, they'd think you're afraid of your wife's driving skills," I tease, knowing fully well he always prefers to be the one driving because I'm not the most careful driver. I'd have let him drive under normal circumstances, but I want to surprise him with this weekend getaway.

"I'll just count my blessings if we don't die," he mumbles, and I give him a smile. Yes, I drive badly, or I should say recklessly. I might even be the poster child for road rage. Of course, Theo probably thinks my skills are just bad because I'm a woman. I shake my head, smirking. I rarely get the chance to drive when he's in the car with me, so I might as well take full advantage.

"I have some not so pleasant news," he says, trying to adjust himself in the seat.

"What is it?"

"Your father called." I frown.

"And?"

"He requests our presence for a family lunch tomorrow."

"Of course. He requests. He never asks." I grimace.

"I'm sorry." Theo gives me a sad smile. My father always calls Theo because he knows he will get a positive response from him. Being one of the mayor's main sponsors gives him some perks, like being able to snap his fingers and expect us to come. My fingers clench around the wheel. It's not even all about money since I could pour my own resources in Theo's office, but the connections tie us to Martin Ashby.

"It's okay. We'll do the usual in and out." I try to appease him. As if it's not bad enough that Theo needs him, he doesn't like the man. Mainly because he's noticed he doesn't care about me at all. Theo's mentioned the issue several times and has told me he wished we could cut ties entirely with him. But given his influence... I bide my time, though. The moment I notice that my father is putting too much pressure on Theo, or threatens him, I snap.

"I don't know why such short notice. I'm guessing Martin has other guests and wants to parade us around."

"Of course. Why else would he even acknowledge us? Don't worry, we can put up with it for a few hours. But now, at least for today, we can enjoy ourselves."

"You plan on keeping me in the dark about this surprise of yours?"

"Oh, yes!"

We're now winding down a path next to some woods. The place should come into view at any moment now. Given that it's the only house in the area, Theo immediately realizes what I meant by surprise.

"You rented a lake house?" I give him a knowing smile.

"We've both been under a lot of stress lately. I thought that maybe if we're away from all the noise, we could relax."

He suddenly leans into me and gives me a very loud smooch.

"Love you, babe," I laugh.

"Yeah, well, wait until you see the jacuzzi. I made sure there was one." I lift my eyebrows suggestively. We'd had some sexy times in a jacuzzi on our honeymoon. You see, I'm trying to earn brownie points here to distract him from the mess I made.

We pull into the man-made driveway and park the car.

"Babe," he says, inhaling the fresh air. "Best idea ever." I wink at him, and we proceed to unload our small bags from the car.

I'd initially rented this for the whole weekend, but since we need to be at my father's house tomorrow, we might as well make the best of this. It's almost mid-May, and the weather is warm enough for the outside jacuzzi. In fact, we may get away with some lake action too, if the water isn't too cold.

We enter the house, and after checking the rooms, we drop our bags in the master bedroom.

"Shit." Theo stops suddenly. "I don't have any swimming trunks."

"Don't worry, already packed them." I remove our swimming suits from my bag, and we quickly change.

The jacuzzi is located right in front of the house, on the porch, overlooking the lake. It's a fantastic view.

After we get in, I snuggle to Theo's side, and we stay like that for a moment.

"Babe..." he starts, his hand going to my bare stomach. "Would you be willing to go for a fertility checkup?" I lift my eyes to meet him, and I am momentarily at a loss of words. "The both of us, of course."

I don't know how to reply. I've been putting off for so long, giving him a proper answer, I don't know how to respond to this. More than me saying yes to this, there are several things I'd have to seriously consider, like my reliance on coke.

"You really want to get pregnant, don't you?"

"I've always wanted to be a father, and I'm not getting any younger. I thought you wanted kids too..." He lets the sentence hang, and I feel the unspoken reproach, so I immediately lie through my teeth.

"Of course, I do. I just hoped it would happen naturally, you know, now that I'm off birth control."

"It's been six months, and it's not as if we haven't tried."

"You're right. I guess I didn't really keep track," I lie.

"B, please tell me if this isn't what you want."

"Of course it's what I want. I'd want nothing more than to have your child."

"I'm glad." His arms tighten around me. "So, what do you think of my suggestion?"

"We should do it. We should make appointments when we get to the city."

"Thank you!" He kisses my temple before peppering kisses on my whole face. "Thank you, thank you, thank you!"

He turns me around, so I'm straddling him. He leans in and gives my lips a nibble before resting his forehead on mine.

"You really make me the happiest."

Oh, Theo... if you only knew.

We're in bed, wrapped in each other's arms. Discussing children with Theo has made me realize the depth of his desire to be a father. In turn, it solidifies my decision to wean myself off drugs, get clean, and actively try to get pregnant. Who knows, maybe I'll be a good mother.

A part of me is afraid that I won't love the child, but at the same time, considering my feelings for Theo, it seems impossible that I wouldn't love any part of him.

The only outstanding issue is my dependence on coke. I'd had a few lines in the morning, after trying to go a couple of days without. My determination hadn't lasted long. But now, I am once again motivated. Although, honestly, I'm not looking forward to at least a week of feeling like shit.

I look up at Theo's sleeping form, taking in his chiseled jaw with just a hint of stubble and his so exceptionally long lashes. My fingers itch to trace the planes of his face, but I don't want to wake him. Not when I've worn him down so much. I smile to myself, just remembering the feeling of his massive body on top of mine. Ever since we'd discussed our attitudes to sex more in depth,

Theo's tried to treat me less like a porcelain doll and more like a woman. Which, in turn, has left me in a state of perpetual satisfaction.

I slowly and carefully get out of bed and make my way to the bathroom, intent on brushing my teeth. It's a split of a second later that my instincts go into full attention mode. Creaking. I hear creaking. There's no one else in the house and no one else in the area. Dressed only in a satin nightgown, I quietly go to my bag, searching for the hidden compartment where I usually keep a pocket pistol. I check for ammo, grimacing as I count only five bullets.

I take another look at Theo in bed and decide against waking him. Treading carefully, so I don't make any type of noise, I look over the baluster to see a few men looking around the house's bottom floor.

"*Ay cabrón, tenemos que terminar esto antes de que el jefe se de cuenta de lo que pasó,*" one of them says.

"*Estúpido,*" one of the men insults the other. "*Si no fuera por tus ideas no estaríamos en esta situación. ¿Quién te dijo que puedes disparar a cualquiera? ¿Si alguien* escuchó?"

"*Carnal... Estamos en el medio de nowhere. ¿Quién podría escuchar?*"

"*Ay cállate. Sabes qué pasa si nos regresamos sin prueba que este gringo esta muerto.*"

I understand enough to know they're after my husband. *Theo, what did you get yourself into?*

From what I can tell, the men each carry a 9mm. And I still don't know how many there are. Fuck! Fuck! Fuck! I quickly shoot a look at the master bedroom door and debate what to do. If any gun goes off, Theo will wake, and he might come barging in the middle of the shooting. I'm torn, but as my mind wrestles with what to do, I know I can't waste any time. The men are already on the stairs. I see three.

Three men. I'll have two bullets left. I just have to hope they didn't send more than three people. The men are still bickering, not very quietly either. It's quite apparent they're low-ranked cartel people.

Taking advantage of their lack of attention, I take position and aim.

I manage to hit two of them, with the third moving around as he sees his partners fall to the ground.

"*Hijo de puta,*" I hear the other say as he takes a few stairs at a time to reach the landing, making him on the same level as me. He points the gun towards me.

Simultaneously, the master suite door opens, and Theo looks at the cartel guy and then at me, his eyes widening in understanding. It all happens in less than a second. The cartel guy immediately changes his focus, turning his gun towards Theo. I move as fast as I can to push Theo back inside the room, and with a cry, I shoot the guy, luckily hitting the hand holding the gun. His own gun goes off, and whether it's my movement or his lack of aim, the bullet only grazes my sidearm.

"Bianca!" Theo screams, but I try not to mind him. I turn once again towards the intruder and put a bullet through his head.

I open the door to the room and see Theo on the floor, looking in horror at me.

"You're bleeding." He points towards my arm, but I wave it off.

"We need to leave now!"

"What..." he starts, but I just drag him, quickly picking up the car keys from the vanity.

"Now!"

Theo frowns but doesn't argue. He pulls on a pair of sweats, and we immediately leave the room, making our way downstairs and towards the car.

While we go down the stairs and over the other two cartel men's dead bodies, Theo surprises me by picking up their weapons and taking them with him.

"Wait here," he says, and I'm almost tempted to tell him off, but seeing Theo take charge in this situation is practically unreal. His stance changes almost immediately, checking the premises for any other intruders. When he's satisfied there's no one else, he waves me over, taking my hand.

We quickly dash towards the car, him in the driver's seat and me in the passenger. He doesn't waste any time putting it into gear and driving us off.

There's one second where I realize just what happened and the fact that I slipped from character. I immediately try to rectify it by making my body shake and willing myself to cry.

"I killed them..." I say in what I hope is a shocked voice. "What happened, Theo? Who were those men? I..." I let my tears flow freely.

Theo is intent on the road ahead, but he pauses just enough to give a command.

"There's a phone in that compartment. Take it out and dial Marcel."

Internally, I'm frowning at his request (not a request though), but with shaky fingers, I do as Theo says.

"Put it on speaker." I do.

"Do you know what time it is, Theo?" Marcel's voice comes through.

"We have a problem." Theo's voice is so severe but composed. I don't think I've ever seen him like this.

"I guessed," Marcel replies drily.

"You were right. We were attacked." There was a pause.

"Are you all right?"

"Yes. Three men. Latino," Theo says, and I add in my best attempt at seeming scared, "They... were... speaking... Spanish."

"Fuck. I didn't think they'd retaliate that quickly."

"Me neither."

"Are they dead?"

Theo gives me an odd look before answering in the affirmative.

"I'll take care of it." I quickly give Marcel the address of the lake house, and we hang up.

Theo doesn't talk to me for what seems like an eternity, driving into the night, until he suddenly pulls over on an abandoned road.

I will my tears to continue to spill, to continue to keep up my pretense.

Theo bangs his head on the steering wheel.

"Theo...?" I ask tentatively, but his voice when he replies scares me.

"Stop!"

We spend a few more minutes in silence. The only noises in the car are my sobs and Theo's harsh breathing.

"How?" he finally asks, lifting his head to look at me as if he's never seen me before. His eyes are steely and unyielding. It's a side of Theo I've never seen, and suddenly, I don't know what to do.

"You killed them," he states.

"They were going to kill you!" I yell at him, thinking that an emotional response is the expected one in this scenario. I've seen movies. I've seen how people react after such frights, and I hope that my impression convinces him.

"I heard them," I continue, my voice taking on a bleak note. "They were there to kill you." I grab his arm. "Oh, what have you done, Theo?" He's still looking at me as if weighing my words.

"How did you kill them?"

"My... pistol... you know the one Drew gave me."

"Tell me from the beginning," he demands, and I realize this is my chance to make him believe me.

"I got out of bed..." I start between silent sobs. "I thought I heard steps downstairs. But it couldn't be, right? Who could have been there? I suddenly got super afraid it was a thief or something. I didn't even think; I just went for the pocket pistol I always carry in my purse. You know the one... There were three of them. Oh Theo, when I heard what they were saying, how they were going to kill you... I just reacted. I aimed and prayed to God; I got them. But then one got away and... Oh, Theo, he almost shot you! I don't... I can't..." I start crying in earnest, and Theo takes me in his arms.

"Shush. It's okay. We're both okay and alive."

"Who were they, Theo? Who wants to kill you?"

"Just some bad people who don't approve of my policies," he says as if it's the most normal thing to just kill someone for disparate opinions. At that moment, I realize I don't know Theo at all.

"We're going to a hotel," he says, and I just nod. A while later, still on the road, he adds, "Never do that again. Don't you dare try to put yourself in front of a bullet for me? Am I clear?"

"Theo..."

"Am I clear?"

"Yes."

19

THEO

Waiting for Marcel's phone call, I sneak a glance at Bianca, where she's lying on the hotel bed, still shaken from what happened. Her entire body is stiff, and she darts her eyes around, almost expecting another attack.

After taking care of her small wound, I try my best to soothe her, but the shock doesn't seem to wear off. Or so she says. So many things have gone wrong tonight. So many things have happened that I simply can't wrap my head around.

She killed three men.

I didn't analyze the cartel men's bodies, but for a simple civilian to put down three criminals is just beyond me. I've seen trained professionals in my day struggle with hitting targets in that amount of time.

No matter her explanations, something doesn't add up.

"Are you okay?" I ask as I sit next to her and hand her a glass of water.

"Yes... just in shock, I guess." I put my hand over hers to comfort her.

"You just went through massive trauma. It's understandable. You should sleep."

"I can't..." she whispers.

"Wait here," I say and quickly go to my car. I remember

140

Marcel leaving some sleeping pills there. They should help her rest.

Returning to the room, I hand her the pills. "Take these, they'll help you rest."

She eyes the pills and almost reluctantly takes them.

"Thank you," she murmurs.

We lay on the bed, and I spoon her from behind, waiting for the pills to kick in. It doesn't take long for her breathing to regulate. I slowly get out of bed, leaving the hotel room again.

I head to the car, and I look at the dashcam footage, seeing the three men exit a vehicle and haphazardly organizing their attack. I try to look for some clues in the footage when Marcel calls.

"Can you talk?" Is the first thing he says.

"Yes, why?"

"I'm at the lake house with a cleaning crew. Damn, that aim," he whistles his appreciation. "I never knew you had it in you," he says, and I frown at his praise.

"I didn't kill them."

"What are you saying? If you didn't kill them, then..."

"Bianca."

"Are you certain?" Marcel asks, and I get the feeling that whatever Marcel is seeing there isn't great.

"Yes, positive."

"Man... I don't know how to tell you this."

"I'm on my way. I'm not far."

"Your wife?"

"Sleeping at a hotel."

"Good. This is... you'll see."

I end the call and head back to the lake house. That is precisely the issue. I don't want to see it. Somehow, I know that what I will find at the lake house will forever change my relationship with my wife.

It doesn't take me long to get there, and I see a few other cars, probably the cleaning crew, in the driveway. Marcel comes to greet me.

I quickly tell him my version of events and ask, "How bad?" He gives me a small grimace.

"I think we may have found our sniper," he says, and I abruptly turn to him with a questioning look in my eyes.

"Marcel..." I start, but he stops me.

"Don't say anything until you see this."

We enter the house, and I see everything exactly as we'd left it.

"I told them not to touch anything until you got here." I nod.

We go up the stairs until we reach the first two bodies. I crouch down to look at their injuries, and I'm shocked by what I see.

"This... how?"

"It's a clean kill shot. Both of them actually. Do you know what the odds are to get that aim, not once but twice?"

"Not great, I'm guessing."

"Extremely rare." He waves over a young man standing by on the sidelines.

"Jacob, you do this all the time. What does this shot tell you?" Marcel asks for his opinion. A feeling of dread takes shape in my stomach.

"That's a pro shot. And I mean pro, pro shot." Marcel thanks him, and I give them leave to deal with these two corpses.

Jacob and another guy come over with what looks like a body bag. They lay it open on the floor and, almost carelessly, they dump one of the bodies inside it. They do the same with the other one. It strikes me as almost inhuman the way they treat the bodies, but then I remember that it's their job. By now, they've probably become too desensitized to it... to death.

"Now, on to the third guy. You already told me that she shot him twice." Marcel snaps me to attention, motioning for the second story of the house.

We get to the top of the stairs, and I see exactly what those shots had been. One shot to his wrist to remove his weapon, and then another kill shot to the head. His hand has a glaring hole in it, suggesting just how clean the shot had been. I slowly peruse the other gunshot wound, and I'm amazed at the alignment of the bullet. Squinting, I look at the distance between the wound and each eye. It's almost mathematical in precision.

"Again, what are the odds that someone got three perfect kill shots in these conditions? None, unless..." He lets it hang, and I fill the gap.

"Unless it's a professional."

"This doesn't look good, Theo. Not only that, but we have her at the scene of Martinez's shooting too."

"What are you trying to say? That my wife is some sort of trained killer?" I ask, sounding a little more defensive than intended.

"All I'm saying is that the evidence is piling up... and it's up to you whether you believe it a fluke that she got those shots, or not."

"Damn..." I mutter.

"And I've been thinking..." Marcel frowns, bringing his hand to his forehead.

"What?"

"Remember the schoolgirl? I want to watch the footage again." I look at him suspiciously for a second before I realize what he's hinting at.

I barely nod, a little taken aback by the potential conjecture. Marcel tells the rest of the crew to finish the job, and we head to his car.

Leaving the house behind, I see more staff in special equipment going towards the house with cleaning supplies. These guys sure are thorough. I wonder where Marcel found them.

"I have a laptop with me," Marcel mentions as we get to his car. He opens the computer and plays the footage again. Surely enough, we first see the footage of my wife going inside the hotel and then exiting.

"She was in there for two hours," I say, realizing she couldn't have taken a shower for that long.

"And then..." Marcel plays the footage for the day of the shooting, where we only see the schoolgirl leaving, but not arriving. We pause on the frame.

"Her height matches," Marcel adds. I squint at the still, but I can't make out much else.

"That would mean she had another disguise going in."

"Or she didn't use the main entrance."

"Damn... okay. Let's say it was her. How did she even know I was meeting with Martinez, or where I was meeting him?"

Marcel and I think on it for a second before we both look at each other in horror.

"The bug we found!" He's the first to note.

"We thought it was the opposition... Shit."

"Your wife... how well do you know her, Theo?"

"Not at all, it seems... but how? I still can't believe it. *How?*"

"You don't just become that skilled overnight, Theo. She's had years and years of practice."

"The apartment Rico followed her to. Did you find who it belongs to?"

"Not yet, most likely, I'll get a reply on Monday." I nod and then frown again.

"So, let me get this straight. My wife's not cheating on me, but she *is* a trained killer and a liar. Fuck me, I don't know what's worse."

"You're taking this surprisingly well."

"Trust me, I haven't fully internalized it. My whole marriage is a farce. Who knows how many other lies she's told me?"

"Don't let her know *you* know. We need to be careful if we want to find out more."

"At this point, I'm terrified what more I could find out."

"There's something I can do to help," Marcel says and opens a briefcase, withdrawing a tiny device. "It's small but packs a punch. Integrated GPS and listening device. Might help."

"Thanks," I mumble before adding, "I should head back. I can't have her wake up and not find me there. Especially now."

"I agree. I'll take care of the rest here. Just... be on alert. We don't know how dangerous she is. Or worse... if she works for someone."

"Wait... You actually think she might have been sent by someone?"

"That skill... there are a handful of people who can do what she does, and they all come with an extreme price tag. We can't let our guard down, especially now that we're going deeper into the Jimenez shit."

He's right. I hadn't even thought of it from that angle until now.

"Fuck! Fine, I'll be careful."

I leave the lake house, trying to block all thoughts during the ride to the hotel. I wasn't lying to Marcel when I'd told him I hadn't internalized the information. Because it's absurd. Yet... all evidence points to the absurd as truth.

Who are you, Bianca?

I quietly enter the hotel room, take off my clothes, and slide into the bed next to my wife. Instinctively, she snuggles closer to me.

An image suddenly appears in my mind.

The moment I'd opened the door at the lake house when I'd seen her aiming the gun at the intruder, her expression had been cold... blank. I superimpose it to the image I have of *my* Bianca—sweet and innocent.

It doesn't match. They are two different people.

I just had the worst realization that the Bianca I love might not even exist.

So far, Bianca's maintained her facade. It's funny because, for all her pretense, she's never once asked me to notify the police. She has tried to get some information on what Marcel did with the bodies, but I shut her down.

She doesn't need to know for now.

Because my own wife may be a cold-blooded killer, the less she knows, the better. I can't believe she might have planted bugs on me. How long has she been doing this? Tracking me? Listening to conversations? There are so many questions going through my head right now, but I cannot allow myself to crack or show that I am in any way suspicious of her. I have to treat her as I've always done and figure out who she really is.

I almost want to laugh.

My wife, a killer, and a liar.

Hey, at least she hasn't slept with another man, my inner voice tells me. I'm almost mad at myself for being relieved she's not having an affair.

But yes, if I'm being frank, I'd rather she be a killer than a cheater.

What does that say about me? That I'm just as fucked up like her?

Yeah, I'll take that.

But more than anything, I'm disappointed. A disappointment so deep, I feel like a part of my heart has withered and died. After spending most of my teens and early twenties in what could only be described as hell on earth, doing everything to survive to see another day, I'd thought she was my peace, my salvation.

Instead, it slowly dawns on me that I'd exchanged one hell for another. I can never escape the violence or wash away the blood.

I'm startled out of my thoughts by a beeping sound that indicates we're running low on gas. I furtively glance at Bianca, and she has her bag on her lap, her hands nervously fidgeting with it.

"Gotta fill the tank," I say, and she just nods absentmindedly.

"I can't believe after last night, we still have to meet my father."

"Yeah... me too."

We resume our silence until we reach a gas station. I get out to fill the tank. After it's done, I signal her that I will pay and distance myself from the car. Call it instinct, but I know that she makes a grab for her phone the moment I'm out of sight. I can even see the movement.

Instead of entering to pay, I hide next to the building and open the app Marcel had installed on my phone, clicking in to listen to what's happening in my car. I hear Russian, and immediately, I record so I can have it translated later.

"не могу говорит. думаю что муж знает. он увидел мне убить три человека." Her words seem hurried, her accent quite flawless, but hey, what do I know about Russian?

A brief pause, and then I hear my name *"Да, Тео был подозрительный. ити один завтра. Пока."*

After she hangs up, I send the recording to Marcel and tell him to give me a translation before heading to pay. I'm inside the store for maybe five minutes when the message comes through with the translation.

Can't talk. My husband knows. He saw me kill three men; Yes, Theo was suspicious. Go alone tomorrow. Later.

Marcel follows the text with.

This isn't good. Convince her you don't suspect a thing. If she's a Russian implant, it could really blow in our faces.

I reply that I'll try before deleting all the messages.

Not even a day ago, Bianca and I were planning to visit a fertility doctor to expand our family. Suddenly, not only is she a killer, a liar, but she might also be a fucking Russian spy.

I school my expression and go back to the car. Inside, Bianca gives me a timorous smile, and I have the urge to both strangle her and kiss her.

Kiss her?

Yeah, I must be as sick as she is.

I've been playing the same role for too many years. I know how to control my expressions to appear timid, shy, introverted. And yet, why does it seem so hard to maintain this mask right now? I feel like I'm suffocating. Like Theo's always waiting for me to slip. After my crying performance last night and the minimal interaction with Theo, I think I overdid it. But I keep going.

At the same time, I also want to know what the deal with Marcel is. I've met him often enough over the years, but none of our encounters have denoted that Marcel is familiar with these types of issues. The way Theo has made it sound is like Marcel doing the clean-up is a regular thing.

One thing is for sure, though. I can't afford to show any holes in my persona. It's also why I had to let Vlad know the thing tomorrow is off. I need to act as normal as I can in the near future.

We're now in my room at my father's house. Theo is in front of the mirror, tying his cravat. I'd donned one of my summer mid-thigh dresses, going for a laid-back yet not too casual look.

As soon as we get to the house, we're greeted by my father's assistant who tells us to take some time to get ready, that there'll be other guests. We'd expected there to be other guests because my father only invites us when he wants to show off a family man's image. It's good for business, or so he always says.

"Do you have any idea who the other invitees are?" Theo asks me, finally breaking the torturous silence.

"No, but don't worry. We do what we always do. Smile, make small talk, and then we leave."

"Indeed." His eyes follow me through the mirror, and I muster the courage to go up to him and touch him. Theo and I have always had a very tactile relationship and keeping a distance would immediately mean admitting something is wrong.

My hands go up his crisply white shirt to settle on his biceps.

"We can do this." I raise myself on my tiptoes to briefly touch my lips against his. He doesn't move, doesn't even react, a glint of something in his eyes. We stand staring at each other for a long moment before his hand encircles my waist, and he tugs me in for a tight hug.

"We're a team," he whispers, almost without conviction.

"Always." I smile into his chest, hoping those words will always stay true.

"Okay, enough of this. Let's go down and face the crowd."

He offers me his arm, and we go towards the large sitting room on the ground floor.

My father's house is massive. It has over forty rooms; most of them only used when my father throws one of his extravagant parties. A double spiraling staircase is in the middle of the hall-way. As we descend towards the great hall, I spot a few figures shaking my father's hand and starting towards the sitting room.

When we arrive, it seems we are the last ones to do so, and everyone's eyes are suddenly on us.

An elderly gentleman is talking to my father, next to whom I see another man around Theo's age, his hand clinically touching the woman next to him. Another two men, already deep in conversation, are on an opposite couch.

"Here are my daughter and son-in-law." My father stands and comes to us with a big smile on his face. The other people stand as well.

Let the acting begin!

My own lips immediately stretch to their full ability, and I see Theo putting on a pleasant smile as well.

"Gentleman," my father begins, clearly about to make the introductions.

"Bianca, Theo, these are Rocco Agosti and his son Enzo Agosti, and the lovely lady next to him is his wife Allegra." He motions towards them, and I'm almost taken aback by the identity of the guests.

Rocco is a portly man with gray hair that has to be about sixty, if not more. His son, though, doesn't resemble him in the least. He is quite tall, with a muscular built, yet it's his face that's entirely too surprising. If I were a normal woman, I might have swooned. The symmetry of his features coupled with his coloring are a dangerous combination. He has an olive skin tone that's accentuated by his vividly green eyes and dark hair.

Pretty boy... very pretty. Too cute when compared with his wife. She's small and frail looking, her bones too breakable. Her face is passable, I suppose, but compared to her husband, she is just... forgettable.

"Agosti, Bianca, and Theodore Hastings." My father completes the first round of introductions.

"Pleased to meet you, Mrs. Hastings." Enzo purrs in accented English, taking my hand and kissing my knuckles. I'm already forcing myself to smile, but my cheeks must look unnaturally compressed at his gesture. Theo's arm tightens around me immediately, and he steps in to shake Enzo's hand, deliberately taking his attention from me.

"Italian, right?" my husband asks.

"Born in the States but raised in Sicily," Enzo answers, showing white teeth and a dazzling smile. I narrow my eyes at him, not quite understanding how someone can look like that. I then shift my gaze to his wife, and she seems utterly indifferent to her husband's flirtatious charm. Odd.

"And these two gentlemen," my father continues, "are Matthew Gallagher and his son Quinn Gallagher from Boston." Both father and son are incredibly fair, their looks the opposite of everyone in the room. They are handsome, in an Aryan way, but their stance tells me they are also deadly.

Then realization dawns.

Well, fuck me!

If this isn't a mob meeting...

I haven't had much interaction with the Italian or Irish mafia, but it seems that my father is quick to rectify that. I'm not dumb. I can read between the lines, with Enzo and his Sicilian upbringing, or the Gallagher men from Boston, who I am sure are packing ammo right as we speak.

Yet my smile doesn't waver. Theo doesn't react either, but I'm guessing he doesn't realize what's happening. His only tell that he is a little out of his comfort zone is that he keeps me glued to his side, the arm around my waist digging into my skin.

I want to tell him he has nothing to worry about, even though any sane woman would admit Enzo's looks are blinding. So, to mollify him, I lean into his shoulder, letting my cheek rest a little on his arm.

"Come, let us sit. We have much to discuss. Mr. Ashby has been singing you both a lot of praise. I can see why he is such a proud papa," the fat man says, and I almost gag when he utters proud papa. If he only knew...

We go to sit on the couches, presumably until called to the dining room. I take a seat next to Allegra, and I see Theo being ushered next to the Agostis. The Gallaghers are directly across from us.

After staring intently at my husband, Quinn Gallagher starts the conversation by asking the oddest question.

"You seem remarkably familiar, Mr. Hastings. Have we met before?" Quinn's face shows traces of a rough mob life. Two white lines bisect his left eyebrow, and his nose has seen better days, potentially before being broken several times. My gaze goes directly to his knuckles, and my suspicions are confirmed. Fighter. But then I'm startled by a thought, and my head snaps in Theo's direction, zoning in on his knuckles as well. Odd...

"Oh, he was in Boston at Harvard; maybe you moved in the same circles?" I quickly jump to Theo's defense.

Quinn laughs.

"Oh, I doubt that.... never mind." I give him one of my *Yes, drop it* smiles.

"Harvard, huh?" Enzo starts. "Is that where you met your delectable wife?" His question throws me off a little, mainly because the wording is inappropriate.

"We met in this very house, in fact. Her father introduced us."

"Such a pity I didn't know you earlier, Mr. Ashby." Enzo turns towards my father and adds.

Everyone laughs. I fake a laugh too, but looking at his wife, I wonder what type of marriage they have that he so blatantly disregards her. She doesn't seem to mind it, though. I would even go as far as to say that her smile is the most genuine one until now. Odd again.

Theo looks in my direction at his comment, his eyes zoning in on my face.

"What can I say, I'm a lucky man," Theo finally says, and the topic is dropped.

The conversation goes on for a little while before we finally head to lunch, and my father reveals his true intentions for this meeting.

21

THEO

After the events of last night, I never thought I'd have another shock in the form of my past staring right into my eyes. Quinn Gallagher is someone I'd known in passing more than a decade ago, and I really hope he won't continue with his line of questioning. If he does, I'll just have to shrug it off and go with *I have one of those faces* lines.

Bianca's intervention has saved me a reply, but her manner of conversing with these people is somehow off. She's being extra solicitous to them. Does she know any of them? I'm particularly taken aback when Enzo Agosti makes some blatantly flirtatious comments towards Bianca, with his own wife standing right next to him.

The whole affair reeks of something more than just a family lunch. I know that Martin dips his fingers in a variety of projects, some of them skirting the line of legality, but the Gallaghers' presence here tells me this isn't merely a matter of loopholes.

I know of their empire in Boston. Who lives there and doesn't find out, or mingles with their likes, even unknowingly? I'm also aware of their personal brand of illegality, which has been thriving in that area since the NYC mob busts in the 80s and 90s that made it outlawed here. And somehow, because of that, I have an inkling as to why I'm needed here.

The Agostis' presence, though? That's a mystery.

Not long after meeting Martin's guests, the butler ushers us all towards the dining room.

Again, I can tell Martin is up to something because he has made sure the seating arrangement puts me next to both Rocco Agosti and Matthew Gallagher, with Bianca next to Enzo Agosti and Quinn Gallagher.

I'm almost tempted to protest, but then I remember she may as well be the deadliest of the room and decide that she can take care of herself. The look she gives me, though, suggests she's not entirely pleased with the arrangement. Enzo's young wife is left to sit next to Martin.

We go through the first two courses making small talk until Martin turns towards me and steers the conversation towards my current career goals.

"It's quite impressive what you've achieved at such a young age, Mr. Hastings," Rocco comments.

"It hasn't been exactly easy," I reply carefully.

"I understand that there are certain topics you are very passionate about."

"Yes, that's correct," I agree, waiting to see where this is going.

"My husband is very involved with the community," Bianca interjects. "He's of the opinion that public servants should always work in tandem with their communities, not only for them." She gives me a smile that shows her pride in my work.

"That is a very commendable stance," Enzo adds, looking at my wife as if she were the dessert that is yet to come. "We, too, deeply believe in such collaborations with our public servants. In fact, over the years, we've developed close relationships that have benefited communities and neighborhoods immensely."

"What is it that you do again?" I ask, and Enzo gives Martin a long look.

"We dabble in everything. But mostly, we own a chain of restaurants and hotels downtown. We've been looking to expand, however."

"My son is correct. Ours is a family business, and we have long been involved in hospitality," Rocco says proudly.

"Where are you thinking of expanding?" This time, Bianca asks the question.

"Oh, here and there, but mostly, we were looking into Upper Manhattan."

"Gallagher here is also thinking of expanding his business, and New York has proven to be the perfect place, with Agosti's help, of course." Martin inclines his head at Rocco, and Matthew nods.

"I wish you luck. I know how hard it is to procure any type of space in Manhattan, least of all enough space for a hotel or restaurant." I'm trying to be friendly and yet distant. There must be a reason why Martin had us come here, and I'm willing to bet it has to do with the expansion plans.

"We're in the process of buying out another family-owned business, and Matthew has given us leave to use his resources."

"That's great," I say and then decide to just go for it. "On the off chance of sounding rude, I will be direct. What is it you want from me?"

"Oh," Martin laughs, almost nervously. "I told you he was smart."

"As mentioned earlier," Enzo starts, his accent thicker than before. "We, too, care about the well-being of the community and would like nothing more than to see it thrive. We've seen your track record when it comes to your policies against crime, especially against homelessness and prostitution."

"Yes, that's correct. I've been campaigning religiously to get the people off the streets. Studies have shown that places rife with homelessness and prostitution are most likely to provide a conducive environment for other crimes. My goal is for my constituents to feel safe in their homes and in their neighborhoods."

"Ahh, I knew you'd understand." Enzo claps. "It is hard, no, to get the people off the streets." I don't have to reply as he continues, "What you need is someone to do the groundwork for you."

"That's why we have NYPD," I add drily.

"And you've had NYPD for almost two hundred years. Tell me, has it helped all that much?"

"It's the way it is. I won't sit here and sing praises to the police.

I know there's bureaucracy involved that simply weakens the system, but what else can be done?"

"Mr. Hastings, I trust you are familiar with the protection system in Sicily?"

"You mean mafia protection?" Oh, here we go to the root of the issue.

"Indeed. I've spent most of my formative years in Sicily, and I've gained a significant understanding of such practice's pros and cons. In fact, I can mostly see the pros."

"Of course, there are pros." My words are perhaps too biting. "For the people offering protection, not those who truly need protecting."

"Alas, that was in the past. It's a new century, a new era. We can learn from our mistakes and make it so that everyone benefits from such a scheme."

"So, what are you proposing, in fact, Mr. Agosti?"

"We can help you with your goals of emptying the streets and keeping the crime rate low."

"We... who is we?"

"At this point, our family has entered a partnership with Gallagher's family. By joining our forces, we can supply enough manpower to ensure the streets are safe and that residents are no longer fearful."

"And what how will everyone benefit from this, exactly?"

"As I've said, the neighborhoods will be considerably safer. We'll gain from the proceeds from the protection fees, while you? Well, you'll certainly benefit from having such a perfect record of keeping your promises."

"But that's not all, is it?"

"Well, we would certainly appreciate it if our businesses stay, shall we say, police-free?"

"That's a lot to ask for meeting for the first time, Mr. Agosti."

"Certainly." Rocco leans forward and takes over. "My son has done a great job of explaining the issue so far. We plan on being most accommodating, should you decide to help us."

"One thing I am not entirely certain of. What is Mr. Gallagher's interest in New York? And what does he stand to gain? So far, he's only been the one supplying in this scenario."

I expect Matthew Gallagher to be the one to take the floor this time, explaining his side. It's still Enzo, however, who does the talking. Again.

"Mr. Gallagher is famous in Boston in the underground fighting scene. He wants to move some of his arenas here, in NYC, and our family has offered up the venues."

"I see..." I say, and I more than see. They are merely scratching the surface with the information they're giving.

"Then you see how beneficial this would be for all of us. Martin's told us about your wife's foundation too. I'm confident that certain allowances can be made regarding that as well," Enzo says, eyeing my wife once more. It also doesn't escape me that he's on a first-name basis with Martin out of everyone here.

"Then allow me to say I have no interest in this scheme of yours," I say, standing to leave. "Bianca, let's go!"

She gives me a questioning look, maybe because what I'm doing is rude and probably because I've never behaved in such a way with her father. I don't know whether she gets it or not, but both men sitting next to her are mobsters. Quinn, I know, and he's a deadly bastard. Enzo, while I'm not familiar with him, I can tell from this short interaction that he's shrewd, maybe too intelligent, and he's the brain behind everything. Bianca stands to follow me when Martin finally speaks up.

"Theodore, Bianca. SIT DOWN." His voice shows he isn't playing around, yet both Bianca and I are still on our feet.

"Theodore, I think you forget who got you your current position." Martin looks at me, daring me to go against him. "You..." His gaze moves towards his daughter. "You forget the shit I buried for you when you were younger." Bianca's face falls.

While I do indeed need his support, I could do without it if it meant going against my principles. I'd done that once in my life, and I'd promised myself never again.

"I don't care about your money or connections," I say, and he smirks.

"Then how about your wife going to prison for murder?"

"Excuse me?" I exclaim. Bianca's face is now blank, devoid of any feelings. Everyone around the table turns to look at her expectantly.

"Auch lass didn't peg you for a wild one," Matthew Gallagher finally speaks, chuckling.

"What do you mean?" I ask him and then look at my wife. "Bianca?" She doesn't react.

"Tell him. Tell him, my darling daughter, how you poisoned your nanny when you were ten. You do remember, right?"

"Bianca, is this true?" I look at her, begging her to say no. She finally raises her head to look at me.

"I'm sorry, Theo."

"No... no..." I mutter.

"So, let's try again. Are you amenable to what was discussed here?"

I don't speak for several seconds, still looking at my wife. I'm still hoping she'll deny it. But she doesn't. She just sits again, as if nothing happened.

"Fine," I eventually answer, taking my seat once more.

Slowly, bit by bit, I'm not only losing the person I thought I loved, but I'm also losing myself.

Theo looks at me as if I disgust him.

After my father lets that bomb drop, we both sit once again, and negotiations start. I've always known my father's businesses weren't legal. Hell, if he can get rid of a body so quickly, it makes sense that he isn't a model citizen. But now? He's blatantly flaunting his connection to the Italian mafia. If that isn't enough, he has to also get involved with the Gallaghers.

Now that Enzo has revealed their plans and how the Irishmen will be involved in the business, I'm sure the arenas they want to install in New York are for to-the-death matches. I'd heard about them before; their type is prevalent in Boston and Philly, with some pop-ups in New Mexico and Nevada. They have an impressive audience, and the fighters can make big bucks in the ring. I can see why they'd want to move this to NYC too; the reach would be incredible.

Still, I can't help but worry about Theo and how they're forcing him to conform. For a moment, I wonder if Vlad knows about this, since he always has the scoop on everything that happens in the city. He's got to have known, so why didn't he say anything?

The men are now going to my father's study to hash out the details over a drink. I'm almost tempted to follow them, but I know they wouldn't let me in on the private talks. I'm left with Enzo's wife, and better than nothing, I decide to take advantage of this to get more information on Agosti.

"We didn't really get the chance to talk before, with the men going about their businesses," I start, plastering a smile on my face and hoping it looks genuine.

"Oh, please!" she replies, and unlike Enzo, she has no accent. "You don't need to butter me up for information."

"I don't?" I raise my eyebrow at her, surprised by her candor.

"You think I didn't notice Enzo making eyes at you? He wants to fuck you if you didn't catch on by now," she says flippantly, as if it's the most normal thing.

"And you're okay with that?"

"Why wouldn't I be? We're only together to maintain an image. We both have separate lives," Allegra huffs. "I'm going to give you a piece of advice. What Enzo wants, Enzo gets. If you want to save your husband, you know what to do."

"This is a very odd conversation," I add, trying to lighten the mood. What the actual fuck? Is she seriously playing wingman for her husband, hoping to guilt me into sleeping with him? Odd doesn't begin to cover it.

"I prefer direct. I'm sure you're a smart girl. Enzo will be the head of the Agosti family soon. There are a lot of benefits to becoming his mistress."

"I think I'll pass," I murmur and redirect my attention to my cup of tea.

Her lips curl into a malignant smile.

"You might want to reconsider."

Realizing that Enzo's wife might be just as crazy as the rest, I quickly extricate myself from the dining room and head towards the study, hoping to eavesdrop on their conversation. But as luck would have it, I leave the devil's mate to come across the devil himself.

"Just who I wanted to see!" Enzo exclaims, his gaze moving up and down my body with interest. I want to snort, but I remember I have to keep up appearances. It won't do me right to get on Enzo's lousy side so early on.

"Mr. Agosti." I incline my head and try to move past him.

"Enzo, *please*." He grabs my arm, holding it firmly. I squirm a little to let him know I want him to let go, but he doesn't. I almost sigh aloud. Fine, let's see what he wants.

"Enzo, if you would, *please* release me." I bat my eyelashes at him.

"If you ask so nicely..." He lets go of my arm, but not before he backs me into one of the hallway's rooms.

"Enzo..." I say again, with a little more frustration than before.

"I have to say I didn't expect Martin's daughter to look like this." One of his hands comes up to my face to caress my cheek, and I catch it mid-air.

"I must remind you I'm married."

"So what? So am I." I purse my lips. This won't be easy.

"Yes, but unlike you, I love my husband." I try again to move past him, but he has me caged.

"I loved my wife too..." he almost whispers. "And yet that didn't stop her, or me for that matter." Why do I feel like there's more to their marriage than meets the eye?

"I can't give you what you want, Enzo." I try to be more direct, hoping he will understand.

"And that's exactly why I'll enjoy the challenge. Must admit." His hand goes to my throat, slowly tracing from one side to the other. "I've never had a lady killer before. You got me curious... How will you taste?" His head dips down, and before his lips meet my skin, I manage to flip him around so that he's the one backed into the wall. He laughs.

"I knew you were feisty."

"You're not used to *no*, are you?" I ask.

"Can't say I am." He's still sporting an amused expression. He's playing me. He hasn't even tried to overpower me.

"Then, I should make it clear. I am *not* interested. I am *not* playing hard to get." I enunciate each word.

He studies me for a few seconds, probably deciding the veracity of my words, and then he smiles again.

"Don't worry, *cara*, I don't force myself on women. Should you ever tire of your husband, though..."

"Yeah, sure, I'll give you a call," I reply sarcastically before stepping away from him and watching him leave.

I don't understand what his game is. Enzo Agosti is an enigma. And I don't like enigmas.

23

THEO

"What the hell, Bianca? Do you realize what I just agreed to?" I bellow when we're back in her childhood room. She's currently sitting on the bed, staring towards the wardrobe, but not seeing anything.

"You killed your nanny?" I ask, disgusted by what I'd learned. "At fucking ten years old?" The more I learn about her, the more I realize I have no idea who the woman in front of me is.

I'm pacing the room, shouting expletives, but she just remains silent, her face blank.

"Say something for God's sake," I plead. "Just say something!"

There's a momentary silence where we just stare at each other, breathing hard from my frustration and Bianca looking entirely unbothered by anything.

"I was eight," she finally says. "I was eight when she started being too friendly with me." I look at her, a feeling of dread taking shape in my gut. Please let it not be what I think it is...

"Before that, she never bothered me. She said I was a devil child and that no one could save me. I didn't really care whether she interacted with me or not; at least she wasn't in my space. I think it happened when she realized that no one cared about me or what happened with me..."

I finally go over to the bed and sit, putting my hand on top of hers to comfort her.

"At first, it was just light touches. She would undress me and study me. And when I'd refuse, she'd hit me. I didn't back down for a long time, but I think at some point, I realized that the pain wasn't really worth it. It was just a few minutes of her touching me. Nothing more. I could just bear it and think of something else. But then, one day, she brought her boyfriend with her." The way she recounts the events is mechanic, but I can see her left eye twitching as she stares at the wall. She *is* affected.

My heart weeps for what I know she's about to say, yet I have to listen.

"She ordered me to sit on my knees, naked, and with my arms raised in front of the bed." She points to the spot in front of the bed we're currently sitting on, and I don't even want to imagine a young Bianca doing that.

"I didn't know what was happening back then. I was too young. They made me sit like that while they had sex on my bed. I couldn't move or make any sounds until she allowed me to. I had to watch them rut like animals for minutes on end. When their grunts stopped, I was almost afraid of what would follow..."

"Babe..." I say, trying to let her know she doesn't need to continue.

"She stopped him before he finished. Instead, she told him to ejaculate on me. *It will be fun,* she said. And he did. He came all over me. Of course, I didn't know what that meant, but it still felt wrong. *I felt gross.*"

My own eyes feel damp as I listen to her talk. I want nothing more than to embrace her and make her forget everything.

"Someone called my name in the house, and they somehow stopped. I don't know whether they were going to do anything more or not... But I knew I couldn't allow it to go on. I tried going to my father, but he ignored me. I just knew that if no one would help me, I had to take things into my own hands. I put rat poison in her food. She died almost instantaneously. My father had to finally man up to do something, so he just made her disappear, I think. That's when Drew came into my life. And partly the reason why I needed a bodyguard."

"B... I don't even know what to say." I take her hand and

entwine our fingers. "I'm so sorry you had to go through that. If anyone's guilty of anything, it's your father."

She finally looks at me. "I'm a monster, Theo. I've always known that. But now I'm dragging *you* down." She averts her eyes, almost as if ashamed.

"B, don't you dare say that! It's not your fault. None of it."

"How can you say that when I've gotten us trapped like this? My father... he owns us."

"Don't worry, we'll figure something out." I put my hand across her shoulders and tug her head under my chin.

"We're a team, remember?"

"Even if one half is a monster?" She repeats the word monster as if that's all she is.

"Even then."

"I wish it were that simple, Theo," she whispers. "We just got thrown into the middle of a battle that neither of us wants any part of."

"We'll get through this. I promise."

"What about your integrity, Theo?"

"There are things that are more important than that..."

24

BIANCA

I've finally admitted to Theo a truth about myself. At least this is a truth he can live with.

It's weird though, I hadn't thought about Jenna, my former nanny, even once in quite a few years.

Over time, I've grown increasingly frustrated that I'd chosen poison to dispatch her. She should have suffered far worse for what she'd done. The regrets have piled up for years, always thinking of how I could have tortured her and made her pay. It's also probably why a lot of my assignments during those years had been child molesters. I've been able to choose some of my targets based on those specific criteria. Every person I've killed during that time has been a stand-in for Jenna. They haven't gotten a quick death, but a long, drawn-out one.

For the first time ever, I prefer blades to guns for their ability to inflict consistent damage and pain.

The most extended bout of torture lasted eighty days. Eighty days in which I made sure that the predator rued the day he first looked upon a child. Eighty days in which I removed all semblance of humanity from him, stripped him of his skin in small stripes, and turned it into a canvas on which I'd carved his sins. Eighty days that he'd survived on IVs and emergency interventions because why should he die faster?

Vlad had put a stop to my overboard activities when I'd spent hours trying to resuscitate the scum just so I could hurt him more.

I was a monster, but I made no excuses.

Theo, though? He's kept my demons at bay.

Being with him has somehow freed me of Jenna's ghost. And now, it's just something that had happened to me. It's in the past.

After telling him the circumstances of Jenna's death, he takes me into his arms and tries to comfort me.

Again, strange.

I haven't said this to him so that he'll comfort me. I want him to know I'm not entirely a savage. I don't just kill indiscriminately.

He holds me into his arms for what seemed like forever until I suggest we leave.

"I don't want to be here any longer than needed."

It isn't until we're finally home that he opens up about what was discussed in the study.

"So wait, they want you to get them a meeting with the mayor?"

"Yes. They know I have a close relationship with him and that he was a friend of my parents."

"I'm so sorry, Theo. I never knew my father would go so far."

I'm sitting at the table in the kitchen, a cup of hot chocolate in my hands. After making his own coffee, he joins me at the table.

"I can't say it was totally unexpected."

"What do you mean?"

"B, don't tell me you've never known your father was involved in illegal stuff."

"I mean yeah, sure, I had my suspicions, but I never once believed he would force you into this. Especially by blackmailing you... And it's all my fault."

"It's okay. I told you, we'll get through this. But I have to ask..."

"Yes?" I look up into his eyes, and he hesitates slightly.

"What else does he have on you?" Of course, he would ask that. I remember my father hinting at lots of other skeletons in my closet.

"Would you believe me if I told you I don't know? Even with Jenna, my nanny, I had no idea he even knew that *I* poisoned her."

Theo is pensive for a while before speaking. "We have to find out everything he has on you; otherwise, we'll be at his mercy indefinitely."

I nod.

"I'll do that. It's my mess, and I'll be the one to fix it. But... just don't leave me. I couldn't bear if you left me, Theo." His hand comes on top of mine, and he squeezes.

"I seem to have a very increased tolerance to things when it comes to you, B... Just... don't betray me."

"I could never betray you, Theo. Always for you and with you, never against you."

My assurances flow from my mouth, hoping they're enough to convince him, especially now when things are so precarious. If killing those people would solve the problem, I would do it in a heartbeat.

But even I can recognize that murder isn't the solution in this particular scenario. The best we can hope for is to play them at their own games.

"We can't just let them walk all over us," I add, hoping he already has a plan.

"One step at a time. I'm going to have to talk to Marcel about this, get his angle too."

"Are you sure? Do you trust him?" It's not that I don't know who Marcel is to Theo, but this information is too sensitive.

"Of course. I'd trust Marcel with my life. Besides, two minds can work better than one."

"Three, you're forgetting me!"

"B, I don't want you involved in this. You could get hurt."

"You could too! And it's my fault you're involved in this in the first place. I won't stand by and watch you strut in the den of wolves by yourself." He sighs deeply.

"Fine! But don't do anything without talking to me first. Don't think I didn't see how Enzo was eating you up with his eyes."

"Deal! And don't worry. Enzo and I have reached an understanding," I say as I stand to put my mug in the sink.

Theo grabs me suddenly. "What understanding?" His voice is tense, and if I didn't think the situation was dire enough, I might have teased him for being jealous.

"Down, boy. He understood that I'm not interested. Although I have to say the dynamic between him and his wife was entirely off," I add my observation.

"She's sleeping with Martin."

"What?" I let out a scream.

"I'm fairly sure of it. Enzo doesn't care, though."

"Why do you think they're sleeping together? I didn't see any signs during dinner."

"Except them sitting next to each other?" he asks, and I have to agree that it was unusual. "It was also something Enzo told Martin when we left. He said to remind Allegra that their son has a piano recital on Thursday. It seems she's staying with your father."

"Good Lord," I mutter, suddenly overwhelmed by the many surprises of the day. Who would have thought? Allegra was a beautiful woman, but with my father? Ew. What she sees in that cold reptile is beside me.

"That reminds me. What do you make of the Irishmen?" I ask him, suddenly remembering Quinn's interest in Theo.

"Truthfully..." Theo starts, "I couldn't say which ones are more dangerous, the Agostis or the Gallaghers."

"Did you hear about them in Boston?" As far as I knew, Theo had spent a considerable amount of time in Boston before and during college.

"Not really, but then again, we didn't move in the same circles."

"It was odd that Quinn said you looked familiar."

"Who knows..." He leaves it hanging, but somehow, I'm not convinced. Both Quinn and his father are men of very few words. If anything, the fact that he'd spoken that question aloud means there's something behind it.

But I can't dig any further. Theo is clearly not comfortable with the subject.

2 5

THEO

"I managed to get a list of all the tenants." Marcel pauses. "I also cross-referenced it with people actually living there. However, she didn't make my job too hard. The apartment is in her mother's name. It's number eighteen."

I take a deep breath, digesting the information.

It had been hard to hear about her childhood, but did it justify her actions? I feel like a war is raging inside me on whether I can accept and forgive Bianca's actions. And somehow, I know deep down that the apartment will shed light on my dilemma and not necessarily in the right way.

"Keep Rico on her. I'm going in there when she's at work." If Rico's constantly onto her location, I can avoid meeting her.

"Sure. It's code-locked, by the way. Eight digits. Might wanna make a list beforehand." Marcus chuckles.

"Anything else?"

He shifts his gaze around the office in his usual bored manner.

"I might have gotten a hit with Jimenez's men. The people I got on the case have some info, but I'm just not sure how reliable."

"Info about what?" I ask almost too anxiously.

"Incoming batch of girls for his bordellos. Shipment is supposed to come into the port in two weeks."

"Why do you think the info might not pay off?"

170

"Theo, when was the last time we had this type of info on Jimenez? Reliable insider info? It's too good to be true."

"I guess you're right." My shoulders slump at the thought. After so much time hunting Jimenez, I finally get *something*, and it might not even be legit.

"How many people can we get on this just in case the tip pays off?"

"I'll look into it. Not too many since this is under the table. I have some people who owe me favors." While I'm not involved personally on groundwork, I've made it my job to get to know as many officers as possible, knowing that someday I'll need their loyalty to bring down Jimenez.

"I talked to Vlad, by the way. Wanted to check if he knew Bianca after the phone call incident."

"And?" Vlad is someone I'd met through Marcel, but I know his reputation, and I also know that Marcel trusts him.

"He couldn't tell me anything, as expected. But he did say that she's not a danger to us. At least that excludes insider work."

"That's good to know... although I do think you're a little too paranoid with your insider work. With her father, I just don't see her as a Russian spy."

Marcel shakes his head, amused. "Especially with her father." His expression gets serious. "The Jimenez thing is too big. I can't help suspecting if anyone who gets close to us might be a potential implant. They already know we're onto them. The attempt on your life should prove as much."

"We still don't know whether those men were sent by Martinez or Jimenez. Any luck yet on the ID?"

"No, illegal immigrants most likely. From what you told me, they barely knew how to use a gun."

"So, it makes Jimenez less likely."

He nods. "If he saw you as a danger, he wouldn't send amateurs. And he has enough resources to afford professionals."

"I agree. I would say it's someone from Martinez's side. Family maybe? Someone who knew about the meeting and connected the dots."

"That's just the thing. I can't find any family on Martinez. But..." he starts, lost in thought.

"Let's retrace this a little." Marcel's brain works differently, but his insight is always invaluable and spot on. So, I go along.

"We contacted Martinez, and he agreed for an exchange of information. One million for a list of suppliers on Jimenez."

"Then he showed up ready to kill, with an empty drive," I add.

"He never intended to give the info, so why the meeting?"

"Shit." I get up from my seat, an idea entering my mind.

"Fuck! I can't believe this. Yeah, they never intended to give us the real shit. They wanted to know who's sniffing around and take them out. We made the arrangements through proxies, so he couldn't know who I was."

"Until you went there."

"What if we got this wrong?"

"I don't like where you're going..." Marcel comments, but I can see he has the same idea I do.

"Martinez was Ortega's right-hand man. He wouldn't act on his own. And the meeting... It was simply to draw me out in the open. Why would Martinez want that?"

"He wouldn't," Marcel adds. "But Jimenez would. Before this, he only knew you were after him as chief commissioner. Now, he knows you're after him off the books too."

"It gets worse. If Martinez wouldn't act without consent, then Ortega must answer to Jimenez too. Fuck!" I curse aloud. "It means he controls another cartel. Maybe not even just one."

"It makes sense, though, if you look at the big picture." Marcel suddenly spreads sheets of paper all over my desk. "Look, we've had reports of activities that relate to Jimenez from five different states. But we've never been able to connect it to his people."

"So, he has other cartels under his control. How do we even begin to get someone with that power and that reach?"

"We don't." Marcel suddenly smirks. "At least we need to change tactics, stop the offensive. If we put the attempt on your life into perspective, it sure looks more like an attempt to scare you rather than to actually kill you."

"You're right. They want us to stop digging. What are you thinking of?"

"You told me about what happened at dinner with Agosti and Gallagher. What if we used them to force Jimenez into the open?"

"Competition?" I ask, finally seeing where Marcel is going.

"I can assure you Agosti's family business is nothing remotely related to restaurants and hotels." He chuckles. "I'm sure you too know of a few clubs owned by them. Not to mention the many underground bordellos they operate, right in the heart of Manhattan. Now that they plan to expand the business, they'll need more suppliers."

"But that's the thing, we don't know Jimenez's suppliers."

"Yes, we don't. But I'm sure Agosti can find out. Just drop a few hints here and there about Jimenez, and how there might be a conflict of interests where they're concerned."

"That's a great idea. But are you sure they'll bite? What if they actually develop a partnership?"

"One thing you need to understand about the Famiglia is that they don't deal well with outsiders or with people encroaching their territory. The Gallaghers are an exception because they deal in different vices. There's no competition."

"I see. Then it might just work."

26

THEO

Here it is—the moment of truth.

What are you hiding, Bianca?

I'd been messaging back and forth with Rico all day to ensure I came here when she was at work. As Marcel's mentioned, the apartment is password operated. I'd made a list earlier of possible combinations, and with a sigh, I plug them in. I try her birthday, her mother's birthday, our anniversary, our wedding day, and none work. I'm almost scared this will get stuck if I keep trying the wrong combinations. I finally plug in my date of birth, and surprisingly, it opens.

I make my way inside almost hesitantly. It's like now that I'm here, I don't want to find out. But I have to, so I push through.

There's a hallway and what seems to be three bedrooms. Okay, nothing ominous so far. I start with the first door, and when I open it, I'm blown away.

Actually, blown away doesn't even cover it.

Inside is the biggest weapons collection I've ever seen outside military facilities. I take in the rifles and guns on display, and cases upon cases of what I can only presume is ammunition and more weapons. There are knives, traps, swords, weapons I don't think I've seen before, and other devices that I'm sure are just as deadly as the others. What the fuck is this?

Not understanding what I'm seeing, I video call Marcel.

"You there yet?" he asks and then frowns, possibly because my face exudes the shock I feel.

"You're not going to believe what I'm seeing."

"What?" He almost laughs, but as I switch to the rear camera, I can see his face drop.

"Holy shit!" he exclaims. "Theo, do you realize what those are?" he says in awe.

"Which ones?" I ask, considering there are too many.

"Those rifles on the wall. Man, that's military-grade equipment. You can't get those on the regular market. And those... wait, go to the right." I move the phone around to capture the entire room, and Marcel is almost fangirling at the sight of the knives.

"Those are Japanese daggers. I'm willing to believe they're extremely rare too," I grunt, mostly because I've never been interested in guns, and I don't know much about them.

"This is easily a couple million *just* in weapons." Marcel drops the bomb, and I feel my mouth gape open.

"What? A few million? Are you crazy?"

"No, I'm telling you, that's not cheap shit."

"It's like an entire arsenal..."

"An entire arsenal for an entire army. For one person?" He shakes his head, and I follow his logic. This is too much in the realm of superlatives for just one person.

"What could she possibly do with this?"

After filming the entire room, some portions in detail, I tell Marcel I'm going to the next bedroom.

"This looks ordinary," he says, almost disappointed, as I open the second door.

"Yeah, it's just a bedroom." I go through the drawers, the closet, but it's just a regular sleeping space. I'm about to leave when something catches my eye from under the bed.

"Wait." It's like the corner of a box. I put the phone on the bed, and I get on my knees to slide it towards me. It looks like a shoebox. I open it just to say I checked it.

Inside, I find a bunch of tiny packets filled with white powder.

No... I shake my head, feeling some wetness in my eyes. Surely no...

"Theo, are you there?" Marcel's voice startles me. I grab the phone, and I immediately click to show him what I found.

"Is that...?" His eyes are the size of saucers. I don't say anything. Instead, I open a small packet and put a little of the powder on my tongue, thus confirming my worst fears.

"Positive. It's coke."

"That much? What is she, a dealer?" Looking at the amount she has stashed here, that would be the conclusion. But somehow, the truth is even direr.

"No, I think it's hers."

"You're shitting me. Bianca, a drug addict? Have you ever suspected?"

"No... never." But as I say this, past episodes are coming back to mind, of her sleepless nights, of her hands sometimes shaking, of her irritability. It makes sense now, though. It all ties in.

"Theo..."

"She's a high-functioning drug addict, Marcel. My wife of three years is a freaking drug addict. Who knows how long she's been on these things, with her having a double life and all?" My voice is bitter and full of disappointment. Who is she even?

"I'm so sorry, Theo," he says, and I can tell he means it. But this changes everything.

"Let's see the last room. I don't think there's anything worse to find out now."

I think I spoke too soon because the moment I open the last door, I almost drop the phone.

"Double Holy Shit. Your wife is like a master spy," Marcel says because the room is an entire closet of different looks. Or yet, better said, disguises.

"I gotta go. I'll talk to you later." My words are strained as I pocket my phone and take a step inside the room, heading straight for the mannequin in its center. Pink hair. Purple mini dress. Fishnets. Doc Martens.

It's...

Pink.

My knees give out, and I drop on the floor.

Pink... The prostitute I'd fucked over seven years ago. And I'd met Bianca less than five years ago. I frown, unable to take this in.

Bianca is Pink.

Did she...

My head keeps shaking at the notion, but I can't even deny it with the evidence in front of me. Why? Why would she do that?

I stand there for what seems like an eternity before my phone rings.

"She's on the move," Rico tells me, and I mechanically reply with something.

I'm still dazed, but I remember to take a picture of the outfits before getting out of there. *Evidence*, I tell myself.

I feel sick to my stomach, to my head. And most of all, to my soul.

I thought my heart had been irrevocably broken when my parents had been murdered right under my nose.

But this?

It feels like my soul is being snatched out of my body.

It feels like I'm drowning in a sea of misery. And as I sit in my car a few minutes later, my head resting on the wheel, I keep repeating.

"Let it be a dream. Please let it be all just a bad dream."

I t's not a dream.

I've texted Marcel to meet me at the office, not trusting myself to speak and drive, or speak, or drive.

But I manage it.

I drive without killing myself, which might just have been a mercy in this situation.

I trudge my way inside my office to find Marcel already waiting for me there.

"Shit, Theo, what happened to you?"

"I just found out my wife used to be a prostitute, is currently a drug addict, and has a collection of weapons to rival a military base. Does that cover it?" I give a sad smile and plop myself into the chair.

"Wait a minute...a prostitute?"

"As you heard. A prostitute I fucked, too, years before I met Bianca." He stares at me before bringing his hand to his chin, stroking pensively.

"Do you think there's a connection?"

"Hell if I know. But doesn't it seem like a perfect coincidence? More than anything, I realize what a fool I've been. God, how many lies? I don't even know her..."

"Theo, calm down..."

"How? How can I calm down when I find out my wife isn't remotely who I thought she was? Pink... the prostitute, was the exact opposite of Bianca. God! I really thought she was this soft-spoken, shy girl, struggling under her father's thumb, waiting for me to save her... That sounds so fucked now that I say it out loud, but she played me. She played me so well, knowing exactly what to do to get under my skin. She only showed me what I wanted to see. I wanted her to be helpless. I wanted her to be innocent..." My hand goes to my face, and I try to massage my temples. There's a throbbing in my head that only seems to intensify. "Who *is* she?" I whisper.

"Are you going to confront her?"

"I don't know... I don't think I'm capable of anything right now." I think for a moment and realize I need to know more about Pink. Why? Maybe to torture myself even more.

"I'm going to give you some time. This isn't easy to accept," Marcel says and, at some point, leaves the office. I don't actually pay attention. I might have nodded at him...

An image springs into my mind.

"Bianca Ashby, will you do me the honor of becoming my wife?" I was on one knee, my hands holding the ring box in front of a stunned Bianca. She'd looked extraordinary that night. Her long, black hair had gleamed in the moonlight. Her eyes had sparkled with warmth and love and everything I'd ever wanted.

"Yes! Yes!" she'd cried. "A thousand times, yes!" That was the night she'd become mine.

But it has all been a lie. A terrible bitterness assaults me as I realize she's never actually been mine.

I still can't wrap my head around why she did it. Why she went to this extent to live a double life. Was I just a smokescreen for her activities? Had she seen me as an easy target? She'd certainly known my weaknesses and had manipulated me to fall for her. Was anything that came out of her mouth real?

So many questions, and for a time, I allow myself to be overcome by grief.

The Bianca I love just doesn't exist.

Sometime later, I manage to pull myself together long enough to approach this more calmly. One look out the window tells me it's already night—just the perfect time for what I have in mind. I know I need answers from one more place before I confront her.

I put on my blazer and stride from my workplace, heading determinedly to my car—my destination club Palace.

Taking my phone out, I hesitate before sending Bianca a short text that I'll be working late. At this point, I don't even know what she might be capable of.

I get to the club, and it doesn't take long for the bouncer to check my name against their customer list. For a strip club, Palace is incredibly anal about its privacy, probably because so many important people in high positions are customers. Another reason might be the fact that the upstairs rooms function as boudoirs for those seeking a little extra.

Once inside, I figure my best chances at finding some answers are by asking the manager and maybe talking to some girls.

It's not easy to find my way to the manager's office, and indeed, it's not easy to convince him that I'm not some psycho obsessed with one of their girls. I actually have to show him my credentials for him to give me a chance.

"Pink, you say?" He purses his lips.

"Yes, around five years ago," I add, not entirely sure when she stopped working here.

Or if... but that's something I'm not ready to consider just yet.

"I think I may remember who you're talking about. But only because she was very odd."

"Odd? What do you mean?"

"She was always by herself, never interacting with any of the other girls. Didn't really care about tips or other opportunities. In this business, that's very odd. If my memory serves right, one day, she just disappeared. Stopped coming altogether."

"And do you remember when that was?"

"Not sure, but it was a long time ago."

"Thank you. Are there any girls who were here at the same time as her?"

"Let me see..." He goes to his computer, probably checking his employee charts.

"Yes, there is one. Anais. She's actually working tonight." Before I leave, I get a description of the girl and her dancing schedule and head towards the main stage of the club. Taking a seat, I now wait for the show.

Halfway through the set and three girls left until Anais, I am bored out of my mind. I keep checking my watch, and the time seems to move even slower than before. I almost groan in frustration.

I raise my head and scan the club, my eyes zeroing in on pink hair. I blink twice, clearly not seeing right, and it disappears.

Of course, at this point, I'm probably hallucinating. I'm clearly running on borrowed energy. One just needs to make a list of everything I found out in one week, my attempted assassination notwithstanding, to conclude I'm owed a respite.

I settle a little more comfortably into my seat.

Out of nowhere, I feel a hand on my shoulder from behind and hot breath in my ear.

"Long time no see, handsome." My head almost snaps at that sound. Surely not? I take a deep breath and turn around. Surely yes.

Pink, in all her glory, fishnets included.

I struggle to keep a straight face.

"Pink!" I will myself to exclaim, surprised, but glad to see her.

Inside my head, questions pile on top of questions. Does *she* know *I* know? What is she doing here? Fuck... Fuck...

She drapes herself on top of me without any preliminaries, her ass digging purposefully into my crotch. The proximity allows me to take a good look at my deceiver.

Her pink hair is styled as it's always been—short bob with bangs. The difference in makeup, the green contacts, and the fake beauty mark on top of her upper lip make her unrecognizable.

At least I wasn't that stupid. I reluctantly tell myself.

Her face contouring is harsh, making her naturally soft face all angles. No way I would have ever considered Pink to be Bianca if proof of it hadn't stared me right into the eyes.

"You still work here?" I make my best attempt at conversation. Even her voice sounds huskier than usual, or maybe it's the acoustic in the club.

"Of course," she lies and smiles seductively, her hands roving about my body. *What is her game?*

"Tired of that girl of yours?" she asks with a pout, and it takes all my willpower to control my expression. She's got to be the ultimate liar. There's absolutely no tell, no trace of guilt even. It's then that I decide to turn the tables on her. Maybe it's petty revenge, but she has brought it on herself.

"She's... bland," I reply, my fingers teasing her jaw before jerking her closer. My mouth is now maybe one inch away from hers.

"Want me to make it better?" She licks her lips. I immediately capture her tongue in my mouth, sucking on it. Her hands wrap around my neck, and I bring her closer to my body, my mouth devouring her in a punishing manner.

"Upstairs!" I say, and she slowly nods, probably still dazed from the kiss.

I grab her hand and all but drag her upstairs, where an attendee asks us what we are in the mood for.

"Torture chamber," I say, knowing that's the one place I hadn't gone to with Pink in the past. While our encounters had been wild, rough, and sensual, we'd never ventured into more dangerous territory. Honestly, I'd never thought something would ever crack my carefully built control, but Bianca is awfully close to unleashing a storm. There's a reason I always held back...

But somehow, I know my little deceiver can take it.

"Hmm... feeling frisky?" She purrs on my arm as I lead her towards the room.

"You have no idea, babe."

27
BIANCA

I've just gotten home when I receive a message from an old contact that my husband is asking questions at the Palace. At first, I'm stunned, my mind wondering why he's there.

Does he suspect anything?

Why would he go back there?

Initially, I convince myself to go there as Pink to investigate the circumstances, and should the situation require, alleviate any concerns regarding Pink's identity.

I've even taken more care than usual with my get-up, wanting to look as different from Bianca as possible.

There's no way he knows... I keep telling myself.

But as I get to the club and see him looking all manly and delicious, I can't not take advantage of the situation and pretend to be Pink for a little longer...

Maybe he'll even punish me for being a naughty girl.

And now?

Now, Theo's taking me to the torture chamber—so-called because of its myriad of toys and props.

I've seen it before. I've longed for Theo to take me there. But he never has.

Until now, that is.

Maybe I *should* be worried he's willing to sleep with another woman. But considering that the woman in question *is* me, the implications just don't hit me as they should.

I'm simply happy to be here. Maybe too happy.

And he is going to *fuck* me. Not make love. *Fuck!* And I can bet it's going to be dirty as hell.

We enter the room, and I giggle at the sight of the interior, imagining Theo doing wicked things to me in all those scenarios.

There are benches and chairs made to maximize both pain and pleasure. There's a cross in the form of an X at the back of the wall, while in the middle of the room, like a low chandelier, there's a suspension bar. Both sides of the room are fitted with different instruments to inflict pain—crops, whips, bars, and others I can't even name. A shiver of anticipation runs through me.

"What are the limits for today?" he asks, his fingers caressing the nape of my neck and making me shiver.

"None." I feel him smirking against my skin, his lips skimming the sensitive spot just below my ear.

"Remember your safe word?"

"Hmm?" I whimper, already a slave to the sensations he wrings from my body.

"Safe word?" he asks again.

"Yes... Lemon."

"Good," he whispers, and he turns me to face him.

"Strip down and get on your knees." His entire manner changes, his voice unyielding and commanding.

This is the Theo I like to fuck.

"Yes, sir." I quickly undress and take off my shoes, remaining only in my fishnets. I'd come braless, and the sight of Theo eyeing my erect nipples tells me it was the perfect decision.

I quickly kneel in front of him, waiting for further instruction.

"Eyes on me," he says, and with two fingers, he tips my jaw, so I'm looking straight into his eyes.

"Take my cock out and put it into your mouth." His smooth voice leaves me breathless, and I can only do as commanded.

My hands go to his office pants, and I lower the zipper, pulling down just enough to take his straining length out.

I give it one light stroke before bending forward and

taking the tip into my mouth, my tongue gently swiping across the underside. I give a few licks to the head before moving lower on the shaft and sucking his balls deep into my mouth.

A hissing sound escapes him, and I take it as encouragement to continue my ministrations. I'm sucking on the head when he suddenly commands me to stay still.

His hands go into my hair (and I'm thankful I fully secured my wig in place) before taking control and fucking my mouth.

In and out, his movements are aggressive yet controlled. I gag when the tip hits the roof of my mouth and spit pours down my chin, and it seems to make him even more demanding. My eyes are tearing up from the pressure. His grip tightens on my scalp, and I know he's close. With a low groan, he empties himself down my throat.

"Swallow," he commands.

I do, looking up at him as I lick the remains of his cum from my mouth.

"Good girl." His thumb caresses my cheek in appreciation.

"Now, to the bar."

On shaky legs, I get up and head to the suspension bar. He cages me on both sides, locking my wrists into place and leaving me exposed. I'm already achingly wet, but I know my relief will be a torturous bliss.

He steps away from me, admiring me.

Slowly, he divests himself of his own clothing, his shirt, and then his pants and underwear. He is indeed a spectacular specimen. His broad shoulders are complimented by toned arms and a defined stomach.

My eyes take him in, how the V of his pelvis leads to his magnificent cock, jutting proudly and erect once more. His movements are unhurried, almost leisurely.

Naked, he strides to a table, taking a few items. Coming to stand in front of me, he looks me in the eye for a second before his mouth is on me.

His tongue clashes with mine in an open kiss that has me tugging at my restraints, wanting to weave my hands into his hair.

His teeth nibble at my bottom lip before he puts enough space between us to tie a blindfold over my eyes.

"Good girl," he praises me.

Deprived of my sight, I try to focus on his touch. He trails what feels like a feather from my neck, down my torso, giving special attention to my nipples.

They tighten in response, and a moan escapes my lips.

"Tsk, Tsk. We can't have that," he says before bringing over a gag and placing it in my mouth.

"You're much prettier when you're quiet," he whispers in my ear before a sharp sensation assails me in one nipple, then in the other. A cold metal chain brushes against my belly, and I realize he has used nipple clamps.

"Are you wet for me, sweet girl?" His voice is almost hypnotic, and I just nod, feeling my panties soaked. I expect him to check for himself, but he doesn't. Instead, he takes a few steps back and stops.

I wait.

He's clearly using this to his advantage, screwing with both my mind and my senses.

My impatience gets the best of me, and I squirm within the confines of my cuffs.

Then I feel a stinging pain on my ass. A muted sound comes out of my mouth, blocked by the gag.

Theo grasps my fishnets from behind with both hands and tears them in one motion, my panties going quickly after. Cold air meets my bare bottom for the first time, but he doesn't waste any second flaying me over with the crop once more.

The immediate pain makes me yank my chain forward, but the afterburn is deliciously addictive.

I push my ass up into him, signaling my approval, and he hits me again. And again. If I was soaked before, now my pussy's flooding my thighs with my juices.

Suddenly, the spanking stops, and I feel his fingers glide over my abused bottom, slowly massaging the flesh.

One hand sneaks between my cheeks, encountering my wetness and spreading it around.

"You want my cock, sweet girl, don't you? Your pussy is begging me to fill it up," he whispers in my ear, and his words only serve to make me more aroused.

With one last slap on my ass, he moves away from me, his absence immediately a source of frustration.

I want to protest it somehow through my body language, but before I get the chance, Theo lifts me, his hands on my butt, placing my legs on each shoulder, his face inches away from my core.

He blows a few times, the warm air of his breath caressing my slit. With one long lick, he dives in, sucking my clit and making me thrash in his hold. Every touch of his tongue sends me on the brink of the abyss, each time a little bit deeper.

Until I fall.

My throat contracts, trying to make the sounds that describe the myriad of feelings pooling in my pussy. And Theo doesn't stop. He laps and laps until he wrings a second orgasm from me. He stills for a second before biting down on my clit while at the same time yanking on the chain holding my nipple clamps together. The combined pain wrecks my body as it mingles with my last orgasm's aftershocks and makes me climax again.

I'm panting. As much as I can, considering the gag.

Theo slowly puts me down and then proceeds to remove the blindfold and the gag, before finally opening up my wrist cuffs.

I am so spent, I melt to the floor, but Theo has other plans.

One hand is suddenly at my throat, and he lifts me up until I'm lined up with the wall. His other hand comes up to my face, tracing the sweat dripping down my face before offering his fingers for me to suck.

"Giving up?" he asks, and I shake my head.

"What, I didn't hear?" The hand at my throat tightens, restricting my airflow just enough to make my voice sound hoarse as I answer.

"No, sir."

"Good girl." He gives me a half smile before his face changes again.

"Hands and knees. Now."

I immediately comply, stumbling on my hands and knees. Theo comes behind me, and I feel his hands kneading my ass cheeks.

He guides the head of his cock and lines it against my entrance but doesn't push in. He glides it against my juices and my battered clit, and it elicits a loud moan from me, half pleasure, half pain.

He finally slips the tip in, just barely, and my channel immediately contracts. I don't even stop to wonder why he's not using a condom, as he'd always used before with Pink. He slams into me in one mighty thrust that triggers my orgasm, my walls tightening around him. He continues to thrust in and out of me, the only sound indicating his pleasure his harsh breathing.

He pushes himself so deep inside my body, my vision becomes impaired from the sweet pleasure. But just as I get used to his brutal use of my body, he pulls his cock out.

I whimper at the sudden loss, but from the corner of my eye, I see him take a bottle of lube from the table. Coming behind me again, he lathers the liquid all over my butt, slowly massaging it towards my hole.

His thumb slips inside at the same time his cock enters my pussy again. He strokes me deeply, his finger increasing the pressure until suddenly his cock is out of my wet heat and pushing against my hole.

The initial sensation of pain gives way to stretching and ultimately to fullness.

He works his cock against my ass until he's all the way in. He then fucks me so deep, when another orgasm hits me, I almost pass out. In fact, the moment he pulls out and flips me on my back, I'm entirely too powerless to do anything.

I watch him get to his feet, his hand fisting his cock as he takes himself to completion. Hot spurts of semen burst from his shaft and onto my face and neck.

He crouches once more, looking at me almost affectionately before saying, "Good girl."

Then he retrieves his clothes, puts them on, and leaves.

I'm still on the floor, fucked within an inch of my life, and struggling to keep my eyes open.

28

THEO

I flick the light on as I enter the apartment. After leaving Bianca at the Palace, I'd gone around driving to clear my head. Having my way with her like that should have made me feel better. But if anything, I feel worse.

I feel... cheated.

I slowly make my way inside, not thinking whether Bianca is home yet or not. I'm honestly not in the mood for a confrontation right now.

But as I reach the living room, it's to see her sitting quite daintily on the couch, a book in her hand.

"Theo! I was worried," she says, a mask of concern on her face.

"Really? Why?" I ask drily.

"It's late, why else? After what happened at the lake house..." She trails off.

"I'm fine," I simply say and make for the bedroom. Halfway there, I stop, turning slightly towards her. I don't know what comes over me when I say the next words, "I fucked a whore tonight." I watch her face slowly morph into a combination of expressions, as if she's trying to find the right one to fit my confession. She settles on an amused one, regaling me with a fake laugh too.

"Ha, ha, you're funny, babe." I just raise my eyebrows at her, waiting for her to continue.

"You're not mad that I fucked another woman?" I repeat.

"Theo, what are you saying?" She makes another attempt to laugh it off.

"Or maybe," I start as I walk towards her, planting myself in front of her. My thumb goes to her freshly scrubbed face.

"You're not mad because *that woman* was actually you."

"Theo..." she stammers, and for the first time, I see a trace of real emotion on her face.

She knows she's caught.

"Whatever are you saying? Have you been drinking?" She puts the book next to her and stands, attempting to bypass me.

"Really? That's all you have to say?" I grab her hand and fling her back on the couch.

"What about these handprints on your lovely throat?" I move her hair to the side to trace the evidence of her guilt.

"Theo... I."

"No." I cut her words. "Let's have it now that we started it. I know... Pink."

I watch her eyes widen, her head shaking in denial.

"Don't insult me further by denying it. I know... everything."

"How?" She finally composes herself, and the change is immediate. It's like she's an entirely different person.

Neither Pink nor Bianca.

Her expression is cold, detached.

"Your apartment," I simply state.

"I see. Marcel?" she asks, probably realizing who'd done the investigation. I nod.

"What do you think you know, Theo?"

"What... you've got to be kidding me," I say, suddenly pissed at her. How dare she be so calm, so uncaring?

"I know you are Pink. I know about your drug problem, and I also know that you are some sort of Russian killer. Does that cover it?" I ask her sarcastically.

She gives a mirthless laugh.

"Wow, I have to say I never imagined this day would come. Or how it would proceed."

"Just tell me one thing... Why me? Why go through so much trouble just to get to me?"

"I wanted you." Her answer shocks me. "I wanted you, so I got you, the only way I knew how."

"By playing a hooker. For God's sake, B!"

"I told you. I wanted you." She shrugs.

"Then, why the whole innocent act?"

"I wanted to keep you, too."

"So what, you figured the hooker could fuck me while the innocent could marry me?"

"Well, isn't that exactly how it happened?" She has the gall to smirk at that.

"You lied to me. God... I don't even know what's true anymore. You told me I was your first kiss, your first everything. Shit..." I curse aloud.

"I do admit that maybe I wasn't *entirely* truthful. But I didn't lie about *that*. You were and still are the only man who's *ever* touched me."

"Entirely truthful? Are you hearing yourself? What's *wrong* with you? Our entire marriage is a lie," I say, exasperated, and watch her eye twitch.

"Since everything is out in the open, I might as well be honest with you." She raises her eyes to look at me.

"I'm not normal. You are correct. I don't feel remorse. I don't think I ever have. One psychiatrist diagnosed me with Antisocial Personality Disorder. I guess in popular culture, that's what you'd call a sociopath." She is completely serious as she talks. "I'm not a Russian assassin, by the way. I am mostly a freelancer. Although... I do have close ties to the Russians," she says proudly, and I'm just standing in front of her, looking flabbergasted. "I used to take on more assignments in the past, but I haven't worked as much ever since I married you. Now, I just do it to take the edge off every now and then. Like a hobby." The way she speaks about murder is how any other woman would talk about a grocery list.

"You killed Martinez," I state, and she shrugs.

"I'd kill anyone to keep you safe."

"What the fuck... B, that's not normal."

"I told you. I'm not normal." She frowns.

"Those bugs were yours, weren't they? That's how you knew about Martinez in the first place. How long? How long have you been tracking me?"

"Since we got married. I had to keep you safe." Arguing further seems like a moot point when her reasoning seems to be mainly keeping me safe... by killing people. I push that thought away and bring up the other topic.

"What about drugs? I still can't believe I never once suspected you used..."

For the first time, she appears to be ashamed.

"That... I'm trying to quit."

"Fuck!" I say once more, pacing about the living room.

"Now that all is out in the open, we can improve our relationship. I can be Pink for you every time you want." She licks her lips suggestively, and I'm just... stunned.

"You really don't understand, do you?"

"What? You know the truth now. I don't have to hide anymore."

"You *hurt* me, Bianca. You lied and manipulated me into marrying you. You're a fucking killer, for God's sake. And you want us to just continue as if nothing happened? As if I'm not looking at a stranger right now?"

"Well... yes." She cocks her head to the side as if contemplating the idea.

"This isn't real..." I throw my hands in the air.

"There's no relationship anymore, Bianca. There never fucking was one, it seems," I tell her even though my own heart is breaking as I say this. "There's no us. I want you *out*. Out of the house, out of my life. I never want to see you again. It's over."

"But Theo..." she protests, but I've had enough. I don't recognize my own voice as I yell at her.

"Get the fuck out. Don't even think about coming near me again. You disgust me."

I turn my back and leave her, heading into one of the guest rooms for the night and locking the door. Isn't it funny that now I'm worried she might even kill me?

I laugh at my own stupidity and maybe at how this all fits. Perhaps it's fate, after all.

My own wife, a sociopath... a cold-blooded killer. A pretender.

Yeah, maybe it *is* karma.

Since I am the biggest pretender of them all.

BIANCA

I don't know how I left the apartment or where I am. I've never seen Theo so upset, so inconsolable. When he'd told me to get out and that I disgusted him, something broke inside me. My chest cavity feels constricted for some reason.

I stand for a minute and punch myself in my breast to alleviate some of the discomfort. Am I having a heart attack? There's something to be said about the state I'm in... I've never felt like this before. Can someone feel like dying when they're very much alive and physically uninjured?

I've had my fair share of wounds throughout the years, caused by different weapons and to varying degrees of concern. Not even the worst pain I'd withstood when Vlad and I had been stranded in New Mexico with no medical equipment but a bottle of whiskey and our knives.

He'd dug out a bullet from my thigh with his blade and poured alcohol on it, and I'd somehow refrained from crying out. Now?

I shake my head and stumble forward, gripping the wall of the building near me for support.

There's something wet on my face. I touch my hand to it and realize it's tears.

I'm... crying? I've never cried unless I was pretending.

Never.

I panic, my breathing out of control. What's happening to me? Did I finally break?

I try to put one foot in front of the other to make my way to my other apartment, but my entire body is too stiff. Why I'd walked instead of driven, I don't know.

Out of the fog that shields my mind, I hear a whistle. I frown but keep walking. The whistling seems to intensify. I take a second to look around and realize I passed the 5th Avenue Station, so I must be around 62nd Street. I keep my pace until the whistling comes directly from behind me. Just as I'm waiting for it to pass me, a hand grabs my arm painfully and shoves me towards the alleyway.

Great.

I jerk my arm around to free myself, but it only makes my assailant treat me more roughly. I hit the wall, and pain radiates from my shoulder blade.

Shit. I wince.

Raising my head up, I see an older man with an unkempt appearance leering at me.

"Let me go," I say, quickly taking in all escape routes.

"Now, sweet girl. Out at this hour ain't safe." He slurs his words, but what hits me is his appellation—sweet girl. My mind hones in on that word, and everything seems to fall away.

His hand goes to my shirt, his hurried movements aggressively ripping the bottom material. It's enough to wake me up from my mental fog. My arm shoots out, and my elbow catches him under his chin, causing him to fall backward.

At this moment, I could run if I wanted to. I could leave him here and take off.

But I don't.

My eyes must be glazed with a crazed look because as he sees me approaching him, he takes a step back.

My punch goes next, hitting him in the stomach. Then I knee him in the balls until he's curled up at my feet.

"Please..." he whimpers.

I don't stop.

My fists go at his face for what seems like forever. I hit and hit and hit, all the pain in my chest intensifying and making me go harder and harder.

I feel bone crunching.

The skin on my knuckles is slowly peeling away as I slam into him. His zygoma is crushed, bits of it flying as I keep hammering. I only stop when I feel a softness swallowing my knuckles and realize I've likely reached his brain. With a harsh breath, I let myself fall next to his body. Dead. He's dead.

I killed him.

I'm a monster.

I'm disgusting.

Theo's words keep replaying inside my head, and my tears fall uncontrollably.

It doesn't take long for me to realize I need to do something about this, so I quickly grab my phone and dial Vlad.

"I... killed him," I say between sobs and hiccups.

"B?" he asks, concerned, and I hear movement. "Where are you?"

I give him what I think is my location, and he tells me to wait. The hand holding the cell drops, and I stare at the massacre in front of me.

I'm disgusting.

I keep looking at my handiwork that I don't realize when, sometime later, a car pulls over. Vlad and his bodyguard Maxim step into the alleyway. I turn to look at him and see that he averts his gaze as soon as he spots the bloody corpse, his hand shielding his eyes. I can only imagine what seeing this does to him.

"Harsh, little goddess, harsh!" He shakes his heads and barks some commands in Russian to Maxim.

He notes my almost catatonic state and takes me into his arms to bring me to the car. Meanwhile, Maxim collects the corpse, placing it in the trunk of the vehicle.

"I'm sorry," I whisper, and he sighs.

"Don't worry about it now."

That's the last thing I hear before everything goes black.

W hen I come to, it's to find an unknown man tending to the wounds on my hands. I struggle to snatch my hand away and get out of bed, but the man just gives me a strained smile.

"*Yeshyeo net.*" Not yet.

"*Pochemu?*" I croak, asking him why.

"*Est eta.*" He gets a pouch and rummages in it for what looks like some pills. I shake my head. I don't think I need anything else.

"*Est!*" he commands me to take the pill.

"*Shto eta?*" I ask as he peels off the foil and hands me a glass of water.

"*Za galavi i protiv infektsi*" His voice is matter of fact, and I don't protest anymore. I take the pills, and that's when Vlad comes into the room.

"*Sposiba Sasha. Idti.*" He nods to the man, Sasha, and comes to stand next to my bed.

"You fucked up, *malyshka.*"

I hitch my knees up and rest my back against the headboard of the bed.

"Theo knows... everything." I sigh, realizing this is still the reality I find myself in. I keep hoping it was just a bad dream.

"How did he take it?"

"He kicked me out. Said he never wants to see me again."

"Will he go to the police?"

"I... I didn't even think about that..." I mutter. "I don't think so..."

"This isn't you *malyshka,*" Vlad says, his tone full of disappointment.

"I... I need help, Vlad."

Vlad purses his lips and regards me skeptically.

"Help?"

"I need to detox. I need to show him..." I say, my voice trembling a little. "I can't give up on him. I won't."

"Don't you think the ship's already sailed?"

"No... no." I shake my head furiously. "I can't let him go..."

Vlad sighs aloud and gets up.

"If that's what you want, I'll help you."

"Yes, it's what I want."

"Well, then. Gear up for the worst week of your life, B." He leaves me alone, saying I need rest.

What I need is Theo. I want him to hug me to sleep. I want him to tell me it'll be all right.

I can't control my tears as they spill once more down my face.

I once thought I had absolutely no feelings.

I still do, but there seems to be an exception.

Theo...

30

THEO

After last night's events, I'll be the first to admit I had the worst sleep. Hearing everything from Bianca's lips had been like a punch to the gut.

I neglect my work the whole morning; instead, I look on the internet for information on sociopaths.

The more I read, the more I realize how everything fit—the drugs, the violence, the lies.

What breaks my heart the most is reading that sociopaths aren't capable of feeling love. They can pretend, but they will always value themselves above all else.

Bianca had said she'd wanted me. And so, she'd done everything to get me, violating every moral law possible in the process, some legal ones as well.

Now, the question is what to do next... Marcel's been the only one I've told about my problems with Bianca, and I've yet to talk to him about confronting her. Considering all she's been involved in, the natural course of events would be to turn her in.

She is, after all, a killer.

My mind is telling me that such a person shouldn't be left roaming around free, but my heart can't even fathom the notion that Bianca would be locked behind bars for manslaughter... if not even worse. I don't know what that says about me. Here in my lofty position within NYPD, and I'm basically fostering a murderer.

So many times, I find myself glancing towards the phone, ready to make the call. But I just can't. It seems that no matter how many times I try to live righteously, I always give up.

It's around noon when my phone rings.

"Mr. Hastings, a Mr. Quinn Gallagher is here to see you," my secretary informs me. I freeze for a moment, my first intention being to not see him. But considering the circumstances, it might be more beneficial to see what exactly he knows or thinks he knows.

"Bring him in," I reply and close the connection.

I don't know how I'm still functioning, caught between my duty and the mob, Jimenez gunning for me, and then my wife turning out to be a fucking sociopath.

Honestly, if only I could bring myself to turn her in, I'd be rid of two problems... both the mob and her. And therein lies the issue.

I can't.

I look up to see Quinn Gallagher stride in my office, looking as menacing as he did on Sunday. His dirty-blond hair looks uncombed and disheveled. Although I think the length is supposed to hide the many scars marring his face. He's wearing a basic black T-shirt that outlines his outrageous muscles and nondescript jeans. He'd be a handsome man if he didn't look like he's escaped jail. Or maybe he has, who knows.

"Mr. Gallagher." I motion for him to take a seat. He doesn't say anything, his light-blue eyes staring at me. He finally nods and sits.

"To what do I owe this visit?" I ask, folding my hands in front of me. Quinn's lips slowly drag themselves upwards.

"I think you know well why," he finally replies.

"I can't say I do." I feign ignorance.

Quinn snorts before adding, "Sure... Barnett." My expression freezes in place at that name. It's one I haven't heard in more than a decade.

"Barnett?" I slowly ask, trying to keep my face from giving away how unnerved I am.

"Stop!" He puts his hand up, his eyes closing as if he's at the end of his rope. "Let's skip the whole denying phase. I know who you are. Or..." He looks me up and down. "Who you were."

I purse my lips. "I don't know what you're trying to do here..."

"You know... when I saw you, I immediately realized it wasn't the first time. But then I had to think real hard to remember where I knew you from." He smirks, probably knowing he already has me. This was what I'd been afraid of all along. He then goes a step further and pushes a photo onto the desk towards me.

I take a look at the photo, and my eyes suddenly go to his in question.

"You could imagine my surprise when I came across this picture. You were my uncle's favorite champion." He nods towards the picture that shows a bloody man full of bruises next to a man in a suit posing for the cameras.

"I left that life behind me," I answer tersely, but he continues.

"Looking at your circumstances right now, it doesn't seem that you have. Also, that wife of yours... Does she know about your past? I'm guessing not. Although, based on what I've heard, you're both cut from the same cloth."

"I don't know what you're talking about," I say again, trying to see what he knows about Bianca.

"Oh, come on. I think you found the only female who made her first kill at ten. Tell me, do you exchange notes on your victims?" I can see he's doing this on purpose to rile me up, so I don't answer.

"Not judging." He shrugs. "In our world, it's rare to have your hands clean of blood. I'm simply curious at your dynamic." He pauses and studies me. "It's not every day that you see a pairing such as yours. Hell, if my wife were like that, I wouldn't have spent the last few years locked up." Quinn points to some tattoos on his arm, probably to show me proof of his years behind bars. Seems like my initial impression has been proven right. He *did* do time.

"Your wife turned on you?" I ask, and his eyes seem to darken at the mention, but he just shrugs it off.

And just like that, I'm back to my initial dilemma. Even if I could stomach turning Bianca in, I'd be just a hypocrite, since my hands are also stained with blood.

"I'm curious though, what happened to the actual Theodore Hastings." He changes the topic.

"He's dead," I answer, and he lifts his eyebrows suspiciously.

"I didn't take you for the treacherous sort, *Mr. Hastings.*" The emphasis on my last name is not lost on me, but I feel compelled to clarify.

"Not by my hand. You probably realize how he ended up dead."

"That's true... now that I think about it..." He looks me up and down, "My uncle used to rave about you. Quiet, hardworking. You never gave him any problems... Until the day you disappeared."

I purse my lips, not liking where this is going.

"You do realize my uncle still owns you, don't you?" Quinn asks in a bored manner, and my hands clench into fists.

"What are you going to do about it?" I ask through gritted teeth. He knows he has me, so his smile is pure evil.

"Eh." He waves his hand. "I'll have none of that. We need you more in a suit than in a ring. My uncle will just have to live with the disappointment. You, on the other hand... let's just say you behave."

"So, that's why you came here? To threaten me into submission?"

"Not at all. I just wanted to remind you that things rarely stay truly buried. You can enjoy what you have now, or... you can lose it all." He gets up to his feet as he says that.

"I guess we'll see each other soon, Mr. Hastings. A pleasure." He tips his head and exits my office.

I'm left alone, and my mind retakes me to that night when I'd found my parents killed in the kitchen. I can't help but ask myself if revenge is worth everything, even selling my soul to the devil. But just the picture of my mother shot in the head and my father lying in a pool of blood is enough to remind me what I'm fighting for and why. I can take whatever they dish at me as long as I get Jimenez's head on a platter.

I never really cared much about my current life except to prepare my revenge.

Not until Bianca, anyway.

Now, there's nothing left to lose.

31
ADRIAN

In the aftermath of my parents' murder, I learned one thing. No matter how smart, a kid is just a kid. And no one takes a kid seriously.

I'd spent so much time trying to make the police see that there was no robbery, but it was soon apparent they'd never listen to a fourteen-year-old. Not even when I'd told them about the stranger, Greg, and the list my parents had given him.

"This isn't a conspiracy theory, kid," one cop had told me.

I'd had to grit my teeth and move on, knowing that I had to do it myself if I truly wanted to make a difference.

But being a minor, the system had other plans for me. Most of which involved a succession of foster homes in the Boston area. I'd been in two homes before I eventually realized it wasn't for me. The first one had been fine, if fine is defined by the minimum required to sustain life. I'd been moved from that one when there had been one too many arrivals, all of them under ten.

The second home, however, housed another three teenage boys. I realized from the first meeting that once bullied, always bullied.

They'd taken one look at my scrawny self, scoffed, and made my life a living hell. I'd been there three months before cuts and bruises accumulated to such a degree that normal activities became a chore. I would trudge my way instead of walk because I probably had some broken bones. For those kids, *that* meant weakness, and it was open season to do worse.

The night I'd escaped, I'd barely been able to move. I'd stolen a bike and pedaled as fast and as much as I could until I'd crashed at some point.

Maybe it'd been my luck, or retrospectively my misfortune, but the spot I'd fallen had non-ironically been near Basilica of Our Lady of Perpetual Help.

I'd lost consciousness at some point, but I'd woken up to find myself on a warm bed, with all my wounds taken care of. They'd taken a good look at me and understood I was a runaway, and as such, they'd offered to let me stay there.

The Basilica also had a grammar school in which I'd promptly been enrolled. It all seemed too good to be true until I'd realized just how I was supposed to pay for my upkeep.

For a bony kid who'd always been picked on, the chance to learn how to fight while making money on the side seemed like heaven sent literally.

I also saw it as my chance to make something of myself, so I could get to Jimenez in the future.

I trained, maybe harder than everyone in my quarters. It wasn't long before I had my first successful fight. After that, it was a series of easy wins, most of them due to an ever-increasing muscle mass and a sudden growth spurt.

By the beginning of my sixteenth year, I was as big and thick as any of the older fighters. This seemed to entertain the elders as they gave me matches with more seasoned fighters each time. When I'd won my hardest victory yet, I'd also taken the notice of a certain Andrew Gallagher. He was visiting for new recruits when he'd decided I'd come with him.

From my small game fights to Gallagher's pit fights, there was a world of difference. I quickly understood that in this new environment, it was kill or be killed.

Literally.

Andrew's pit fights weren't your regular MMA fights. They

were vicious, fight for your life type of battles. This was where the real money was made. There were several arenas in use throughout Boston, each of them alternated for different fights. The legality or illegality of it was as glaring as making minors fight for their food.

But I recognized it for what it was—my chance at surviving in this cutthroat world and making connections while doing so. I'd quickly realize what the name Jimenez meant in the underground world. And if there was one way to fight a fire, it was with fire.

From my first fight, my first kill, my first foray into pit fights, I strove to become the best.

Andrew's pet, they called me. They weren't wrong. I was biddable but deadly. In their minds, the best combination.

It's been two years now. Two years in which I'd fought almost weekly on Andrew's stage. Two years in which the corpses had accumulated, and my hands had bathed in blood. Two years in which I watched my humanity seep out of my body with each strike of my fists.

I look at the swollen skin on my knuckles and sigh, dragging the bandage over and securing it in place. I stand and take in my meager accommodations. It's a small room with a single bed and an adjacent bathroom. For all my earnings during these years, I prefer a Spartan lifestyle. I go to the bathroom and take out some ointment from the mirror cupboard. I scrutinize my battered face for any open wounds, applying generously at the corner of my mouth and under my eye. The last bastard I'd fought had gotten me good in the face a couple of times.

The more successful I became in the arena the less time I had between fights. Logically, it didn't make sense if you had your fighter's top shape in mind. But these pits maximized on usefulness. For them, everyone had a shelf life, so it was better to squeeze every bit of profit before it was too late.

My last fight had been a mere four days ago. And yet, tomorrow I'm scheduled for another one.

With a sigh, I leave my room and head to the gym to continue my training.

The minute I enter, an older man looks me up and down.

"You Andrew's boy?"

"Yes, sir," I answer, having learned that respect goes a long way with these people.

"What's your name?"

"Adrian Barnett, sir." He squints his eyes at me and purses his lips.

"And when's your next fight?"

"Tomorrow night."

"Good, good. We have a new recruit. Andrew wants you to train him, show him the ropes."

"A new recruit?" I ask. Weird. Fighters aren't usually supposed to train new recruits.

"Yeah, well... he'll have more chances if you help him. He's a bit gaunt if you ask me. Don't know what he's doing in a place like this. But hey, boss says to do it, we do it." I nod slowly in understanding.

"Come now, let me show you to the lad." He heads to the back of the gym, where the weights are, and he points at a kid struggling with a pair of dumbbells that can't be over twenty-five pounds each.

When he sees us approach, he stops and wipes the sweat from his brow. He looks... healthy, unblemished. Not a usual condition when you're out of the Basilica, especially to advance to this level. This immediately tells me he didn't come in the regular route.

"Oh, hey there." He gives a hesitant smile that neither me nor the old man return.

I take a second to study the boy. He's got shaggy long hair, a couple of piercings in his ears, and some random tattoos on his skinny arms.

"This here is Barnett. He's gonna show you the ropes." The man looks between the two of us and shakes his head. "Don't get yourself killed, kid." He turns and leaves me with him.

"I'm Adrian Barnett," I say and put my hand out to him. I know people in this place get off on intimidation, but I can't help but feel for the kid when his slender frame is so obvious in the gym.

"Theodore Hastings. But call me Theo." He returns my handshake, and I can feel him trembling. Somehow that makes me give him a small, assuring smile.

"Well, Theo, let's get you started, shall we?"

FOURTEEN YEARS AGO

"Are you fucking kidding me?" I punch Theo's shoulder as he opens the door to the room.

"What the fuck, man?" He jumps back and scowls at me.

"Do you really have a death wish?" His hand goes to massage the spot I hit, and I see him cringe in pain as he heads towards the bed. "Don't even tell me you tried your last fight. You were just taking hit after hit..."

He collapses on the bed, clearly tired from his fight.

I shake my head and am about to head out when I hear muffled sobs. I half-turn and see Theo with his head in the pillow.

"Shit, dude, are you okay?" I immediately ask.

"It's all my fault..." His hands clench into fists, and he smacks the mattress.

I don't even know what to say to comfort him.

When Theo arrived two years ago as a scrawny kid ready to take on seasoned fighters, it had been solely to rebel against his parents. His wealthy, well-connected parents. Apparently, for a posh kid, it's not enough to get a few piercings and ink on your body.

No, the best way to rebel is to throw yourself headfirst into pit fighting, where the chances of getting out alive are against you. Honestly, the only reason Theo's still standing today is because I haven't given up on him. I've trained and trained him until he could hold his own. Well... in the first year, it was mostly me nursing him to health and teaching him how to *not* get killed.

It all changed, though, when his parents were killed in a car accident. Theo blames himself for it because he wasn't there. If you ask me, that's bollocks. I'd gone through the whole blaming myself routine too. In his case, the accident couldn't have been prevented.

In mine, maybe...

Now, it seems that Theo is dead set on getting himself killed in the ring. I don't understand him. He's already been accepted into Harvard but decided to defer his enrollment to fight in this dump. At least I have an ulterior motive for being here. Him? He's wasting away his potential.

I've tried to tell him that on a number of occasions, but he always assumes I'm telling him he's weak and takes offense.

I've stopped.

That doesn't mean I've stopped taking care of him. He's my best friend, and he isn't fit for this world.

A few days later, when we're training in the gym, he tells me of his upcoming fight. I'm holding the training targets, and he's aiming to catch me off guard.

"No way," I say, incredulous that anyone would allow such a pairing. My hand slips, and his punch barely misses my cheek.

"Fuck." Theo laughs. "Why are you so surprised? Do you know this Bull dude?"

"Do I know him? Theo, have you been living under a rock this whole time?"

"I'm serious. I've never heard about him before."

"He used to be a champion here a couple of years ago. Never got to fight him though, before he got moved to Nevada."

"Then what got you so spooked?"

"Dude, are you kidding me? The guy's a tank. He's easily twice your size. What were they thinking to pair you two?"

"Maybe they see my potential," Theo adds with a wink, but I can see he's getting scared.

"When is it?" I ask, not really wanting to know. In Andrew's pits, the rule is that you can never renege on a fight unless you're dead. Which doesn't leave much hope for Theo.

"Tonight," Theo adds casually, removing his gloves and taking a sip of water.

"And you're not resting?" Never mind that I'm scared of him fighting Bull, but there's no way he has any chance if he goes into the ring already tired.

"That's it. You're not doing anything for the rest of the day." I lead him to the bench and make him sit. "Conserve your strength."

"You'll be there?" he asks almost hesitantly.

"Of course." I try my best to mask my worry, not wanting him to pick up on it and influence his morale. But truth is... deep down, I know that Theo's not going to make it.

It's close to midnight when I take a seat on the bleachers in the arena. Theo's fight is supposed to start soon. From the corner of my eye, I see him give me a little wave before heading to his side. Turning slightly, I also take in Bull. Like his name, the guy is huge, his muscles bulging from what I doubt is genuine effort. Still, to stay in the game for so long, you gotta be good. Hell, better than good. You gotta be the best.

The match quickly begins, and I see Theo try to make up for his smaller size with his speed. He's dodging left and right Bull's attacks. I'm at the edge of my seat, hoping he can score some blows on him before Bull does. Theo manages an uppercut when Bull least expects it and proceeds to throw another punch to Bull's temple.

Yes! My fists clench in excitement. He can do this.

Come on, Theo!

They circle each other a few more times before suddenly, Bull is in front of Theo, and with one punch to the stomach, throws him to the ground. Theo coughs up some blood and tries to stand, but Bull is on him, pummeling away. My eyes are wide as I realize that Theo's not even fighting. He turns his head slightly and catches my eyes, giving me a hint of a smile before his head drops to the ground, and his eyes close.

"We have a winner!" The crowd is cheering for Bull, but I can't hear anything. Theo's dead. Why is he dead? Why did he give up? I move mechanically towards the back of the arena, where the dead fighters are taken before being disposed of. On my way, I see Andrew, who stops me with a hand on my shoulder.

"That kid had a death wish," he says, looking towards the ring. I barely have the power to speak when I ask.

"What... do you mean?"

"Why he'd ask to fight Bull... it's beside me. I'd planned to have you fight him next weekend." He shakes his head as if he can't quite understand Theo's decision before moving forward and leaving me rooted to the spot. Theo had wanted it. He'd willingly sought death. Why? But I know the answer. The guilt had been too much for him.

I'm later in my room, still numb from the events in the arena. I've bribed some workers to have Theo buried in the cemetery next to the Basilica, hoping this will at least offer him some peace in death, even though his will forever be an unmarked grave.

Usually, the defeated aren't even given the privilege of being buried, some immediately being disposed of in of the crematories in the city, while others are sold for different purposes. Apparently, corpses have their uses.

I give a bitter laugh at the notion.

Undressing, I plop myself into bed. I shift for a while, trying to find a good position when I realize there's something under the pillow. Frowning, I lift it to find a big envelope.

I open it, and I'm amazed to see documents: a passport, social security number, university acceptance. Theo's stuff.

I continue to look through them, and I see a letter addressed to me.

Dear Adrian,

I'm sorry. I'm not sure you'll ever forgive me, but I'll have to take the risk.

I realize I've never valued my identity and my privilege. You were right. I was selfish.

Which is why I hope you can make the best out of it. (Don't worry, no one will miss me!)

You don't have to be a criminal to fight criminals.

I hope you'll take this chance to fight bad with good.

P.S. Classes start in two months! I already picked your courses. Hope you like political science and law.

You can do it!

Your only friend,
Theo

I feel tears run down my cheeks. That idiot! He actually wants me to take his place. I crunch the paper in my fist.

Idiot.

TWO MONTHS LATER

"Hi, where can I register for freshman orientation?" I ask the lady at one of the stands.

"You're at the right place!" she says with a bright smile. "What's your name?"

"Theo... Theodore Hastings." I cringe at my own voice, but she doesn't seem to notice.

"Perfect. Let me get you your ID." She sifts through some papers before handing me a university ID that has a picture Theo had uploaded for me as well as a bunch of freebies and stationaries.

"Welcome to Harvard!" She waves as I go.

Two months ago, Adrian Barnett died in the pit. Theodore Hastings made it out alive.

You were right, Theo, I don't have to stoop to Jimenez's level to get him. I just have to get up high enough.

BIANCA

I don't know how much time's passed. Vlad's given me one of his guestrooms, a room bare except for basic necessities. He's advised me how tough the next few days will be, and yet I don't believe him.

As I lay in bed now, my skin drenched in sweat, my body heavy and lethargic, I almost want to beg him to either give me a line or put a bullet through my brain. It's been a while since my mind started playing tricks on me, a fogginess clouding my sight and making me lose track of everything around.

I'm in and out of consciousness.

I sleep and sleep and when I wake, I want to sleep again. At some point, I have to admit to myself that it's not just my body that yearns for that rest, but my mind also doesn't want to face reality.

Whenever I find myself awake, my mind immediately takes me back to my last conversation with Theo. I keep hearing his words, again and again. They keep replaying in my head like an anthem.

"You disgust me!"

I've never made excuses for my behavior before.

I've always thought that I am what I am, why should I change? I kill because I enjoy it. I take coke because I enjoy it. I love Theo because I enjoy it.

Maybe that's the problem... It always goes back to what I'm

enjoying. I don't think I've ever done anything that doesn't result in *my enjoyment,* no matter how much I've professed that I've always put Theo's well-being above my own.

Alone in my continuous torment, I realize I never have.

I've been overconfident. I've assumed he'd never find out. I've assumed he'd always be mine.

And now he's *not.*

Why? Why can't he overlook it? Why can't he accept me?

But I know the truth deep down, just as I've known when I've changed my personality to suit him. I've known he'd never go for me, the real me.

I'm bawling at this point. Big, fat tears streaming down my face. I can't do this. I can't ever do this.

I struggle out of bed, almost tripping on my way out.

"Vlad!" I yell, banging on the door. "Vlad!" I keep on hitting the door.

"Bianca?" I hear Vlad respond once the door opens.

I don't stop however, now hitting his chest instead.

"I can't do it, Vlad. I can't! Please don't make me do it!" I cry out, sobs wrecking my body. When all my energy is spent from my tantrum, I collapse at Vlad's feet.

"B, come on, let's put you to bed." He gathers me in his arms and puts me to bed.

"Please..." I beg him. "One line. Just one. I need out of my head. I can't bear these thoughts, Vlad." My hands go to his blazer, and I plead with him at this point. I don't want to hear Theo's voice telling me how disgusting I am anymore. I don't want to see his face full of disappointment, of hate.

"I can't, B. You have to push through. It's only been two days. It's going to get better, I promise."

"Why would I? He hates me. He... He can't stand the sight of me."

"But you said you weren't going to give up on him. Remember?"

I shake my head. "It's pointless. He's never going to forgive me, is he?"

"Shh, B, come on, sleep." He tugs my head towards the pillow, holding me for a little longer.

I sleep more, waking up only to eat and drink some fluids. Sasha, Vlad's doctor, comes by a few times to check up on me, but he doesn't say much.

I'm still having bad dreams. And when I'm awake, my mind immediately goes to Theo.

I've asked Vlad if he's tried to contact me so far, but he has refrained from replying.

In my few moments of clarity, I can understand Vlad's thoughts. He doesn't think I can ever get Theo back.

It's a new day when I wake, or so I think. From what Vlad's told me, this is the third day of my detox. To say I'm craving a line is an understatement. From the moment I open my eyes, I notice the trembling in my body. The fact that my eyes can't focus well on things. But mostly, I become singularly focused on getting more dope.

It's pure instinct when a guy comes in later to bring me food. I wait for him to give me his back before I grab him by the throat, stealing his gun.

I'm still a sweaty mess, but I'm a sweaty mess with a purpose.

I yank open the door and head for one of the warehouses. I know Vlad's house like I know my own. And I know he always keeps some product on hand for emergency deliveries. I just have to make my way to the edge of the property where the warehouses are located.

I only make it to the back garden before Vlad catches up with me.

"Please don't stop me, Vlad," I plead with him. I must look a fright, and I feel my fingers trembling on the trigger of the pistol in my hand.

"Put the gun down, *malyshka*, you can't shoot shit right now, and you know it." He smiles at me and cocks his head. I raise my hand and try to point it at Vlad and the guys behind him.

"You don't want to do this," he continues and removes his cell phone from his pocket, dangling it in front of me.

"Please, Vlad. You don't get it. I can't do this!" I don't recognize my own voice when I'm speaking.

Vlad just shrugs at me and dials a number, showing me he's putting it on speaker.

"Hastings here," the voice says on the other end, and my eyes widen in surprise.

"No..."

"Mr. Hastings, just the man I wanted to talk to." Vlad smiles, and I take a step towards him, whispering *no* again.

"What is it, Vlad?" my husband asks in a clipped manner.

"I have something of yours." He looks at me. "Although, she's a little damaged."

"No..." I keep shaking my head.

"What are you on about, Vlad?" Theo asks, and Vlad winks at me.

"Bianca, do you want to say something to your husband?"

"Theo..." I say his name, the hand holding the gun coming down on its own.

I take a step towards the phone, my focus suddenly changing from dope to Theo. I don't make it though. At some point, while in motion, I feel a figure sneak behind my back and a needle poking my skin.

I almost fall to the ground before someone catches me, but I manage to yell one more time at the top of my lungs.

"Theoooo!"

ADRIAN

It's been three days. Three days since Bianca's left the apartment and hasn't picked up any of her things. Three days in which Bianca hasn't as much as called or left a message.

I should be glad—cutting the ties so efficiently.

But I can't.

I miss her.

I can't sleep. I can barely eat. And when I'm at home, all I do is look at photos of us.

Pathetic, I know.

She never loved you. I try to tell myself. *She's not capable of it.*

No matter how much I try to come to terms with it, I can't.

I'm in my car, heading to a meeting, when my cell rings.

"Hastings here," I activate my Bluetooth headpiece and answer.

"No..." I can hear a vague sound in the background.

"Mr. Hastings, just the man I wanted to talk to." When the voice comes through, I realize who it is. I frown, trying to think why he'd reach out to me. My relationship with Vlad is casual at best.

"What is it, Vlad?" I ask, a bit tersely.

"I have something of yours," he says and pauses. "Although

she's a little damaged." Something of mine? Now that's unusual. But I'm curious, so I ask.

"What are you on about, Vlad?"

"Bianca, do you want to say something to your husband?" Vlad says, and my hands clench on the steering wheel. Why would Bianca be with Vlad? Then I hear a small "Theo..." followed by a loud wailing "Theoooo!"

My foot hits the brake without even realizing. I look left and right and decide to pull over to compose myself.

"Vlad? What's the meaning of this?" I can barely breathe, thinking of all possible scenarios. Her voice... Lord, her voice.

"I told you... your wife is a little damaged."

"What do you mean by that? Tell me?"

"Do you care?" he asks casually, and I curse under my breath. "Vlad, just tell me!" I demand, and he chuckles.

"If you want to know, you can come by. I'll text you the address. It's up to you." He hangs up the phone.

I'm stunned for a moment before I hit the wheel in frustration.

Please be okay, Bianca, is all my mind can process at the moment.

I don't even think; I copy the address and input it in my GPS, changing direction and heading straight to Vlad's house.

So much for a clean break

The entire way to the address Vlad provided, I'm wrecked with worry. What could have happened to her? Is she ill? Did she get herself into trouble? Is she in trouble with Vlad? How exactly do they know each other?

When I finally arrive at the destination, armed guards greet me, who perform a rudimentary search on me.

Of course.

Then, one of them escorts me into a very normal-looking mansion.

"Where is she?" I bark when I spot Vlad at the entrance. He gives me an amused smile and looks at his watch.

"It only took you a half hour. Any traffic violations, Mr. Law and Order?" I grit my teeth at his sarcasm. "I mean, never let it be known that I'm heartless." He cocks his head to the side as if thinking about something. "Come, she's sleeping now."

He leads me towards a room on the other side of the house. I'm so keen on finding out what happened to Bianca that I'm not even taking any precautions, like assessing my environment or keeping my eyes on potential dangers.

Vlad opens the door to a small room, and on the bed, I see the figure of my wife, sound asleep.

"What's wrong with her?" I ask as I near the bed and take in her ragged appearance. Her hair is knotted and messy, her clothes damp and clinging to her form. Her face is pale, her lips chapped and dry. I immediately run my hand on her forehead, noting she is feverish.

"She's detoxing," Vlad answers, leaning on the door frame. "We had to sedate her because she stole a gun and attacked me."

"What?" I whip my head around to regard him.

"Come, let her rest. She'll be as good as new by the end of the week. You must have a lot of questions and as it happens, I'm feeling mighty generous."

He stands and motions me out, leading me to what looks to be a study. He shuts the door behind us and takes a seat at his desk, telling me to do the same.

For a second, there's only silence, and I see him staring very intently at a pendulum on his desk. Then, as if he remembers I'm still in the room with him, he turns to me and gives me a jolly smile.

"Now, where were we?"

"Maybe on the why Bianca is here," I answer drily. It's clear to me that no one means her harm here. If they had, she wouldn't be sleeping peacefully after pointing a gun at Vlad. On that point, I'm relieved. But I still want to know what Vlad is willing to impart.

"I've known your wife for over ten years." He pulls a drawer, taking a pack of gum and popping one in his mouth. Chewing on it, he continues, "She's what you'd call my friend."

I frown at this. Over ten years? Friend?

Hell no.

Even as a dude, I have to admit that Vlad is an attractive guy. There's no way...

My suspicion must be written on my face because Vlad scowls and stops my train of thought.

"Easy, boy. It's probably not what you're thinking of. I mean... ew. No offence, but I'm not one to exchange bodily fluids... with anyone." He makes another disgusted face at the thought before continuing, "I don't know how much Bianca's told you but... we used to be partners."

I release a breath I didn't know I was holding at his confirmation that they're strictly platonic, although I mentally chastise myself for even caring.

"In...?" I ask, and he shakes a finger at me.

"You know exactly in what." No incriminating evidence. I chuckle but let him have his way.

"Then I guess you also know she's a sociopath," I carefully add, watching closely his body language.

"Of course," he readily agrees, popping another piece of gum into his mouth. "That's why we were partnered in the first place. You see, we share a similar affliction, Bianca and I. But my case... is a little more volatile," he casually says. "Our temperaments were opposite, but complementary. And we worked perfectly together."

"What was she, fifteen, sixteen? How can someone that young do that?"

He drums his fingers on the surface of the desk. One glaring thing about Vlad is that he can't seem to stay still.

"Did she tell you about her nanny?" he asks, and I nod.

"Then you realize it's not too young. By that time, she'd already had years of training. I'll be honest, I've never seen anyone with a better aim than B, only when she's not coked up though." His use of her nickname grates me, but I have to admit that he knows things about her I don't. I can't deny that they have a special bond.

"How long has she been using?" I ask what has been on my mind for days now.

"Honestly... I don't know. It's not her first rodeo with coke, though. She's had on and off periods with it, but she's never truly been off it, I think."

"Why though? What would prompt her to do this... any of this?" I ask, almost exasperated.

"She's not normal, Hastings. She's not and never will be. You have to come to terms with this if you want to be with her." I want to correct him and tell him we're already over, but I let him continue.

"For people like us, it's hard to conform to normality. To social norms. We just need a trigger and off we go. Hers was the nanny. Drugs... let's just say they help us be less apathetic. When all you know is a sea of nothingness, you'd do anything to cause a little wave."

"So that's how you're justifying her being an addict?" I ask, shaking my head at his logic. "By that logic, you should be one too."

His eyes are on that pendulum again.

"We all have different drugs. Mine just don't happen to be an illicit substance." He doesn't elaborate on that.

I sit still for a moment, digesting what Vlad's saying. But I still can't help myself. I want to understand. Hell...

"How can I even contemplate being with a person who manipulated and lied to me? She isn't capable of empathy, of love."

"Is she not?" he asks, his eyebrow raised. "Don't get me wrong, I'm not sure she's capable of those things either. But I've known her long enough to see how irregular her behavior is towards you. For someone who kills in cold blood, the instinct to protect is entirely antithetic. And yet, all she's ever done has been to protect you."

"What about you, then? If you say you don't feel either, why are you helping her?"

Vlad chuckles, shoving yet another piece of gum in his mouth.

"I'm governed by a very simple rule of retribution, or *an eye for an eye*. The only difference is that I pay back those who help me in kind too. Bianca... she may not be normal, but she's the most loyal person you could ever find. Don't let other inconsequential things detract from that."

"You call murder inconsequential?" I add sarcastically.

"In the grand scheme of things? Yes. And if you knew who those she dispatched were, you would see that the world is a better place without them. One thing I can promise you, though, is that she's never, ever, hurt an innocent person."

I think on that and reply, "I think we can agree to disagree."

"I'm disappointed, Hastings. I wouldn't have taken you for a narrow-minded type of fellow."

"Again, I wouldn't call disapproving of murder narrow minded."

"And yet your past says otherwise." I freeze. What does he know?

"What do you mean?"

"You know exactly what I mean." Slowly, his mouth curls upwards. "But alas, I cannot make your decisions for you." He stands, and I can see I'm being dismissed. "You should know though, she's doing the detox for you."

"She should do it for herself, not for me." I stand as well, ready to go.

"It's up to you." Vlad shrugs and says with finality, "I thought you could use a different perspective. My job here is done."

"Just... take care of her."

"Always." He gives me another charming smile before seeing me off.

34
BIANCA

"You're finally awake." I open my eyes to see Vlad staring down at me, his face expressionless.

"How do you feel?" he asks, going to the bathroom and bringing me a wet towel. I take it and wipe my face, feeling the sweat cling to my skin.

"Much better. How long was I out?" He looks at his watch.

"Almost thirty-two hours now."

"You're kidding me." I stare at him, but he just shrugs.

"It's gotta be the sedative. The coke must be out of your system by now, though, so that's good. Although..." He pauses to think. "I'm not letting you out of my sight for another couple of days."

I slowly nod. I remember pieces of my embarrassing outburst, and I cringe.

"I'm sorry about before." Vlad waves his hand as if it's nothing.

"It's not as if I expected you to be a model patient. Your husband visited by the way."

"Theo?" My eyes widen. "You're serious?" He pulls the chair from the desk next to my bed and positions himself in front of me.

"Why? How?"

"I called him."

"And he came?"

"Uhum. He was quite worried about you. Maybe not all is lost..."

"Not all is lost... you mean..."

"I'll help you. I'll help you win that husband of yours back. But I need a favor for that."

"Anything," I readily agree, and he nods.

"Good. I will exact a promise from you," I frown at his request, shaking my head.

"What promise?" I ask, trying to see why he'd go to such an extent.

"You'll know when the moment comes." His head turns toward the window. "Do I have your word?"

"Of course," I say, maybe too fast. Who knows what Vlad will ask me. But at this point, I'd be willing to give him anything.

"Great!" His face immediately changes to accommodate a smile. "Now, on to more serious concerns."

I drag myself in a sitting position. While my mind is no longer as clouded as before, I can't say I'm in top shape. I'm also in dire need of a shower. But if Vlad says it's serious... chances are it's serious.

He takes out his phone and plays a recording. I listen attentively and ask.

"Is that...?"

"Yes. It's your arms dealer."

"Not my arms dealer," I have to correct it with a scowl.

"You were the one who almost fell into a trap. You don't get a say."

"I could have handled myself."

"I have no doubt, you would have also attracted unwanted attention to yourself." I don't reply, knowing he is right.

"Okay, so *my* arms dealer."

"As you see, I managed to get some information out of him. He was looking specifically for Artemis."

"Yeah, to get to you and what was that... Chimera? Who's that?"

"That's what I am most concerned about. Chimera was my previous partner."

"I didn't know you had another partner before me."

"It's not common knowledge. Chimera just disappeared one day."

"So, why would they want you or Chimera? From what I understand from that confession, I was just the means to an end."

"That's my question as well." He shuffles some files and gives me a dossier full of pictures.

"What's this?" I ask, and he just nods for me to open it. When I do, I immediately frown. I turn page after page, and I am greeted by massacre after massacre, one worse than the other. One, in particular, is almost something unlike anything I'd ever seen. A torso riddled with small, clean-cut holes is propped on a chair in a dark room. The ribs look to have been removed beforehand. And the holes? They look meticulous, hand-carved ones. Instead of arms, human legs had been sown at the torso's sockets, making it a monstrous amalgamation. And instead of toes, human fingers had been added. It's a massacre, but it's also a work of art.

"That is Chimera." Vlad points at the pictures in my hands. "He wasn't just an assassin. He was the boogie man. His job wasn't just to kill, but to send a message. Look at the next page."

I do, and I notice teeth—human teeth arranged in the form of a C.

"That's his mark."

"Shit," I whisper. Even to my eyes, which have seen countless sick shit... this is something different.

"You were partnered with *this?*" Vlad purses his lips.

"Things were different back then. But the issue is that Chimera disappeared over ten years ago."

"Before I became your partner," I say, and he nods. "And why would anyone be looking for Chimera *now?*"

"That was my question, as well. It's clear that whoever is looking for Chimera has some insider information; otherwise, they wouldn't tie Chimera to Berserker or Artemis."

"Do you think it's someone out for revenge? You said Chimera was used to send messages. That means that the people who got the messages were left alive. At least I'm assuming."

"Not necessarily. But I did think of that as well."

"And?"

"It gets worse." He takes another file, and I see *CONFIDEN-*

TIAL written on it. I open it to see a report from what looks to be the FBI. It details a few gruesome murders in the Tri-state area. I'm about to ask Vlad what I'm looking at when I turn the page, and I suddenly understand.

Teeth.

The mark of the Chimera.

"Look at the date." There are a total of four murders, stretching from two years ago to last month. My eyes snap back to Vlad's.

"I kept thinking about it. It couldn't be coincidental that they were looking into Chimera after so much time. I asked some questions here and there, and my sources came back with this."

"So, Chimera is back?"

"No. Chimera is not back. That." He points at the FBI file and then at the previous folder. "is not Chimera. It's a copycat."

"How do you know? Maybe Chimera suddenly decided to make a reappearance."

Vlad lifts his eyebrow. "I know Chimera. He's out of commission."

I frown. This doesn't make sense at all.

"But who would know about Chimera's work after all this time?"

"That is my question, as well. But I wanted you to know the details too. Chances are, if they tried once, they would keep on trying to get to you. Better be on guard at all times."

"Can't you get in touch with the real Chimera?"

"No. At least not yet. Chimera is..." Vlad shakes his head. "He isn't like us, not really."

"Like us?"

"He felt. Too deeply, one might say. In our line of work, no one is truly sane. To do what Chimera did, however..." He trails off.

"You'd have to be really deranged."

"Exactly. And Chimera's feelings were his downfall. He went off the rails." Vlad shakes his head. "I really don't know what would happen if I brought any of this up."

"Do you need my help?"

"For now, no. I just need you to be on guard. You already have too much on your plate."

"Tell me about it," I mumble and Vlad takes the files away from me.

"Which brings me to my second point. The Italians."

"So you heard? How am I not surprised." I roll my eyes.

"What can I say, I have ears everywhere. Your father is an idiot if you ask me."

"Tell me something new..."

"There's gonna be a war soon. How's that for new?"

"What?"

"Did they tell you why the partnership with the Irish? It's not really their style."

"Not in detail. Why?"

"Because Enzo is trying to eliminate the other families. He wants to be Capo Dei Capi. But he needs support. Influence. Soldiers. You really think they didn't come to me first?"

"Of course they would. Why didn't you agree?"

"You know I find human trafficking distasteful." Vlad makes a disgusted face. "But more than that, their main enemy is the Lastra family."

"Lastra..." I repeat, trying to remember where I'd heard the name.

"They own Upper Manhattan."

"Wait!" I put my hand up, realizing where I know the name from. "Why are they, enemies? Didn't one of Agosti's daughters marry into the Lastra family?" I knew this because, after the unsettling lunch at my father's, I'd done some research on the Agostis.

"You are correct. But she's dead. And coincidentally or not, they blame her husband, the Lastra Capo, for it."

"Are they right? Did he do it?"

"No. I don't think so. I'd even go as far as to say that Enzo could have had her killed just to have a reason for conflict."

"Damn, I thought Italians drew the line at family."

"They do when they're male." Vlad curls his lip at the notion. "If they're female, they're either marriageable or unmarriageable, whereby they live out their lives in a convent."

"You're joking."

"No. They are strictly used as currency. That's why I think Romina might have outlived her purpose."

"I didn't realize Enzo was so ruthless. Smart? Yeah. But not heartless."

"The thing with Enzo is that you can never get a good read on him. He's just *that* smart."

"Is that why you didn't agree to help them? Because you don't trust him?"

"That is part of the reason. Also, I'm honor-bound to the Lastra Capo."

"So, you'll take their side in the war?"

"I haven't decided yet. I can pay my dues by simply not aiding the other side."

"Yeah, well... both me and Theo are currently stuck on their side. The old man kept some evidence on me that's currently keeping me out of jail."

"Bianca, Bianca..." Vlad tsks at me in disapproval. He's always criticized me for being careless. "Do you think your husband will keep playing along now?"

"Honestly? I don't know. I wouldn't even hold it against him if he didn't," I add uncertainly.

"Good thing you have me," Vlad smirks. "I have a plan that might just solve *most* of your problems."

"Really?"

"Let's see..."

He starts and outlines what could, in fact, solve *all* my problems.

35

ADRIAN

"I hear you, Marcel. But I still don't see how this is going to play out," I say into my Bluetooth headset as I steer my car towards the parking lot.

"Trust me. Enzo definitely has something up his sleeve," he comments.

I sigh and thread my fingers through my hair.

"Fine. I'll update you!" I say and disconnect the call.

I get out of my car and head towards Enzo's office. They weren't kidding when they were talking about their restaurants. This one is a high-end one on Madison Avenue. I'd heard of it before, but I'd never connected it to the mob before. I guess that goes to show just how embedded in society they are. The usher greets me, and I tell him who I'm supposed to meet. After confirming my ID, he shows me to the back elevator, punching some code, which takes me to the building's third floor.

As I step out of the elevator, I am met with an open plan apartment, of which the kitchen seems to take a significant portion. Enzo is right in the middle of that kitchen, full gear on. He removes a tray from the industrial oven, and the smell wafts towards me.

It smells... intriguing.

"Hastings," he says in that Italian accent of his. He puts the

230

tray on the table for cooling and frees his hands. He quickly checks his watch and his mouth curls up, noting. "You're early."

"Did I disturb your baking party?" I add drily, but he just shrugs, taking off his apron and motioning me to the sofas.

"If you'd have been on time, the cake would have had time to cool down. Now you'll just have to wait."

"I didn't take you for the baking sort."

"My wife loved baking. Now it just allows me to relax," he says nonchalantly. "But alas, let us get back to business. I trust you received the file I sent you?"

"Indeed."

"Do you have questions? I thought it was pretty straightforward. Those are our current locations, but shortly we will have a few more places opening. Of course, I shall update you. All in due time, however."

"That's not exactly what I wanted to talk to you. I've already flagged those locations as per our agreement. There is something that bothers me."

"Go ahead." Enzo takes a pack of cigarettes from the table and lights one, crossing his legs and regaling me with his undivided attention.

"I'm not entirely sure how much you've heard about the recent disturbances," I start carefully. I don't want to rush into the meat of the issue lest Enzo suspects I have a personal stake in this.

"How recent are we talking?" He drags deeply from the cigarette and releases a cloud of smoke.

"It's been a couple of months now. The reports have been trickling in."

"Let's say I have an idea of what you're talking about."

"There's been an increase in street disturbances. Word is that a new gang is in town," I continue.

"But it's not," he states, and I nod.

"Yes, it's a cartel we've been watching for a while now. They're trying to set base in New York."

"You're pretty well informed, Chief." Enzo takes another drag and heads to the small liquor cabinet next to the window. He turns to me with a question, but I shake my head.

"I'm driving," I simply say. He pours himself a drink and settles back on the sofa.

"I've been informed of this new cartel trying to get into our territory. It's interesting to see you know too." He smiles slowly but continues, "So, what's your issue?"

"Your part of the bargain is to help keep crime low. These people are only driving it up." I keep my voice steady, hoping he won't ask more questions.

"So it is. Let's do this. Tell me what you know, and I will tell you what I know. Tit for tat, very simple." He makes it sound simple, but somehow I doubt this is an equal exchange.

"My sources tell me these people are part of the Ortega cartel. We don't know much because their people don't talk. We do, however, know that they're mainly involved in sex trafficking."

"I see." Enzo regards me for a second before giving his own side. "Ortega isn't your problem. Jimenez is. I've noticed changes in the market since he's started encroaching in the area. But no one can actually vouch for the man. He's never been seen in person. He's more like a myth if you will." Oh, how I know. I've been chasing this myth for twenty years. Few have reported seeing or interacting with him, with most of them probably lying through their teeth.

"How do you deal with a myth then?"

Enzo's mouth spreads into a wide smile. "You're lucky, Hastings. Your enemy seems to be my enemy, as well."

"Really?" I drawl, realizing how well Marcel had predicted this.

"Let's just say we're competing in the same market."

"Then I gather you've already thought how to deal with him?"

"Of course. Jimenez is a dangerous enemy because he doesn't show himself. He only works through intermediaries."

"So, you plan to make him show himself?"

"Exactly. My wife's birthday is in two days. We've been planning a bash for a while now, thinking to lure Jimenez into a cordial partnership." He looks me up and down critically. "You should join us and bring that lovely wife of yours with you."

"That's a very impromptu invite. But thank you nonetheless."

"What can I say. Law enforcement isn't very high up on my list for pleasant company. But I shall make an exception for you. We're to be partners, no?"

"Of course. We'll make sure to be there."

"I'll have the invitations sent to your office."

We quickly wrap up when Enzo receives a phone call that he's needed at one of his locations, but not before he packs me half of the cherry tart he baked.

I get in my car and head to Marcel's office at the D.A.'s. When he sees me come in with the cake, he raises his eyebrow in amusement, and I shrug.

"Who knew Enzo was a baking enthusiast."

"That's funny," he says, but he takes the tart from me and proceeds to cut it in pieces. "It's actually delicious," he praises it, his mouth full. I take a small amount as well, and I have to agree. It's not bad at all.

"Sweets aside, what did you manage?" Marcel reclines in his seat, and I make myself comfortable across from him.

"He's after Jimenez as well. It seems he's been planning for a while to get close to him."

"I assumed as much. There's no way Enzo wouldn't know what happens in his own territory and if there is anyone who threatens his business. Most probably, there's been some sort of communications between him and Jimenez."

"You think? With how elusive Jimenez is?"

"Definitely. The Agostis are very well connected," Marcel remarks.

"Then it would make sense why he thinks Jimenez would make an appearance at his wife's birthday party," I say, musing. When Enzo had casually mentioned Jimenez coming to the party, I hadn't taken it too seriously.

"Did he say so?"

"Yeah, he belatedly invited Bianca and me as well. It's in two days."

"Shit!" Marcel curses under his breath, and I have to agree. The situation isn't optimal. I might actually need to bring Bianca with me.

"Do you think she'll agree to come?" he finally asks.

"I don't know. Last I saw her, she looked pretty rough."

I'd tried my damned best to get the image of her looking half-dead in that bed.

I'd had to keep myself from checking up on her again. Although, with recent developments, it looks like I might have to do just that.

"Does she know why you've been after Jimenez for so long?" I shake my head.

"I don't think she knows the details, only that it's personal."

"We should still try to get her on board. It would look too suspicious if you showed up without her."

"I know, I thought about that as well." I sigh aloud before saying, "I'll reach out to Vlad tonight, maybe see her tomorrow."

"Good. I have to say I was astonished when you told me about Bianca's relationship with Vlad."

"He assured me it's always been strictly platonic," I feel compelled to add, and I see Marcel fighting a smile.

"And that was the most important thing for you, wasn't it?"

"Of course," I answer too readily and catch myself. "Shit..." I laugh. "This situation has been messing with my brain."

"You're not a saint yourself, *Adrian*." Marcel arches an eyebrow at me. "Maybe cut her some slack." Marcel had been the first to call me out on some irregularities in my background, and the only person to know my true identity. What began as a slight rivalry soon grew into an unexpected friendship.

"I don't think her killing people bothers me as much as her manipulating me. From what she's told me, her first kill was definitely warranted. The others? I don't know. Vlad assures me they weren't innocent. But she *lied* to me. She put on an act. I don't even know the real her, and that's the main problem."

"Then get to know her. The *real* her."

"Easy for you to say," I mumble, crossing my arms defensively. Since when is Marcel Bianca's biggest supporter?

"Sometimes, maybe even monsters deserve some redemption," he says, more to himself.

36

BIANCA

I cock my pistol and shoot. One down. I move one meter to my left and repeat the movement. Two down. I do it again and again until I've finished the row.

Then, I head to the targets to check my results. Bull's eye. Every single one of them.

I release a breath I didn't know I was holding. My coke-free body can still hit the mark. My abilities haven't been compromised.

I have to admit that one of my biggest concerns has been that without coke, I will suddenly stop being me... especially in the field.

Today is the first day I've picked up a gun since the withdrawal fiasco, and my fingers don't tremble. No, in fact, my vision is sharper, my awareness has increased. Maybe being drug-free isn't so bad.

"Guess who's going to be here in about thirty minutes." Vlad's voice takes me by surprise, and I look back to see him heading towards me.

"I told you it would work, didn't I?" He winks at me.

"How did you even know?" Some of the things Vlad knows sometimes take me by surprise. It's like you can't hide any secret from him. Which is also how he'd devised his plan.

"I have my ways. Now, you might want to change into something else." I look down at myself and notice how sweaty I am. Ever since my head had cleared, I'd been using Vlad's gym. I was now only wearing a pair of gym shorts and a sports bra.

"Fine, I'll meet you in a few," I say and jog towards my room.

Thankfully, Vlad had brought some clothes from my apartment. I'm halfway across the lawn when a car pulls up in the driveway.

I stop and crane my neck. Getting out of the car, I see Marcel and Theo, both dressed in their immaculate suits. Vlad must have seen them too because he catches up with me and sniffs me.

"You don't smell *too* bad."

"Thanks," I say drily. Both Vlad and I go over to the men and quietly greet them before heading to Vlad's office. I just hope that Vlad's prediction will be accurate. As we head to the room, I realize that Theo keeps avoiding my gaze. He's bound to talk to me, though.

"So, gentlemen. Welcome to my humble abode." Vlad begins with his usual theatrics, and I see Marcel and Theo roll their eyes.

"Thanks for arranging this," Theo replies. I stand next to Vlad, keeping my face blank and waiting to be addressed.

"Well, now that you're both here." Vlad stops to muse before adding, "Fancy seeing you too, Marcel." Marcel just gives an almost imperceptible nod. "Let's get down to the meat of things. Hastings, you said it was urgent to talk to Bianca."

"We've been invited to Allegra Agosti's birthday party, which is tomorrow. Enzo was hoping Bianca would be able to join when he extended the invitation," he says without even glancing at me once, all the while addressing Vlad.

"So, you came here to see whether Bianca was well enough to attend?" Vlad asks. I have to say, I'm particularly amused by how this exchange is taking place.

"Yes, and I see she's looking much better." Theo finally swings his eyes to me but only briefly. I decide it's time this stops.

"You really want me to accompany you?" I ask, my voice steady and devoid of emotion. He gives a strained nod but still avoids meeting my gaze.

"You could at least look me in the eye and ask," I feel

compelled to add, seeing how he likes to pretend I'm not present and have no agency.

Theo's practically fuming at my words, but he grits his teeth and turns to me to ask.

"Could you please come with me to Enzo's party?"

"Fine." I shrug. I don't care why he's asking me, although Vlad did tell me some specifics. I only care that we'll be forced to share a space. Then I can begin my seduction anew. Yes, that is indeed perfect.

"Good. I'll pick you up tomorrow at eight p.m." Theo turns to leave, but Vlad tsks in his usual manner, making him draw to a halt.

"Really, Hastings, I didn't take you to be so hypocritical. Not too long ago, you were bedeviling your wife, but now you need her help. Why don't you tell her exactly why you have to attend?" Vlad's manner is relaxed, but his words are cutting. I can see Theo's shoulders tense before he simply answers.

"It's for work. Bianca probably already knows I've been trying to get someone named Jimenez for a long time now. Enzo's event might prove to be just the place."

"Good. Now try again, but without the lies," Vlad takes a few steps towards Theo and adds.

At this, I turn sharply towards Vlad. He's never mentioned anything else when he's outlined our plan of action. What is he talking about?

"I don't know what you're talking about," Theo replies, but his expression is closed off. Marcel, however, has been on the sidelines this whole time, observing. Odd.

Vlad takes one more step, now wholly within Theo's personal space. I see his stance a second before he acts, throwing a punch at Theo.

My first instinct is to grab the first weapon I see from Vlad's desk, so I take one of his pencils, ready to draw blood. Just as I'm about to move, I see Marcel showing me a stop sign with his raised palm, followed by a hand motion towards the ensuing fight. I finally focus on what's happening and see Theo entirely holding his own against Vlad. They're both approximately the same size, but Vlad is the one with a lifetime of experience.

But what I see leaves me cold. Theo dodges almost every single attack, even the more complicated ones. At the same time, he gives as good as he gets. The only reason they're not entirely bloody and wounded is because they seem to be evenly matched in skills.

After what seems like an eternity of seeing one of the best fighting matches I've ever seen, they stop, both panting.

"Anything left to say, *Adrian*?" Vlad retreats to his desk, where he procures a handkerchief and proceeds to gracefully wipe the sweat from his face.

I see Theo's eyes widen a little, and I frown.

"Adrian?" I finally speak. It feels like everyone is onto something, and I'm the only one not knowing what's happening.

"Why don't you tell her, *Hastings*. Or wait, that's not really your name, is it?" Vlad turns to me with an expression of fake concern. "I fear you've married him under false pretense, little goddess."

I'm... intrigued.

"What do you mean?"

"Shall I, or shall you?" Vlad nods towards Theo, and I can see the tension radiating from him.

He doesn't speak, so Vlad does the honors.

"Let's see from the beginning. Tragic tale. Michael and Paulina Barnett. Killed in their home after a supposed robbery gone wrong. Left behind one son. Adrian Barnett. After some foster homes, he found himself fighting to the death for the Irish. Andrew Gallagher if I'm not mistaken. I met him a time or two, not the most pleasant fellow." Vlad scrunches his face in annoyance before continuing.

"Where was I... oh yes. This Adrian fought for Andrew for four years. Apparently, he had almost weekly matches. Can you imagine the body count?" Vlad turns to me when he asks that, and I'm mentally already doing the math, and it's around two hundred ish. Not bad. Not bad at all. I'm almost impressed.

"Then he just disappeared. Poof." Vlad makes a sound, and I

raise an eyebrow. Get to the point already. "Around the same time, Theodore Hastings enrolled into Harvard."

"Pretty tale, but I don't see the point," Theo finally says, but Vlad isn't done.

"The point is that Michael Barnett was involved in a project to take Jimenez down. Allegedly, he compiled a list of high-level officials and wealthy patrons investing with Jimenez."

"So what, you're saying I'm this Barnett guy?"

"I'm not saying. You are. That little physical exertion was my proof. But if you want more..." Vlad says before heading to his safe and opening it, withdrawing a folder. Within the folder are a few photographs that he hands directly to me. All of them depict the same man, in various injury stages, and within a fighting ring. While the man in the pictures is bulkier and more massive than Theo, there's no doubt they're the same.

"So, you're Adrian Barnett?" I cock my head and study my husband, suddenly seeing him with new eyes.

He's... perfect.

My eyes eat him up as I realize just how similar we are. He's killed before too. I instinctively lick my lips. He knows what it's like to take someone's life.

Not all is lost.

We can be together.

And we can kill together.

Oh, my God!

I'm already lost in a fantasy scenario, imagining what it would be like to have Theo... no, Adrian at my side on a mission. I'm deep in when I vaguely hear him speak.

"How do you know that?" He looks at Vlad, who just shrugs.

"Maybe you haven't noticed until now, but there are no secrets I don't have access to."

More words are exchanged, but I'm still within my own fantasy, so I don't register what's being spoken. Instead, I act on instinct and fling myself at Theo... erm, Adrian. I wrap my arms around him. I feel him tense for a second before untangling himself from my grasp.

I only pout, Pink style, and plaster myself to his side. He turns and frowns at me.

"Why are you doing this? Have you not heard a word until now? I'm not Theodore Hastings."

"I know. Now we can be together." I hug his arm tighter.

"What?" he exclaims and shoves me away. I cock my head and frown.

"We're not that different. You kill. I kill. We're the same."

"We're not the same, Bianca. I killed out of necessity. You kill because you like it."

"Was it really a necessity? Who pointed a gun at you and forced you to kill? And don't tell me there wasn't a moment when you felt human life seep through your hands, and you didn't enjoy it. "

Theo's about to respond when Vlad intervenes.

"Enough of that. I think we have more important things to discuss. Don't worry, Hastings, your secret is safe here. Now, let me put things this way. You want to get Jimenez. I want information on Enzo. I think we can help each other."

37

ADRIAN

I'm trying my hardest to resist this proximity to Bianca. She's still at my side, and her scent keeps on invading my nostrils. When I first saw her, I couldn't believe how good she looked. I was almost taken aback by my body's response to seeing her again, even if it's only been days.

So, I try to ignore her.

I don't address her, and I don't look at her.

But then Vlad happens.

I should have guessed he had something under his sleeve when he sparred with me. I just didn't realize how much he knew about my old identity.

And now Bianca knows too. I'm almost apprehensive about her reaction. But then she throws herself at me, saying how similar we are, the expression on her face almost dreamy. I'm caught in her eyes for a second.

Just for a second.

Then I remember she can't feel.

And now, Vlad's saying he wants to help with Jimenez. I almost snort. Why do I feel that I can't trust him? There's just something about him that rubs me off. Mostly when he seems to be too cheerful without reason.

"So, let me see if I have this right. You want us to bug Enzo's house. How do you even know the party's going to be at his house?" I ask. I'm surprised that Marcel has been quiet this whole time, but he seems to be more interested in observing than participating.

"I knew about it long before you did. Rest assured; it's going to be at his home."

"But why don't *you* do it?"

"Enzo and I aren't the best of friends." Vlad smiles ruefully. "Thankfully, he has no idea you know me, or believe me, you wouldn't be invited either."

"We'll do it," Bianca readily agrees, and I frown at her.

"We *won't* do it," I correct, and she cranes her neck to look at me.

"I'll do it then," she says, shrugging, and her ready support of Vlad is getting a rise of me.

"No." The word slips my lips before I even think it through.

"What? I'll do it, don't worry," she dismisses me by redirecting her attention to Vlad, and I'm... flabbergasted.

"No," I say again and add, "Why should we do anything for *you?*" I motion to Vlad, a little more aggressively than I would have liked.

"I said I'll do it, for fuck's sake. You don't need to concern yourself with it." Bianca's exasperation fuels my own unreasonable ire.

"That's it, children." The subject of my displeasure intervenes, and my lips compress in irritation. "Hastings, if you don't want to get involved, don't worry. Bianca can do this on my behalf. On the other hand, I also won't give you any information on Jimenez."

I snort at his vanity. What does he think he has that's so valuable?

"What kind of information could you possibly have?"

"Nothing much..." he starts sarcastically. "Only the location of the club he frequents."

"You're bluffing," I accuse, given how elusive Jimenez has been for years.

"Am I..."

"He's not bluffing," Bianca affirms, and Marcel shifts nervously in the corner.

"I'd trust his word," he adds on a strained tone, but I don't have the time to ponder that.

"So, what will it be? The offer will expire in five... four..."

"Fine." I put one hand up to stop him, while the other rubs at my temples.

He smiles.

"I knew you'd come around. You and Bianca will make a wonderful team." He winks at her, and my fists clench. Why is he winking at her?

"Enzo expects Jimenez to show up at the party," Marcel interjects, and Vlad shifts his focus towards him. Is it just me, or is there something going on between the two of them?

"He won't. But that doesn't mean all is lost. I'm sure he'll send someone close to him."

"How do you know?" I ask.

"I have eyes on Jimenez. He hasn't left his location, and no arrangements have been made for him to leave anytime soon."

"Damn," I mutter. Not that I trust Vlad, but all will be confirmed tomorrow.

"Now that we've decided to work together, we can start planning." Vlad goes around his desk and shuffles some files, withdrawing a big sheet of paper.

"Is that...?" I ask, squinting to get a better view.

"Yes. The plans for Enzo's house. You need to be in and out of the office without raising an eyebrow. Best to be prepared." Okay, wow. Vlad certainly takes himself seriously.

As he spreads it onto the table, we all get closer.

"It's quite similar to Martin's house," Bianca notes, and I have to agree. They're both two-story mansions, but Enzo's seems to have a more traditional design.

"Where does his father live?" I ask.

"With his mistress in the city. This used to be the family home for the Agostis, but now it's only Enzo, his wife, and son who live there."

"What about the other sister?" Bianca suddenly chimes in, and all eyes are on her.

"Which one?" Vlad carefully asks.

"The unmarried one. When I looked into their family, there

were three sisters, and two were married. What happened to the third? Catalina was her name, I think."

There's an immediate silence, and Marcel's shoulders stiffen for a second. Vlad seems to take note of this when he answers.

"She disappeared. Years ago. Probably dead if you ask me."

Odd.

As Vlad says this, Marcel immediately averts his face but not before I catch a glimpse of pain on his features.

"Back to the blueprint. This is the ballroom where the party will most definitely take place." He points to the east wing of the house.

"Now here," his finger moves to the west wing, "is the study. It's on the same floor, but it's separated by the kitchen and the drawing room. You'll need to pass those without seeming suspicious."

"How many people invited?" Bianca asks.

"From what I heard, at least a hundred."

"Good, they're our best cover. Worst-case scenario, I'll distract Enzo."

"You're not distracting him. We'll do it together." Just the image of Bianca and Enzo together in an intimate setting is enough to make my temples throb.

No, that's not an option, especially with how Enzo was eyeing my wife at lunch.

"I thought you said you didn't wanna do it."

"I changed my mind," I retort. I realize I'm probably sounding infantile right now, but I don't want her near Enzo.

"So, it's settled. In case of an emergency, there are options." Vlad walks us through all the nooks and crannies of the house and shows us how to use them to our advantage. He insists that the bugs must be placed in Enzo's study, in the drawing room and in the kitchen.

"The kitchen?" I ask, curious.

"You'd be surprised by how the staff gossip. Especially in households like this."

"Okay. Sounds good," Bianca agrees, but then suddenly asks, "They'll search us for weapons, no?"

"Yes, they will. Likely metal detectors too," Vlad replies, and Bianca purses her lips.

"What type of bugs do you have?"

"Non-metal," Vlad smiles sheepishly, and I chuckle.

"Can I borrow your 3D printer? I need at least a pistol."

"Take an obsidian blade. That should pass muster."

Bianca scoffs at this. "You know I don't like blades."

"You do when you must." The back and forth between the two of them makes me feel like an outsider. I also cannot help but notice how different Bianca is. She exudes a serenity that she didn't have before. She's also forward and bold.

Is this the real her?

"What about him?" she suddenly asks and points at Marcel. "He's not coming, is he?"

"No, I'm not," Marcel replies.

"Then what is he doing here?"

"He's my *trusted* friend." I emphasize trusted to let her know precisely what she's lost. She doesn't seem to react, though, and *I* end up being the one annoyed.

We finalize the plans, and Marcel and I turn to leave. I see Bianca look at me with an indescribable expression on her face. I shake myself and force myself to disregard it.

Later, when we're in the car, Marcel mentions the visible tension between Bianca and me.

"Did it go how you would have expected?" he asks, and I have to think for a few seconds.

"Yes, and no. Yes, because I realize I don't know *this* Bianca at all. Who would have imagined that I would be pouring over blueprints with my wife, planning to install listening devices in an Italian mob boss' home? No, because even knowing what I know, I can't help but still feel drawn to her."

"She is completely different. I think it's mostly her countenance and her voice. She no longer has that upspeak that always made her look insecure."

"You're right now that you mention it. The cadence of her voice is completely different. Also, emotionless."

"Really?" Marcel gives me a side look. "I thought there was enough emotion in her when she jumped on you."

"Did you even hear what she was saying? She was romanticizing killing. What does she think? We can suddenly become Mr. and Mrs. Smith?" I ask almost absentmindedly, but I notice Marcel frown.

"Man... don't tell me you don't know the reference." When he doesn't answer, I add drily. "I forgot you have no life outside your work. It's about this couple who are both secret assassins and get their happily ever after."

He chuckles at my brief description. "You say that, but I don't think I've heard you talk about separation or divorce yet."

I ponder his words and have to admit he is right. While I saw our relationship in limbo, I didn't dare to think beyond that.

"I guess it's inevitable." I allow uncertainly.

"Is it? We'll see." Marcel says cryptically.

"What about you?" I give him a conspiratorial smile.

"Me? What about me?"

"Come on, don't tell your reaction to Agosti's sister was nothing. Did you know her?" The moment the words are out of my mouth, Marcel tenses, his fingers almost trembling on the steering wheel.

"Oh, really?" He tries to put on a fake smile.

"Yeah, what was that about?" Why I don't drop it, I don't know. Maybe because in all our years of friendship, I've never known Marcel to even look twice toward a woman, least of all react to one.

"I knew her briefly. A long time ago."

"So mysterious. Did you guys date or something?"

"I wanted to marry her," he says quietly.

"Shit! What happened? Vlad said she's missing?"

"I don't know... I still don't know." He repeats the words, his voice straining.

"Man..." I'm about to say when Marcel suddenly hits the brakes, and we are both flung forward. Luckily, our seatbelts stop us from serious injury. I immediately get out of the car to see if we hit an animal or something, exhaling in relief when there's no evidence of impact.

"Shit. That was a close one!" I mention as I get back into the car.

Marcel is bent over the steering wheel, his head cradled between his arms. I can hear him sobbing softly.

"I'm sorry. I'm so sorry," he keeps repeating. I want to comfort him, but I know he doesn't like to be touched, so I just sit next to him in silence, waiting for whatever ghost of the past is bothering him to disappear.

That night, I realize just how little I know about my most *trusted* friend.

38

BIANCA

"Do I look okay?" I look in the mirror, adjusting the hem of my dress. It's a black cocktail dress with a cinched waist, reminiscent of 50's-style dresses and a flaring skirt. I'd left my hair hanging down my shoulders and kept my makeup light, only applying some mascara and red lipstick.

"Of course, little goddess," Vlad replies almost mechanically from his seat on the chair. He's swirling bourbon in a glass, not really paying attention to me.

"Vlad!" I turn to him and wait to get his attention.

"What?" He finally snaps out of whatever trance he's been in.

"Never mind." I shake my head and lift my skirt to reveal a pair of biker shorts. I proceed to sheath the obsidian knives I'd reluctantly accepted instead of a 3D-printed pistol. I had to be smart with this, so I sheathed one right on my inner thigh. We'd also decided to place the bugs in my cleavage since it was the least likely spot to be searched. For my bag, I'd chosen a small clutch that had a camera within the bag logo. While Vlad hadn't been too particular about that, he hadn't denied being curious about who Enzo would invite.

"I don't remember you mentioning a conflict with Enzo before," I add. I've been wondering about that since yesterday's meeting.

"It's not exactly a conflict as much as it is a mutual under-standing to not get in each other's way."

"But? There's more. He *did* come to you with an offer. So, spill."

"He only came to me out of necessity and because I'm already established in the city. Our problems stem from years back when he first got married. We used to be friendly before that, but he accused me of sleeping with his wife *of all things*. We got into a fight, didn't end up very pretty."

"Did you?"

"Hell no. You've met the bitch. She's the sleaziest piece of shit I've ever met. She came onto me so many times and then told him *I* was the instigator." He shakes his head in disgust. "Truly vile." I'd never heard Vlad speak that way of a woman. For him to call her a bitch... But I'd met the woman... and she's sleeping with Martin now. Really, what did I expect?

"He didn't believe you."

"Nope. They'd just had a kid and accused me of taking advan-tage of her emotional state and whatnot."

"I'm surprised he didn't pursue it further. He seems the type."

"He did, for a while. But he quickly realized he'd have to fight the entire city. It's not a secret now that his wife sleeps with anything that walks. On that note, I'd keep your husband away from her. She doesn't take no for an answer."

"If he knows she's like that, why didn't you reconcile?"

"By then, pride got in the way. And he already got involved with people I don't particularly care for or approve of. And there's also that vendetta of his against the Lastras. Safe to say we have conflicting interests."

"I see. I'll take note of that."

"Just don't be too obvious. Enzo is many things, but a fool he is *not*. Make sure he can't see through your facade."

"Don't worry. I've had enough practice." I smooth over my skirt, and Vlad lets me know Theo is already outside. Or should I call him *Adrian* now? I think it might take me some getting used to. At least now, I can make sense of where all those repressed control issues come from.

"Break a leg." Vlad winks at me before heading to his study.

Since I've been staying with him for a few days now, I can't help but notice that something might be wrong with him. There are moments when he seems lost in his head, but it's more than daydreaming. It's like he's in a trance. His good humor also seems more strained than usual.

Heading out of the house, I put my concerns out of my mind, focusing on the mission first.

Exiting, I see Adrian, black tuxedo on, leaning on his car and waiting for me. When he looks up and sees me coming towards him, his expression changes ever so slightly, and I know he likes what he's seeing. I have to be incredibly careful, though. This will be our first real interaction with all cards on the table. I have to show him how good it can be between us—the real us.

"Let's go!" he says, and I get in the car—one step at a time.

"I envy you." I start by trying to find some common ground. He seems surprised, so I just continue, "You can kill with your bare hands. I wish I could do that." When he hears that, he frowns, his mouth changing shape as if he wants to say something but just shakes his head.

"You envy *that*," he asks as if not quite believing my words.

I must try harder.

"Yes. You have the advantage of strength. My punches can *barely* do any damage. I usually bank on speed, though," I say, proud of myself for also inserting a small praise. He must see that I don't hold his past against him. It's actually very attractive.

"Sure... so you've never killed anyone barehanded?" he asks, not quite looking at me, but then again, he's watching the road. I take this as a sign he's willing to engage in conversation.

"Not really. I usually only use guns. Sometimes knives. Don't like knives, though. Too messy," I answer immediately. The homeless man I'd killed a few days ago does come to mind, but is that kill even noteworthy? It was too one-sided.

"So, you don't like blood?" he inquires, and for a moment, I panic. He was a fighter. That means blood. What if he likes blood? What if he will hold it against me that I don't like blood? Well, not necessarily don't like, but it's sticky, and it stains and... A flash of brain matter smeared on my knuckles almost makes me want to gag.

"B, it was just a question," he says after a while, his eyes regarding me with concern. I realize I'd been fidgeting while I was debating in my head what the best answer was. Real. I have to be authentic. I let out a breath and tell him just that.

"Then why kill at all? If you don't enjoy the blood? Why seek it?"

"It gives me a purpose."

"Purpose?" He frowns at my word choice. Yes, I have to be real. Why is it that now that I'm sober, my brain seems to respond to things differently?

It feels odd.

"Yes. You remember Drew, my bodyguard. After Jenna's death, he taught me how to channel my anger in meaningful ways."

"Killing?"

"Well, yes. He knew I would probably do it again, so he did what he thought best at the time."

"Go on."

"Drew introduced me to the Russians, and then I got partnered with Vlad. Many of our assignments were strictly Bratva enemies, but I got to choose my targets after a while. So, I sought the vilest predators and took them out."

"Predators?"

"People who prey on children. On innocents. It was the only time I felt something. Yeah, I don't care about blood and gore... much. But I do care that those people suffer. I've probably done my fair share of torture at some point. But usually, I prefer a neat kill."

"This isn't a normal conversation." He smiles to himself.

"I'm not normal, I told you." And then I frown. "You're not *normal*, either. For someone who claims to have empathy, how do you reconcile those deaths on your conscience?"

I don't think much of the question, merely curiosity. But for him, it doesn't seem to be. His expression immediately darkens.

"Why do you think I ever reconciled it?"

"You haven't? Sorry, I just don't really understand. I know how I function because I don't really care. I don't assign the same value to human life that other people do. Vlad is the same. You're not... and yet? You must have killed a couple hundred in your time in the pits."

"That I did." He's silent for a moment before continuing, "You have your purpose, and I have mine. And so whatever sacrifices I made along the road were for that purpose."

"Getting revenge on Jimenez?" He nods.

"What after then?"

The car stops at that exact moment, and I see we've arrived. Adrian turns to me and regards me for a while. I see in his eyes that he hasn't considered the *What then?*

We exit the car after handing the keys to a valet. There is indeed a security check, and they are insanely thorough. Luckily, my dagger is on my inner thigh as they pat my outer. After we successfully pass security, I loop my arm through Adrian's, and we proceed inside.

"Act natural," I tell him as I feel him stiffen. I don't want to consider that he might actually be disgusted by me physically, so I push that thought away.

"There you are." Enzo comes up to us in the hallway, beaming. He shakes Adrian's hand and kisses both my cheeks.

"You look spectacular as always, Bianca," Enzo praises me, and I have to remember to plaster on my social smile. I forcefully tug my lips upwards, and I see Adrian watching me, a smile playing on his lips. He's learning my cues.

"Please enjoy yourselves."

He turns to leave, but I clear my throat and ask, "Where's the birthday girl? We need to wish her a happy birthday. Right, darling?" I bat my eyelashes at Adrian, and he tightens his hold on me.

"Indeed. And where's the special guest?" Adrian changes the topic, asking about Jimenez.

"Allegra is probably with your father around here, somewhere," he answers, and he doesn't seem particularly put off by his wife's blatant infidelity. "The special guest has failed to make an appearance. An intermediary has shown up, however." Enzo seems more disappointed at Jimenez's absence than at his wife's cuckolding him. Odd.

"Maybe we can all get together later on," Adrian suggests, and Enzo accepts before excusing himself to greet other guests.

"Let's do this." I take his hand again, and we enter the ballroom.

39

ADRIAN

Enzo leads us into the ballroom before excusing himself to greet the rest of the guests. We step into the big room, and there are already too many people. I see a lot of familiar faces, some of them deeply entrenched in local and national politics. It figures that Enzo's connections would include the most powerful men.

"I should have expected Martin to make an appearance," Bianca states, nudging me towards the couple on the dance floor. Martin is twirling Allegra on the dance floor, both of them already seeming intoxicated.

"I don't recall seeing your father drunk before," I add, pensively. Martin's always been the stoic type, too set on control to relinquish any to alcohol.

"He doesn't drink in public. Or at least he didn't used to. *Clearly*, Allegra has changed that." We're not the only people staring at them in dismay. I shake my head and try to scan the room for other familiar faces, making mental notes.

The party is full of older men, most of them accompanied by younger counterparts. Not a surprise there. The surprise is seeing respected people from politics, especially men I'd personally met at the mayor's office. At no point had I suspected they were involved with the mob. This goes to show how deep the corruption runs in this country. And I'd bet that the women hanging on their arms are *not* their wives. My lips turn up in distaste, and I sneak a quick glance at Bianca to gauge her reaction.

She's as blank as always.

"Let's get some drinks and mingle for a while," she says and points towards the bar at the end of the room. I nod, and we head there. Bianca gets a glass of champagne while I get a bourbon.

"I hope you don't plan to actually drink that," she whispers.

"Why?"

"Rule number one: you never drink on a mission. Just pretend to drink and every so often. empty it into flowerpots."

"But the flowers..." She doesn't let me finish as she pinches me.

"Empty it in the flowerpot," she says a bit more forcefully before turning her head and plastering a big smile on her face. I take her cue and turn my attention forward to see Allegra and Martin heading our way. Both look giddy and flushed from the dancing.

"Bianca!" Martin exclaims and hugs his daughter. Bianca's expression immediately turns sour, but she doesn't shove Martin away. Instead, she pats his back almost reluctantly while looking at me for help. I shrug. I've never seen Martin like this, and I don't know how to deal with him. He seems to whisper something in her ear before Bianca turns to me.

"We'll be right back. He has something urgent to talk about." She doesn't seem too glad to go with him, and I wonder what the urgent thing is.

It's only when they're out of sight that I realize I'm left with Allegra. She puckers her lips at me before scrunching her face.

"I think I'm going to be ill. Can you help me to the restroom?" she slurs, and my shoulders slump in resignation. I take her arm and let her guide me to one of the bathrooms. Since I know fully well where all the bathrooms are on this floor, I'm surprised when I see that she's taking me in a completely different direction. Is she that drunk that she doesn't remember where the bathroom is in her own house?

I'm about to ask where we're going when she points towards a door and gleefully says, "There," and then dashes for the door. I take a moment where I wonder if I should really go there, but somehow I feel bad leaving a clearly inebriated woman to her own devices, no matter how repulsive.

And so I follow through.

As soon as I close the door behind me, there's a quick movement in which Allegra reverses our positions and thrusts me into the room, which I now see is just a sizable closet storage, before she locks the door.

What?

"I've been watching you," she purrs in a much clearer voice than before.

"Mrs. Agosti." I try to put some distance between us.

"Come on, your wife isn't here. I know you've been watching me too."

What? When? I don't think I've ever spared her more than two glances, tonight included, and I try to tell her exactly that.

"I'm sorry. I think you got the wrong impression," I explain, using my hands to gesticulate and keep her at bay.

"Mr. Hastings. You are so, so naughty," she says in that weird voice of hers as she keeps advancing towards me, deeper into the storage closet until I'm backed against the wall. Shit. She puts her hands on my pectorals and gropes me. I grip her arms and attempt to stop her again by pushing her and trying to bypass her in my way to the door. Her arms suddenly come in contact with my shoulders, and she pushes me against the wall.

"You like to play hard, don't you?" she half-moans, fitting herself against my body, her hand going directly to my crotch this time. Good Lord, I don't hit women, but I truly want to smack her right now.

"No. And I would appreciate it if you kept your hands to yourself," I say through gritted teeth, trying to control myself so I don't hurt her.

She doesn't seem to register my words as she squeezes me through my pants.

Okay, that's it. I'm not playing nice anymore. I'm about to push her away when the closet door forcefully opens, revealing Bianca.

She takes one look at us, and her eyes cloud with fury. She

doesn't waste any time ripping Allegra off me and grabbing her throat, pushing her against the wall and almost lifting her off the floor.

"You think to touch *my* husband?" Bianca's fingers tighten around Allegra's neck, restricting her breathing.

"Agh." Allegra makes a choking sound, but Bianca doesn't stop.

"What? I didn't hear you?"

I can see the defined veins in Bianca's hand as she applies further pressure on Allegra's throat, and I realize she *will* kill her if I don't stop her. I make a grab for her hand, saying, "Stop. You're choking her." At my words, she suddenly turns towards me, cocking her head in confusion.

"You're defending her?"

"No, but you're killing her right now." I tug her hand, and Allegra falls to the floor, gasping for air.

Bianca snatches her hand out of mine and crouches near Allegra, so they're now on eye level.

"I see you again making a pass at my husband, I *will* end you. Do we understand each other?" Bianca enunciates each word, and Allegra looks at her in disbelief.

"You're a crazy bitch. Fucking crazy bitch... What the fuck?" Allegra says between ragged breaths.

"Yes. I *am* a crazy bitch. And guess what? Crazy bitches have nothing against chopping your body one part at a time while you're still alive. You want to fuck my father? Go ahead. You as much as look in my husband's direction, and I will make it so that even wild animals will scoff at eating your remains. Are we clear?"

Allegra nods her head emphatically, Bianca's words clearly having an effect on her.

"Run!" Bianca urges her, and Allegra does as she's told, leaving my wife and me alone in this goddamn closet.

I'm thankful it's done, to be honest, and I'm about to head out when Bianca stops me.

"Did you touch her?" she asks, her eyes pinning me to the spot.

"What? Of course not," I say casually, and I make for the door.

Bianca once again grabs my arm and twirls me around, so I'm against the wall.

"Did you fucking touch her?" What is wrong with the female species? I get rid of a predator just to get myself yelled at by a jealous woman.

Wait... I suddenly stop at that thought.

Jealous? Is Bianca jealous? Because that would imply feelings, and she's not capable of that. Or...

"No," I answer once again, and she starts her tirade.

"Good, because God help me if you ever so much as..." I stop her mid-sentence when I take advantage of my superior strength and switch us around, so she is now the one pinned to the wall. My hand goes at her throat, enjoying the feel of her soft skin and her throbbing pulse.

"If I ever so much as?" I ask, brushing my cheek against her hair.

"If you ever as much as look at another woman," she starts but can't seem to continue as my fingers massage her pulse.

"Yes?"

"If you ever..." she moans, and that's when I attack.

"Let me tell you. If you ever think I would stoop so low as to break my marriage vows, even when my wife is a fucking sociopath, then you are sorely mistaken." I release her and step out of the storage closet, heading directly for the bar.

This night just can't get any better, and we haven't even planted the bugs. As I beeline for the bar, I see a disheveled Allegra talking to Enzo, her body language suggesting she's playing the victim.

Enzo looks at her with obvious distaste. I shake my head at the scene and continue on my way. I order another bourbon, this time tipping the glass back and enjoying the amber liquid's burn.

Man... I gotta admit, though. Bianca looked so hot, all aggressive and jealous. It almost makes me want to try it again, just to see her all worked up.

Almost.

Because I know she would actually kill the other woman. Why am I not more bothered by that, I really can't say.

After finishing the drink, I take a few minutes to compose myself before seeking Bianca to complete this mission and get out of here. Since Jimenez isn't present, there isn't a reason for us to linger around.

I exit the ballroom and look around until I'm at the entrance of the drawing room. There are a few ongoing poker games at different tables, and I finally spot Bianca by one of the tables, rooted to the spot.

I make my way towards her and realize she's looking at something with an odd, longing look on her face. I turn my attention towards the table and see one of the men spreading some white powder into a clean line before rolling a one-hundred-dollar bill and sniffing it off the table.

Bianca's mouth opens ever so slightly, and her feet move. I quickly realize she's craving this, being that it's only a few days since she's detoxed.

As her feet take her towards her addiction, so do mine.

40

BIANCA

After Adrian storms out of the closet, I rush after him. At some point, I lose sight of him in the throng of people, so I walk around here and there, trying to see if I can spot him.

We still need to complete the mission!

I somehow end up in the other wing of the house and close to the study.

Should I...

But then I shake my head. I need to do this with Adrian. Show him we can be a team.

I head towards the drawing room, as it's the only one I haven't checked.

The moment I walk inside, I can already tell the atmosphere is different. There are multiple tables spread around the room, similar to a casino. People are smoking inside, and the entire space is a hotbox. I step inside and take in the participants, my eyes scanning for Adrian. When I see no sign of him, I turn to leave but not before seeing a flash of white.

I'm not even conscious of my own actions. My feet take me forward until I'm in front of the table. A man is spreading cocaine onto the surface, preparing to inhale it. My hands clench at the sudden urge to move and partake as well.

I put one foot in front of the other, my eyes never leaving the

260

white powder. Just as I'm about to reach the man sniffing the drug, someone pulls on my arm and twists me around.

I come face to face with Adrian, his eyes intently watching me, his hand coming up to my face for a light caress.

"Close your eyes and breathe," he says in a low voice, and I do. I then immediately feel his lips on mine, his mouth ever so lightly brushing against mine before his tongue strokes the seam of my lips, opening them for his invasion. The moment our mouths fuse together, I forget about everything. The magic powder is but a distant thought.

I don't want this to end. I tighten my arms around Adrian's biceps, clutching at his suit's material, my body begging him to never let go.

But he does.

I hear hands clapping around us, and I look to see a number of the older men at the poker tables are whistling and clapping at our public display.

Adrian excuses us and takes me into the hallway. He doesn't say anything, and I feel compelled to fill the void.

"Thank you. For distracting me." He just grunts in acknowledgment before lowering his head so he can whisper in my ear.

"Don't thank me. I managed to place one bug," he whispers, and I almost feel disappointed. "Let's go through the kitchen and into the study."

We quickly make an excuse to be in the kitchen, and while Adrian chats up the staff, I manage to stealthily place two bugs, one to the back of the fridge and one under the sink. After giving him a sign, he excuses himself, and we head to the study in the west wing.

"So far, so good," he says when he sees the hallway clear.

Three doors down, we come to a stop in front of the study. I signal him to open it while I stand guard.

He turns the knob ever so slowly to avoid making too much noise, but to our surprise, it's locked.

"Of course. We should have realized he wouldn't leave his study open during a house party?" I whisper angrily.

"What then?"

"Move aside and stand guard." We switch places, and I remove a couple ivory pins from my garter.

I'd remembered last minute to add them, but now they come in handy. The pins are extremely thin, sharp, and sturdy, making them the perfect mini weapons for metal detectors.

They can also do a lot of damage if used properly.

Although I'd never tried this before, maybe they can be used to pick a lock too.

I use the first pin as a tension wrench and insert it in the lower half of the lock. Then I add the second pin, and I jiggle it continuously while adding pressure on the first one. It takes about a minute or so for the first pin to give and a clicking sound to announce that the door is now unlocked.

I creak the door open and signal Adrian to follow me. When I turn, he's looking at me with an expression akin to awe.

"Impressive," he says in a hushed tone as he enters the room.

Enzo's study has a traditional European design with luxurious Italian furniture that blends New and Old World materials. I look around and see countless upon countless shelves of books.

"You think Enzo reads all this?" I ask, trailing my hands on the spines of the books. They're in different languages, too.

"He's very eloquent. I'd wager that yes, he does read them." I shrug at Adrian's words. My first impression of Enzo hadn't been a good one, but from our short interactions, even I could agree that he could teach rhetoric to the Greeks.

"We need to find a few spots that he's unlikely to touch," Adrian notes, scrutinizing the space.

"Look for dust," I say and head behind his desk, where a massive floor-to-ceiling block of furniture houses a bust of Machiavelli. My hand feels for the back of the statue, and there is indeed dust. I take out a bug and place it at the base of the figure.

"One down." I turn to see Adrian crouching on the floor at the desk's foot, where the study's feet seem to be slightly uneven.

"You think there's enough space?" I stoop down to see what he's doing. There clearly isn't enough space for a hand to place the bug.

"Wait," I say and remove the obsidian blade from my thigh. "This should be just about thin enough."

Adrian takes the knife from my hand and carefully places the bug, adhesive side up, on the blade.

Carefully, he lowers it and inserts it in the crevice. The fit is very tight, but with a little pressure, the bug remains in place when he withdraws the knife.

It's not visible either. I sigh in relief. The less time we're in here, the better. Now that it's all done, we can leave before we're caught.

"Let's go." I nod my head towards the door, and Adrian follows me. Opening the door slightly, I look to see if there are people in the hallway, leading him out with me when I realize it's empty. It's only when we're once again close to the ballroom that tension drains from both our shoulders.

I look at him with a conspiratorial grin that he returns, and we high-five.

"What has you so giddy, lovebirds?" Enzo surprises us from behind.

"Nothing much," Adrian replies. "Is the man Jimenez sent around here? I'd like an introduction," he continues, and Enzo's mouth immediately curls up in disgust.

"He's around here somewhere. Unpleasant fellow if I may say so myself." He shakes his head before continuing, "I tried talking to him when he arrived, and he had the gall to tell me he's not here to socialize. I am the host!" Enzo exclaims, clearly scandalized that his Italian etiquette has been breached.

"I thought the whole purpose of this was diplomacy," Adrian adds, and Enzo agrees.

"It was supposed to be. Clearly, they had other ideas. I made sure to have someone follow him, though. Just in case he decides to do something." Enzo pats Adrian on the back and leaves us. I can clearly see this situation bothers him; he doesn't even try to flirt with me.

"Too bad you don't know who to look for," I say.

"Since we've fulfilled our purpose here, we might as well go," he adds, clearly disappointed that he didn't manage to meet Jimenez's substitute.

He puts his hand at my lower back and leads me towards the exit. We're in the foyer when a shrilling scream explodes from the west wing of the house. Even with the overlapping voices engaged in conversation throughout the house, the shriek is loud enough to jolt everyone to attention. Both Adrian and I look at each other before we spring into action, going towards the direction of the sound.

Going deeper into the west wing, we follow the other people in front of us until we notice a small crowd in front of the study with Enzo in front of the door, trying to tell people to keep their distance. His jaw tightens when he sees us, but he calls us over.

"There's no way to say this." Enzo starts, and he looks as if he's trying to find his words. "Maybe only Hastings should go in."

Wait, what? What's going on?

"What's happening?" Adrian asks, and Enzo grimaces.

"There's a body in the study."

"A body?" My eyebrows shoot up. "We're going in," I declare, and Enzo might have wanted to add something, but I already push past him and open the door.

What greets me is a sight I don't think I'll ever forget. I wish I had a polaroid camera, really, to immortalize this. It's like all my childhood dreams come true, but a little bit bloodier. Remembering the small camera embedded in my purse, I slightly angle it to capture the mess on the floor.

I'll print this later.

As I focus on the scene before me, the first thing I notice is the bodiless heart, lying a few steps away. A trail of blood leads from the heart to the corpse.

The body had been put in a sitting position on the floor and propped against the study. The shirt is gaping, revealing a big hole in his chest where the heart used to be. Higher still is the centerpiece. A big T is carved on the forehead of the man.

My eyes quickly scan the body for other signs of injury, curious about the cause of death. Adrian's nudge makes me realize that Enzo had closed the door behind us and is looking at me expectantly.

He probably wants me to burst into tears or hysterics.

"Can't say I'm surprised my father died a traitor's death," I add drily, and both men frown at me.

"Are you all right?" Enzo finally asks me, and I wave away his concern.

"Bianca?"

"Do you know who did it?" I ask as I go towards the body and crouch next to it.

"No. I called the tech guy, and the cameras were out all evening in this wing." Yeah, probably because of us, I mentally add.

"He's still hot to the touch; it couldn't have been too long since it happened."

"Yeah. I gathered that when I saw the heart still leaking blood when I came here."

"Who found him?"

"One of my staff. She said she saw a shadow in the hallway and wanted to check. She found the door to the study half-open and then, you know. Poor woman, she's likely traumatized for life..." he says and regards me. "But you're not," he adds curiously, and I stand to give him an honest look.

"How well did you know Martin?"

"Not that well, he was mostly acquainted with my father... and my wife."

"Don't worry, you didn't miss much. To be honest, anyone could have done this to him." I point towards the T on his fore-head. "He's always been involved in shady dealings. They finally bit him in the ass."

"Whoever did this, however, wanted an audience. Likely to make an example of him."

"You're right. Which means... Martin wasn't the only one involved with whoever branded him."

"It's a long shot to draw that conclusion," Adrian counters Enzo's argument, but he isn't deterred.

"Maybe, but why *my* house to send a message? When there are so many people present involved in *my* dealings. We won't know, though, until we find who killed Martin."

"Did your wife hear?" I ask, curious about how tight her relationship with my father was.

"Not yet. I'll take care of her later."

"What are you going to do with the body?" I hope he doesn't say I'll have to deal with it.

"I already sent for a crew. They'll clean everything nicely, and I'll forward you the details for the funeral home," Enzo says, his eyes still on the corpse. "You're going to have a funeral, no?" He raises his head towards me to ask.

I turn towards Adrian and see the same understanding in his eyes. We need to.

"Yes. Thank you for doing this."

"Don't worry about it."

I take one last look at the scene, and with a sigh, I head towards the door. Just as I open it, I see a hysterical Allegra rushing towards the study. The other people who'd been waiting around for the spectacle had likely dissipated thanks to Enzo's security. But now, there's no one to stop Allegra from seeing Martin in the study. Well, technically, *I* could. But I don't want to. Instead, I kick the door wide open with my foot so she can make her way inside.

She stops in the doorway, her wild eyes assessing. A moment passes before she screams. I look back and see Enzo casually shake his head as if this were the last thing he would have liked to deal with.

Allegra collapses to her knees, still focused on Martin's lifeless body. Slowly, she crawls towards his heart and cradles it to her chest, murmuring some crazy shit.

I quickly look up to see both Adrian and Enzo's shocked expressions.

"Allegra..." Enzo starts, almost exasperated. "You need to put that down."

"No." She shakes her head vehemently, her hands holding the heart reverently.

"Now we can be together forever," she whispers to the heart as she holds it next to her face, smearing blood on her skin.

Enzo rolls his eyes and takes his phone out to dial his security. Soon, a few men step forward and try to take the heart out of Allegra's hands without doing much damage. She holds onto it even tighter, her fingers digging into the organ's muscles and denting it a little.

Well, if this isn't a spectacle.

They finally manage to get Allegra to drop the heart, and they quickly restrain her.

"Take her to her room and call for her maid," Enzo orders before turning to us.

"Sorry for that... she's probably just shocked," Enzo adds, a little embarrassed. I don't say anything in return, merely nodding. There was more than shock to that performance. Not my business, though, as long as she stays away from Adrian.

I look up and beckon him to go—too much excitement for one night.

41

ADRIAN

Bianca parks the car in Vlad's driveway, and we both get out. She'd been adamant about driving since she'd smelled some alcohol on my breath. It's moments like these when I genuinely question her lack of empathy.

But I digress.

There are far more critical things to do now than for me to mentally debate how much of a sociopath my wife truly is. I shake myself from those thoughts as we meet up with Vlad in his office. Bianca has already called him to let him know we're coming.

"My condolences for your father, little goddess. I'm so sorry you didn't get to kill him yourself," Vlad taunts Bianca, and she only gives him a droll look.

"Yeah, well, there goes my lifelong goal of murdering my sire."

With these two, it's hard to tell when they're joking about murder or not, especially since most of the time, they are *not*.

"What did Martin want when he took you aside?" I ask, as I remember.

"He wasn't making much sense, to be honest. You noticed how drunk he was. That was highly unusual for him. He started saying how he got lured by the money and that he shouldn't have done something... I have no idea what it was."

"Do you think he was afraid? Maybe he knew what was coming?"

268

"Maybe." She ponders this and turns to Vlad. "We need to hear the recordings. Whoever killed Martin was in there not long after we planted the bugs."

"I already prepared them." Vlad casually leans back in his seat and hits play on the computer.

There's a lot of static noise, followed by our voices as we leave the room, and then after some fast-forwarding, we hear Martin's voice.

"You came sooner than I expected," Martin slurred.

"I only do as *mi señor* demands," another male voice responds. The use of Spanish could be an indicator of who the other man is.

"He kept me around for so long as his circus animal... Always fearing when he was going to strike."

"You should have known it was going to come. Eventually. Especially after you refused to hand over your daughter."

"I didn't refuse it," Martin immediately counters. "*He* didn't want to meet my conditions. But then, I screwed him too, didn't I? When I gave her to Hastings? He's probably still bitter about that, isn't he?"

"You overestimate the impact of your petty revenge. No, that's not why I'm here."

"Oh, I know why. It's because of Agosti, isn't it?" Martin gives a bitter laugh. "You don't like that I switched teams."

"Then, you know what to expect... how a traitor gets treated."

"You think I didn't know you were coming? I wanted to go out on my terms." Martin says before some movements indicate a struggle.

"*Hijo de puta!*" the other man exclaims.

After, the audio picks on some noises that are likely the man doing the physical damage to Martin's body. Vlad stops the recording then, and we're all perplexed.

I'm shocked at the contents of the audio. Did Martin want to sell Bianca? What kind of fucked-up shit is that? How could he even contemplate that? Especially given his wealth, what more could he possibly want that he'd be willing to trade in his own daughter.

"Well," Bianca starts, and she doesn't seem the least affected by what she'd just heard. "We know the assailant spoke Spanish. We just need the list of invitees to see who it might have been."

"And how do you intend to ask for it?" Vlad asks. "Enzo will want to know why Spanish, and you can't very well say that you bugged his office."

Bianca strokes her chin and thinks, and within seconds, her eyes light up, and she reaches for her phone.

"Enzo. Yes, it's Bianca. I just remembered something that might be useful. Before he was killed, my father took me aside and told me he had some money problems, and some Spanish person was after him. Yes, I'm sure he said Spanish... Do you think you could check the invitee list and forward me the names of Spanish or Spanish speakers? Are you sure? ... And the times match? ... Do you happen to have a picture from your CCTV? ... Yes, thank you!"

"So?" Vlad and I ask at the same time

"You're not going to like this."

"Spill, B!" Vlad seems as anxious as I am.

"Enzo told me that the only Spanish-speaking person he could name off the top of his head was Jimenez's substitute, and the man following him lost him around the time Martin turned up dead. After that, he just vanished."

My eyes widen as I take in the new information.

"Martin and Jimenez?" Vlad's eyebrows shoot up. "Now, *that* I didn't think of."

"Did you?" I ask Bianca, and my words come out a little harsher than I intend.

"No, not at all." She frowns as she thinks. "I didn't always pay attention to whatever garbage Martin had involved himself in, but I would have never believed him to be *that* deep with the cartel."

I believe her. She has no reason to lie, considering her strained relationship with Martin.

"Replay the conversation!" I turn back to the computer, and Vlad clicks on play again.

"There!" I stop him, and you can hear Martin say again, "*He didn't want to meet my conditions. But then I screwed him too,*" *didn't I? When I gave her to Hastings. He's probably still bitter about that, isn't he?"*

"He was planning to sell me to Jimenez?" Bianca narrows her eyes.

"It must have been around the time we started dating. Although I really don't know what he means by *giving you* to me."

"I think he means forcing our meetings. Let's face it, after he introduced us, you were forever a fixed element in the house. *That*, I didn't even have to manufacture myself," Bianca adds ironically, and looking back, I have to agree. Martin had been trying to force a proximity between us. But why?

"Why you?" Bianca voices my own question. "The question now is whether Jimenez was bitter just because it wasn't him or because it was *you* specifically."

"And why would Jimenez want you?" I shudder to think of the possibility. No, better not let my mind wander there.

"Why does anyone want a barely legal girl?" she says with a shrug, and Vlad finds this the best time to joke.

"It might have been better if your father had given you to Jimenez." When none of us are replying, he further adds, "He would already be dead. Come on, you think B would have spared him?" he addresses to me.

"Probably not..." I respond.

"We need to figure out what connection Martin had with Jimenez," Bianca says before looking at her phone and frowning. "Wait. Vlad, I'm forwarding you Enzo's pictures. Pull them up on the screen."

Vlad complies, and the CCTV pictures show a silver-haired man in a tuxedo mingling around the guests. Swiping through the images, he finally stops at one that shows a close-up of the man.

"Shit," I exclaim, moving closer to the screen to make sure I'm not wrong.

"Anyone you know?" Vlad turns his head towards me.

"Yes...I knew him. At least I think so. He's older now, of course. But I knew him more than fifteen years ago."

"Who is he?"

"He was a priest at the church that took me in after I left foster care. He's the one who helped me get back on my feet and train for the small league fights. Why would..." I trail off, not making sense of any of this. Why would Jimenez's man help me after his own boss killed my family?

"Maybe he wasn't working for Jimenez yet?" Bianca offers, and I shake my head.

"No, I don't think so. He never spoke with a Spanish accent back then, never even used Spanish words. If he wasn't under Jimenez, why try so hard to mask his speech?"

"But that would mean..." Bianca starts.

"That Jimenez has known who I am all along."

"Wait!" Bianca suddenly remembers something and puts her clutch on the desk, her fingers working the opening mechanism and removing what looks to be a memory card.

"Can you play this as well? Now that we know what he looks at, maybe we can get some clues from what my camera filmed." She hands the memory card to Vlad to plug it into his computer.

"I didn't know you were filming as well," I add.

"Cozying up to the enemy is only ever for information gathering. Let's face it. Enzo may be all nice and polite, especially given Martin's death in his house, but he's still going to be the enemy after this ends."

"Fair enough. I like that you're so thorough," I admit, my voice filled with admiration. And I am.

I don't know whether it's because she's stopped pretending or because she's drug-free, but this version of Bianca is competent and scary.

But I find that I like that too.

Vlad signals that the video has been downloaded onto the computer and plays it for us.

"Lucky we weren't there for long," Bianca adds drily, realizing that we can't just fast forward it as we did with the audio.

Our eyes glued to the screen, we keep watching.

"There. See that man?" Vlad points to the silver-haired man in the far right of the frame. "When is this?"

"It must have been when I was talking with Martin. He was watching him."

We continue to watch frame by frame, and the man appears a few more times in the background. Most of the time, he was in Martin's vicinity. There's one instance, though, when we were in the drawing room, the man was present, this time watching us.

"Shit!" Bianca curses and purses her lips. "Vlad, whatever you know about Jimenez, I think now it's time to spit it out. This is getting out of hand."

"You wound me, little goddess. So little patience."

"Vlad!"

"Fine, fine. I told you I'd give you the club he frequents. It's called The Block, and it's in Atlantic City. And it's a little more... on the wild side. Other than that, I know a few of his businesses, but honestly, half the time, the information I get on him ends up being a fake rumor."

"How do you know this club is legit, then?"

"I have very close sources that attest to the information."

"Perfect. I'll wait until the funeral, and I'm going," I say.

"We're going," Bianca corrects. "I'm not letting you go alone."

"I can handle myself just fine."

"Fine will get you killed. Don't worry, I'll be your bodyguard."

"Bianca... seriously?"

"I'm extremely serious. You're not going anywhere without me. And that's final." She folds her arms over her chest, suggesting the conversation is over.

I throw my hands up in exasperation, and Vlad chuckles.

"I'd do as she says. She can be exceedingly stubborn. But do keep her from drugs." I shake my head in resignation, not that I was planning on putting too much resistance anyway.

"One condition, though," I add, needing to set some boundaries.

"What?" Basks, looking at me all innocent. Sure...

"No killing. No killing Jimenez, or any other man." Now, she pouts.

"Why? At *least* Jimenez," she pleads.

"No. I didn't take Theo's identity and got so far in my career for nothing. I want to see Jimenez prosecuted to the full extent of the law for his wrongdoings. It's something I promised myself when this all started."

Bianca rolls her eyes at me as if this all seems too much for her, but she eventually relents.

"Fine. No killing." She sighs and looks so dejected, as if I just took away her favorite toy.

Right around then, Bianca's phone rings, and she mouths that it's Enzo again.

"Yes? So fast... Oh, I didn't realize you could find that out so fast... No, I really don't know... Thank you for this update... Yes, tell them to forward me the details... I'll see you at the funeral."

Sighing in a bored manner, Bianca relates what Enzo told her, "Apparently, preliminary results show cyanide poisoning. They found vast amounts in his mouth, so they're suspecting a suicide pill."

"So, that was the noise we heard in the audio..." I muse aloud.

"Even in death, Martin simply has to have the last word." Bianca sounds disappointed.

"Now what?" Vlad suddenly asks, and Bianca and I share a look.

"We have a funeral to plan. Yay," Bianca replies with fake enthusiasm before stomping her foot in frustration.

"Do you know what this means? I have to fucking pretend to be sad that the old man is gone. Fuuuuck! I need to buy eye drops."

"I think you're not the only one who's going to attempt to shed fake crocodile tears." I've known Martin close to ten years, and he's never struck me as the type to inspire that sort of emotion in a person.

42

BIANCA

Adrian is right. I'm definitely not the only one crying my eyes out.

At this point, I've already used up two bottles of eye drops. Adrian is holding onto my arm with a stern look on his face as I hunch over the coffin, sobbing at least audibly if not visually. But I'm not the only one putting on a show. On the other side of the coffin, Allegra is wailing like a banshee. Somehow, I doubt her love for my father had been that strong.

Enzo is sitting next to the row of chairs. The ceremony just ended, and they're ready to lower the coffin into the ground. Finally, I'd be rid of the old man forever. I have to mentally tell myself to build up the patience to withstand this display.

I'm surprised Adrian hasn't tried to dissuade me from going this far, but even he knows that appearances have to be kept.

We invite everyone back to the house. I'm thankful, though, that Adrian is doing most of the entertaining, and I can take a break. Fake crying does take a toll on you.

Of course, Allegra seems to get the memo as well when she passes out in the drawing room. I have to wonder if this is part of the act, or she's too worn out from the crying. Enzo is currently picking her up from the floor, none too pleased to be put into this position, and deposits her on one of the sofas.

"She took it pretty rough, didn't she?" I ask sarcastically after he leaves her and heads to the refreshment table.

"She's been hysterical for days."

"How long were they together?"

"That I know of? A few months." He pours himself a glass of wine and casually leans against the wall. From the corner of my eye, I see Adrian talking to some old men. He catches my eye and glares at me for some reason.

He's probably mad that I'm throwing him to the wolves.

"I don't know what she saw in him." I shake my head at the mental image of Allegra and Martin. Allegra is around my age, for God's sake. The entire situation is too disgusting to contemplate.

"My wife has unusual tastes in men." I detect almost a smile as he says the words, but it's quickly gone as he asks me. "I'm curious about you, though."

"Me?" I feign ignorance and give him a small smile. Again, Adrian scowls at me from across the room. What's wrong with him?

"You were almost too calm when you saw Martin... heartless, so to speak. And today, you were worse than Mary at Jesus' crucifixion. So, which one is it?"

"Enzo, a woman must preserve an air of mystery at all times."

"Indeed. I just find it odd. Martin commits suicide before having his heart carved out and a T branded on his forehead by the henchman of a drug lord."

"Considering Martin's implication with you, I think it's not surprising he would have availed himself to the services of a cartel."

"Touché." Enzo laughs. "But I do wonder. Why did you conceal the suicide?"

"It's rather simple. Martin wanted to end up on top with that stunt of his. I merely ensured he wouldn't be able to crawl from the bottom. Pun intended," I say with a straight face, but Enzo's eyes twinkle with merriment. He shifts a little closer, and that's when I hear a throat being cleared.

"Enzo," Adrian greets him with a deadly stare, to which Enzo just smiles. "My wife must be tired after suffering so much. I think it's time she rested." He puts his arm around my shoulders and doesn't wait for Enzo or me to reply, steering me up the stairs.

"What about the other guests?" I turn to him and ask.

"They'll eventually find their way out."

"You didn't have to be so rude. Really, Enzo was just being polite."

"Too damn close for polite," Adrian grumbles, and I suddenly realize what this is. My lips stretch into a smile, and I let myself be led by him.

"This...?" I ask when I realize he's stopped in front of a guest room.

"I remember what you told me about your childhood room. You might prefer to rest here." I look at him for a second, trying to decipher what I'm feeling right now. There's a warmth in my chest...

"Thank you," I say, suddenly shy. I open the door and dash inside, closing it behind me.

What was that?

I fan myself a little, and I go into the ensuite bathroom to look in the mirror.

My cheeks are red.

I turn on the faucet and clean my face, removing the mix of dirt and eye drops.

Taking Adrian's advice to rest, I take off my clothes, remove the mini pistol from my boot, and place it under the pillow. One hour of sleep should be enough to forget about this fiasco and those people to leave. I mean, let's face it, no one, absolutely no one, is mourning Martin. I doubt even Allegra feels even a smidgen of tenderness towards him. He was just an awful and distasteful person.

I wake up a while later, and I head downstairs. It seems that most people have left. There's only Marcel and Adrian in the middle of the hallway, engaged in conversation.

"Bianca," Marcel acknowledges me with a nod that I return.

"Is everyone gone?"

"Yes, a while ago," Adrian tells me as he goes towards the bar and pours himself a drink. "I talked to most people, and no one seemed suspicious."

"And here I thought his enemies would at least come to gloat." I sigh and cross my arms. "I went through all the files in his office, and there isn't anything incriminating." For the past three days since Enzo's party, I'd scoured every inch of the house, trying to find at least some evidence of Martin's relationship with Jimenez.

"Martin was many things, but careless wasn't one of them," Adrian adds.

"There's only one place I haven't managed to look in." Marcel and Adrian look at me expectantly. "His safe."

"Safe?" Adrian frowns.

"I don't think anyone knew about the safe. I didn't until I snooped around. It's hidden in his dressing room."

"Have you tried opening it?" Marcel asks, and I shake my head.

"I couldn't. It's one of those high-tech ones. It has biometrics."

"Then how can we break it? We need to see what's inside."

"Don't worry. I couldn't, until *now* that is"

"What do you mean?"

"I needed the funeral home to release Martin's body for the wake," I say and motion them to follow me to the kitchen. I open the freezer and remove a bag containing Martin's fingers.

"You cut his fingers?" Adrian's mouth snaps open in shock as he watches me take a plate and shake the bag so that the fingers fall into the container.

"Only the thumbs and the pointers."

"Good Lord!" Adrian's hand goes to his forehead, massaging his temple.

Marcel, on the other hand, doesn't seem at all fazed. I narrow my eyes ever so slightly.

Whatever. One less person to criticize me.

"Fine! Let's get this over with!" Adrian shakes his head in disgust. I wonder why, though. It's not like they're smelly...

"We can't... yet," Marcel intervenes as he studies the fingers. "Too frozen. We need to leave them to thaw first."

I scrunch up my nose as I look them over and realize he's right.

"Let's microwave them," I suggest, and Adrian slaps his forehead this time, letting out a loud sigh.

"I don't mean like *that*," I immediately add. "The defrost setting. It might work."

"No," Marcel says pensively. "We can't risk the heat damaging the fingerprints." Okay, that does make sense.

"You're right. We can wait for a couple of hours more. We should probably move them until then, though. I don't think the staff will react too well to detached body parts laying around." I take the plate with the fingers and motion the guys to follow me to Martin's room.

"This is huge!" Marcel exclaims when he enters.

"Wait until you see the dressing room." I motion towards the door at the end of the room and show them where the safe is.

"There's probably a fortune here only in watches." Adrian looks at the glass case in the middle of the dressing room that displays Martin's collection. I'd wager it's a couple of million just for the watches.

"It makes you wonder what he keeps in the safe if he leaves the valuables outside," Marcel notes.

"It must be business related. There was absolutely nothing anywhere else. To be honest, considering his suicide method, he was prepared to die at any point."

"I wonder why he was willing to risk death by crossing Jimenez. It's clear that he knew what he was getting into," Adrian says, and Marcel and I agree.

"We just have to hope the safe will give us some info. Otherwise, dead men tell no tales."

I move a bunch of his clothes to reveal a hole in the wall, with the front of the safe sticking out.

"That's... a big safe." The safe is at least one and a half meters tall and probably stretching another meter in the back.

We decide to sit around and wait for the fingers to thaw, checking every now and then.

The downside is that it also doesn't take long for them to smell. Adrian turns his face and gives me a reproaching look.

"Hey, I didn't have any other option, okay?" He shakes his head before saying, "I'm not touching that, just so you know."

"Pussy," I mutter, and Marcel coughs uncomfortably in his fist.

"Don't worry, big guys. I brought gloves." I remove a pair of medical gloves from my pocket and slip them on. "Let's see now." I pick up a thumb, and I study the texture, rotating it around. If I wipe it well, it should be fine. I go to the closet and grab one of Martin's shirts, wiping the finger on it.

"Let's try now." Both men watch me as I approach the safe with the thumb and press it onto the pad. I wait and... nothing.

"Shit. Can you bring the plate here? This one isn't working." I proceed to try each finger after carefully wiping all moisture traces from them, but without any luck.

"I think the prints must have been destroyed in the process," Marcel notes, taking one thumb and placing it in the light. "Look, the print is only partial."

"Fuck!" I say, not expecting this. After going through the trouble of desecrating the dead, something even I hadn't done before, and this isn't working. I sigh, trying to think of alternatives.

"Then what?" Adrian asks, and an idea comes to mind.

"We blow it up."

"What?" They both turn to look at me.

"Let's evacuate the house, and we try to blow up the safe's front door."

"Where do we even get any explosives?"

"I might have some..." I say sheepishly. "I had an explosive stage as a teenager," I add ironically and roll my eyes. "There might still be some left in the basement."

Marcel shakes his head and steps forward to scrutinize the lock. "We risk damaging the inside if we're not careful. Let me have a go at the lock."

I look at him skeptically, but we don't have anything to lose, so I nod.

"Do you have any tool kits?"

I quickly go to the basement and bring him everything that

might help. When I come back, Marcel looks at the different tools and tests for their size. He then takes a few screwdrivers and digs into the control panel of the vault. He removes the outside cap, and I can see some intricate wiring that's probably controlling the safe's functions.

He uses a few more tools to dig inside the panel. I don't understand what's happening, but suddenly, there's a click sound, and the door opens.

"Shit, man!" Adrian is in awe, and honestly, so am I.

Marcel opens the door, and inside are rows upon rows of files. Marcel takes a few out and hands them to me. I'm looking at the documents in my hands, not really paying attention when I hear Adrian yell for us to step back.

I don't register what happens exactly, but I'm thrown to the back of the room by an explosion coming from the direction of the vault. Adrian's hands are wrapped around me, cushioning me.

"Fuck! Fuck! Fuck!" I mutter when I see the vault in flames, the whole room surrounded by smoke and burnt paper. I turn around and see Adrian against the wall, his eyes closed. I don't even think when I shake him.

"Theo... Theo, wake up. Please wake up." My hands go all over his body, trying to see if there's any hidden injury. I'm hyperventilating at this point. "Theo..."

"Agh..." He coughs a few times, and the tension leaves my body. He's all right. He opens his eyes and looks at me with worry in his eyes. "Are you okay?"

"Yes, because of you. How are you?" I get up and try to help him to his feet. He winces when he tries, and his hand goes to his midriff.

"I'll be fine. Marcel?" I then remember Marcel was there too and even closer than me.

"Fine!" he says, and I see him on the other side of the bed, with barely any injuries. He must have jumped when Adrian yelled.

Now that everyone is safe and sound, I hurry outside and grab a fire extinguisher from the hallway. I remove the safety and spray it all over the clothes, putting out the small fire that had erupted.

"I should have seen this coming," Marcel says ruefully. "Of

course, a high-end vault like this would have a safety installed in case of a break-in. Especially if the information is highly incriminating."

"We still have this." I wave the envelope that Marcel had managed to pass to me before the explosion. "Considering how many more there were inside, it's not much. But maybe it's something."

"Let's see." Adrian still doesn't look right, but the prospect of opening the envelope is too tempting. I'll make him get checked out later, I promise myself.

I open the envelope and dump its contents on the bed. It's a bunch of IDs: a passport, a driver's license, some subscription cards, an old Boston metro card, and a couple sheets of paper. I look at the IDs, and they all have the same name.

"Greg Sullivan," I say aloud, frowning at Martin's picture next to that name. "Weird."

While the guys are still perusing the cards, I grab the two sheets and skim them, quickly realizing they both contain high-profile individuals: senators, governors, business executives, etc. There are a few names on the list that are crossed out.

"Look!" I hand the papers to Adrian and Marcel, and they also peruse the names.

"This... do you think it's blackmail? Why else would all these people's names be in the same place? What do they have in common?"

"No... it can't be..." Adrian looks at the documents as if he'd seen a ghost. He quickly takes the passport with Greg Sullivan's name on it and puts them side by side.

"What?" I ask.

"The night my parents were killed, I overheard them talking to someone. They said they had a list of all the names involved with Jimenez, and they wanted to go public, but they were afraid for me. They ended up giving the files away as insurance."

"To whom?" I frown. How could he know they're the same files?

"To someone named Greg..." He raises his head and gives me an odd look. This just got a whole lot more complicated.

43

ADRIAN

"We need to do further testing. I'm sending you to get a scan. For now, I'm mostly worried about your ribs and your right hand." The doctor writes down the order for the x-ray before telling us he'll be back later on.

Bianca had insisted on an ER visit when she'd seen me wincing a few times when moving, even though I'd said I was okay. Sure, there was some tenderness around my chest, but I've suffered worse in the past.

I'm now sitting on the hospital bed, pulling my shirt back on and avoiding Bianca's gaze.

"I don't think it's *just* your ribs and your right hand. What about your upper back? You smashed directly into the wall with your back." She shakes her head.

"I'm sure the doctor knows what he's doing."

"No," she starts adamantly. "I can't have you broken. What if he misses something?"

"Bianca, calm down."

She'd nagged me all the way to the hospital and almost bullied the hospital staff into looking at me as soon as possible. By the way she was speaking, you'd think I was bleeding out. In fact, when we'd come through the emergency entrance, she'd immediately gone to the reception, and straight-faced she'd said, "My husband

283

is broken. I need you to fix him. *Now!*" For a moment, I thought she'd pull a gun on them.

I tried to calm her down, but she'd been belligerent until a doctor had seen me.

I may have been annoyed at this type of behavior under any other circumstances, but coming from Bianca, it was a little too endearing to get mad at. Especially since I *actually* believe her concern is genuine.

It had all happened so fast. Marcel was taking out the contents of the safe; the next, I noticed a countdown on its display. When I'd realized the imminent danger, my only thought had been to get Bianca as far away from the explosion as possible. I'd only managed to grab her and make for the floor when we'd both been flung to the other end of the room.

And then there had been the shock of finding the envelope with the list of names. I hadn't quite registered the pain as I'd been too caught up remembering that long-ago conversation my parents had had with Greg.

"Marcel is compiling information on every name on that list," Bianca relays this as she gets off the phone with Marcel. He'd refused to get a check-up, saying he was completely fine.

"I'm still not sure how he managed to avoid that blast altogether," she adds, and I have to agree. I didn't see exactly what happened with him, but it's impressive that he's wholly unharmed.

A nurse comes by, and she tells me to follow her to get the scan. Bianca starts behind us too, but the nurse shakes her head.

"I'm sorry, ma'am, but you must wait here." Bianca's eyes widen a little in disbelief, and I can almost tell she won't accept this.

"It's fine, B. Wait here," I try to tell her gingerly, afraid she might cause a scene. She scowls at me but reluctantly nods.

We go to a different floor, and they take x-rays of my ribs and my right hand. After I'm done, the nurse accompanies me back to my bed.

"That was fast," Bianca notes when I lie down again.

"They don't usually take long," I say almost absentmindedly.

"I wouldn't know." Bianca shrugs.

"You've never had broken bones?"

Given her profession, it would be almost abnormal to not encounter that sort of injury.

"Oh, I've had plenty." She waves her hand as if it's nothing, and my head snaps in her direction. "But I've never gone to a hospital for them." I mean, I can empathize with that.

When I was fighting, we couldn't go to the hospital because they would alert the police. But we still had a makeshift clinic special for the fighters. After all, if you lasted longer, you could make more money for them.

I'm curious how she got them treated, though. Maybe Vlad had doctors working for him?

"Then how did you deal with them?"

"Usually, they happened while on a mission, and Vlad or I would make do with whatever materials we had. I think I've been lucky so far, though. I've only popped my shoulder a few times, broken my left wrist a time or two... but it wasn't something too bad."

"You mean you never had them looked at by a professional?"

"Well..." She thinks about it for a minute. "A surgeon once told me I shouldn't worry about it?"

"A surgeon?" I stare at her in disbelief.

"Yeah." She tugs her shirt, so her shoulder is exposed, pointing at a white puckered scar. "Got shot once. It was pretty messy because the guy couldn't find the bullet. He told me that compared to that, a dislocation isn't *that* bad."

I'm... shocked.

She tells this in an emotionless voice, as if she's just reciting some random facts. I'm even more shocked to realize that the many scars that she'd blamed on childhood accidents were *not* actual childhood accidents.

Remembering many of the marks on her body, I now realize how gullible I'd been. Or maybe, better said, blind.

I, better than anyone, should recognize a knife or bullet wound, given my experience both in the force and during my time under Andrew. But of course, my sweet, sheltered wife couldn't have possibly gotten shot or stabbed.

"What about your other scars?" I find myself asking. "The ones you said were childhood accidents."

"Oh... let me think. I don't have *that* many. I'm good at my job." She looks at me offended, as if I'm questioning her abilities. "Let's see. The one on my thigh is from a bullet. There's the big one on my back from a knife... oh, and there are also the smaller white ones on my chest and belly. Those are from some *very* shallow knife wounds. They scarred quite prettily, actually."

She's about to take off her top to show me, but I stop her when I spot the doctor coming our way. She pouts for a second but doesn't continue.

"Doctor." I nod at him, and his expression doesn't look too good.

"Mr. Hastings. I fear I don't have good news. I've looked at your scans. You do display some cracking in your ribs and wrist. But what I'm most concerned is the bone that hasn't healed." He turns his tablet towards me and pulls up my chest x-rays. He points to some circled areas in blue.

"These are your new injuries. But these..." He now points towards some areas in red. "These are old injuries that never healed properly. Have you had any breathing problems? Pain in your chest when you try to inhale and expand your lungs?" I shake my head.

"Good... that's good." He almost sounds relieved. "Given your extensive previous trauma, it's imperative that you avoid anything that might cause further injury." He explains that badly healed ribs could affect my lungs and, worst-case scenario, restrict my breathing.

"He will do just that!" Bianca is quick to assuage the doctor, her hand on my back.

"Now, on to your wrist scans. These are better. I can still see a lot of remodeled bone, but it's been set properly, so it shouldn't trouble you. There's only a hairline fracture on the distal side of your radius and should heal on its own. That's why I'm going to recommend you wear a hand brace instead of a cast. Don't put too much stress on it, though, because it *will* worsen."

I nod as the doctor describes everything I need to do. He ends up only prescribing me some pain medicine and advising me to be careful while my ribs are healing.

We thank the doctor, and after he leaves, Bianca crosses her arms and raises an eyebrow at me.

"And you were saying about *my* injuries...?"

"Why are you so satisfied with yourself?" I grumble.

"Because maybe at some point, you'll realize we're not so different, you and I." I stare at her for a moment, trying to gather my thoughts for a reply, when her phone goes off again. She puts one finger up before accepting the call and putting it on speaker.

"There you are, little goddess. Marcel told me you encountered some problems."

"Yeah, we're about to leave the hospital," Bianca replies.

"Good. Come by, will you? I think we've found something with that list of yours."

"Fine. We'll be there soon." She hangs up the phone, and I voice something that's been bothering me for quite some time.

"Why does he always call you a little goddess?"

"It's from my code name." She leans in to whisper in my ear, "Artemis. One day, he just called me that, and I went with it." She shrugs as if it doesn't seem entirely too intimate.

"I don't like it," I tell her, and she frowns at me.

"Why?"

"I just don't," I complain and cross my arms.

"Fine, I'll tell him not to call me that anymore." She takes her purse to go.

"Just like that? No objections?"

She doesn't seem to understand what I'm trying to say as she replies nonchalantly, "Why would I object? You don't like it, so I'll tell him to stop."

"Never mind." I stand to go.

We get to Vlad's place, and we find him and Marcel in front of the computer, focused on whatever is on the screen.

"There you are," Vlad says without looking up. "Come see this." We both go around the desk, and Vlad points towards the document he's pulled up.

"So, there are a total of eighteen names on the list. We've

managed to track all of them." He shows us pictures of the two sheets of paper containing the names, with six of those names being crossed out.

"What did you find out?" I ask, hoping they found something.

"All of those twelve names we can make out were important men in the public functions or heads of businesses twenty years ago."

"Were?"

"Some are dead now, and most have retired already. I've also talked to my IT guy to try to make out the crossed-out names."

"This isn't much," Bianca notes, but Vlad quickly puts up his hand to stop her.

"Not finished, please. The working theory is that these people were involved with Jimenez at one point. Marcel and I started looking at each person's finances. If they invested with Jimenez, there must be some type of evidence, right? We didn't manage to go through all, *obviously*, but the three people we did manage to investigate gave us something."

"Something?" I ask, and Vlad pulls up financial statements next.

"We noticed the three have something in common. Around twenty years ago, they started making regular yearly payments to an offshore account." He points to the amount, and it's staggering. Each person would wire two hundred and fifty thousand dollars each.

"Shit! Blackmail?" Both Vlad and Marcel nod.

"And the offshore account?"

"Still working on that. But if my theory is right... and it probably is." Vlad starts in his usual self-assured manner. "We're going to find similar payments made by the rest of the people on that list."

"What would Martin be doing with this? Insurance?" I wonder aloud. It doesn't make sense.

"No... not insurance," Bianca finally speaks, and her insight brings a whole different angle to the problem. "My father was never poor, strictly speaking, but he went through a rough patch when I was a child. I remember because that was around the time he started being meaner than usual, and he would complain a lot about money. Can you check Martin's accounts from around that time?"

"You really think *he* was the one who blackmailed these people?" The names on the list belong to politicians... people in power. How could Martin...

Shit.

I remember Martin's widespread connections, and how everyone seemed so subservient to him. Retrospectively, maybe he did have something on them?

"I only have access to public information now, but..." Vlad is focused on the screen, trying to access some data. "B's right. There was a rough patch around twenty-two years ago. He was losing more money than he was making. He was almost contemplating insolvency at that point." He shows us some financial statements that show millions in debt. "Then, he was suddenly on his feet again." He scrolls through more statements, and the date on the one that shows him on plus is... eighteen years ago.

"The timeline would match," Bianca states. "So, let's say that Martin made some bad investments, was losing money, and needed urgent capital. He got that list with people who were clearly involved in illegal things, and he blackmailed them. We can account for that four-year lag in profits because his debts were just too big to be wiped clean immediately."

"That would be the logical conclusion," Vlad agrees. "Although, I still want to run the rest of the names to confirm this."

"I'm curious about the other six crossed names." Marcel stands to pace around the room. "And is Jimenez involved?"

"I think there is one way to find out." Bianca's face suddenly lights up, and I sigh. I'm learning her facial cues, and this can't be good. "We interrogate some of the people on the list. They should be able to give us info on Martin and Jimenez."

"That's a great idea, little goddess!" Vlad exclaims, rubbing his hands together in excitement. There's a one-second pause before Bianca gives him a blank look.

"You can't call me a little goddess anymore. He doesn't like it."

She raises her hand and points her finger at me—way to throw me under the bus, B.

Vlad immediately chuckles.

"Are you jealous, Hastings?" he coos at me, and I close my eyes to maintain my calm.

"Aww, don't worry." He pats my back in a mocking gesture. "I've seen her naked, and she doesn't do anything for me."

The moment the words are out of his mouth, the hand now sporting a brace shoots out and wraps itself around Vlad's throat, almost lifting him from his chair.

His expression is still amused when he says, "No offense, B." Then, he turns his gaze from her to me, and in a deadly voice, he utters, "Take your hand off me, Hastings, or I won't play nice."

Before I can say anything, Bianca intervenes.

"Don't you dare, Vlad! He just came back from the doctor. Adrian, let him go!" She taps her foot and waits expectantly. I reluctantly let go, and Vlad is back in his seat.

"Now, make up!" Her command seems to have the same effect on Vlad as it has on me. I give him a side-eye and reluctantly mumble something.

"Great. Now that we're done with the family drama, we can focus on Bianca's suggestion." Marcel intervenes, barely able to hide his laughter.

"Yes, take your husband with you and go do your thing." Vlad massages his neck as if I'd applied Herculean force on it.

"Nope. Can't do that. *He just came back from the doctor!*" Bianca reiterates, almost outraged that Vlad would suggest such a thing.

"Well, I can't go. Marcel can't go. So, either you go alone or take him." He nudges his head in my direction.

I want to reply, but Bianca once again speaks, "Why can't Marcel?"

"He's not made for these things..."

"I guess you're right." She frowns at the notion before adding, "Then, I'll go alone."

"You're not going alone," I finally say.

"No, no, you're not coming," she scoffs at me as if it's the most absurd thing.

"Yes, I am. If I'm not going with you, then I'll go alone."

"Alone?" Her eyes widen at the possibility, and I realize I know exactly how to get her.

"Yes. You know, it's probably going to put a strain on my arm and my ribs... but I'm sure I can do it alone too."

"No! You're coming with me. I'll take care of you."

"Fine," I reply, trying to seem indifferent but inside, I'm smirking.

I think I'm getting the hang of how *this* Bianca operates. And it's kind of fun to push her buttons.

"Good one, Hastings!" Both Marcel and Vlad nod at me while Bianca looks a little confused. She doesn't even know what she's just given me.

"Now... who are we paying a visit to?"

"You're welcome to choose from here." He gives us an updated list of their professions before looking at his phone and adding, "My IT guy just confirmed that the rest have outgoing payments to the same offshore account too. Once we got the pattern, it was fairly easy for him to check for the same thing."

"Let's see. We want someone willing to talk," B says as she scans the new list and settles on a name. "Former Senator Wolfe. I remember him. He used to come to our house all the time when I was younger."

"Yeah, I know him as well..." I add drily. He was an old man who had to include Jesus in every single conversation. We'd had a few disputes under the guise of debates over the years. He retired some eight or nine years ago, last I remember.

"Have your IT guy get all information on Wolfe, and then we'll act." Bianca nods towards Vlad.

It seems that our visit to Atlantic City will have to be delayed... again.

44

BIANCA

According to the information Vlad's IT guy provided, Wolfe is seventy-four years old, married for forty of those, and the proud father of three children. He currently resides in Tampa, Florida. I'm working on memorizing his personal details while Adrian is getting changed. We decide to come back to the penthouse before heading for our four a.m. flight to Tampa.

I haven't been back here since our fight, and on the drive back, he'd felt compelled to add, "Don't think any of this means I forgive you." I hadn't said anything because I never expected him to... at least not this soon. I just have to work harder to prove to him that we belong together.

So far, our teamwork has been exemplary if one looks past Martin's death and the vault's explosion.

"Are you done?" I look up to see him button up a white shirt and fold his sleeves.

"Yes." He nods and drops a backpack next to me. "I packed some essentials."

"Good. Me too." I show him the small case luggage I'd prepared. "I'm checking this one in. It has everything we will need for the more unsavory parts of the journey." Unsavory being the code word for blood and gore. I'd packed some of my guns, ammo, and a couple knives. He frowns when he gets my meaning.

"How will it pass airport security?"

"They have my name flagged, so they never check it," I explain how it's like a subscription you pay for if you know the right people. For someone who needs to travel with weapons nine times out of ten, it's necessary.

He grunts in acknowledgment, but he doesn't seem too thrilled about my reservation. It's probably the lawman in him. Even though he's seen some sides of the underground world, Adrian is still innocent of many of the dealings that happen around us.

We leave the apartment and drive to the airport. We'd already decided we wouldn't stay there longer than a couple of days. Adrian had been quite vocal about that because he's anxious to go to Atlantic City and find Jimenez. I hadn't argued, mainly because where he goes, I go.

Once we get to the airport, we park the car, pay in advance for a few days, and head towards the check-in area.

"Are you sure it's going to work?" Adrian keeps eyeing my luggage.

"Trust me, it will work," I assure him for the thousandth time.

"I don't think I do..." he mutters under his breath but drops the issue.

Going through security is a piece of cake, and we soon take our seats in the flight.

"See, I told you there was nothing to worry about."

"I still can't believe you can just bribe airport security." He shakes his head, but I catch a glimpse of a grimace.

"How's the pain?" I point at his chest, and he shrugs.

"I took some painkillers. It's fine now."

"Don't overdo it," I chastise him slightly.

The plane takes off, and I see Adrian close his eyes.

Okay... so he doesn't want to talk. Not that I blame him too much, considering everything that happened this week. I still can't believe the old man made his fortune through blackmail, although it's not surprising.

I'd never concerned myself with his business. And he was never concerned with mine.

The only times we interacted was when he notified me of an event or a dinner I needed to attend with him to present the perfect family image to the world.

The more I think about my childhood, the more I regret I wasn't the one to put a bullet between his eyes. It would have been so satisfying...

"What did Vlad mean?" My thoughts are interrupted when Adrian tilts his head and looks at me through hooded eyes.

"When?" I try to remember what instance he's talking about but can't.

"When he said he's seen you naked."

"Ah! I've seen him naked, too. It's not a big deal. We were often in such close quarters with each other, we didn't have any privacy. Especially during missions in remote areas." I hope he doesn't think there's anything between Vlad and me. I mean, we're basically siblings.

Adrian is silent for a moment.

"Was this before we were together?"

I try to think back, and maybe... I don't really remember.

"Mostly," I reply.

After Vlad became Pakhan, we rarely went on missions together, so in a sense, I'm not lying.

"I see..." Adrian replies and purses his lips. What's going on? Is that a good *I see* or a bad *I see*?

"You must understand that nothing ever happened." I try to placate him further.

"How would you feel if I told you I had this close female friend, and we've both seen each other naked?"

A red mist covers my sight. My hand clutches at the armrest when I say, "I'd kill her."

"See?" He lifts an eyebrow at me.

"But..." I start, not seeing how these two situations compare.

"If this," he points towards me and then towards himself, "is going to work in any way, you'll have to try to put yourself in my shoes every now and then."

I grumble some type of acquiescence and drop the subject. How am I supposed to put myself in his shoes? I'll probably have to make a list of all the things he dislikes and memorize it. Would it be too much to ask *him* to make a list? One furtive glance at his stern features discourages me from voicing aloud that particular thought. He already thinks I'm a monster; I shouldn't add crazy to the mix.

Trying to salvage the time left on the flight, I change the topic and bring up something I'd been wondering for a long time.

"I've been meaning to ask you," I start, almost testing the waters. He turns ever so slightly towards me, so I continue, "How come Marcel is so involved in this Jimenez hunt?"

"He's my best friend," Adrian says automatically. "But to answer your question, Marcel found out that I was Adrian Barnett incredibly early in our friendship. I ended up telling him the entire history and why I was chasing after Jimenez. He's been helping me since, especially with his connections in the D.A. office."

"How does he know Vlad, then?" I ask, another mystery I haven't been able to crack.

"I don't know exactly. He said they're old friends."

"And you don't find that odd? *I* didn't know about their acquaintance until very recently." And I know mostly everyone in Vlad's life, not that there are that many people.

"Marcel has his secrets, but he's always been loyal to me," he adds with confidence.

"Hmm..." Adrian's trust in Marcel is ironclad. And yet, I have this nagging feeling that I'm missing something. Why is he so dedicated to finding Jimenez? Just for his best friend? It seems like a perilous task to undertake just to be of help to someone... I realize I can't voice my doubts anymore because I'd be doing so in vain.

But I'd have to monitor Marcel.

***

We land and after getting the luggage, we go to rent a car. After signing the agreement, we start on the road.

I input the coordinates for Wolfe's home, and then we head to

Palm Harbor. A quick glance at the community shows it's mainly retired people, so we have to keep that in mind to blend in.

"I guess Martin sucked him dry," I say as Wolfe's house comes in sight. It's very modest, especially considering the other neighboring houses.

"The first attempt is friendly, all right?" Adrian gives me a look while trying to find a parking spot, making sure I'm on the same page. We'd argued a little on the drive here, but we'd resolved to do it his way at first, and if it doesn't work, then we'll do it my way.

We get out of the car and knock on the door. After a few knocks, an old lady opens the door and greets us.

"Mrs. Wolfe?" Adrian inquires, and she nods. "I'm Theodore Hastings, and this is my wife Bianca Ashby. We'd like to talk with your husband. Is he at home?"

"Yes, yes, just a second. Please come in." She shows us to the living room and tells us to make ourselves comfortable.

We sit, and I take in my surroundings. Everything looks typical of a suburban home. There are family photos everywhere.

By all intents and purposes, it seems as if Senator Wolfe is a family man. There's also an unusual amount of religious paraphernalia, lots of crosses and the Bible in at least a dozen editions.

The sound of coughing brings my gaze towards the doorway, where an elderly man is holding onto the wall, seemingly walking with difficulty.

"Senator Wolfe." Adrian stands to shake the man's hand. Wolfe doesn't seem to be in top shape, but maybe this will be to our advantage.

"Hastings, right? Good to see you again, boy." He then looks at me and narrows his eyes. "Ashby... I heard about Martin. My condolences." I just give him a nod and watch him position himself on the opposite couch.

"What brings you here?" he asks, and I look at Adrian, keeping my mouth shut and giving him the stage.

"We've discovered a list among Martin's belongings," Adrian starts, and the effect is immediate. Wolfe's face pales, and there's a slight trembling to the hand resting on his knee.

"And?"

"Your name, along with other high-profile people, was on said list. We were wondering if you could provide us with some information..." Wolfe immediately stands, faster than he should have been capable of.

"Out!" he says. "Get out of my house! Now!" His hand points towards the door, and Adrian purses his lips, not yet moving.

"I don't think I made myself clear, Senator. We already know you were paying off Martin. What was it, quarter a million a year? How could a mere public officer have that much money to spare?" I know he's bluffing right now, but damn if it's not working.

If before we only theorized that Martin was the one blackmailing these people, now we know for sure. Wolfe promptly retakes his seat with a defeated look.

"What do you want?"

"The truth. Starting with why you were on the list in the first place."

"I... I can't," Wolfe stutters.

"Can't or won't?" Adrian rises to his feet and casually walks to the fireplace, above which are many family pictures. He takes one of the frames.

"You have a lovely family..."

"Please! It's over, just leave me alone," he pleads before turning towards me with venom in his eyes. "And you? I should have expected that any offspring of Martin's would be as vile." I'm slightly taken aback at this. Adrian interjects.

"You'll address my wife with respect, Wolfe, or you will find that you won't like the consequences." Adrian's voice suddenly booms, and my cheeks warm at his defense.

"Y-Y-You..." Wolfe sputters. Adrian moves in front of him, pointing to the family photo.

"Now, let's try again. Why was your name on the list?" I casually slip a gun from my back and play with a silencer. Wolfe's eyes go wide like saucers while Adrian looks resigned. He gives me a silent sign to not act.

"I... You can't tell anyone this, please. You can't tell my family. I'll be ruined."

"We don't care about that, Wolfe. Come on."

"I used to go to this club... it was a club that auctioned people for... sex." His cheeks go red at the admission.

"And?"

"I..." His eyes go back and forth from Adrian to my gun, and he swallows deeply. "I bought boys." His head drops at this.

"Boys? Define boys."

"T-T-Teenage boys." My hand immediately tightens on the gun, and it takes all my self-control to not shoot the fucker at once.

"Who was providing the boys?" Adrian continues to calmly ask, but I can see how much this bothers him.

"Jimenez... He has sex rings all over the East Coast. He arranges auctions, but..."

"But Martin got that list somehow." Wolfe nods.

"I see." Adrian stands and puts the picture back in its place.

"You won't say anything, right?" Wolfe looks at both of us. Adrian motions me towards the door, so I stand as well.

"Goodbye, Senator," Adrian says, and we leave.

In the car, the atmosphere is tense. And I simply have to ask, "Can I kill him?"

Adrian's hands splay on the wheel, and he sighs deeply, his eyes determined.

"Yes." Well, that's surprising. Giddiness overcomes me.

"Thank you!" I grab his arm and hug it to my chest in an impulsive gesture. Adrian spares me half a glance before focusing on the road, but his mouth has the slightest hint of a smile.

We check into a hotel, and I outline the plan.

"This lasted less than a day. You were great," I praise him. Honestly, I was impressed by how he handled the situation. Not so impressed with how I hadn't been able to kill him, but there's always tonight.

"You think you'll be fine on your own?" he asks after I tell him what I intend.

"I'd rather you didn't witness me... doing that," I add ruefully. I know that our working together on this case implies coming face to face with a lot of violence. At the same time, I'd rather he didn't have a picture of me killing this old man.

"If you're sure..." He doesn't look entirely sure himself, but I wave him off. I know what I'm doing, and now that I'm clean, I'm also much more aware of my surroundings. I can be in and out with no one finding out.

Later at night, I leave the hotel room, taking a long-winded way back to the senator's house to avoid detection. Once I'm there, it's easy to get inside the house.

I go to the second floor where the senator's bedroom is and see him in bed with his wife. He's lying face up and snoring loudly.

My right hand goes to my small pouch, and I withdraw a small syringe. I'd read up the senator's file and had noticed he had a heart problem. Then I'd realized what the best way to end him would be—a shot of potassium. A natural death for a foul human being.

Pity...

I put my left hand over his mouth and watch his eyes jolt open and widen at my presence. I give him a smile as I push the syringe into his neck.

As I watch, it doesn't take long for him to fade. I check his pulse with two fingers, satisfied with myself when I find none.

This wasn't a rewarding kill. He got what he deserved for purchasing underage boys for sex, but he was already old and decrepit. Even if I could inflict more pain on him, his body wouldn't have taken it, so it would have been in vain. Pity... that he was punished decades too late.

I get back to the hotel room and see Adrian already in bed, resting on his side.

Is he asleep?

I slip inside and tentatively wrap my arms around him from behind, putting my head on his back.

"Done?" His voice surprises me. So, he is awake.

"Yes," I whisper.

His hand comes on top of mine, and I steel myself for the rejection, thinking he'll push me away.

But he doesn't.

His hand just rests over mine, giving me warmth I'd never genuinely appreciated before.

45

ADRIAN

We arrive back in NYC early the next morning. After we'd communicated our findings to Vlad and Marcel, Vlad had been adamant about checking other names on the list.

"You need repeated testing to prove a hypothesis," he'd said. I hadn't been too happy, mainly because I was sure about it. It seemed pretty clear cut from where I stood.

Those people have all been involved with Jimenez at some point, and then Martin had profited by blackmailing them. The only thing we'd check is whether all the names on the list were guilty of the same crime or different ones.

"But aren't you curious?" Bianca had asked when I'd brought up that point.

"Why would I be? These people may have been involved with Jimenez at some point. But that was over twenty years ago. Even if the information gave us insight into what type of businesses Jimenez ran, it's still in the past. I doubt he kept everything the same."

"You're right and wrong at the same time," Vlad had said. "You're right in that the information would be indeed outdated, but you're wrong in that it would *still* be viable. A leopard doesn't change its spots, no matter how many years pass. And in our world, if you're good at something, you keep doing it. Jimenez has never been caught. He's never even been *sighted* so far. Law enforcement knows about him, but they can't catch him because they don't know what he looks like. If that's not success..."

While I see Vlad's point of view, I don't want to go about gallivanting and crossing each name off the list.

But Bianca has other ideas. And somehow, I can't let her go alone, no matter how deadly she thinks she is.

And so, we've paid a few more house visits, and for the next four days, we manage to speak to another six people, the only living ones on the list.

Again, none are too willing to talk until we proceed with a little persuasion. Only one other man was involved in the sex rings, while the others were merely guilty of investing in Jimenez's illegitimate businesses or backing up illegal arms dealings.

All of which will look just as bad if they're to be released to the press, fact that we've made clear to them. Luckily, even though we're required to use a little more force than we would have liked to, no one ends up dead.

In my book, that's a victory.

And so, here we are again, piecing everything together and making sense of the empire that Jimenez rules.

"His main sources of income appear to come from human trafficking and illegal arms trade. Not very surprising there," Bianca says after she finishes making a diagram with all the people involved.

"And that's where The Block comes into play." Vlad drops this into the conversation casually, and we all turn to look at him.

"What do you mean?"

"Oh, I forgot to add that by *wild*, I meant that it's mostly used to auction people off. It's truly a dissolute dump, considering all that goes in there. But it's also one of the most exclusive auction clubs that Jimenez owns."

I frown at him. "And you just thought to mention this *now*?" What is Vlad playing at?

"Of course, where would be the fun of giving you everything served on a platter?" He tilts his head in a challenging manner, and without even thinking, I take a step forward.

Bianca puts her hand on my arm and shakes her head.

It takes me a second to cool down.

And that's when I remember Vlad's MO—*quid pro quo*. He doesn't do anything for free... Maybe that's why he was so adamant about checking the whole list. And whatever we found must have been quite crucial for him to feel that he owes us a piece of information.

I sneak a glance at Bianca to check her reaction, but she's as expressionless as always. She knows him well enough not to be offended by this. Or at least she's not showing it.

"What else do you know?" I eventually ask, trying to subdue my temper.

Vlad doesn't answer but opens the drawer and throws two bracelets towards Bianca and me. Both of them have a cursive B imprinted in diamonds on a round piece of gold.

"Those are your invitations. It's *that* exclusive. Wear them, and you're in."

"And how did you manage to get these?"

"I have my contacts. But does it really matter?"

Honestly, no. Vlad could keep his secrets since it's clear he has his own agenda and is probably pursuing something too. I don't care as long as he's transparent with us.

Which he isn't exactly.

It makes me wonder how Bianca could be such close friends with him. Just as that thought takes shape, I remind myself that Vlad doesn't feel anything, either. It's easy to forget that when he mimics feelings and facial expressions so well.

He *almost* seems normal.

When I look now at Bianca and him, I see a world of difference. Ever since Bianca hasn't felt the need to pretend anymore, her default expression has been... blank. There's rarely anything reflected on her face. Vlad, on the other hand, seems entirely too ordinary, even in a room with people who know he's anything but.

That makes him dangerous.

"Fine. Bianca, tomorrow we're going to Atlantic City." She gives me a brief nod.

As I turn to leave, Vlad calls out again.

"Don't you want to know what the crossed-out names were?" he asks in an amused tone.

"You managed to read them?" Bianca inquires, getting closer to Vlad.

"Yes. Nothing new, but Marcel and I confirmed that they all died around the time Martin came into possession of the list."

"We were thinking that they probably refused the blackmail and fought back. In return, Martin killed them," Marcel speaks, crossing his arms from the other corner of the room. I'd almost forgotten he was there, but then, Marcel always maintains a distance between himself and other people.

"Basically, the old man was the piece of shit we already knew he was," Bianca scoffs.

"Thought you'd like to know." Vlad smirks.

I announce that I'm leaving, but not before I wave Marcel over for a quick word.

"I don't trust Vlad," I tell him.

I didn't trust him before, but now? I don't care that B's known him for ten years and whatnot. And it's not about me being jealous.

It's really not.

"I don't like how he just inserted himself in this. Sure, he had some info, but... something isn't right," I tell him.

"Don't worry. He's difficult, I'll allow. But he's never screwed over Bianca, and, by extension, he wouldn't mess with you."

"Just how well do you know him?" I ask, suddenly Bianca's words about their friendship ring in my ears, making me doubtful.

"We were sort of neighbors growing up. You could say we were childhood friends." Marcel shrugs as if it's not a big deal.

"I'm still not sure... But if you say it's fine, I'll trust you."

"I promise," Marcel responds solemnly, the corners of his mouth going up slightly.

I give him a nod, and I turn to leave. I saunter towards my car as if waiting for something...

It never comes.

I'm almost pissed at myself when I get inside and start the car. I've been waiting for Bianca to come after me and say something...

anything, really. Ever since we've gotten back from Florida, she's been more distant and emotionless than usual.

Is that even a thing?

She's barely talked to me if it isn't pertinent to the case. And after Atlantic City, it's unlikely we'll be in proximity again.

When I'd found out about her double life, I'd decided it was over. It had been a painful decision to take because I realized that I'd spent years loving someone who didn't even exist.

But I'd done it. When I'd told her to get out of my life, I'd meant it. Who would have imagined that we would be thrown together again? I've gotten a good look at the real Bianca these past few days, and while she isn't the woman I fell in love with, she is... intriguing.

I know about her childhood trauma, and I wonder how much of that shaped who she is now. Because while I do believe she's not normal, I don't believe she has *no* feelings. Her moral compass is clearly screwed, I'm not going to lie.

But sometimes I see something in her eyes, and I almost believe she loves me.

Almost.

Or maybe it's my wishful thinking. How pathetic is that?

I get back to the apartment and get ready for bed. At least I know that Bianca has been sleeping in her own apartment and not at Vlad's. With my growing distrust of him, I don't think I'd be able to stand the thought of her there.

As I try to drift to sleep, I think of what the future holds. Finally getting Jimenez for all his crimes and giving my parents the justice they deserve. As for Bianca... I think the time will come to say goodbye.

***

The following morning, I pick up Bianca in my car, and we head to Atlantic City. When I see her carrying a massive suitcase with her, my eyes widen.

"What's in that?" I ask, pointing towards it.

"Everything we might need. Disguises, because we're not

walking in there for everyone to recognize us, weapons, and other small things that should help us."

"Small things? I'm afraid to even ask."

She gives me a beaming smile, replying, "Don't."

I shake my head but drive. It's a couple of hours until Atlantic City, so we hash out our plan.

"Remember, no killing," I add to make sure we're on the same page. Bianca frowns at me, probably because I'd agreed with her dispatching Wolfe. True, I'd been too disgusted by what he'd done to contemplate an alternative. But we didn't need to draw unnecessary attention to ourselves this time. The *no killing* rule should be enforced.

"Fine," she grumbles. "But if I don't get to kill anyone, then you don't get to act the hero either," Bianca continues.

"Hero? What do you mean?" I sneak a glance at her, and she has a challenging look on her face.

"As if you wouldn't try to save those people from the auction block. Please, I'm well aware of your good Samaritan syndrome."

"I don't know what you're talking about," I add, a little bit baffled that she'd think I'd do anything to jeopardize this when I'd been looking for a chance to come face to face with Jimenez for twenty years.

She turns towards me and narrows her eyes. "Sure. Whatever you say. It's not as if you haven't been helping strays ever since I've known you."

"That's not exactly true."

"You had six cats when I met you. *Six*. All of them from rescues."

"Those are animals..." I mumble. "And I had to give them up because of your allergy."

"Yeah, if it wasn't for my allergy, we would probably have more than a dozen cats by now. Who knows how many dogs too."

"Do you like dogs?" I suddenly ask, realizing I don't actually know the answer to that.

"I don't know..." she says. "Maybe... Some are cute... I don't know." She's fidgeting, and her answer is all over the place.

I just asked her if she liked dogs. I shake my head. Sometimes I don't understand her.

"Anyway, it's not just cats. Let's not forget that homeless man you set up with a job and an apartment. Or the lost child that time during our date. You spent four hours looking for his mother. Four hours of *our date*." One look at her, and it's clear she's still holding a grudge.

"What was I supposed to do? I work in law enforcement. I couldn't have left him alone."

"You could have handed him to someone else."

"I didn't trust anyone else."

"See? That's what you always do. You see someone in need, and you have to go be the hero. It's not as if you didn't do this with me too. Remember that first dinner? When I was being picked on? It's a pattern." She's relentless. I didn't realize she'd been keeping track of this.

Truth is, most of the time, it's not even a conscious effort. I know what it's like to be picked on, to be the underdog, so when I see someone in a similar position, I feel like I have to act. This is also why my career is so rewarding to me. I've managed to help people so they wouldn't have to make tough decisions like I had to.

I know what it's like to sell your soul for survival, and it's something I'll have to always live with. If I can help one person avoid that type of fate, then it hasn't all been for nothing.

"Okay, okay. Maybe I do... tend to help others. But this is far too important. I can't risk anything going wrong," I say eventually.

"Good. Then we are in agreement." She gives a brisk nod, and we continue in silence.

We soon reach Atlantic City, and we head directly to our motel to check in. There's one word that can describe the atmosphere here—gray. Everything is so commonplace, as if the presence of sin has erased all types of color from this place. There are more dilapidated buildings than not, including the hotel we're staying at, and I can't help but wonder why Jimenez would have chosen this place.

The room we manage to get is a double with two twin-sized beds. For all its bareness, this place is packed.

Bianca drags her huge luggage and dumps it on the bed. She opens it and shows me what she's brought.

"You're going as Pink?" I ask when I see her pink wig and the outfit she used to wear at the Palace.

"I felt it would be fitting." She grins, and I purse my lips in response.

Of course, it would be fitting.

"Just for the record." She puts a finger up to get my attention. "I never worked as a prostitute there. I was just waitressing."

"Really?" I ask ironically.

"Yeah, I only served drinks. I *did* do you on the side, but it wasn't in my job description." She seems so proud of herself that I just shake my head.

"Why did you do it, though?" I never got a straight answer from her. Why go to such lengths?

"I wanted you. But you would have never fucked me as Martin's daughter. I had to improvise." She shrugs.

"Was it worth it? Living a double life?"

"Of course," she answers immediately. No remorse. Nothing.

"What else is in there?" I change the topic, not wanting to dwell on her confession.

"These..." She removes a fake beard and a pair of glasses. "As well as these..." Next are some temporary tattoos on a piece of paper and a wig. "are for you."

"You want me to put *that* on?" I motion towards the long-haired wig.

"Yes. Don't worry. I'll make you look like an outlaw." She smirks and motions me to sit on the other bed. I look at her suspiciously but relent. We need to be discreet, so the disguise goes.

"Let's see," she says as she concentrates on applying the fake tattoos all over my neck and arms.

She then focuses on my face and carefully applies a dark fake beard before finally adding on the wig. I'd never realized how much work goes behind these disguises. Just the amount of time Bianca takes to make sure the wig is safely in place is astonishing.

After she's done, I stand and look at the mirror.

I look... strange. My hands go to my new hairline, and I'm impressed by how sturdy the wig placement is. It makes sense why Bianca's never budged as Pink, even when we'd engaged in more physically demanding activities. She'd tied the long hair of the wig in a tail at the back of my neck. The beard changes my face completely. It's not too long, but it still covers my entire jaw. Those two, coupled with the multiple tattoos that now mar my skin, make me appear a completely different person.

"And these." She hands me a pair of glasses with a golden hue, and I put them on. After I turn towards her to gauge her reaction, she gives out a loud whistle.

"I'd fuck you," she says unabashedly, those words meant to be her approval.

I grunt and then watch her as she transforms herself into Pink.

For her, there are a few other challenging aspects. She starts out with a very bold makeup to change her face's physiognomy before adding a pair of green contact lenses and finally the Pink wig.

She strips to her underwear, and I have to swallow hard as I take in her flawlessly toned body.

She takes off her bra, and I mutter a curse under my breath. She's not even trying to be sexy; she's clearly focused on dressing herself up, yet I can't control myself. I shift ever so slightly to alleviate the discomfort in my pants, but I don't look away from her.

She puts on a lacy black bra that hugs her breasts and then adds the trademark fishnets. She then dons a sparkly purple dress that barely covers her ass.

"I always wondered why Doc Martens," I say as she sits to tie her boots.

"You'll see." She winks at me and then goes to rummage through her suitcase again. She pulls up a bunch of weapons and throws them on the bed in front of me. She looks at each of them before settling on two pocket guns and a small knife, which she then sheaths inside her boots. She then adds more ammo in each boot before she looks at me, grinning, "Done!"

She twirls around, and I'm again surprised by her transformation. We both look entirely different.

"Boots are perfect to store weapons; that's why I usually only wear boots."

"No killing, remember?" I have to add to which she snorts.

"We need to be prepared for every eventuality," she counters, and I let her have her way.

Lastly, she puts on a choker and touches the pendant until it emits a tiny red light.

"Is that?"

"A camera. We can research faces later." I nod, glad she'd thought about this.

By the time we finish getting ready, it's already late.

"Don't forget this!" Bianca flings the bracelet in my direction, and I snap it around my wrist before leaving the motel room.

If anyone asks why we're there, we've convened to say we're looking for a third party for our relationship, but hopefully, it won't get to a point where we have to prove we're serious about that.

We take a cab that drops us at the address Vlad had given us. From the outside, it looks like an abandoned factory. Some windows are broken, and the paint is peeling off the walls.

"Here?" I ask, amazed at what I'm seeing.

"Exclusive, remember?"

We make our way to the door, and we knock. A small window opens, and they ask us to show the bracelets.

We do, and we're then welcomed inside. The man at the door gives us both a ticket with a number.

Immediately, as we enter, there are stairs that lead towards the basement.

So, the actual club isn't in the factory...

We come to a stop when an expansive room bathed in red light opens before us. There's security personnel at all access points.

The room itself has a big stage in the middle and tons of space around, along with some seating areas and VIP areas in the form of balconies.

As we take a step inside, the man next to the entrance asks to see our bracelets. When we show them to him again, he takes us to an alcove that leads to a VIP balcony with a direct view of the stage.

We settle in the chairs, and I take in the view from our vantage point. VIP boxes are scattered around the room, all of them being able to zoom in on the main stage. The box itself is made up of a bench that surrounds it and a table in the middle. There are a few pairs of binoculars on the table, probably to zoom in on the auctions. Next to it is some sort of catalog.

I pick that up, and I'm disgusted to see it lists the schedule of the entertainment. My eyes quickly scan for the auction, which starts at twelve, and it goes successively from adult males and females, to virgins, and lastly, to children.

Bianca must have noticed my expression; she snatches the booklet from my hands and quickly skims it.

"Shit," she mutters. She quickly checks her wristwatch and turns to me.

"It's almost ten." So, we need to wait about two more hours for the auction to start. According to Vlad, if something is interesting on offer, Jimenez is very likely to appear. How we'll recognize him, I don't know.

"What's at ten?" I lean into her to look again at the schedule.

"It says Freestyle, whatever this means," she answers.

Just then, the waiter comes, and we order a bottle of champagne so we can blend in.

The room's lights suddenly change to a deep blue, maybe announcing the beginning of whatever that Freestyle is.

"Maybe it's a strip show?" Bianca says, her eyes focused on the stage.

"I guess we'll see."

Someone comes onto the stage, and the music quiets down.

"As always, we have a freestyle event where everyone can participate. For today's spotlight, I'm going to draw the lucky number."

I turn to Bianca and narrow my eyes. She lifts the pieces of paper we'd received and shows them to me.

"Tonight, you will get to see... number 54." Bianca shakes her head, and I almost breathe in relief when it's not our numbers being called. I don't even know what it's for.

We turn our attention to the stage again, and an elderly man climbs onto the stage with a woman who could be his granddaughter.

"Since you've been chosen for tonight's spotlight, you can invite other people from the audience to take part with you," the presenter tells the man.

He seems lost in thought as he scans the crowd and settles on another couple close to the stage—the presenter motions for them to get up on the scene.

"Let's see what this Freestyle is all about," I muse aloud, and Bianca chuckles.

"It sure isn't a rap competition," she says as the people on the stage take off their clothes.

"Okay... definitely not a dance competition either," I add.

The young woman is now naked and on her knees in front of the old man, sucking his cock. The other couple is also newly naked.

The woman is on her back, her head directly under the young woman and licking her, while the man fucks her.

As I look around, I realize that most of the other people on the floor are now engaging in an orgy.

"We should have seen that coming," Bianca adds drily, and I can only nod as I take in the debauchery before my eyes.

Bianca's hand is suddenly on my thigh, and she nods towards the other VIP boxes, where people are in all kinds of positions, doing the same thing.

But what she's pointing at is so disgusting, I nearly gag. One man has a young boy in a collar and leash and orders him around. The boy can't be more than ten. I can't watch as I see him lower himself on his knees in front of the man.

Bianca can't either, and I hear an almost sob coming from her lips. I turn to look at her, and her face is ashen, her eyes wide and practically brimming with tears.

"What the fuck is this?" she whispers. The more I look around, the more people I see engaging in fucked up and unnatural acts.

The waiter comes and brings our champagne. We both try to collect ourselves while he's here. He pours the liquid in two glasses and suddenly gives us a pointed look.

"You're not participating?" My mouth almost drops open as I realize the implication.

We *have* to participate.

Bianca is quick to react, and she gives him a dazzling smile, her hand roaming on my chest.

"We were waiting for the champagne. Everyone has their kinks, right?" She winks at him, taking a sip from the glass and turning to kiss me.

I part my lips, and she transfers some of the champagne in my mouth. We continue kissing, and I think the waiter's convinced because he takes his leave. She leans back and looks at me.

"I don't know how we're going to do this," I admit. Just knowing what's surrounding us... it's almost too much.

"We have to give them something. They're watching." Bianca slightly nods to the floor, where I see the presenter behind the stage with the waiter whispering something in his ear.

"We can pretend, right?" I ask her, trying to convince myself more than anything. I'm sick to my stomach just thinking about what *kids* are doing in this place.

"I think this is a test," she whispers. And I have to agree. You have to be a certain kind of depraved to engage in an orgy that has children around.

Bianca's hand squeezes mine before standing and tugging her dress over her head.

Shit...

S he drops it on the floor and now stands only in her lacy bra and fishnets. She gives me a sad smile before climbing in my lap, one leg on each side.

My hand goes to her back, and I hold her close.

"It's okay," she whispers, her mouth seeking my throat. At the exact same time, I look ahead and see at least a few people focused on our box. I guess there's no way out of this if we want to keep our cover.

"Don't take anything else off," I tell Bianca, as my hand goes up and down her spine in a stroking manner. "I don't want them to see you."

My other hand finds her jaw, tipping it so that my mouth can fit over hers. I brush my mouth over hers once... twice... and she giggles.

"Your fake beard tickles."

"Are you serious?" A smile plays at my lips, and I'm starting to forget my surroundings.

"I think I know what I'd like to try..." she whispers with a mischievous smile on her face, and I know exactly what she's hinting at.

In no time, I switch our roles so that she's now seated on the padded bench, and I'm on the floor on my knees. I spread her legs and kiss from her ankle towards her inner thigh. Her quick intake of breath tells me I'm heading in the right direction.

I sneak a glance up, and I see her head's already fallen back, her mouth half-open. Finding her center, I rip the fishnets, as I always do, shoving her panties to the side. Looking to draw this moment out, I nuzzle my face between her lips, inhaling her scent.

My tongue traces her entire contour before settling on her clit. I suck it into my mouth, nibbling at it with my teeth. Her thighs clench around my head, and I'm spurred forward, licking, and devouring her juices. I insert two fingers inside her, and it takes only one motion for her to come around me. I can hear the echo of her moans feeling the air and drowning everything else out.

I give her a few more licks before she fists my shirt and brings me up for an open-mouthed kiss. Her hands go to my zipper, and she takes my cock out, stroking me from base to tip. I'm so lost in her kiss that it only takes a few pumps for me to come.

"Shit," I mutter, opening my eyes and looking at Bianca's puffy lips and glazed eyes.

"Better than drugs," she whispers and licks her lips.

Just then, the voice of the presenter echoes in the room again.

"I hope everyone's managed to come." He chuckles at his joke before introducing the next entertainment.

The stage is now empty of the previous couples.

"What's next?" I ask Bianca as I slide next to her after putting myself together. She's also put her dress back on and is now looking at the schedule.

"It says Dungeon." She frowns. "Who came up with these names? And is this supposed to be some kinky shit?"

I think we've had enough kinky shit.

Knowing we got each other off while crazy motherfuckers were there engaging in God knows what with children makes me feel shameful and disgusted with myself. I can also see that even Bianca isn't as unmoved as she always wants to appear and might need to put in some effort to maintain a poker face.

The presenter continues with the introduction of the Dungeon.

"Here at The Block, we aim to please every vice. And for our second entertainment of the evening, we have the Dungeon. Once again, please check your numbers as you might very soon get the chance for premium dining. Here and Live!"

As he finishes speaking, a chair is brought up to the middle of the stage.

Two big men bring forward another man, dragging him towards the chair and securing him with metal chains. The man has a collar around his neck that seems to feed electric stimuli into his body if he struggles. After settling the man in the chair, they bring forward an electric grill followed by a table with different utensils.

"Is that?" My eyes widen, and I think I finally get the implication.

"I will once again explain the rules for those who are new. A few numbers will be drawn for the chance to dine on our terrific prisoner. Along with the numbers, you will also receive a body part from which you can eat. The number which is lucky to get the heart will go last and will get the chance to personally carve it out of our lovely prisoner." He waves his hand towards the man in the chair, whose expression is that of pure terror.

The presenter calls out numbers, each one being delegated a

body part from which they can take their pound of flesh. Some get the right leg, some the left, some the hands, and so on. Once they hear their number, they all head to a portion of the stage, awaiting their turn.

Bianca and I are at the edge of our seats, religiously checking our numbers, so we're not chosen.

"And lastly..." He builds the anticipation. "For the heart... Number 103."

Shit.

I look down at my number.

103.

Bianca's eyes snap to mine, and so fast I can barely register, she changes our tickets and stands to head for the stage.

"B!" I yell after her, but she doesn't even look back.

I watch, stupefied, as person after person takes a turn at the man in the chair.

Most of them take little bits of meat, cooking it on the grill and eating it in front of an audience.

By Bianca's turn, the man is still alive but barely.

"And now, for the highlight of this event. Miss..." He motions towards Bianca, and she answers, "Pink."

"Miss Pink is going to have the honor of carving out the heart. The rules are simple, young lady. You must not, at any point, kill him before taking out the heart. Think you can manage?" The presenter is treating this like it's game night, and this is a quest.

"I can manage," Bianca replies in her expressionless manner.

The crowd is going crazy, saying she doesn't have the guts, others asking what a woman's doing up there, and so on.

Bianca doesn't seem bothered as she goes to the table next to the grill and chooses a small knife, testing its sharpness on her own thigh. Once satisfied, she licks the blood off it and turns towards the man in the chair.

Many people are clapping at her display, but they stop when she kneels in front of the man and studies him. He now has holes in most areas of his body, including one on each cheek.

How he's holding on I have no idea... but I'm pretty sure they must have fed him some sort of drugs for him to withstand this type of pain.

Bianca takes the knife and slowly makes a deep incision from his sternum to his belly. She then cuts thoroughly through flesh and muscle to reveal his ribcage. At this point, the crowd is going wild, with the presenter egging them on.

Bianca casually goes back to the table and picks up a drill, which she then uses to cut through his ribs. How she even knows to do this, it's beside me...

I watch in awe and terror as she calmly takes a retractor and widens the gap between the ribs to reveal the man's beating heart. He's still alive... but his shallow breaths indicate that he won't be for much longer.

The presenter quickly checks and announces to the whole crowd that he's still breathing, praising Bianca's technique.

Once the heart is in full sight of everyone, Bianca steps aside and lets them watch for a few seconds. She knows this is all for show, and she's giving them exactly that.

Before going back, she gives me a quick look and mouths, *I'm sorry*. It doesn't hit me for another moment, but she's apologizing for not keeping her promise not to kill anyone.

She leaves all instruments on the table and turns to the man, her right hand going straight for his heart and ripping it from his chest in a bloody shower—everyone gasps at the barbaric display.

The man's eyes, a second ago wide with terror, are now stuck forever like this.

Bianca's standing in the middle of the stage, the heart bleeding from her hand. Her eyes look at me, but it's like she doesn't see me anymore.

When the presenter prompts her, she goes to the table and cuts the heart in half, spreading it on the grill. She tends to it for a while until it's clear it's done. She grabs a knife and a fork and cuts into it, bringing the bite to her lips. Her mouth opens, and she starts chewing and swallows.

To anyone else, she probably looks unconcerned with what she's doing, maybe even enjoying it. But I know better. I see her eye twitch like I've seen it before in extreme situations, and I know.

I know she's doing her best to keep her calm.

Just like I know what a sacrifice she's made *for me*.

When she's done, she leaves the stage amid raging applause from the crowd. She comes back to our box, quietly taking her seat.

"B... are you okay?"

"I'm fine," she says in a small voice. This time, her eyes are no longer blank.

They are bleak.

46

BIANCA

"**Y**ou're not doing that." Adrian paces around the motel room, his face muscles taut.

"It's our best bet. What did we succeed yesterday? I swear not even bleach can remove those images from my eyes, and I've seen *a lot...*" I say, shuddering at the thought of last night's events.

After almost gagging on that man's heart, I've tried to put myself together and not show how much I'd been affected by what I'd done.

There are some things that even *I* consider too much. Adding cannibalism to the list now... I almost want to hurl just thinking about it.

And it *all* had been for nothing.

After the auction had started, we'd watched, observing every single person bidding. But without any additional information, there's just been no way to weed out Jimenez. We might know he's usually at the Block, but if we don't know what he looks like, we're back to zero.

We'd ended up leaving disappointed and maybe with a little more baggage than we'd come in. Which is why I thought of *this* plan.

Remembering Martin's words that Jimenez had wanted me, I decide that what better way to draw Jimenez out than to put myself on the auction block, hoping he'll be the one to buy me. If I go as Bianca Ashby, the odds of him hearing and participating are much higher. And probably our best bet if we ever want to get to Jimenez.

"I know... Fucking hell," Adrian curses aloud.

"I'm not letting you do that. You saw what they do with the people they auction off. They fucking dress them in skimpy clothes, put them on display, and then give them to their new owner in a fucking leash. B..." He shakes his head. "No, I won't have you do that. Absolutely not."

"You do realize we have no other way," I try to explain it to him. "We don't *know* what Jimenez looks like. How are we going to catch him?"

"Then, we won't. I'd rather give that up than know the danger you'd put yourself through. No! And it's final!" He leaves the room and slams the door in his wake. He's probably going to clear his head.

He always does that when he gets too heated. I sink on the bed and sigh. It's the only way, but I can't make him see that.

I also can't have him give up on this. It's been his goal for years on end.

No... I have to do this. Only then will he be able to be happy... with me. I smile to myself. Yes, if I manage to get Jimenez for him, he's finally going to accept that we're meant to be.

Chewing on my inner cheek, I start planning. He'll never approve this, but I'll just do it first and ask for forgiveness later.

I take out my phone, and I dial Vlad. I've been sensing some tension between Adrian and Vlad, and I'd rather he not catch me calling him.

Indeed, Vlad's not always too forthcoming, but even when he intentionally leaves out information, I know he won't send me into the lion's mouth.

"You idiot," I start. "You knew where you sent us, didn't you?"

Vlad chuckles on the other end.

"I'm guessing it didn't go that well?"

"I had to fucking eat a human heart. You call that well?"

"You got the heart? Pfff..." Vlad sighs aloud.

"And here I only got an arm last time. Lucky you." He whistles, and I'm shocked.

He's been there too?

As if knowing my train of thought, he adds, "You didn't think I'd send you somewhere I hadn't already been."

"You've been there?" I ask in disbelief. Why? This is contrary to everything I know about Vlad.

He doesn't answer, but I'm not too concerned right now, since that's not what I want from him.

"You *did* realize when you sent us here that the chances of us actually finding Jimenez are null."

"I know," he says casually, as if it's a game.

"Then why did you?"

"Your husband wanted information. I gave him what he wanted."

"Fuck you!" I say, and he just laughs. Of course.

"Anything else?" he asks in that amused tone of his.

"Yes. I want to auction myself off."

"Woooow. You really went the extra mile."

"How else are we to draw Jimenez out?" I add sarcastically, but Vlad stuns me.

"I knew you'd go for that."

"What do you mean?"

"I mean... in the beginning, I have to admit, I exchanged the info for the club because it was convenient, but after hearing Martin's words, I realized this would be your best chance at catching Jimenez's eye."

"So, you planned this?"

"Planning? No, come on, B, you know me. I'm not a planner; I'm an opportunist. It just happened that the puzzle pieces fell into place on their own."

"Great..." I mutter, but then get to the meat of the problem. "Since you assumed I would auction myself, you must have researched how."

"Now, that *is* planning." He baits me, but I don't reply. "I've talked to someone. I'll text you the info. But I'm curious. Did that husband of yours agree to this?"

"No, he didn't."

"Sneaky... You *do* do sneaky best. I'll tell my guy to expect you this afternoon. He'll take care of everything."

"Thanks," I say and hang up.

Vlad is definitely up to something. Ugh. Too complicated to think about this right now. I have one job: to get Jimenez to buy me, and then... well, I don't know what then, but one step at a time.

All I can think of is Adrian's expression when he gets Jimenez.

"Bianca," he would say, his eyes full with love. "Will you marry me again? Renew our vows." He would get down on one knee and propose to me again. I would jump on him and pepper kisses all over his face, saying, "Yes" a million times.

I shake myself from my fantasy, now more motivated than ever.

———

I drag my suitcase full of weapons on the bed and proceed to arm myself as best as possible, opting for the smallest but deadliest weapons I have. This is one of those instances where a knife is more useful than a gun. I'm also making sure to add some listening devices in case I manage to drop a few backstage.

After I'm satisfied with my arsenal, I leave Adrian a quick note, and I slip out of the room before he returns, stealing his bracelet so he can't go to the club at night.

Vlad's already texted me the instructions. I'm to go to the club's location, ask for a certain Diego, and show him a code I'd received via text.

As before, I have my bracelet on.

When I arrive at the abandoned factory, I knock, showing the bracelet and asking to speak with Diego. The bouncer looks me up and down before giving me a brisk nod and guiding me to a different part of the club that I hadn't seen last night.

A man is waiting for me in front of the door.

"Diego?" After I show him my code, I ask, and he opens the door to take me inside.

The room is bare except for a few items. It's also the size of a closet.

Maybe it is a closet...

"Vlad told me you want to sell yourself," he adds as he goes to a big bag in a corner and removes a white gossamer dress, some face paint, and a neck collar like the one we'd seen on the auctioned people the other night.

All the auctioned girls had worn some type of sheer dress, but the colors had been different. Some had worn white and some red, for obvious reasons.

"It's a dummy." He indicates towards the neck collar. "It will emit light pulses, but it will not actually electrocute you. So, you must pretend if anyone activates your collar."

"I can do that," I add drily. It's what I've been doing my entire life. He proceeds to show me how to manually remove the collar in case I need it off.

He then explains how everything will go down. I'll wear that see-through dress, and I'll have to paint my face and body to seem bruised. He emphasized the fact that I must seem unwilling.

"I've already spread word of your presence, as per Vlad's instructions," he adds before leaving me alone for a few minutes to change.

"Wait. What about weapons?"

"You can't take anything with you. I'm already running a risk with your fake collar. Vlad said you can handle yourself." He shrugs and leaves.

Damn.

And damn Vlad. He could have at least warned me... What's his actual game? I mean, sure, I can handle myself, but I will feel a little bit too empty without any weapons...

I shake my head and take everything off.

I take some blue, yellow, and purplish paint and do my best to emulate some bruises. I add them on my arms, my neck, and on one cheek.

Just to be sure, I add a few smaller ones on my legs. Then I take the red paint and streak some blood in my hair.

After I add the collar and the dress, I look at myself in the tiny mirror Diego had provided, and I'm pleased with what I'm seeing.

He eventually returns and nods at me in approval.

"You'll now be taken with the rest of the captives. Once you're there, you're on your own. I can't foresee who will buy you, or if whatever you have in mind is going to work. Whatever happens, I don't know you. Are we clear?"

"Sure."

He then connects a leash to the collar and tugs me out of the closet and deeper underground. Wow... I would have never believed all of this was under the abandoned factory. It's tunnels upon tunnels.

At some point, we take a right turn, and I see cages on each side of the walls. As we walk, I sneak a glance and see tens of people huddled together in one cell.

Diego suddenly stops at one of the cages, opens the door, and roughly thrusts me inside before locking up and disappearing.

I quickly get my bearings and look around. The cage is less than ninety square feet, and there are about five other girls, all of them wearing the same white dress. I see this as my chance to gain more insight into how Jimenez acquires his captives, so I start with a shy greeting.

"Hi," I say and notice that the girls aren't even looking at me; instead, they're forcing their gazes to the ground.

I frown and try again. "Hi there. Do you speak English?" I add that because maybe they're foreigners. No response. They keep ignoring me as if I hadn't spoken a word.

"Don't expect an answer," the girl closest to me whispers to me.

"Why?" I lower my volume to match hers.

"We aren't allowed to speak to each other. They're afraid of getting punished."

"Punished?"

"The guards... they must not hear us speak," the girl continues, her eyes looking outside the cell for any movement.

"How long have you been here?" I ask her, following her

example and looking anywhere but at her. I also see the cage across ours and notice the women are all wearing red, not white.

"I arrived here yesterday," she whispers, and at that point, two guards appear and aggressively open the cell.

"What did I say about talking?" He smirks down at us, and the girl next to me instinctively huddles closer.

"I was asking about food. I'm hungry." I quickly make up something to take the fire off the poor girl.

"Really?" He looks me up and down in a lascivious way and grabs me by the collar, one hand trailing down my chest. Shit...

"*Cabrón, déjala. Es blanca,*" the other guard says, implying that those wearing white can't be touched.

"*Pues qué quieres que haga? Mírala, me lo pide,*" the idiot continues, and I thrust myself backward, trying to avoid his roving hands.

"*Hija de puta!*" he curses and backhands me.

Hard.

This time, the force of his slap catches me off guard and throws me sprawling on the cage's floor. The other girls all scurry to the back to avoid any punishment.

My hand goes to my cheek, and I feel the sting of it.

I want to spit out what I think must be blood and kill the fucker.

But I can't.

So, I pretend.

I sob my heart out.

From the corner of my eye, I see the guard who hit me unbuckle his belt, and for the first time ever, something akin to fear grows in the pit of my stomach.

"*Cabrón,*" the other guard tells him off again, this time more annoyed.

"You're lucky," the douchebag says, palming and stroking himself in front of me. He stares at me for a few seconds before he locks the door and goes to the cell across. He takes one of the women wearing a red dress and drags her directly in front of our cell's door. He shoves her to her hands and knees and gives me a satisfied gleam.

"See what you caused." He lifts the red dress and throws it over her hips so that her ass is exposed, and without any preliminaries, he impales himself in her.

She gives out a pained wail, before falling silent when he grabs her collar once again, and her body spasms from the electrical stimuli. Her head is hung low as she stares at the ground. His grunts are the only sounds filling the air now.

I tilt my head, watching the scene in front of me with tears on my cheeks. I don't care about the woman being raped in front of me.

Not personally.

Though the act itself goes against everything I believe in, and so, I *will* remember the face of this fucker. And he *will* die by my hand.

The other guard just watches as he pumps in and out of her. He finishes with a moan and clutches at the hips of the woman to stabilize himself.

"*¿No te cansas de mirar?*" He gloats to his friend while zipping himself up. He then shoves the woman in her cage and gives me another heated look before leaving.

Now I realize why Diego gave me a white dress. That *could* have been me.

Hours pass before we're mobilized towards the main area of the club. Hours in which I don't try to talk to the other girls again, not after that display.

We're given food once... if that can be called food. It's no wonder why some of these girls look so skeletal.

I scrunch my nose at the food, but I refuse to eat it. God knows what they could have put in it. The guard who comes to take the empty food containers is the one who was only watching earlier. He sees my untouched food and raises an eyebrow.

I refuse to acknowledge him, or anyone, really. I need to preserve my strength.

After the unsuccessful dinner, the cages are emptied one after another, until our turn comes. Guards come in and hook leashes to our collars, and then they proceed to lead us down the corridor in a prisoner row. They take a few turns before we are led in another room that I'm guessing is connected with the stage.

We're the only ones here, so I'm thinking the other people have already been auctioned off, and our category is next.

The guards bark some commands at us and tell us to stay put. Immediately, one after another, girls are led by their leashes towards this huge double door.

I'm trying my hardest to listen to everything that goes around me while still trying to look as terrified as the girls in front of me are.

At this point, I have no notion of time...

In fact, I'm almost bored waiting for my turn. When the guard comes for me and tugs me towards those same double doors, the only feelings brewing in my chest are anticipation and curiosity.

Behind the double doors is a vast room, the size of a basketball court. It's mostly filled with technical equipment, and a few people are running around checking things. I also see the electric grill in one corner.

The guard leading my leash passes me to last night's host, looking mightily disinterested until he hears my name uttered. Then his eyes widen, and his mouth curls up.

"This should be interesting," he says, and he takes the leash. I again do my best to look scared and intimidated by all the men around me. He pulls me towards the backstage, and without warning, he pushes me onto the stage.

I stumble in the process and fall precisely in the middle of the stage, where the light focuses on me.

"Ladies and gentlemen, the latest addition tonight. The daughter of the notorious Martin Ashby. Someone personally plucked the little bitch from her posh mansion and dropped her on your laps. Let's see how much you're willing to pay for her."

The crowd shout, and with my hair covering most of my face, I cower and furtively look around. I can see the VIP balconies, but the lighting makes it hard to discern who's inside.

At this point, the host's already raising my value, and people are clamoring for it.

It's all going so fast I can't keep track of who's bidding.

"**S**ix million." My head snaps around at the number, and I hear the host again.

"Anyone else?..." No one dares to raise the number further, so he declares, "Sold! To *El jefe*." To the boss? Hope blossoms in my chest.

Two bouncers come and take my leash.

One walks behind me and one in front of me. They take me off the stage, and they lead me back to the tunnels.

Strange...

As I look around, I realize it's an entirely different area from where the cages are located. Even though this is still underground, the pathway is better lit, and instead of cells, there are doors on each side of the hallway. The bouncers stop in front of one of the doors and knock.

"Come in," a voice says from the other side. One of them opens the door and leads me inside. I have to blink twice to let my eyes accommodate to the blinding light.

The room is decorated in a Louis XIV style with a huge double poster bed full with gilded curtains. The furniture is just as ostentatious. At the back of the room, I can make out the figure of a man. His back is to us, in front of what looks to be a decanter.

The men push me inside the room and silently take their leave, closing the door.

I take a few steps inside to get a better look at the man. Something isn't right...

The host clearly said I was sold to the boss, but the man in front of me doesn't look old enough to be Jimenez. In fact, he seems to be around Adrian's age.

Carrying a glass in his hand, he slowly turns around, and his eyes look me up and down.

Yes, definitely not old.

"Who are you?" I ask, doing my best to memorize his face. His most distinctive feature is the scar that bisects his right cheek. He's not an unattractive man, but there's something about him...

There's a glint in his eyes that makes me instantly wary.

"Who am I?" He chuckles and casually goes towards the bed,

where he makes himself comfortable and continues to watch me. I'm tempted to glare at him, but I need to remain in character.

"Yes..." I try to make my voice tremble.

"Your new master," he says simply, and I decide to prod a little further.

"You are... Jimenez?" My voice is small, and I square my shoulders so it looks like I'm intimidated.

"You could say so." He smirks.

"Jimenez is my father." His hand shoots up, and with a movement of his finger, he beckons me to him.

I obey—finally, some reliable information.

"Wh-what do you want with me? Daddy told me he refused your father once," I lie.

"Did he now..." he says in a bored voice.

"Kneel. If you're a good pet, I may tell you."

I kneel in front of him, and he laughs.

"My, aren't you obedient."

His hand moves to my face, and I have to steel myself, so I don't instinctively recoil at his touch.

"I wonder... who put you in white." He shakes his head, amused.

"You see... it wasn't my father who wanted you. You were supposed to be *mine. My* wife." His face suddenly shifts, and he regards me with a disgusted look. "But he gave you to *him* instead."

"Why... why would Daddy promise me to you?" I whisper, hoping he believes my helpless act.

"Because he owed my father. You don't think he became that rich on his own. As if..." He scoffs, "And then he had to go and screw everything up."

Suddenly, he flings the glass to his right, and it breaks into a thousand pieces when it meets the wall. I flinch on purpose, but with both of his hands free now, he grabs onto the flimsy material of my dress and rips it in the middle. Tsk, tsk... too soon.

"Wait," I wail. "Please! I need to understand... Daddy, no..." I shake my head, and tears are already falling down my cheeks. I deserve an Oscar for this performance.

"How did he even get involved with Jimenez?"

Jimenez Jr., aka the man in front of me, looks put off by my questioning, but thankfully, he indulges me.

"You're so naïve..." His hand again goes to the skin around my throat, tracing over the collar and going downwards.

Please, just answer the fucking question, my mind screams.

"You must have thought your daddy was untouchable, didn't you? I heard about the way you mourned him." He talks to me as if I'm a child, which, honestly, isn't all that bad. It means that my act at the funeral worked.

"They met at Princeton. They were in the same fraternity. Your daddy would be nowhere without mine." Okay, I can work with this...

"No... Daddy was a good man." I want to bite my tongue for even voicing that aloud.

He shakes his head at me, pursing his lips.

"Sure he was, sweetheart." He takes hold of my leash and tugs me forward until I fall onto him.

I guess talking time is over. He rolls the leash around his knuckles a couple of times, and I can't help but follow its course, now standing too close to him for my liking. My eyes roam my surroundings, and I quickly scan for anything useful to make my escape.

The glass...

I look to see a few bulky pieces among the myriad of other shards. Might work.

"I'm going to enjoy breaking you." His mouth is next to my ear as he whispers, "I'm going to fuck you into submission... you're never going to see the light of the day again." He studies my face as he says this, his words full of malice and resentment.

One of his hands goes to my ripped dress to fondle my breast, while the other clenches around my throat, above the collar. He flips me on my back onto the bed in one sudden movement, his body looming over me.

Okay, time out.

He takes advantage of my disorientation to settle between my legs.

No, we can't have that.

Calmly, I take his face in my hands, and I smile at him. He seems disturbed by this, especially when I bring his face closer.

"You wish, bastard," I tell him before applying all of my force to roll over with him. I manage to get almost halfway before he pushes against me, and I fall back down, but not before disentangling my legs.

Good.

"Fucking bitch." He tries to hold onto me without success. I curl one fist, and I catch him right under his jaw, stunning him for a moment.

I take advantage of that to push him off me and stand. He clutches his jaw in pain, and I know I can't waste any time.

My hand goes to my collar and rotating a small wheel that Diego had shown me, I quickly pull it off me, using the leash to tie his hands in an eight loop, making sure it's secure enough. His whole body now thrashes under me, and with my elbow, I hit him as hard as possible in the temple. I see his eyes roll to the back of his head and sigh in relief.

He's out.

I pick up two relatively bigger shards of glass and head towards the door. Sure enough, two guards are standing next to it. They react immediately when they see me open the door, but I move faster.

I let them come after me inside the room, thinking it might help disperse the noise.

I take a few steps back and then lunge for the first man, jumping on him and going straight for his throat.

It's one fluid motion later that blood gushes out.

This has given the other guard enough time to take his gun out and aim it at me. With one hand, I quickly turn the limp body around to cushion the bullets, while with the other, I pat him down in search of his gun.

When my fingers finally wrap themselves around the cold steel, I wrench the weapon free of the guard's trousers and aim for my target. The man crumples to the ground, and I take one second to catch my breath before grabbing the other gun as well.

I'm about to finally exit the room when I remember my state of deshabille, so I take one of the fallen guards' jackets and wrap it around my shoulders.

Now the hard part begins.

I go down the corridor, and I try my hardest to remember all the turns we took when we came here from the stage. I think I got it at some point, but I'm met by other guards who yell "Intruder" when they spot me.

I aim both guns and shoot, taking two out and wounding another before taking cover behind one of the bodies.

I check the guns for ammo, disappointed to see one is out. Shit. I abandon that pistol and search for another with the dead man. I don't have time to check again before the shots start.

There's only one way out of this.

I drag the body with me a few meters, sneaking a few glances in the direction of the targets up ahead. Five people. Two in the back and three of them advancing towards me. They keep shooting, so I count to three and ditch the body, running at full speed towards the guards ahead.

I fling myself towards one of the men and stoop down at the same time, distracting him and taking a kill shot from down below.

I immediately shift my focus to the other two while taking advantage of the shelter of the body next to me. Since it's such a straight tunnel, I can't use anything else as a shield, so I have to jump from person to person to avoid a direct hit.

These men, though, aren't great shots, that's for sure. I'm already tired, and my movements are becoming sloppy, so for them to not get even one good shot at me... that's on them.

Not that I'm complaining.

A few more kill shots later, and I find myself next to the entrance of the club. Remembering the way out, I make a dash for it, killing a couple more people on my way, including the bouncer at the door. When I'm finally out of the abandoned factory, I don't stop running.

I hear people being mobilized behind me, but I try not to pay attention too much, focusing instead on my remaining stamina and making the best of it.

Since the factory is in the middle of fucking nowhere, I find myself on the highway, and I know there's little hope of finding a cab around here.

I stop for a second to catch my breath and look around. Nothing... some abandoned buildings on the horizon, but that's it.

Fucking Atlantic City!

I need to keep moving.

My rib cage constricts my airflow from running at full speed without stopping. I can probably last another ten minutes at this pace.

My whole body aches.

And if it's not enough that there's perhaps an army of men on my trail, I also see a car coming at full speed and lowering one of the windows to fit a gun through it.

Shit!

Given my physical condition, I'm not fast enough to duck before the bullet grazes the skin of my left shoulder.

"Mother fucker!" I curse aloud through labored breaths. "I can do this!" I tell myself, even though I start a mental countdown until my body will shut down.

I aim one gun towards the car with my remaining strength and shoot at the one tire and then a second. The car makes a screeching noise as the driver tries to maneuver it, and I know I've bought myself *some* time.

With one last deep breath, I take off again.

I don't even manage to cover a few meters when the sound of another car draws my attention. The vehicle in question is driving on the opposite lane, and it's getting closer and closer to me.

I chuckle in relief and run full force towards it.

Adrian opens the passenger door just long enough for me to get in. He then reverses the car and drives at full speed, leaving a storm of bullets in our wake.

I'm still breathing hard from the previous exertion, and I'm trying to calm my body down. My wound is also bleeding, as I feel the liquid trickling down my arm under the jacket.

After a few dummy turns, Adrian parks the car at a gas station. He stops the car and looks straight ahead with a blank expression on his face.

What's wrong?

I frown at this, not understanding his behavior.

"I'm fine," I add to break the silence. He doesn't answer, so I continue, "Really. You should have seen how many I took out." I give him a smile, hoping he'd say something...

"You fool..." He finally spits out the words and grabs me from across the seat in a bear hug. "You fucking fool... how could you even think to do this?" His arms are around my torso, and he's squishing me. Not that I'm not enjoying it, but it's pressing a little on my wound, making me visibly wince.

"Ah," I mutter unconsciously as pain shoots through my arm.

"Shit. Are you okay? Where are you hurt?" He pats me down, looking for any sign of injury. His face is fraught with worry, and I can't help but smile.

He *still* cares.

I let out a dreamy sigh, which he immediately interprets as a pained sigh, and tugs at the jacket.

I help him take it off, and the moment he sees my torn bodice, he stops, his expression frozen.

"Tell me nothing happened," he pleads in an anguished tone. "Please tell me nothing happened to you." He tugs my head under his chin, holding me to his chest.

"Nothing happened. I promise," I whisper.

"You're sure?" He flattens his hands on both sides of my hair, looking at me with moisture in his eyes. "Don't ever you do that again. Ever... You have no idea what hell you put me through, B. Please... Never again."

There's just so much emotion in his voice that I can't help but promise him just that.

"Yes, never again," I mumble, enjoying the warmth of his body. The comfort of safety lulls me to sleep, and I can't help but succumb. "Promise..."

47

ADRIAN

Bianca's crazy if she thinks I'll allow her to put herself in danger to get *some* information. There's not even a guarantee that Jimenez would be the one to buy her. Just thinking about her proposition makes my blood boil. After seeing that there was no reasoning with her, I decide to leave and clear my head. Otherwise, I may have exploded.

Funny how I've always prided myself on being too level-headed, but this new Bianca has a unique ability to make me lose my calm. I don't think we've ever had an argument in all our marriage, mainly because Bianca has never expressed a divergent opinion.

Now that I think about it, I realize how everything we've done has been me suggesting it and her going along. She's never challenged me about anything. And it's all because she was trying to please me.

I give a bitter laugh at the notion.

It feels like I've been in a relationship with a robot, not a person.

At the same time, I have to admit to myself that the real Bianca is something else entirely.

She's unapologetically raw and without polish. She's smart, capable, and a little bit too impulsive.

And I find myself liking it... liking *her*.

Not to mention, our chemistry has never been more potent. In bed, we're the perfect match. Outside of it... I haven't yet decided.

At this point, I've been roaming for what feels like forever. A quick glance at my watch, and I realize I've lost over two hours just going around in circles. Hoping that Bianca's also had enough time to accept the foolishness of her plan, I head back to the motel.

"Bianca?" I ask as I open the door and enter the room. I frown when she's nowhere in sight. Her entire luggage is haphazardly thrown on the bed.

"B?" I creak the bathroom door, but she's not there either. Where could she have gone?

I put all her shit back in the suitcase when I notice a note on the night table. I pick it up.

I know you won't like this, but I'm going back to the Block.
I won't be long.
Sorry in advance.
XoXo,
Bianca

I crumple the paper in my hand and grind my teeth. Sorry in advance? How can she even write that?

"Why... Why would you fucking do this?" I say to myself, squeezing my eyes shut to calm the rage inside me.

"Fuck!" My fist flies out and connects with the wall, leaving a small crater behind that fractures into smaller fissures all around.

I can't even feel the pain radiating from my knuckles. It takes me a while to calm myself, after which I register that she's not been gone for that long. All I need is to go to the club and get her.

I search frantically for the bracelet, only to realize she must have taken it with her, purposefully keeping me away from the club.

"Bianca..." I mutter, sliding on the floor, my hands massaging my temples.

How could she do this to me? *How?* I keep asking myself. She knows how much I'd protested against her going, and yet she openly did it.

She doesn't care, a small voice inside my head tells me.

It's something I've noticed with her. If she gets fixated on something, she doesn't care how or who she hurts in the process; she just goes ahead with it.

I pray so hard I'm not too late when I reach the club, and even though I don't have a bracelet anymore, I try to get inside.

"Bracelet?" the bouncer demands when he opens the small window in the door. Of course, I wouldn't be welcomed in without the bracelet. As much as I try to bullshit, the only response I get is the window being shut in my face.

And when I prowl around for other hidden entrances, I find myself face to face with a group of guards who demand I leave the premises. Well, not as much as demand, as they push a gun in my face and tell me I have five minutes to disappear.

Out of viable options, I do the only thing I can think of... I very reluctantly call Vlad. Since he was the one to give us the entrance bracelets, maybe he knows what I can do to find Bianca.

"I expected you to call earlier," Vlad says the minute the call gets through.

"You knew about this?"

"You're slow, Hastings."

"You're telling me you knew what she was up to, and you fucking let it happen?" I'm getting too heated. What kind of sick friendship is this?

"I let it happen?" Vlad scoffs at me. "I don't think you realize that there's no letting anything happen with Bianca. She's always going to do things her own way. I merely accommodated her so it would be safer."

Even I have to admit that Vlad is right in one respect. No one can stop Bianca from doing something she wants.

"How?"

Vlad sighs and informs me of his arrangement with one of the guards at the Block, assuring me that until the auction, Bianca would be taken care of.

"And after? What if it doesn't work? Anyone can buy her. Don't tell me you haven't thought about that."

"The odds are in her favor," Vlad answers simply.

"The odds? What's this, a lottery? We're talking about the safety of *my wife* here. *Your friend.*"

"So, now she's your wife again? Interesting."

"Vlad!"

"Let me put this differently. Given all the known variables, the probability that Bianca's going to be sold to Jimenez is higher than her being sold to a random person. I don't expect you to understand."

"You know what? I'm sick of your half-truths and omitted information. I don't know what you're after, but from now on, leave Bianca and me out of it."

"If that's what you want..." He chuckles. "Don't worry about Bianca. She can take care of herself."

He hangs up, and I hurl the phone into the nearest wall, watching it splinter.

I go back to where I parked the car and resolve to wait around until I know the auction is over, then hope that Bianca can get out of whatever situation she's in.

Maybe I can even intercept her while she's being moved by her buyer?

Too many thoughts go through my head at the same time. The precariousness of the situation makes me entirely too anxious.

I drive around, at some point, stopping to get some food and water. She might be thirsty or hungry or both... I also get a few energy drinks for myself, already foreseeing a late night. A few miles later, it again dawns on me that she might be injured or sick. I find the closest Walgreens and buy everything I can possibly think of.

The cashier gives me weird looks as I keep on piling things at the checkout, including bandages, saline water, superglue, pain killers, some paracetamol, and some ointments. I'm basically buying one of each.

After I pay the bill, I head out with two full bags, loading them in the car's backseat for easy access. I look at my watch and see it's just a little bit after one a.m.

Remembering the schedule from the night before, I loiter around the abandoned factory again, parking somewhere close but out of sight and driving around every half hour.

I sip my energy drink, checking the time almost every five minutes. It's well into the night that I hear gunshots coming from the direction of the factory.

I immediately start the car and drive in towards the noise. As I get closer, I see another car opening fire at someone running on the other side of the highway before having its tires shot down. I don't know how, but I know for sure that it's Bianca they're shooting at.

Without even thinking, I reverse my car and go on to the opposite lane. The closer I get to the moving figure, the more horrified I am by her condition. She's wearing a black jacket over a white dress that almost reaches the floor. She's virtually limping as she trudges her way forward. She recognizes my car as she stops and changes direction, coming straight at me.

I stop by the road and open the passenger door. She jumps in, and I drive at full speed, hearing more and more bullets aimed at us.

I don't know how I manage to avoid all the shots, but somehow, I do. When I'm out of range, I keep driving around to make sure no one follows us. I exit the highway and do a few rounds within a neighborhood before parking at a gas station.

As I stop the car, I'm breathing hard. The shock of what just happened still hasn't worn off as I raise my hands and look at my trembling fingers.

I can't even bear to spare a glance to Bianca, knowing that once I see the state she's in, my heart will break. We sit in silence for a while, and I'm getting progressively more concerned that she's not saying anything. I'm even afraid to ask her if she's all right.

"I'm fine," she finally utters the words I'm dying to hear. I close my eyes and take a big breath.

She continues, "Really. You should have seen how many I took out." What? Is that what she's concerned with now? Does she think I care how many people she killed?

"You fool..." I mutter, and not being able to help myself any longer, I grab onto her arms and drag her towards me, hugging her close, more for my benefit than hers.

"You fucking fool... how could you even think to do this?" Pressure builds between my eyes, and I hold onto her even tighter.

"Ah," she whimpers, and I'm jolted back to reality. Is she hurt? What's wrong?

"Shit. Are you okay? Where are you hurt?" When she's not replying to my question, I look for myself, surveying her clearly swollen cheek and internally wincing.

I continue to probe at her, almost wrenching the jacket off her shoulders in my attempt to look for further injuries.

She stops my hands and removes the jacket herself. But when I see that her dress is torn in the middle, her breasts hanging out, her entire upper body bruised, I lose it.

"Tell me nothing happened," I beseech her, already feeling myself spiraling into the what-ifs. "Please tell me nothing happened to you." I don't know what to do anymore. I feel so helpless, seeing her in this state and knowing I did nothing to stop her. I hold her close to me, and I rock back and forth with her.

"Nothing happened. I promise," she whispers, but I don't believe it.

"You're sure?" I cradle her head between my hands and look her in the eyes, praying she's not lying to me. "Don't ever do that again. Ever... You have no idea what hell you put me through, B. Please... Never again." I implore her at this point, but I don't care. The thought of losing her... I can't even contemplate that.

"Yes, never again," she assures me, but I don't know if I believe her. "Promise..." She trails off, and I feel her drop, limp in my arms.

"B?" I ask tentatively, and when she doesn't answer, I shake her. "Bianca?"

"... stop... tired... sleep," she mumbles incoherently, and I let out a deep sigh. She's fine.

I then notice the blood on her arm and the gaping wound right below her shoulder.

Shit.

I carefully place her in her seat, buckling her seatbelt, and then I drive back to our motel. It's not entirely easy taking her inside, especially with all the blood. I try to cover her as best as I can with the jacket she's wearing, and I proceed to carry her inside.

When I reach our room, I'm overwhelmed with a sense of pure relief. I put her on the bed and make another trip to the car to take the shopping bags, feeling extremely satisfied with myself for having the foresight to plan ahead.

I undress Bianca, and with a wet cloth, I clean her body, feeling a little bit more comforted when I see the paint coming off her skin.

So, this is what Vlad meant when he told me about her preparation. When I've washed her from head to toe, only a couple of real bruises are left. I apply some pain-relieving ointment to those areas, and then I focus on the wound on her shoulders.

The wound is pretty deep. I bathe it in saline water, and then I apply superglue to hold it together until we can get a doctor to look at it. I pinch the skin so that the glue takes and then hold it.

Bianca winces once or twice in her sleep. Once I'm satisfied with the glue, I wrap her arm up with a clean bandage.

Sitting on the floor, I unscrew a bottle of water and take a few gulps.

I keep staring at Bianca's sleeping form and debate how to move forward.

She arouses so many emotions in me that I can't think straight... Not when she's risking her life and putting herself in harm's way. Those hours spent in my car, following the movements of the watch's hands, were the most terrifying of my life. The worry and the countless what ifs... I don't think I ever want to go through that again.

I also realize that for all the heartache she's caused me, I can't have her out of my sight. I'd surely go crazy wondering if she's taking other unnecessary risks. And then there was the moment in the car when I'd seen her so worn out but still smiling at me.

That's when I knew I could never let her go...

I comb my fingers through my hair and let out a frustrated groan.

I'm an idiot. I know I am.

After all she's done to me, I'm still the same besotted fool. And I can't imagine my life without her...

I own up to it. I fully admit it may not be the sanest decision, but it's the best one for me.

I just love her... I love her with her obsessive tendencies and her stubborn streak. I love her with her devotion and selflessness because I don't believe for a moment that she doesn't *feel* love for me. Not when she just put her life on the line to help fulfill my wish.

Who does that if not someone who loves deeply?

I watch over her for a few more hours, and when I see signs she's about to rouse, I take out some of the food I'd purchased before and make her something to eat.

"Adrian?" Her voice croaks as she slowly opens her eyes to look at me. I set the food on the night table next to her bed, and I crouch down next to her.

"How are you feeling?"

"Good... I think. Water?" I hand a bottle of water to her, helping her sit up so she doesn't choke on it.

"Thanks," she mumbles and proceeds to empty the entire bottle.

"Here. Eat this, and we'll talk." I give her a sandwich and watch as she zooms in on the food and dives in with a hearty appetite.

"Easy." I stroke her hair and give her a lazy smile, which she briefly returns before going back for more food.

"You... have no idea... how hungry... I was," she says between mouthfuls of food.

She quickly finishes everything I'd gotten her, and I'm happy to see she's regained some color in her cheeks.

"You did this?" She points towards her bandaged arm, and I nod.

"Those bastards... I was too tired at that point." She tries to excuse her injury as if that's the main issue at hand.

"B... I told you I didn't want you to go." I sit on the adjacent bed, ready to pour my heart out to her.

"I know." She lowers her eyes and actually looks ashamed. As if. "But I couldn't pass this up. I know how much this means to you..."

"And you mean more to me." Her expression freezes at my words as if she can't quite believe it.

"Are..." She quickly shakes her head. "Do you mean it?" Those words are imbued with so much hopefulness, my heart is about to burst.

I take her uninjured hand and squeeze.

"I do," I confirm.

"Still... you told me I disgusted you." Her voice is small as she repeats the words I'd flung at her in anger.

"I was angry... bitter. You lied to me about so many things..."

"How can you? How can you still care about me?" She shakes her head again in disbelief.

"I don't just care about you, B... I love you," I confess, and her eyes widen for a second before tears runs down her cheeks.

"B?" I ask, not knowing what's happening. She gives my hand a tug before lifting it and holding it to her cheek.

"I know you'll probably never be able to believe me, but I do love you. You're the only thing I've ever cared about in this life. I swear to you. I know what I did hurt you... I understand that, and I'm not looking for excuses where there are none. I knew fully well what I was doing."

"B..." I start, but she silences me.

"No, let me. I don't regret what I did... It's true, and it's messed up. Fuck, it's probably borderline insane. But I do regret one thing... and that is that I caused you pain. When you hurt, I hurt. I may not be normal, but *you* are my one link to normal." She brings my hand to her lips for the ghost of a kiss. "You are my tether... and for you, I can try to be better."

I give her a warm smile. Yes, it's fucked up. *We* are fucked up.

But I find that I don't care... Not anymore. All my life, I've searched for some semblance of ordinary... I want to live the typical American life, have a house, a wife, children, and die of old age, retired somewhere in Montana.

No killing, no bloodshed, no mayhem.

No corruption, no mob, and no assassins.

I want a life as far away from crime as possible because that's all I've ever known for a while. But the more I try to avoid it, the more drawn I become to it, without even realizing it. I should have known that chasing after Jimenez would put me on a path of no return.

But as I look into Bianca's eyes, I realize I *don't* want to return to ordinary.

"*We* can try," I finally say. Because she's not the only one who will be navigating this unknown world. And somehow, we'll manage it together.

"I want to take this slow," she adds, almost bashfully.

"What do you mean?"

"I want us to take it from zero... to get to know each other as our real selves. I want to know who Adrian Barnett is, and I want you to find out who the real Bianca Ashby is. No more secrets."

"I'd like that." I cup her jaw and go for a quick peck. "I'll even take you on a date when we get back." I smile at her, and she chuckles.

"Can I choose what type of date?"

"Sure."

"Good." She gives me another quick kiss before she frowns, remembering something.

"Wait. We can't go back just yet."

"Why?"

She proceeds to tell me in detail how her stint on the auction block went, including her meeting with Jimenez's son, and how Martin and Jimenez knew each other from being in the same fraternity at Princeton.

"I've never heard of him having a son," I muse before adding, "Too bad, we can't really use any of that information."

"Not true, which is also why we aren't heading directly back to

New York. We need to go to Princeton and get our hands on one of their old photo albums. When I went through Martin's stuff, there wasn't anything related to his days at Princeton, so I'm guessing the more important things were in his safe, which you know how that ended up. Anyway, if we can find a photobook from his time there, maybe we can also find Jimenez. That was the entire purpose of this mission. Putting a face to the name."

When she explains it like this, I can't help but see the logic of it.

"Fine. Let's rest tonight and head there tomorrow." Bianca still needs some rest to heal.

"No, we need to leave now. I don't think they're going to drop the search for me, especially when it was *el jefe* who I offended." She suddenly springs out of bed and puts on clothes. "Shit," she mutters. "I should have thought of this before... We need to move. Like now!" At her urgency, I pack the rest of our stuff. When we're done, we hurry towards the car, and I leave a big tip at the check-in desk for the almost hole I left in their wall. I guess I don't have the time for apologies.

I get in behind the wheel, and Bianca joins me in the passenger seat.

"Do you know which fraternity?" I ask as we leave the motel and head onto the highway.

"Yes. Sigma something... We'll have to ask around. I remember he used to go to some of the alumni events when I was younger."

"Wait... Didn't Senator Wolfe also go to Princeton?" I'm suddenly struck by that thought, and Bianca's look tells me it just occurred to her as well.

"He did... Shit." She quickly takes out her phone, and I see her about to ring Vlad. My right hand shoots out and stops her before calling.

"Call Marcel," I tell her. "I don't trust Vlad." I expect her to put up a fight about this, as she's always defending Vlad, but she surprises me when she actually dials Marcel, putting him on speaker.

"Marcel, can you please look at the list and tell us where they went to school?"

"What?" he mumbles, clearly barely out of bed.

"We need to know what universities the people on the list went to," Bianca reiterates, and Marcel tells us to wait.

"Do you really think...?" Bianca looks at me and asks.

Honestly, at this point, anything is possible.

"Yeah... I pulled up the file," a sleepy Marcel says. "Let's see... Princeton... Princeton... Shit." A pause. "All went to Princeton."

Both me and Bianca share a look.

"Did they all happen to be in the same fraternity too?"

"Yes. Sigma Theta Epsilon."

"Thanks. We'll call you back."

"I can't believe they missed this the first time," Bianca adds.

"They focused only on jobs and finances. God... there's a real possibility that's where it all started."

It doesn't take us too long to reach Princeton, and luckily, it's pretty early in the day, so when we knock at the fraternity house, we get a response.

"Yeah?" a guy wearing only a pair of boxer shorts answers.

Bianca gives me a wink, and I know she wants me to let her handle this.

"Hi. I'm sorry for coming in so early. My father was an alumnus, and he recently died. I was wondering if you have some old photo albums I could take a look at?" Her voice is almost too sugary sweet, and it seems to wake the guy up as he looks her up and down.

I try to keep my hands to myself. It wouldn't do to go around punching college students...

"Yeah, sure... We got some upstairs. Come in."

"Yo, Mark, what's up." Another guy comes up towards us, but this one is wearing more clothes.

"They want to see some of our photo albums. Her dad was an alumnus," Mark says in a bored tone. The new guy turns towards us and regards us suspiciously.

"Who was your father?"

"Martin Ashby," Bianca replies, and I can see the guys recognize the name.

"No shit... wow. He was a legend."

"Was he?" Bianca adds, a little bit too ironically. But the guys don't seem to notice.

"Yeah, hell... I'm sorry for your loss. I heard about his death."

Bianca tells them to look for class of '82, and they show us to the second floor where there is a library of sorts. The walls are filled with recent alumni pictures.

Mark goes to one wall and pulls out an album with 1982 on its spine.

"Here." He hands it to Bianca.

"Does this have underclassmen or upperclassmen too?"

"It should have the full brothers from that year. Are you looking for someone else?"

"Just another relative. He told me he was in the same fraternity as my father."

"Here." Mark pulls a few more albums spanning the early 80s. "You might find him in here."

They talk about something else and leave us alone, telling us to put them back when we're done.

We divide the albums between the two of us and comb through them.

"Maybe he used another name?" I suggest, but Bianca doesn't even hear me. She's too focused on the 80s album.

"Found it!" Bianca jumps up, a broad smile on her lips. She immediately comes over to me and points to a picture.

"Here. Arturo Jimenez, Class of '81," she says enthusiastically.

When I look at the picture, I'm almost shocked by what I see. He's younger... much younger, but there's no mistaking.

"I know him..." I whisper, not quite believing the picture in front of me.

"What do you mean?"

"I mean, I fucking know this man..." And the most telling feature is a big mole on his right upper lip.

"That's Andrew Gallagher."

Bianca stands and looks at me. "Andrew Gallagher?"

"Or not really..." I add drily. "He's the man I knew under the name of Andrew Gallagher. The man I used to fight for... I swear it's him. But... nothing makes sense anymore."

I feel lost. He was in front of my eyes for so many years... I could have easily crushed him...

"You mean to tell me that both Jimenez and his right-hand man were involved in the Boston fight ring... and they recruited you."

"Yes... but why?"

"That's probably the most important question. They must have known who you were."

"Oh, they definitely knew." I give a bitter laugh.

But it doesn't matter now.

I have a face for Jimenez.

And it will soon be over.

4 8

BIANCA

e haven't been home an hour when Adrian closes himself in his office to drink.

I've stopped by every now and then to bring him some food and water, but even I can see he's in a world of his own, dealing with the information he's learned.

Vlad's doctor, Sasha, has been over to check my wound and stitch it up properly, and even then, Adrian hasn't emerged from the office.

I don't even know what to do with myself in this instance. I've never comforted someone...

How does one do that? And what if he doesn't want me to?

I'm not capable of complicated feelings, and as such, I don't understand them in other people either.

I wish I had someone to call and ask what to do in this situation, but my only friend happens to be as emotionally stunted as me.

I sigh as I remove a tray from the oven. I'd tried to bake a cake. Safe to say that didn't work.

It's half-burnt... but maybe I can cut the edges off? I'd been scouring the internet for things to do for someone sad, and one article suggested baking a cake. And so, I'd resolved to bake a cake. I'd quickly gone to the shop and picked up some ingredients and then proceeded to try.

See, I'm not a bad cook... for food. Cakes are a different issue altogether. It took me three tries to get the batter right, and now I have to deal with the overly burnt bits.

I swear, nowhere did it mention you had to be a professional to do this.

Not one to despair in times of need, I put my apron on once again and start on the frosting. This should be easier as it doesn't involve any funny oven business.

I end up concocting some type of frosting that is a bit overly sweet but passable. I spread it on the non-burnt parts of the cake after cutting them in small shapes.

Satisfied with my work, or as confident as I can be, I decorate a plate. I fill a glass with lemonade, add some ibuprofen for good measure, and then go to the office.

"Adrian?" I ask as I kick the door open with my uninjured shoulder, careful of the tray in my hands. "I made you a cake." I smile, proud of myself.

Adrian's plopped face down on the desk, the half-empty bottle next to him.

I frown for a second, then sigh and put the tray somewhere else before going up to him.

"Adrian?" I gently tap his shoulder, but he doesn't reply, merely giving me a half-moan.

"Okay, mister, you're going to bed." I try my hardest to lift him, but he's double my weight and then some more, so it's not that easy. "A little help would be appreciated," I mumble, but he doesn't seem to rouse.

With great hardship, I manage to get him on the bed or throw him on the bed when I'm within distance. Taking his shoes off, I try to make him more comfortable.

"B?" he groans, shifting around in bed.

"You're wasted," I say, matter of fact.

"I fought for him... I made him *money*," he mutters, clearly referring to Jimenez and his days in the ring.

While I don't know a whole lot about his life as Adrian Barnett, Vlad has implied that he was a successful fighter, often having weekly gigs with barely a respite between. So, Jimenez or

Andrew or whoever he is undoubtedly aimed to squeeze him dry.

Or was that his attempt at killing him, but it just backfired when Adrian wouldn't lose?

I stroke his forehead lightly and place a kiss on his brow. Now more than ever, I'm set on making sure Jimenez won't live for much longer. I know that Adrian wants to get him to pay for his crimes in a court of law.

But how can I allow a man who's made *my husband* suffer like this live?

I can't.

The following day, I try to get Adrian out of bed, but he shuns all of my attempts. He's even taken to ignoring me, sulking all day under the sheets.

When the same behavior, coupled with excessive drinking, continues the next day, I'm out of options.

If cake can't solve this, I don't know what will.

And he doesn't even get to eat my cake!

So, I take to browsing the internet for solutions to my problems once more.

The more I read, the more I know what I need to do. I smile mischievously at the screen. This should get Adrian out of bed with a bang.

Or a meow.

I'm lucky enough that in this country, money can solve everything. It's entirely too simple to make an appointment the next day with a doctor.

"You want me to give you something for your allergies, is that correct?" The doctor, a bald man in his sixties, studies me with narrow eyes. What's so hard about this request?

"Yes," I reply.

"Now?"

"Yes."

"You'll need to get tested to see what specifically causes your allergies..." I already tune out. I look at my watch, and it's almost noon. I need to get everything done before they close all the shelters.

"Look. I don't have the time. I already told you. I'm allergic to cats. Now give me the pills."

"Mrs. Hastings... it doesn't work like that," he continues in that admonishing voice, but I cut him off.

"Sorry, Doctor..." I've forgotten his name. "But I really need to be able to stand next to a cat and not sneeze my lungs out. I would really appreciate it if you'd prescribe me something *now*."

"Mrs...." Oh, for Hell's sake. I pull out a stack of one hundred bills from my bag, which I promptly slap on his desk.

"Yes, I can certainly prescribe some cetirizine. You'll find that it won't make you drowsy and won't interact with your day-to-day activities." He immediately gets to work.

It's funny how quickly he's changed his tune when money gets involved. Now, I'm not actively promoting bribing doctors, especially as a newly recovered addict.

But this is, in fact, an emergency.

I need to pull through with my plan to make sure Adrian quits moping around. Also, because I want him to take me on that promised date... but first, I have to get him out of bed.

As soon as I have my prescription, I drive to the nearest pharmacy, also keeping track of all the shelters around. When I was researching, I had compiled a list of all of them in Manhattan.

I can't just get *any* cat. I need a super cat.

Armed with an entire month supply of cetirizine, I head to the first shelter. I must have really tuned out the doctor because I'm entirely too surprised to see the allergy medicine is syrup and not pills. Well... if it works, it doesn't make a difference.

The clerk at the first shelter shows me around their feline selection, and I can't say I'm impressed. They aren't either if I go by the way they scoff their cat snouts at me.

My nose is a little itchy, but not as bad as before, and it gets progressively better as I go from shelter to shelter.

When I'm at the fourth shelter, I'm greeted by an overly friendly girl, who sings all types of praises to the animals they house. She takes me to their cat area and shows me a couple of adorable kittens.

I pet one of them when a flash of pink snatches my attention. I turn my head to get a better look, and the ugliest cat I've ever seen in my life greets me.

Hairless, her whole body is pale and wrinkly, her big eyes bulging from her bald head.

I look at her. She looks at me. We engage in a battle of spirits, and she doesn't back down. I also notice that she's in a cage of its own, unlike the other cute ones.

"What about that one?" I ask, and I go near the cage.

The girl shakes her head, "I... I probably shouldn't say this because we want all of them to end up in good homes..." Her bottom lip trembles as she continues, "She's been returned five times so far. She's too...aggressive," she says the last word in a hushed tone, and I think the cat senses because it looks at her and bares its teeth.

"See?" she says and takes a few steps back.

"Can I open the cage?"

"Fine. But I'm over there." She points to the other corner of the room where the cuties are, and I shrug. Whatever.

I take the key from her and open the cage. The moment the door swings open, the cat charges me, claws out.

As I crouch to get to her, I lose my balance and end up falling on my back. The cat is now on my chest, one clawed paw up threateningly. I arch my eyebrow at her, and she tilts her head as if she understands me. We stare at each other for a while longer until she decides to finally scratch the hell out of my neck.

That. Hurt.

My hands shoot out to grab the little troublemaker, and I lift her up while she struggles to do more damage.

"Stop!" I command. Once again, she raises her eyes and looks at me. Her pupils narrow into a slit and after an almost nod, she stops fighting. My lips curl up in response.

"I'm taking her," I yell at the girl. She frowns at my voice and tells me to deal with her colleague at the entrance desk.

After sorting all the paperwork, I get to take Miss Troublemaker home. While she's not as aggressive with me, I get why the girl is so afraid.

The moment I let her out of my hands, she goes crazy on the

clerk drawing up the adoption papers. She immediately jump on him and latches onto his skin, leaving clean marks behind.

After we leave the store, I make sure to pet her.

"Proud of you." As I stare into her eyes, a name comes to me. "From now on, you are Maleficent." Or when I'm lazy, Mally.

I give her a wink that she probably doesn't understand, but I'm sure we have our own communication channel.

I'm somehow reluctant to put Mally in the carrier I'd purchased for her, so I settle her on my shoulder after I strap myself in.

"Be a good girl and don't injure me during traffic," I tell her, and she gives my cheek a slow lick.

Yes. She understands.

I start the car to go back home. A few times, I check my mirror and note the same car keeping a safe distance behind. Odd...

I take some random turns to see whether it follows, but I lose track of it after a while. Maybe it's my paranoid mind at work. I shake my head and head home. All the way, Mally keeps purring in my ear, and I can't help but smile.

"**A**drian?" I yell his name when I'm back at the penthouse. Mally is still perched on my shoulder and seems to have really sunk her claws into my clothes, which prevent her from falling anytime I move rather suddenly.

He doesn't answer. Odd.

But when I go towards the kitchen, a disheveled, clearly hungover Adrian greets me, furtively eating some toast.

"Really?" I fold my hands in front of me and ask. Adrian gives me a sheepish smile, and I add, "Well, at least you're out of bed."

"What's that?" He points towards Mally, his mouth still full of toast.

"This is our new friend." I raise my hand to stroke Mally's head, and she gives a tiny yap. Adrian is suddenly alert but looks at me suspiciously.

"Is that a toy?"

"What? No!" I try to get Mally off me, but she doesn't seem to want to detach herself.

"Help?" I ask Adrian, and he joins in the effort to free Mally. Or free me from Mally.

By the time Mally is off my shoulders, she's already in full tantrum mode, and she's growling at Adrian something fierce.

"Mally!" I command her attention. I finally get Adrian a cat, and she hates him? No... we can't have that. "Behave!" I tell her, and she stares at me.

I return the stare, and I think some time passes before Adrian clears his throat.

"Mally?" he asks, lifting the cat slightly to look at her. She's now stopped struggling and regards Adrian with curiosity rather than animosity.

"Maleficent. She's our new cat. She's great!" I feel the need to add that, so he doesn't think I got the most unfriendly cat on purpose.

No, Mally and I have an understanding, and Adrian just needs to join in.

"Is that so?" he asks skeptically. "What about your allergy?"

"I got meds!" I exclaim and show him my syrup. "But she's bald, so... I don't know if she's all that harmful."

"Hmm... maybe." He's now cradling Mally to his chest, and she's almost putty in his arms.

Traitor.

"But why did you get a cat?"

"Because you've been a moping mess recently. I didn't know what else to do to get you out of bed. And here you are, stealing food while I'm not home." I pout and pretend to be upset. He looks embarrassed at my words, and I see a trace of red staining his cheeks.

"I'm good now," he says, but he's not even glancing at me. He's looking at Mally.

There's a moment of panic when I see Mally raise her head and give me a satisfied *He's mine* look.

Lord, did I make a mistake?

"Take me on a date!" I tell him, needing to show Mally who's in charge. But mostly needing my promised date.

"Now?"

"Well..." I start and get closer to sniff him. "After you take a shower."

He looks at me as if he doesn't know what I'm talking about, but when he catches a whiff of his own scent, he doesn't waste any time dumping Mally in my lap, dashing for the bathroom.

"Now. Some house rules." I get Mally's attention, feeling like we need to set some boundaries. "He's mine. You can borrow him." I use my finger to tilt her head up. "But he is *mine*." After what feels like a battle of wills through our stares, Mally is the first to back down, and I give her a nice petting as a reward.

When Adrian is freshly showered and dressed in a pair of khaki pants and a polo shirt, I give him my approval.

We set up Mally with food and water and let her become acquainted with the house while we go away for a little while.

"I'm sorry," Adrian adds once we're in the elevator.

"It's okay. You can be sad. But don't ignore me next time." His hand seeks mine, and he lifts it to his lips for a quick peck.

"You need constant attention, don't you?"

"Maybe..." I frown, realizing that I do need attention... specifically *his* attention.

He chuckles and puts his hand around my waist, tugging me at his side.

"I think I needed some time to come to terms with everything. I just can't believe I spent years under that man, basically being his faithful dog."

"I still don't understand why he would do that.... maybe he hoped you'd lose a fight and die?"

"That's the thing, I don't think he did. He was always the one to push me to train harder, to be better."

"That's odd."

"Yeah. I'll make sure to find out why when I catch him. But now... you have my undivided attention."

"Do I?" I flutter my eyelashes at him.

"I promised to let you choose our date. So, go ahead. I shall be your servant."

As the elevator doors open, he bends at the waist in a faux bow, and I can't help but giggle.

"Let's go to that Italian pizza place we both love," I suggest, leaving my dream date idea for next time. I don't think Adrian will be in the mood to go to a shooting range right now.

See, I can be considerate.

"Sure. Cab or driving?"

"Cab. You can have a glass of wine. Just one, though." I wink at him, and he groans.

"I swear my descent into the whiskey bottle has been a very limited three-day trip. Won't happen again."

We take a cab and head downtown to the restaurant. I suggest this one because we rarely need to book in advance, and it's rather casual.

When we arrive, we're lucky to get a window table, and we order, getting a pizza each and a glass of red wine.

"We haven't been here in a really long time," Adrian states as he looks around.

"We haven't been on a date in a really long time," I correct, and he sighs.

"I'm glad we're doing this... I want to give this a fair shot. Us." He smiles at me, and I feel my cheeks flame.

"Speaking of that. I wanted to tell you something. I quit my job," I say and avert my eyes, not knowing what to expect.

"Your job? At the foundation?" He frowns but awaits my explanation.

"I never liked it. I did it... Well, frankly, I did it because I thought you'd like me better if I was *involved* in the community." He doesn't look at me for a moment, swirling the wine in his glass and watching the liquid move in circles.

"What else?"

"What else?" I ask, not knowing exactly what he's talking about.

"What else did you do because of me?"

"Ugh..." I cringe internally at this; there are just too many things. "I studied social studies and business because you seemed into that." I immediately take a sip of wine, not wanting to see his reaction.

"More. Tell me more."

"I hate fish!" I blurt out, and his eyes widen for a second before bursting into laughter.

"You hate fish?"

"Yes. All those times I ate it with you, I puked it afterward. Fish is just... vile."

"At least now I know what not to cook you anymore."

"Sorry," I mumble, feeling bad because he'd always cook me fish when I was feeling under the weather, thinking it was my favorite food. Instead, it only served to make me sicker and prolong my period of convalescence.

"This is... interesting. What else?" He's amused at this point, so I'm not that worried anymore. All the things I'd done to impress him just roll off my tongue from how I dressed to how I styled my hair and makeup, even to my lack of body art.

"You wanted to get tattoos?"

"Hell, yes. You haven't seen Vlad naked..." I start but catch myself when I see the fire in his eyes at that mention. "He's covered in ink. Every inch of his body is tattooed."

"Vlad? I never realized," he adds pensively.

"He did them in such a way that you can't tell with the way he dresses."

"And even your hair? Come on, B." He veers the topic away from Vlad, and I'm thankful, not wanting any tension tonight.

"Yup. Always wanted to bleach it."

"You should," he says, and I almost drop my fork.

"Really?" He nods, and my excitement gets the best of me, dumping more information that should have stayed hidden.

"I also hated having sex at first," I wince at my own words.

"What, why?" Adrian asks, genuine concern in his voice.

"It hurt too much for the first few times." I shrug.

"I'm sorry. I never realized it." He squeezes my hand.

"It's not your fault. I was very good at pretending. That and I have a pretty high pain threshold."

He anxiously takes a sip of the wine before admitting,

"It *was* probably my fault. I...wasn't very experienced. I didn't know how to read a woman's body."

"Are you for real?" I almost choke on my food when I hear him.

"Honestly, everything I learned was with you... or Pink, I should say."

"I can't believe that." I laugh. Adrian looks at me, curiously.

"We both had no idea what we were doing but were pretending to be experts. Don't you see the irony?" I ask him, still laughing.

"I guess when you put it like that..." That elicits a smile from him, and I shake my head.

"I'm probably going to regret asking this, but what do you mean exactly when you say you weren't experienced?" I almost bite my tongue when I ask this.

Adrian scratches the back of his neck and looks exceptionally uncomfortable, as he says, "Pink was the first woman I went all the way with. I tried in the past, during my fighting days, but it didn't feel right. It was expected of us to blow steam like that." He takes a deep breath. "There was a lot of peer pressure to do it, but I couldn't go through it. I didn't like how impersonal it was—how transactional."

"Interesting..." I say, though inside I am full of glee. Did he just admit he was also a virgin the first time we fucked? I don't want to think about what he means that he *tried* in the past. As far as I'm concerned, that is null.

I'm his first.

Oh my Lord!

He's fully mine. Just as I am fully his.

"Then why Pink?" I clear my throat and ask before I do something stange—like start doing a celebratory dance and shout as loud as I can that I was his first. I'm not sure this establishment would approve that type of behavior.

"Honestly? It was the confidence. You seemed so into it, into me..." He smiles at the memory.

"I was! I'd been watching you for too long. I came up with Pink exactly because I didn't know how else to get your attention."

"Well, you did get it."

"Come on, I can't be the only one to find you hot. I'm sure there must have been other women to hit on you." Yes, please tell me so I can murder them, is what I actually mean.

He frowns, as if remembering. "There were, but I was never interested. Ever since I became Theo, I've been working too hard to pay attention to any of that."

"Then, why *me*?"

"Your presence comforts me," he states. "Remember when we first met? At one of Martin's Sunday dinners." I nod, and he continues, "He somehow put me right next to you at the table. You didn't speak much, but I could feel your presence radiating in the entire room. It was... intoxicating." He takes another sip of his wine. "I couldn't stay away. I told myself multiple times that I didn't have time for any entanglements, especially with Martin's daughter. You weren't someone I could just have an affair with and call it quits."

"You did take a long time to ask me on a date."

"I was only delaying the inevitable."

"That you were." I raise my glass to him, and we clink.

At the same time, my foot slowly travels up his leg—screw taking this slow. I'm getting in the mood when I hear an accented voice behind me.

"Hastings. And with your lovely wife." Annoyed, I drop my foot and turn to give Enzo a dazzling smile. *Please leave.*

"Enzo." Adrian stands and shakes Enzo's hand. He's accompanied by a tall, gorgeous woman, likely a model.

"We were just leaving," I say, giving Adrian a small sign that I don't want him to ruin our date. It's too late, however.

"What a coincidence. We're leaving too. Why don't you join us? We're going to see Quinn's fight." Enzo narrows his eyes at Adrian, and I can see this isn't a mere invitation. Interesting...

Does he even know, I wonder, that his partners are related to his enemy? I almost chortle at the thought but compose myself quickly.

Unable to refuse his invitation, we all get into Enzo's car, after which he tells his driver to take us towards Canal Street.

Once we get there, we're led towards what appears to be a former fire station. After we're vetted, we enter a vast arena full of people yelling at the top of their lungs.

Enzo motions us towards a more secluded area that I'm guessing is reserved for people like him. While not wholly cut off from the other spectators, it still provides a little more privacy than the massive throng of people crowded around the fighting ring.

One glance at Adrian, and I know he's not happy with this turn of events. I take his hand in mine and offer it a big squeeze. He has to know I'm here with him.

Enzo's father joins as well, also accompanied by a model who seems to be a third of his age.

"Do we really have to stay?" I whisper to Adrian and notice the tautness of his muscles when he replies.

"Something is off." He shakes his head, confused. "I don't know what..."

The first round is announced, between Quinn and another man named Sean something. They both enter the ring, and holy moly is Quinn packing some.

I'm busy staring at what is obviously an extremely ripped body when a hand covers my eyes.

"Don't look at other men like that, love. I might have to jump in the ring," Adrian whispers in my hair. I turn around and give him a long kiss.

"You'll always be my number one. Now, down, boy." I smirk at him and pinch him playfully.

The fight starts, and as expected, Quinn wins the first round. The crowd goes crazy. Quinn's movements have both speed and strength, and it's no wonder he's barely sporting any injuries when his adversary is covered in blood.

The many scars on Quinn's body, however, attest to the fact that he's trained hard to get to the level he's at.

The second round starts, and Quinn seems slightly distracted as he keeps looking back to his corner, where his trainer is. It's not affecting his game, as he evades every direct hit while landing some on his opponent. It's clear he's just toying with him at this point.

I have to wonder what the purpose of this game is.

Enzo hadn't been too forthcoming, but I'm guessing it's the arena's inauguration since Quinn himself is in the ring. Odd, though, that I haven't spotted his father yet. Aren't they usually together?

"Do you see his father anywhere?" I ask, scanning the area. Adrian shakes his head and tries to look too. Again, this is odd. Matthew should be in the private box too, watching his son. Maybe he knows this game is just a formality and doesn't think it's worth showing up?

But then doubt creeps in. What if there's more to the Gallaghers than meets the eye?

"We should tell Enzo about Andrew," I suggest. I know we aren't particularly close with Enzo, especially since the whole Martin debacle, but he should have all the details.

Adrian is about to reply when suddenly a couple of shots ring out in our direction.

We both barely have time to react when blood sprays directly into my face. Adrian immediately puts his body in front of me as a shield and pushes me to the ground.

"Down," he commands.

The crowd is frantic, running around and flooding towards the exits. Just as the shots started, they stop. People are still moving around haphazardly, and I can't see if anyone's been hit.

"Adrian?" I ask and try to move him off me while assessing his body for injuries. He just grunts an, *I'm fine.*

Right next to us, Enzo and Rocco are down, both bleeding out. I immediately go to Enzo's side while Adrian takes Rocco.

"I got a pulse," I say and then press my hands against his side, where the bullet must have nabbed him.

Adrian checks for the same with Rocco but shakes his head. Next to Rocco, his companion is also injured. Enzo's, on the other hand, appears to have fled already.

"Call 911," I tell Adrian, knowing that if Enzo doesn't get any medical attention, he'll end up like his father.

"Tell... Allegra... love..." Enzo struggles to get some words out, but his eyes suddenly snap shut, and his breathing becomes more labored.

I keep on applying pressure to the wound until Adrian nudges me and takes my spot. He gives me a worried look before adding, "If anyone asks, I was investigating a tip, and you had no idea what was happening. Clear?" I just nod absentmindedly.

"Act upset... cry. Behave normally."

The paramedics come through, and they load Enzo and Rocco's companion on a stretcher to take them urgently to the hospital.

The police soon follow, but Adrian's rank and his lengthy explanations help explain our presence. After what seems like forever, we're released and given the green light to go home.

We get home, take our clothes off, and immediately go to the shower to remove the blood.

"It was a trap," Adrian says. "The whole arrangement was a trap."

"You think the Gallaghers shot Enzo and Rocco?"

"It's damn smart too. Get rid of the Agostis, and you get rid of the entire competition in New York. If Jimenez wanted to expand..."

"Why not take over an already established empire," I finish his thought.

"If we were wondering whether the Gallaghers were in with Jimenez... well, wonder no more," he says ironically.

I put on a nightgown and go to the kitchen to make us some tea. I spot Mally in the corner, already asleep in her cute little bed. I try to be as quiet as possible as to not wake her.

I bring the cups over to our bedroom and close the door.

"Here."

"Thanks."

"Don't do that again," I suddenly say.

"What?"

"Put yourself between me and a bullet."

He turns to look at me and shakes his head. He takes the cup from my hand and puts it on the night table together with his. Grabbing my face in his hands, he tells me, full of sincerity, "That, I can never promise."

His lips descend on mine, wildly seeking entrance. I'm shocked by his sudden assault, but I return his kiss in full. My hands go to his back, and I'm clawing at his shirt, trying to get as close to his skin as possible.

Adrian pulls back, his eyes glazed with desire. He lifts me and throws me in the middle of the bed. Stretching to his full height in front of me, he takes his shirt off and disposes of it in a corner somewhere.

His pants follow suit, and seeing he went commando, I lick my lips in approval.

Damn, but he's hot!

I don't think I'll ever get used to the way he makes my body sing with just one glance, his presence so intoxicating I could climax just from being *next* to him.

He puts his hands on the bed and advances towards me, prowling with purpose.

To make it harder for him, I back away until I reach the headboard, giving him a saucy grin as I do. He groans loudly and grabs both my ankles, yanking me towards him in one sudden move.

I don't give in easy. Not this time. I let myself go soft for a minute, allowing him to trail kisses down my neck, before using my nails to scratch his back and kick him off me. His arms shoot out to stop my flailing limbs, and we take a tumble that ends up with me on top of him.

Still on the bed.

I want so badly to just melt against him, but I know this is more than sex. This is a mating dance that will reestablish our relationship.

Just as I grind my core on his obvious erection, he grabs my nightgown and rips it off my body. His big hands splay on my back, and he moves me up and down, hitting the right spot to make my eyes roll in the back of my head in pleasure.

Chasing that high, I barely register when he inverses our roles once again, with me squirming beneath him.

"You seem in need of some disciplining," he whispers in my ear before he moves lower.

His mouth travels down to my breasts, where he takes one nipple between his lips. I moan as my legs wrap around his midriff. He palms my ass and brings me into full contact with his cock. I'm already so wet that he smoothly glides between my lips, up and down.

"Inside. Now," I bark out, failing at my own game to draw this out. He chuckles in my ear at my urgency.

"You want my cock, sweet girl?" he asks as he thrusts forward, hitting my clit and eliciting a half-moan from me. "Ask for it," he says, his voice thick and seductive, making my pussy tingle with awareness. He continues to trail wet kisses all around my collarbone.

"I want your cock inside me. Please." I don't even recognize my voice as I beg, but I don't care. It's been too long since I've felt him. All of him.

"Good girl." His mouth covers mine just as he enters my body in one swift thrust. He fills me up to the hilt, and one pump later, my orgasm overwhelms me, my muscles clenching around him.

"Harder," I cry out, and he pistons in and out of me, his tight grip on my ass, bruising my flesh.

I'm holding tightly onto him, enjoying the feel of his cock hitting my cervix and mingling the pleasure with pain when I hear a sudden scratch at the door. My head snaps in that direction, but I try to ignore it, instead urging Adrian to go faster.

The scratching gets louder.

"Did you hear that?" I ask him and point towards the door. He stops and frowns.

"Hear what?"

Something hits the door.

"That," I say, and a mewing accompanies the scratching.

As we both realize who it is at the door, we burst out into laughter.

"Leave it," I say and clench my muscles around him. He moves again, but the meowing intensifies.

"We should see what Mally wants?" Adrian asks, and a red haze suddenly covers my eyes. I arch an eyebrow at him and roll with him, so I'm on top.

I lift myself a little before coming down once more, my hands going to his pecs for support. He grabs onto my breasts and kneads them, the movements sending shivers through my body.

Mally is still throwing a tantrum at the door, but I won't let *her* interfere.

Adrian's hands continue their ascent until they circle my neck. I hum low in my throat, the slight pressure making me come again.

As I ride my pleasure, he takes over, going faster and chasing his own fulfillment.

We both collapse on the bed, and I'm almost reluctant to open the door for Mally, but she seems extremely insistent.

I get up and let her in. She doesn't even look at me as she dashes to Adrian's side.

"Pussies sure love you," I mumble as I settle back on the bed.

"Jealous?" he teases, and I scowl at him.

"Me? Never." And just to be petty, I turn my back to him.

He doesn't waste any time in spooning me from behind and placing Mally in my arms. That's how we fall asleep.

The following days are a blur. We settle into a nice new routine, almost like newlyweds.

Well... newlyweds plus Mally. She just can't help herself. Whenever I'm enjoying some intimate time with my husband, Mally meows, and she's even resorted to breaking a couple of things around the house. It seems that my talk with her didn't take. We might need to rehash some things.

Adrian inquires at the hospital, and it seems that Enzo has survived but is now in the intensive care unit. I've only called Vlad once, and he informs me that with the Agostis out of business, the Gallaghers are currently working to bring over all the Italian allies to their side.

"A storm is brewing," he says.

I haven't told him about Andrew being Jimenez... mostly because Adrian had asked me not to, and I want to honor his wishes.

It's hard because I've never had any secrets with Vlad, but my allegiance will always be Adrian's first and foremost.

Over the past few days, I've been running some errands and fixing things up at the foundation for the new director to take over.

Then, I realized the same car I'd seen when I got Mally is *always* in my side mirror.

I'm on the way back home when I suddenly decide I've had enough.

I hit the brakes and wait a second for the other car to do the same. I then get out and go over, ready to demand an explanation for the stalking.

I knock on the driver's window and wait.

Nothing.

I knock again.

Slowly, the window rolls down to reveal a scarred face I'd last seen in Atlantic City. My hands immediately go to my gun, but it's too late, as I feel a cloth covering my mouth. I struggle as best as I can before darkness takes over.

49

ADRIAN

"The real Andrew Gallagher died at age twelve in Belfast," Marcel voices aloud what I'd been suspecting of a while now. "I have some connections in the UK, and they sent a copy of his death certificate. He would have been fifty-eight now."

We're at his apartment in Chelsea. In all the years I've known Marcel, I can count on one hand the times I've been to his apartment.

It's a sleek, modern, one-bedroom apartment that could belong to a showroom for its bareness. I've always marveled at the minimalist style that Marcel seems to adhere to. We're now in his living room, reviewing some old case files, and trying to make sense of the entire situation.

"So, he stole Andrew's identity," I say, dropping one of the files I'd been skimming through on the desk. "Interesting, though, that Quinn referred to him as his uncle," I add, stroking my jaw pensively.

"At this point, we can only infer that there's some sort of relation between Jimenez and the Gallaghers."

"They acted too fast against the Agostis. They must have realized we knew something."

The attack on Enzo and Rocco had been smartly timed. Both of them had been present in an open space with a lot of people

368

around. With Enzo still in the ICU, it's only a matter of time until the Agosti business falls to Jimenez.

"If Enzo dies, the Agosti territory will be up for grabs."

"The Marchesi are also swiping in to try to salvage what they can. I've had reports that Enzo's wife is already giving orders as Capo. Plus, her family landed in the States the day after the attack."

"It's not going to be pretty. I wouldn't want to be Enzo... if he survives." I grimace at the thought. For all my dislike of Enzo, I can only imagine his reaction at waking up to find his father dead, his partners betraying him, and his wife reaping the benefits of his own demise... Too many betrayals at once.

"You said that Bianca met Jimenez's son." Marcel shuffles some papers, looking for something specific.

"Yeah. Odd considering none of our intel has ever alluded to the existence of a son. From what Bianca told me, he's in his early thirties and has a defining scar on his right cheek. I've already done a partial search in the police database, but so far, I got nothing."

"Look at this." Marcel shows me a profile photo of a man with a scarred cheek.

"What's this?"

"When you described the guy to me, I had my doubts but decided to look into it. He's not in the database because he's never been convicted, but we had a case come in almost three years ago, and this guy was the main suspect. A few women came forward with rape allegations against him. Some of the testimonies had holes in them, so he got away."

"What piqued your curiosity about him?" I ask, knowing there must be a reason why Marcel is showing me this.

"I remembered him from my days as a prosecutor. I was the one handling his case, so I met the guy. Nasty piece of work, no remorse. That he got away on mere technicalities guts me... His name is Carlos Delgado, thirty. Mother was Elena Delgado, father unknown."

"So? That's a long shot to assume that the unknown father is

Jimenez." I arch an eyebrow, thinking he's grasping at straws with this.

"Here." He spreads a few more pictures on the desk, and I see what he means. All of them show Carlos meeting with Quinn in a dark alley, their hands exchanging something.

"When was this taken?"

"Day before the shooting." I frown. Why would Marcel have pictures of Quinn from before the shooting?

"Before?" I ask, trying to mask the doubt in my voice.

"I've had someone watching the Gallaghers ever since they came to NYC." Wait, what?

"Why? Did Vlad put you up to this?"

"In a way. We watched Enzo and, by extension, the Gallaghers." It all sounds logical, given Vlad's blatant interest in Enzo. But why do I feel like it isn't the real reason...

"Maybe one of these days, you'll give me more details into this friendship of yours with Vlad," I add casually and watch Marcel's face fall for a second before he composes himself.

"Maybe..." he answers cryptically.

"Let me send a picture of Carlos to Bianca; that way, we can have direct confirmation without resorting to conjectures." I get my phone out and snap a picture of Carlos, sending it to Bianca.

"Right. How have things been with you and Bianca?"

"Good. She adopted a cat." I keep my answer short and vague, not wanting to disclose more details. Our new relationship is still in its infancy, and I don't want to jinx anything.

"A cat?" Marcel asks, clearly amused.

"Her name's Mally. You'll like her," I add fondly. However, Marcel doesn't seem to share my enthusiasm, as the prospect of meeting Mally has him already pale.

"Shit. Sorry, forgot about that." I shake my head at my thoughtlessness.

Marcel has a pet phobia. I know this because when we first met, I had one too many pets. One time, Marcel had come by my place, and at the sight of the animals racing towards him, he'd fled the premises and had declared my apartment off-limits. It seems that fate is about to repeat itself.

"No worries." He tries to dismiss it, but I can see I've ruined the mood.

I excuse myself and tell him I will update him when Bianca replies.

"One more thing..." Marcel says as I'm about to head out.

"Hm?"

"Carlos is still in NYC. Tell Bianca to be careful."

"Thanks."

Now, that's a worrying thought. Bianca had tried to describe her experience at the Block in as much detail as possible, and I'd been shocked at how close she'd come to being assaulted, first by the guards and then by the man who bought her.

He'd been bent on getting his due since, apparently, Martin had cheated him. I'd tried not to show Bianca just how upsetting those details had been to hear, mostly since it was clear that it wasn't too bad from her own perspective.

To just think of her in such a situation... I still blame myself for allowing her to do that in the first place. I don't care that it did yield results, and we uncovered Jimenez's identity. Not at that potential cost.

After wrapping up with Marcel, I head back to work to complete some paperwork. With everything going on, I'd been on leave for almost two weeks now. Although the amount of work I have to catch up with is outstanding, I leave at around six, thinking to surprise Bianca for dinner.

Since we've decided to give our relationship a try, things have been... too good. We've had various discussions, and we've both confessed the stuff we've done in our past. I'd told her about my childhood, how my parents had done the best they could with me, and that I'd been a happy teen until their deaths.

After that, I'd been placed in foster care, and because of bullying, I'd ended up on the streets only to be taken in by a Catholic church belonging to the Irish mob. I'd described my time in the ring and how it had forced me to grow up and mature. I'd also confided in her my shame at keeping that lifestyle for as long as I did when there wasn't anything forcing me to do it other than my thirst for revenge.

I owed Theo everything.

Not only had he given me a clean slate, but he'd also given me a ticket out of a lifetime of criminality, which was what I'd been looking at had I continued on that path.

In turn, she'd also described her childhood. Her voice had held her usual cool tone as she'd related the abuse and neglect she'd suffered at Martin's hands. After Jenna, she was already looking at a self-destructing path that Drew had helped her avoid by showing her how to redirect her anger. She'd told me as much as she could about her involvement with the Bratva. And then she'd opened up about how her obsession with me started.

I have to admit I'd been a little weirded out by the lengths she'd gone to get to me. But is it normal to find it all just a little bit endearing?

Maybe not... and perhaps the fact that I hadn't reacted negatively to her confessing all the fucked-up shit she'd done from the time she'd first seen me to our first meeting should be the first sign that our relationship will never be normal.

And now that I've had a taste of her brand of abnormal... I'm not sure I'd ever want to go back to normal.

I get home before dinner time, but I'm surprised to find the apartment empty.

"B?" I call out, but nothing. Mally slowly walks towards me and gives me a meow. I pick her up and pet her a little while I look for Bianca. When I realize she's not in the apartment, I check my phone and see that there are no messages from her. I frown. She's usually pretty quick at replying to my texts. I dial her number, and while it rings a few times, it soon goes directly into voicemail.

Okay... not to panic. I'm sure there's an explanation.

I go to my laptop and try to track her phone. The app shows me the phone's last location, and it's not too far off from the foundation.

Maybe she's on her way from work? Over the last few days, she's been organizing a leadership takeover. Maybe her meetings have run late.

I think Marcel must have sown paranoia in my mind when he'd mentioned that Carlos is still in New York.

Yes... I'm sure that's why I'm so frantic about not hearing from her yet.

I wait another half hour, the time it usually takes her to get home from the foundation. When there's still no sight of her, and her phone location hasn't changed, I take my car keys and head towards her.

It's not too long until our locations coincide on the map. I look around and see an empty street. Already a feeling of uneasiness creeps up my spine.

I get out of the car and dial her number. *Please pick up...* I walk around in circles, still ringing her phone when I suddenly hear a sound. I'm barely able to put one step in front of the other towards the bush where the noise comes from.

I take a deep breath and burrow my way through the foliage. I see the phone. I don't see Bianca. I sigh in relief, my worst fears alleviated.

I pick up the phone and notice it's cracked. There's no way Bianca would have just dumped her phone and left it somewhere. No... something isn't right.

"Carlos is still in NYC. Tell Bianca to be careful." Marcel's voice rings in my head.

No... Please let her be okay.

I try to compose myself, knowing that if I let fear rule me, I won't be able to do anything to find Bianca. I slowly look around from the spot where I'd found the phone for any CCTV cameras that might have caught what happened on film. I see two of them overlooking the street.

I know what I have to do. Swallowing my pride, I get in my car and drive to Vlad's. He has the resources to find Bianca. I also ask Marcel to meet me there.

I drive at full speed, not wanting to waste any time. When I get to Vlad's, Marcel is already there. So fast?

"Bianca's missing." It's the first thing I say when I see them. "I found her phone, but no sign of her." Turning to Marcel, I ask, "Do you think Carlos..." Marcel purses his lips.

Vlad, on the other hand, doesn't seem to think this is an emergency.

"Maybe she just got sick of you," he says, joking around. Daggers must be shooting from my eyes as I make my way towards him. He puts his hands up in surrender.

"Chill, Hastings. I got you." Vlad gets his computer, and after inputting password after password, a map appears on the screen.

"What's that?" I ask, looking at the red dot on the map.

"That's Bianca's location."

"But how?"

"Both Bianca and I had a chip implanted under the skin for this exact reason. Because we were partners, the chances of one being used to draw the other out were quite high. We didn't want to take any chances, so we covered our ground."

"That's one of those storage places in the Bronx, isn't it?" Marcel studies the map on the screen.

"I think so," Vlad concurs.

I don't have time for this. The moment I have the location, I do a one-eighty, already heading for the door.

"Do you want to save your wife, Hastings, or go to your own death?" Vlad makes a tsk sound that stops me in my tracks.

"We can't waste any time. You know that the first few hours after a kidnapping are the most important," I address Marcel, who's also seen his fair share of such cases.

"Yes, but there's also the element of surprise. And we can only bank on that if we know the details of who took her. Don't be hasty."

"I can't just sit around, Marcel." My voice betrays the emotion I feel inside. If Carlos took her...

My mind keeps on imagining the worst.

"Patience, Hastings." Vlad shakes his head. "Now, tell me where you found her phone."

I give Vlad the coordinates and watch as he swiftly pulls the CCTV feed. At this point, I'm not even interested in how he's done that. All that matters is seeing what happened to Bianca.

"When was the last time you talked to her?" he asks me.

"Around ten." When she'd told me about her plans at the foundation.

Vlad starts the feed from ten, and we go through the footage until I point out Bianca's car coming to a stop.

"There's another car." Right behind Bianca, another car stops. We watch as she gets out of the vehicle and heads towards the other car, knocking on the window. Simultaneously, a man walks around the car and takes her by surprise, likely with a chloroform-infused material. After she slumps against the man, she's loaded into the car.

"Stop." I point to the frame that allows the best view inside the open window.

"Zoom in." Vlad zooms in, and I spare a glance at Marcel. It looks like him.

"Carlos?" he asks, and Marcel and I nod.

"We need to go there."

"Wait," Vlad says again, and I get annoyed with all his interruptions. He pulls up more CCTV footage, this time from the storage unit in the Bronx.

"There's a lot of traffic." Marcel frowns and asks Vlad to search for other angles.

We see a few trucks pulling up at the industrial entrance. Switching to some inner cameras, the trucks are being unloaded and craters are being carried inside the buildings. There's also an excessive number of staff climbing out of the vehicles.

"What do we know about that storage company?"

"It's been closed for more than a year now and was recently acquired by an offshore account... Do you think?" Vlad looks at Marcel when he asks this, and he nods.

"It could be Jimenez's new operating base," Marcel speculates. "It would make sense why the increased traffic now, since Agosti is out."

"You think he moved in so quickly?"

"To get the best part of a carcass, a scavenger must be the first one at the scene." Vlad's voice turns wistful.

"Thanks for the imagery," I add drily.

"Welcome." He beams.

"You can't simply barge in there. We need a plan," Marcel tells me. "It's likely they have an army in there." He paces around, thinking of something. "Vlad, can you find the blueprints of the building?"

"I'll try," Vlad replies and gets to work.

I head over to Marcel and lower the volume of my voice. "I can't just sit around. What if something happens to Bianca?"

"We'll get her. Don't worry," Marcel says.

"I wouldn't underestimate your wife, Hastings." Vlad's eyes are still on the screen when he calls out.

"Yeah, but even *she* isn't invincible."

Vlad looks up ever so slightly, and for the first time, I detect something more than apathy.

"She *will* be fine." I give him a small nod, the only concession I'm willing to make when it comes to him.

Vlad manages to eventually find the building's plans, and we pore over them, making notes on all the entrances, exits, and how the rooms are connected.

"If Jimenez's already finished with the preparation, then we should expect to meet guards here, here..." Vlad shows us the most strategic placement of people given the open spaces in the building.

"I'll have my people ready. Hastings, how are you with a gun?"

"Decent," I answer. I haven't had much practice since my active-duty days, but those are long past. I can probably hit a target, but I'm nowhere near as proficient as Bianca.

"Hope so. If you've noticed, trucks carrying craters come in every two hours." Vlad shifts back to the screen. "The most straightforward way to access the compound is to hijack one of the trucks and take out the men inside. We'll then replace them and deliver whatever it is they're delivering."

"Sounds good to me. When can we go?" I say, almost too impatiently. I know I should pay more attention to the planning part, but I can't stop thinking about Bianca and what might be happening to her right now.

Vlad proceeds to follow CCTV footage along the truck's route and finds the best spot for the takeover. After we hash over all the details, Vlad phones Maxim and asks him to assemble some people.

A little while later, Maxim comes in with a huge box-like case and opens it for us. Inside are bulletproof vests, guns, and other weapons.

Vlad takes a pair of long, curved blades and sheaths them to his back, in the bulletproof vest pockets that seem to be custom made to hold the swords.

Both Marcel and I don the vests, and we each take two pistols.

"How are *you* with a pistol?" I ask Marcel, amused. I don't recall him ever touching a gun.

"He's good. Aren't you, *Marcel?*" Vlad answers for him, putting a weird emphasis on his name. Marcel seems to be put out by the reply but doesn't comment further.

With everything now in place, we leave towards the convened spot.

50

BIANCA

I struggle to open my eyes. Stifling a groan as a full-on headache hits me, I try to bring my hand up to massage my temple, but I realize I can't.

My hands are restrained behind my back. I blink twice and try to focus on my surroundings. Everything is still foggy. My mouth is dry, a cloth wrapped across it. And as I slowly come to, I remember confronting the car following me for a few days now.

And that man... Jimenez's son.

My eyes finally get used to the room's lighting, and I see that I'm inside what looks to be a cellar.

I turn my head around as much as possible, but there isn't much to see. The room is entirely bare but for the chair I'm sitting on. There are no windows and only one door, right in front of me. There is, however, one camera directly above the door.

I shake my head ever so slightly, seeking to alleviate the discomfort I feel.

They must have drugged me. Fuckers... taking me by surprise. My muscles tense with the animosity I feel towards them. Just wait until I'm free. I'm almost tempted to break my non-messy rule and make them pay for daring to do this to me.

I wriggle in the chair, but my hands and feet are tightly secured. I simply can't do anything right now. I must bide my time and take advantage whenever the opportunity presents itself.

378

I look straight to the camera, and with a jerk of my head, I push my feet into the floor with all my strength and propel myself backward. It works, and I fall flat on my back. I truly hope someone is watching that feed and that seeing proof I'm awake, they come in.

It doesn't take long after my stunt to hear the door opening. Since I'm lying on my back, I can't see who's coming inside. But the sound of someone stepping inside is unmistakable.

"And she's awake," the voice says laconically. I purse my lips, already knowing who it is.

"Mhmm." I make some sounds from behind my gag, hoping he'll take it off.

"Naughty, naughty." He comes deeper into the room and within my field of vision. Crouching next to me, he looks at me with an eyebrow raised.

"You couldn't help yourself, could you?" he asks, studying me. With a sigh, he helps me up so that the chair is now planted on the ground, straight up again. I paint my features into a scowl to show him my displeasure.

"Mhmm," I try to say something again through the gag, and he finally pulls it down. I immediately lick my chapped lips, wishing he would have at least brought some water with him. Well... kidnapping and a five-star hotel aren't exactly synonymous, so I'll just settle for having my mouth free for now.

"Really?" I ask him, ironically.

"You know... I really underestimated you." He threads his fingers through his hair. "At first, I was really pissed about the stunt you pulled. But then, the more I thought about it..., the more I realized how perfect you'd be."

"Perfect? For what?" I need to draw this out until I find an opening to make a move.

"To rule together, of course." He smiles at me before frowning. "I just have to get rid of your husband." The moment I hear that, a coldness that I'd never experienced before spreads through my limbs.

"You might want to start by telling me your name?" I change my voice so that it seems I'm actually interested in his proposition.

He gives me a challenging look, "Carlos."

"Nice to meet you, Carlos," I add sweetly, but not overly sweet. "Honestly, I couldn't care less about my husband," I lie.

"I already have my people on him. But don't worry. I'll kill him myself. I won't make the same mistake twice." He takes my jaw in his hands and tips it up so that I'm forced to look into his eyes.

"Twice?" I frown, but Carlos just smirks.

"He's been a thorn in my side for too long. I should have known that sending someone else to kill him wouldn't deliver successful results," he says almost pensively.

"Someone else? You sent those people to the lake house?" Until now, I'd thought all attempts on Adrian's life had been made by Jimenez.

"Ortega was supposed to get rid of him when he sent Martinez for the meetup, but he failed. So, he sent some amateurs to finish the job. Of course, they couldn't." He shakes his head. "If you want something done right, you have to do it yourself," he mutters, more to himself.

"But why? Just because he was inquiring about your father?"

"Why, you ask?" He laughs sarcastically. "It's more than that... Martin had a deal with Jimenez to merge their businesses. The goal's always been getting onto the New York market, and Martin was the perfect tool. A marriage between you and me would have cemented the alliance, and everyone could have profited. But Martin was a greedy bastard. He thought that someone in a position of legitimate power would serve him better than Jimenez... so he gave you to Hastings."

"Of course, it's not only that. By also allying himself with the Italians, Martin thought he was getting the best of both worlds, legal protection and access to the Italians' resources."

"So, you gave orders to have Martin killed too?" Finally, the pieces are falling in place.

"Yes, but I had my father's blessing for that. Martin was a treacherous dog. Jimenez was happy to get rid of him."

"So, if not for Martin's machinations, we would have been married already?"

"Indeed," he answers smoothly.

"Then tell me, why would I choose *you* over him now?" I change my tactic, trying to seem as mercenary as Martin. He doesn't know about my relationship with Adrian. Few people know. And from the outside, we're the perfect high society pair. I can work with that. "Tell me, what are the perks for... joining you?"

"Why, you'd be a queen, of course. I'm going to take over my father's empire. And you'd be by my side. We were already fated to be, if not for your father." The way he's telling this, it's like he actually believes his delusions.

"Hmm... tempting," I drawl seductively.

"You're quite quick to throw your husband away." He strokes my cheek, and I have to keep myself from shuddering in disgust. I smile instead. "It was Daddy's desire to marry Theo... I couldn't say no."

"And you did everything your daddy told you, didn't you?"

"Of course." I pout my lips. "Why would I marry that stuffy man otherwise?" I feel the bitterness of the words on my tongue as I say them.

"Indeed..." His lips stretch into a dangerous smirk. "You'll have to forgive me if I don't believe everything you say." Hmm, so he's not that dumb.

Fine, I can work with that.

"I wouldn't lie about it. I'm at your mercy, aren't I?" I give him a tremulous smile, showing a hint of vulnerability. I have to make this as believable as possible.

"That you are..." He removes a knife from his back pocket and trails it up and down my cheek. "You're so beautiful... unblemished..." His words are wistful as he focuses on my face.

"Tell me, does it bother you to look at me?" he asks, referring to the glaring scar on his cheek.

"Of course not," I reply, almost too fast. Shit. "I've always had a thing for bad boys," I amend my answer, hoping to stroke his ego a little.

"And you think I got this scar because I was a bad boy?" He chuckles derisively. "On the contrary, I got this because I was a good boy." His gaze moves above my head, and somehow, I know he's not talking to me anymore. "You see... my father said I looked too much like my mother." He laughs at that. "And he couldn't have that... no... not when he raped her so brutally for years that she finally took her own life to escape from him." Shit... that came out of nowhere. "He said I reminded him too much of her... of her screams. So, he branded me."

I don't know how to reply to that, mainly because I don't want to say something that might set him off. So, I let him continue with his soliloquy.

"But do you know what he did for that husband of yours? He personally trained him." I almost frown. Why is he suddenly mentioning Adrian? He clearly has daddy issues.

"You do know, don't you? That your precious law-abiding husband used to kill people in illegal fights." My mouth forms a big O, and I try to show him my most surprised expression.

"What... what are you talking about?"

"So, you didn't know, did you...?" He laughs. "I don't know what he saw in him. *I* did everything my father wanted me to. *I* led his cartel. It was *my* plan to use the Gallaghers to take over New York. And how does he repay me?" He snickers. "He's still more concerned about your husband. He told me to leave you alone because you belong to *him*."

He gets in my face, his lips a mere breath away from mine.

"And you know what? I'm done obeying. *You* are *mine*. The empire is *mine*," he spits out before his lips are on mine, the pressure almost unbearable.

For a second, I feel like I can't do this, but then I remember his threats regarding Adrian. He hates him. He wants to kill him...

Saying *I'm sorry* to Adrian in my mind, I return the kiss. He needs to believe that I'm willing to readily switch sides if he'll ever trust me enough to free me.

Then, it's game on.

His tongue sweeps in, and I have to will my body to not gag as I respond. He seems surprised by my easy acquiescence. Ending the kiss, he slyly looks into my eyes.

"I almost believe you meant it."

"I told you," I say, and eyeing the cross at his neck, I immediately add, "I don't owe my husband anything except my allegiance before God. After you take him out, I'm yours." I hope this will work. He takes a step back and regards me quizzically, as if he doesn't know whether to trust my words.

"That so?" he muses. I take this chance to cement my position.

"Of course. I've only ever slept with my husband and *only* after our wedding vows." I'm banking on him being an honest thief at this point. But seeing that he hasn't raped me until now, or when I was unconscious, I'm willing to bet there's more to him than meets the eye.

He seems pensive as he takes in my words. I'm actively praying to that imaginary God I'd been invoking for him to believe me.

"Kill my husband, and then I'll marry you. Like it was meant to be. I'll be yours."

"Mine..." He tastes the words on his tongue, his lips curling into a wolfish smile. "I like the sound of that. Very well." Yes. One small victory.

He turns his back to leave, and my eyes widen. Wait, why is he leaving? I thought we were on the same page now.

"Wait. Are you going to leave me like this?"

"Why would I *not* leave you like this? I have to say, you've been convincing so far, but I've learned my lesson with you." He opens the door and leaves, locking it behind him.

Fuck this shit, I mutter to myself.

My efforts were in vain. I'm tempted to spit on the floor, just to cleanse my mouth of him, but I know he must be watching. So, I put on my best behavior. I have to think fast. I can't do *anything* from here, and Adrian is in danger.

What could I possibly do now? My eyes frantically search around the room for any idea that might be helpful. But none comes.

Desperation grips me like a fine glove, so I do the only remaining thing.

I bite my tongue.

Hard.

Blood floods my mouth and pours down my lips.

Good.

The first step is done. Then I push myself backward again, making my body shiver uncontrollably, hoping to imitate a seizure.

Sure enough, he's back through the door. He *was* watching.

He cradles my head in his hands and pushes my mouth open, taking hold of my tongue. I continue to make my limbs spasm. He's trying to make sure I'm not swallowing my tongue. My eyes roll back into my head, and I pretend to be out.

He barks some commands in Spanish, and then he unties me.

Good... good.

I moan in pain, half-pretend, half-real since my tongue does hurt.

"Are you okay?" he asks me after I'm free of my restraints. I manage a nod before I make myself faint.

"Shit. *Un médico!*" he yells, and I hear more movement. He takes me into his arms and leaves the cellar with me, taking me who knows where.

I surreptitiously open one eye, and I see that he's rushing me to one of the more furnished rooms with a bed.

He carefully places me on the bed, and I do my best to seem out of it.

"*¡Un médico, pendejo! Ya te lo he dicho. ¿Qué estás haciendo?*" He yells out some more commands.

"*Perdón, patrón.*" Some people apologize, and there's more shuffling.

I'm lying on the bed with my eyes closed, and Carlos is still caressing my forehead.

His movements are... tender. I almost scoff at myself for thinking that.

It's not much later that a doctor finally arrives. After having a chat with Carlos, the doctor examines me, shining light into my eyes and looking at my mouth.

"*Tuvo una convulsión. Déjala descansar y la voy a examinar otra vez mañana. Le voy a dar un analgésico por ahora,"* the doctor confirms my charade.

"¿Doctor, está seguro que no es nada grave?" Carlos asks, making sure there's nothing wrong with me.

"Si, claro. Quiero hacerla una prueba de sangre," the doctor continues, asking to draw some blood from me.

"Dale. Tengo algo que solver, pero mándame los resultados cuando los tienes." Before leaving, Carlos drops by the bed and fastens each hand to the bed frame, effectively limiting my movements. At least my feet are free now.

I'm left alone with the doctor, and I keep my eyes closed, waiting.

"You can stop pretending," the doctor says in accented English. I open my eyes and stare at him. My mouth is sore, and I can still feel the taste of the blood.

The doctor is a man in his forties, dressed in a regular black shirt and jeans. Seeing that he caught me in my ruse and didn't expose me, I don't know what to expect from him.

He looks me over before heading to the door and turning the lock so that no one can enter. I frown. He just needs to take some blood, right?

"Everyone was wondering what piece of ass Carlos brought over." He eyes my restrained wrists and smirks, his hands going to his jeans and unbuckling his belt.

Are you fucking kidding me?

"Carlos won't like that," I say, my words distorted by my injured tongue.

"He doesn't have to know."

His pants undone, he advances towards the bed and work on my jeans. Fuck!

I don't allow him to do much else as I flex my legs and push. He loses his balance for a moment but jumps back on me. I'm prepared for him as I wrap my legs around his neck, applying as much pressure as possible.

"Bitch!" he spits out, his face already going red.

I don't know how long I can hold him like this, so I bend my wrists and hold onto the bed frame with my hands, using it as an anchor.

Then I focus all my strength on my lower body, and I bring his head towards me, banging it against the board. His hands are trying to reach me, and it's getting harder and harder to keep him in place. I breathe in deeply and bang his head once more, this time taking advantage of the momentum to toss him back and off the bed.

His head is bleeding pretty badly, and he's looking at me with murder in his eyes.

My fists curl around the bed frame once more, and at one tug, I realize it's wiggling. I frantically wiggle more and more, hoping to destabilize it enough to pull it from the bed.

The doctor slowly recovers, rising to his feet. The hit to the head must have been relatively good since he's swaying a little.

"Fucking *puta*," he yells before jumping on me once again. Luckily, at this moment, the bed frame comes free from its hinges, and I manage to fling it at him, the panel hitting him straight in the throat. He releases a few choked sounds before crumpling to the ground, clutching at his Adam's apple.

I sigh in relief and take a moment to compose myself. Realizing that Carlos could turn up at any moment, I get up from the bed, bed frame still attached to my hands.

I go directly to the doctor's medical kit and look for a scalpel. I find one, but now cutting the rope holding my wrists prisoner to the board is still hard.

I grasp the scalpel in one hand and try to rotate it so that the sharp side can graze the rope. I do the movement a few times before I notice a cut forming. I continue my efforts on that specific area until my wrist snaps free. I do the same with the other wrist and then throw the frame on the bed.

I'm about to leave, but I give the doctor another kick in the balls just for good measure. He's so far gone he can't even voice his pain.

Now, that felt good.

I open the door and exit the room, not knowing exactly where

I'm going. I hear a few people at some point and hide behind a wall, waiting for them to pass.

The more I walk, the more lost I am.

Until I reach an elevator.

Once inside, I notice I'm on the fourth floor. I quickly press zero to get to the ground floor, hoping there won't be too many people getting in my way.

W hen the elevator doors open on the ground floor, an older man in a sleek, black, two-piece suit greets me. I slowly drag my eyes from his feet to the gun he aims at me, and then suddenly to his face.

"Jimenez," I say, the name slipping from my lips and eliciting a wince of pain.

"And look who's here." He whistles, brandishing the gun around. I immediately put my hands up, hoping he'll see I'm unarmed.

His face is thoughtful for a while, as he says, "You weren't included in my plan. I guess I'll have to make it work." He motions me aside, and he steps into the elevator next to me. He presses 3, and the elevator takes us to the third floor.

Jimenez forces me to walk in front of him and tells me to head to the corridor's end.

"Father!" My head snaps to the side, and I see Carlos heading towards us, his eyes raging with fury.

"I gather this is your doing?" Jimenez asks in a bored fashion.

"She's *mine*," Carlos replies, his jaw locked tight.

"No, she's not. And *you* were about to ruin my plans." Jimenez pushes me as a sign to keep walking, but Carlos isn't done.

"She was supposed to be *mine*," he emphasizes, and Jimenez laughs.

"She was *never* supposed to be yours. The deal was met, accordingly. Martin was a shrewd bastard." Carlos' eyes widen, and I can see that's the moment he snaps. He charges at Jimenez full force.

I take a step back, hoping to avoid getting between them, but a few guards materialize out of nowhere and tackle Carlos to the ground.

They immobilize his hands and drag him in front of Jimenez, who looks at him with disgust in his eyes.

"I never should have taken you on. You're a weakling, just like your whore of a mother was." He spits in Carlos' face, and he struggles against the hold of the guards. "But I did keep you because I needed an heir. Now, I need you no more."

Jimenez lifts his arm and aims the gun at Carlos' chest. The shot echoes throughout the hallway. Carlos' body goes limp, blood leaking from his wound.

"Dump him in the river," Jimenez orders the guards, and they haul Carlos away.

Jimenez slowly turns towards me.

"Now, let the show begin."

And I start walking once more.

51

ADRIAN

It's the middle of the night when we manage to hijack one of the trucks. After disposing of the people inside and stealing their clothes, we're ready to go.

Marcel takes over at the wheel, while Vlad and I go in the back with some of his men. It's not precisely comfortable fitting everyone among the craters.

"Now, let's see what's so precious about these." Vlad takes a metal bar and forces the top of one of the craters off.

"So?" I ask, moving slightly closer to get a look inside.

"As I suspected," he muses and picks up a rifle from the crater. Inside, more weapons are stashed, one on top of the other. "Military grade too."

"That's a lot of weapons," I say, alarm bells ringing in my head.

"It is. But then again, a war is coming."

"And you're sure this is just for that *war?*" Vlad shakes his head.

"No... far too many for an underground war. For an all-out war, though? Not enough."

I frown.

"What do you mean an all-out war?"

"Come on, Hastings. You of all people should know. There is political instability. The alt-right movement is gaining supporters. There have already been so many small gatherings and protests all over the country. But now, they're slowly, very slowly, becoming more organized. It only takes one spark to light a torch."

"You're talking about civil unrest... instigating anarchy. Why would Jimenez want that?"

"Because when there are no rules, those who've never answered to anyone have the most to gain."

"So, you're saying that he *could* profit from anarchy."

"It's a two-way street. Jimenez will financially profit from the initial sales and then reap the benefits from the social unrest."

When he puts it like that, it does make sense. If what Vlad's saying ever comes to pass, it *will* be a bloodbath. Both figuratively and literally, and it could have wider political implications.

"Shit. We can't take any chances," I say, and Vlad grimly nods.

"It will not get to that," he says before amending. "Hopefully."

Marcel announces that we've arrived at the gates through one of the intercoms. They open, letting us pass through, and soon, we're in front of the building.

Someone opens the doors, and we remain in character, carrying the craters out. Vlad's people exit as well, mingling with Jimenez's guards.

"Let's go to the convened room," Vlad says, and Marcel and I follow. While Vlad had been able to hack into the CCTV feed from the street and from around the compound, he couldn't get inside the actual building. He'd told us that he could connect to the network and get access to the rest of the cameras once inside. But he needed the proximity.

We'd studied the blueprints of the building and had memorized all the entrances and exits and the rooms and their capacities.

Once inside a room on the ground floor, Vlad quickly takes out his tablet and connects to the system. It takes a while, but he is successful. He retrieves footage from the hallway and multiple rooms within the building.

We see staff and guards moving about freely, with most rooms either empty or filled with craters.

Vlad shifts from one feed to another.

"There," he says and pulls the feed to cover the whole screen.

Bianca is tied to a chair in the middle of the room. In the far back, a man is lounging on what looks to be a chaise.

"Jimenez," I mutter under my breath.

"Are you sure?" Both Vlad and Marcel look at me for confirmation, and I nod. I'd recognize him anywhere.

Vlad then pulls up the blueprints and works to pinpoint the location of the room.

"Once we're out, shoot before asking any questions."

One by one, we get out of the room and head directly towards the staircase. Vlad's men should have mixed with Jimenez's staff and should be on standby if anything happens.

The moment we open the staircase door, shots start ringing out.

"Duck." Marcel pushes me in front of him, turning around and returning the shots. I raise my gun as well and aim. From the corner of my eyes, I can see Vlad unsheathing his swords, ready to fight.

"Stop!" a voice commands, and the shooting stops immediately. We're all confused, and we see a man coming from the direction of the elevator.

Marcel's gun is fixed on him as he approaches us, but he's barehanded.

"The boss will see you now."

"Why would we trust you?" I ask, and he shrugs.

"You can come with me now and avoid more bloodshed, or you can make it on your own through a storm of bullets. It's up to you."

Vlad is the first one to sheath his swords and take a step forward.

"Ortega, isn't it?" The man smirks at him.

"Vladimir Kuznetsov. Can't say it's a pleasure." Ortega sizes Vlad up, displeasure written on his face.

"It's mutual, I assure you," Vlad retorts.

I look at Marcel to gauge his reaction, and he gives me a brief nod, following Vlad. I go as well.

Ortega leads us to the elevator, pressing 3.

"I won't forget what you did to Martinez," Ortega addresses

me. "I can't do anything now because the boss won't allow it. But best believe it's not forgotten."

I turn my head and don't reply. What's one more enemy in the scheme of all things?

Once the elevator rings that we've arrived at the specified floor, we follow Ortega towards the end of the hallway and inside a double door room.

As soon as we get inside, my eyes search for Bianca, and I find her sitting on a chair in the middle of the room, just like the camera feed had shown us. Her eyes widen when she sees me.

Disregarding everyone and everything around me, I dash to her side and untie her hands.

"Adrian," she whispers her tone slightly off.

"Did they hurt you? Are you okay?" I ask, looking her over to make sure she's unharmed.

"No... I'm fine. But Jimenez..." Her voice is calm, and she shakes her head. I immediately gather her in my arms and turn to where Marcel and Vlad are standing.

As I'm moving, someone claps.

"Wonderful. Just wonderful."

I turn my head slightly, and I see Jimenez approaching us, a cynical expression on his face.

"Put me down," Bianca says, but I am reluctant. "I'm fine." She pushes on my shoulder, trying to extricate herself from me. I relent and put her down. She seems fine on her feet, but I'm still not convinced...

Considering I went through the worst day of my life wondering what might have happened to her, I can't help but want to smother her to my chest. So, even though I put her down, I still sneak my arm around her waist, craving the contact.

Both Marcel and Vlad exchange words with Bianca to make sure she's okay.

"Look at you, lovebirds." Jimenez takes a seat on the chair Bianca had just vacated and looks at us, amused.

"We finally meet again, *Andrew*," I add sarcastically.

His mouth goes up in a cruel smile.

"Ah, you always were my favorite, Adrian... Did you never wonder why?"

"Why, was it your guilty conscience?"

Jimenez frowns for a second before his mouth goes in an O. "I forgot you still believe that nonsense that I killed your parents." He sighs as if it's the most absurd thing.

"What are you talking about? You *did* kill them," I say, almost angry that he'd have the gall to deny it to my face.

"Really? Please tell me how I killed them." What?

"I heard them that night. They were talking about you and a list of people involved with you. My mother was afraid of *you*," I say in an accusatory manner. Jimenez looks serious one moment before bursting into laughter.

"The list. Of course." He shakes his head, still smiling. "Have you never wondered why your mother was so afraid of me?" He tips his head back, waiting for my answer.

"Because she had dirt on you," I reply.

"As if," he scoffs. "You think some *dirt* was going to bring *me* down? No, your mother was afraid for a different reason altogether. She knew that if I found her, I'd take *you*."

"Me? What do you mean?"

"And finally, we get to the meat of the issue. Let me tell you a short story. When I was a young man, I met a woman. She was unlike any other I'd ever known, and of course, things developed until we became inseparable. But she didn't know what I did for a living. Once she found out, she was scandalized that I was breaking the law, and she tried to escape me. It didn't go well for her. But she tried again. And again. Until one day, she succeeded. But you see, when she did manage to leave, she wasn't alone anymore."

"What are you saying?" I barely get the words out, as my brain absorbs the information.

"When Paulina left me, she was six months pregnant. She was clever, I'll give her that. She found a man who married her and gave her the perfect cover. I searched for a long time for her, you know. Most of all, because I wanted *you*. My eldest born," he says, pride showing on his face.

I instinctively take a step back, feeling like I've been hit in the chest.

"What did you say?" I croak. Bianca's hand wraps itself around my arm in comfort. She seems just as stunned as me.

Looking at Vlad and Marcel, though, I can't gauge their reaction to this revelation. Their expressions are blank. If they're just as surprised, they sure aren't showing it.

"Don't be melodramatic. We're family," he dismisses my reaction.

"Is that why you killed them?"

"How many times do I have to tell you I didn't kill them. I would have if I'd known where they were hiding you. But I didn't."

"If you didn't.... then who else?" I shoot back. Who else would have the motive?

"Isn't it obvious, boy?" he asks, almost exasperated. "Let me enlighten you. There was only one other person who knew *you*, Theodore Hastings, were in fact Adrian Barnett. And that was Martin Ashby. He was a smart asshole; I'll give him that. He kept you near and married you to his daughter so he could use you against me."

"You're saying Martin killed my parents? Why?"

"Because of the list, why else? Who do you think was the first name on the list?" Jimenez asks, and I can only turn to Marcel, who averts his gaze guiltily. So, Martin was among the crossed-out names...

Twenty years. Twenty years in which I'd had one thought and one thought only.

Get Jimenez.

I'd been so single-minded about it that I'd walked through life almost like a robot. Each action serving to bring me closer to Jimenez. And now? Not only did he *not* kill my parents, he's also my fucking biological father. How am I supposed to take this in? What's the expected reaction? Because I can't even think straight. Everything I'd ever known is... shit.

"Fuck," I mutter, and Jimenez chuckles.

"I can't say I regret letting you think I killed your parents. You've certainly done well for yourself in the name of revenge."

"Did you know about me? When you were posing as Andrew?"

"Of course. I was alerted to your presence after your parents' death, and I tracked you down. Or what, do you really think it was such a coincidence that you ended up at the Basilica? Please... the moment you walked into Boston, I was aware of your every movement."

I give a bitter laugh. "So what, you were trying to find a way to kill me? That's why you got me into the to-the-death fights?"

"Kill you? Whyever would I kill my own heir? I was making you strong, boy. You needed to grow up and stop seeing life through rose-colored glasses."

"Am I supposed to thank you, then? For making me kill? For making me fight without respite?"

"Of course," he replies indignantly.

"Then, I'm surprised you let me go so easily," I add, realizing that he had indeed let me off the hook when I'd run off.

"I never let you go. I merely watched over."

"Really? Then why now? Why reveal yourself now?"

"Because you've reached a position of power that will allow us to consolidate our empire," he says proudly.

"*Our* empire?" I ask in disbelief.

"You are now my official heir."

"And Carlos? Isn't he your son too?"

"Carlos?" He almost laughs at that mention. "He was just a failed experiment. After Paulina left me, I tried to replicate everything with Elena... Didn't work. But don't worry about Carlos, he should be fish food by now," he adds casually, and I feel Bianca's hand tighten on my arm.

"He killed him," she whispers in my ear.

"And Matthew and Quinn Gallagher? How do they figure in your plans?"

"My father saved Matthew's life when he was a kid. He owed me, and I always cash in. That they saw the advantage of further working with me is their good foresight. But now that I'll have you, they're just extras."

"You actually expect me to join you? Are you screwed in the head?"

"Of course, you'll join me. You're extremely easy to read, Adrian. Did you look carefully at your wife?" He smirks and motions towards Bianca.

Her eyes widen in understanding before staring at me with horror.

"He poisoned me," she spits the words out.

"Remember the myth of Hades and Persephone. She only had to eat a few pomegranate seeds to forever tie herself to the dark side." He goes over the chaise and picks up an empty tea bottle.

"In your wife's case, only a few sips, and she's forever dependent on me."

"What did you give her?" Panic overtakes me.

"She's fine... for now. It's a slow-acting poison. I can give you an antidote for it every thirty days. But if she doesn't take it, then she'll die in excruciating pain. Is that what you want for your beloved wife?" Jimenez's mocking tone makes me clench my fists in frustration.

"Don't. Please, don't." Bianca takes my hand once more and pleads with me. "Don't do this. I'm fine with dying; you don't have to subject yourself to this madman."

"Are you fucking crazy?" I yell at her, taking her face in my hands. "How could you even ask me that?"

"Please, Adrian. Don't..." Her eyes are moist with unshed tears. I don't even understand how she thinks I'd even contemplate refusing him. How does she think I can live without her?

"Fine." I drop my hands and turn towards Jimenez. Bianca makes a grab for my arm, but I push her off.

"What do you want me to do?"

"Why, it's simple. Take over New York."

Just as Jimenez says this, I hear the door of the room open again. We all turn towards the newcomer. Everything then happens in slow motion.

The stranger lifts his arm and shoots Jimenez straight through the heart.

"No!" I yell, rushing at Jimenez's side. If he dies, so does Bianca.

No... No... This can't be happening.

At the same time, Marcel's voice rings out, "Tino, no!"

I put pressure on Jimenez's wound, trying to keep him alive.

"The antidote... please tell me where the antidote is," I beg him, as his life is about to end.

"N..." he starts, but it's in vain. His heart stops beating, and with it mine, too.

I slowly raise my head to look at Bianca and find her sharing my anguish.

"B..." She runs to me and hugs me to her chest.

Jimenez's killer has a proud look on his face and turning to Marcel, he just shrugs.

"Sorry, *fratello*."

52

BIANCA

I'm holding tightly onto Adrian's arm, trying to prevent him from doing anything stupid, especially when the other man is still holding a gun.

I understand his anguish, not because I feel it too, but because I'm aware of the consequences of Jimenez's death.

But do I have anyone else to blame but myself?

When Jimenez had taken me to this room, he'd been nothing but gracious and had started talking to me about his grand plans of taking over New York. He'd started by telling me how he'd managed to ingratiate himself with the Gallaghers. His father, Diego Jimenez, had been an extremely wealthy man in Colombia with tight ties to Escobar. The Gallaghers themselves had long been rooted in the crime scene in Boston.

Matthew Gallagher's father, in particular, had consolidated the foundation for their illegal fighting empire. At some point, though, he'd gotten into serious trouble with a Mexican cartel, who, coincidentally, was also an enemy of Diego's. And so, the Gallaghers had sought refuge with Diego Jimenez in Colombia. Jimenez himself had met Matthew as a child, and they'd become fast friends. And so, a close relationship born out of debt was born. Jimenez had been quick to take advantage of that when he'd wanted to spread his influence into Boston and the East Coast. Using the many connections he'd built at Princeton, he'd amassed a network ranging from the lowest intermediaries to the highest public functionaries.

The list Martin had so carefully guarded? It held less than a fraction of the people who owed Jimenez.

"The key to longevity in this life is to lead from the shadows." Jimenez had proudly related. "You were smart to check the photobooks, I'll give you that." At my small gasp, he'd chucked. "Oh, you think I didn't know? It's all the fault of that disappointment of a son of mine. He just couldn't keep his mouth shut. Because of his carelessness, we had to speed up all of our plans, including getting rid of the Agostis."

"Why didn't you get rid of the photobooks, if you're so smart?" I'd asked sassily.

"I'll take that as *my one* mistake. After becoming Andrew Gallagher, it seemed redundant. The Jimenez name was only used to inspire fear. No one actually *knew* who I was." It seemed off that as proud a man as Jimenez would admit to a mistake. But I'd soon found that not only was he intelligent and cunning, but he was also self-reflective.

Maybe that's why his brand of cruelty was so potent; it was borne out of a distinctly analytical mind. With no one to recognize him, he'd been able to slowly consolidate his empire and annex any adjacent smaller powers. He'd been playing games with everyone, but he'd been the only one aware of the rules.

While he'd not told me the exact reason why he'd assumed the identity of Andrew Gallagher, he'd revealed enough that I realized that the Gallaghers had soon found themselves under his rule. The possibilities had been endless, mostly as Jimenez was slowly but effectively gearing up to take over New York. He'd only had one obstacle—the Italians.

The five families weren't what they'd once been, he'd happily recounted. They'd split the territory amongst themselves, and more often than not, they were at each other's throats, taking every opportunity to wage war amongst themselves. Jimenez had just played on their own weaknesses by sowing a little bit of dissent here, a little there.

Soon, the families found themselves isolated and looking at the outside for support.

It had all been very carefully planned. A character study had given Jimenez the necessary target, banking on Enzo Agosti's desire for monopoly and exploiting his excessive pride.

"Enzo is... *was* an architect, just like me. When you encounter your likeness in every way... Well, it's easy to target the weak spots," Jimenez had said, implying that Enzo was probably dead by now.

"And with the Agostis out of the way, a large part of New York is already mine." He'd smiled at the prospect.

So engrossed in his storytelling I'd been that I hadn't even given one thought to accepting a drink from him. Not when my mouth was sore and dry, my tongue still suffering the aftermath of my not-so-bright plan.

And this is how I find myself now, looking at a long, drawn-out death, thanks to the same trickery I'd been admiring only hours prior.

Adrian tries to shove my hand away and head for Jimenez's killer, but I apply all of my force to keep him rooted to the spot.

"Why?" A painful cry slips from his lips.

But then the assailant shocks everyone when he looks at Marcel and adds an ironic, "Sorry, *fratello*."

B oth Adrian and I are now staring at Marcel open mouthed.

"Marcel?" Adrian croaks, and a prickling feeling tells me this night of revelations is yet to be over. I sneak a glance at Adrian and see his face morph into a myriad of emotions.

The man looks at our shocked expressions and laughs.

"You did good, Marcello. Better than even *I* could have done it," he drawls. Marcel just looks at him as if he's seen a ghost.

"Who are you?" I ask, and he gives a sarcastic laugh.

"Valentino Lastra. At your service." He does a mock of a curtsy with his cane. "Marcello's brother."

Valentino looks to be in his mid-forties, thin and barely holding himself upright, needing a cane to keep straight.

"Lastra?" Adrian asks, his eyes never leaving Marcel. "Marcel, what's the meaning of this?"

"I'm sorry," Marcel whispers, averting his gaze.

"Sorry? For what?" Adrian asks.

"Come on, Marcel. Tell your *friends* what you're sorry for. Or should I?"

Marcel is silent, his eyes distant.

"Marcello here owed me a debt. A *tremendous* debt, I might add," Valentino emphasizes. "And the only way to repay it was for him to shadow you in your quest for vengeance. I knew that *you* were the most likely person to draw Jimenez out. After which, of course, Marcel would report back to me."

The moment he says that I think back to Marcel's actions. Sometimes he'd acted suspicious. But then another thought crosses my mind.

The list...

"Is that why you hid Martin's name from the list? You were afraid he'd stop looking for Jimenez if he knew Martin was the one who killed his parents?" I ask, accusatory.

Marcel flushes, his entire countenance screaming his shame.

Adrian gives Marcel one last look that conveys the disappointment he feels at the betrayal, before turning to his bother.

"Why? Why was Jimenez so important to you?" Adrian addresses Valentino. "Why kill him?" He shakes his head. "You don't know what you've done..."

Valentino scoffs. "Done? I got rid of a plague that roamed this earth. Please... as if everyone isn't better off without him. As to why? It's quite simple. He killed my wife. And do you know *why* he did it?" Valentino's eyes bulge in his head, his expression almost maniacal. "To blame *me* for her death, so that Rocco could turn against me for killing his daughter."

"And now you've condemned *my wife* to the same fate." Adrian's voice is full of bitterness.

Valentino frowns.

"Jimenez poisoned her, and he was the only one with the antidote," Vlad interjects, his voice steady and devoid of any emotion.

Valentino's face falls for a second, but he quickly recovers. In a split of a second, I find myself on my back, with Adrian charging towards him.

He tackles him to the ground, his fists going straight to his face. My eyes widen, and I signal for Vlad to help me get him off.

We must have been too slow because the sound of a gun discharging permeates the air.

We both stop in our track, and we watch in horror as Valentino pushes Adrian off him, breathing heavily. On his back, Adrian groans in pain, but I only see the spot of red forming at his temple.

"No!" I yell and fling myself towards him. "No... this can't be happening...." My hands go to his wound.

A head wound... I'm frantic in my movements, not knowing what to do. I bring my hands to my shirt and rip a significant portion of it, using it to stop the blood and wrap it around his head.

"911... call 911." I don't recognize my voice as I look at his shallow breaths.

Please, Adrian, please! Stay with me!

Valentino drags himself to his feet, a horrified look on his face.

"I didn't mean... It went off..." He keeps on shaking his head in shock.

Then, with a last glance at Marcel, he grips the gun tightly and places it under his chin.

There's only Marcel's voice as he runs towards him before Valentino pulls the trigger, blowing up his brains in front of all of us.

His body falls to the ground, and we're all stupefied at the turn of events.

A pained wail comes from Marcel as he hurries to his brother's side. His face is unrecognizable now, a big exit hole marring his forehead, his brains leaking out.

Vlad's been the only one relatively calm throughout all of this, but even *he* averts his eyes when he sees the amount of blood flooding the room.

With measured strides, he puts a hand on Marcel's shoulder. Marcel flinches slightly, but he's too busy mourning his brother.

"He was dying anyway," Vlad comments. "He had Multiple Sclerosis."

"You knew?" Marcel's appalled look doesn't intimidate Vlad as he continues.

"Valentino knew he was going to die all along. But he wanted to avenge Romina first and clear his name."

Adrian gasps for air, struggling to keep his eyes open.

"Shh... it's okay," I try to tell him, focusing my strength on his bleeding wound.

"Hang on, please," I plead again, and Vlad gives me a tight nod of assurance.

"The ambulance should be here soon," he says and then leaves the room.

I cradle Adrian's head to my chest, while Marcel grieves for his already departed brother.

After the paramedics arrive, I don't exactly know what happens. They try to separate me from Adrian, and I just can't let go.

"Miss, please let us do our job," someone says to me, but I just shake my head. "No..."

"Miss." They repeat and wrench me from Adrian's side. His eyes are closed, and I don't see any sign of life on his face. My breathing grows laborious.

"Please, help my husband," I say between pants, and one of the paramedics takes me aside while they load Adrian on a stretcher.

"Miss, look at me." My eyes are unfocused, and my chest feels constricted. There's a faint noise in my head, and everything is distorted.

"Miss, please breathe. You're having a panic attack." I can't focus on what he's saying. I can't concentrate on anything but the thought of Adrian dying. The idea of a world without him. My breaths become even sparser, and one hand clutches at my chest while the other digs into the paramedic's arm.

"Miss, stop, or I'll have to sedate you." I don't know what's happening, but I can't stop. The only time I catch my breath is to yell Adrian's name. I'm so focused on getting to him, making sure he'll be all right, I don't realize when they inject me with something. Suddenly, my lids feel heavy, and I go under.

My eyes flutter open. I'm disoriented for a few seconds before everything comes back to me. Adrian!

"Where's my husband?" I jump up from the bed I'm lying in and yell. I take in my surroundings and see I'm in a hospital. There are a few rows of beds around, all of them filled with patients. I look at my arm and notice an IV drip, probably with fluids. I wrench the needle from my skin and go towards one of the nurses at the end of the station.

"I'm looking for my husband," I tell her.

She looks me over in a bored fashion and just says, "Don't know," then turns around, leaving me there.

I yank her arm with all my strength and back her into a wall.

"Where is my husband?" I yell at her, and she retaliates by calling security. They tug on my arm to release her, but I keep on crying out, "Where is my husband?"

Finally, after one security guard restrains me, a doctor comes by.

"Your husband is Theodore Hastings?" the man asks, and I give a swift nod.

"He's still in surgery. Here, let me." The doctor gives the guard an okay look and takes me back to my bed.

"Tell me," I beg him, and he sighs.

"Your husband suffered a gunshot wound to the head. Luckily, the bullet only grazed his temporal bone and didn't lodge itself inside."

"That's good, isn't it?" I quickly ask, hopeful at the diagnosis.

"We don't know yet. The bullet did do damage in its trajectory. We can't yet gauge how the injury affected the patient, or if he'll wake up."

"What... do you mean if he'll wake up?"

"The brain is a sensitive organ. It really depends from case to case how the patient will recover. We're doing everything we can to ensure the best care for your husband. But you should, in any eventuality, prepare for the worst."

"Worst...?" I trail off.

"He may become brain dead... at any moment," the doctor professionally tells me. The blow is, nonetheless, lethal. I stumble back onto the bed, my hand going to my heart immediately. I'm trying to regulate my breathing when the doctor continues, "We've seen his file, and he is an organ donor. I wanted to let you know that..." I tune him out. Organ donor? Yeah, that sounds like my husband.

But that means... I can't deal with this.

No...

My hand shoots out and wraps itself around the doctor's throat.

"You *will* make sure he lives. If not, I will hunt down everyone you care about, and I will put a bullet through their skulls. Are we clear?" I threaten in a steely voice. The doctor pales at my words and just nods numbly. I release him, and he scurries away.

Oh, Adrian...

I don't know how I make it to the waiting room on my shaky legs, but once I do, the sight of Marcel slumped against a wall greets me.

"You!" I spit out the words and watch as Marcel's head shoots up, his eyes widening at my presence.

"It's all your fault," I accuse him, launching myself at him. I don't even get to touch him as Marcel pales and flinches away, effectively avoiding my fist. "Fuck you!" I throw myself against him again, but this time, a firm grip holding me from behind stops me.

"Enough, B," Vlad whispers in my hair.

"You knew... you knew everything," I cry out at him and throw haphazard punches. Vlad takes it for a minute before restraining me.

"Stop." And I do... not because I want to, but because my body can't withstand the effort anymore. I sink into him and let my tears flow freely.

"How could you?" I keep on repeating. Vlad continues to stroke my hair, letting me purge my feelings through my tears.

A while later and after I've calmed down, the surgeon in charge of Adrian's case comes out to tell us the surgery's been a success.

"We still need to wait until wakes up to see if there have been any side effects from the bullet, or the surgery." He then tells us that Adrian will be moved to a private salon.

After they bring him to the salon, I tell the doctor that no one else is allowed to visit him but *me*.

Marcel looks at me remorsefully, but I know Adrian wouldn't want to see him either. I could see it in his eyes when he'd learned that his *trusted* friend had been using him this whole time, something inside of him had died. I'm not about to put more stress on him when he needs to recover from such a severe injury. I also let Vlad know that I don't think it would be optimal for him to visit.

I can't say that I know precisely what Vlad's angle had been in all of this. But he hadn't seemed surprised at any of the revelations. I'm not sure I can trust him right now.

I make my own space inside the salon to watch over Adrian and only leave him for a little while when it's apparent that I'm missing many necessities.

I make a quick trip home and pack enough clothes and toiletries for a week and some weapons just in case anyone tries something. At this point, better be prepared.

The first day in the hospital passes without any change. The doctor informs me that some people take a little longer to wake.

And so, one day turns into two, and two turns into three, and still nothing.

I'm almost out of my mind worrying about Adrian that I haven't even had time to think about my own predicament.

On that third day, Vlad gives me a call and urges me to get my bloodwork done to check for the poison. I reluctantly agree and go through the process, but only because I'm still holding out hope that Adrian will wake.

If he doesn't... then what's the point of me living still?

At the end of the week, my bloodwork comes back clean—no

substances found in my system, no drugs or poison. Jimenez had been bluffing.

I almost laugh at the results.

Of course, he had been bluffing.

I don't even get to enjoy the good news because Adrian has still not awoken.

Every day, I sit by his side. Sometimes I read to him, sometimes I tell him stories of our life together. Sometimes I just beg him to come back to me.

It's all in vain.

And I can't help but feel that it's all my fault.

———

Two weeks go by like this. Neither Marcel nor Vlad have tried to come to the hospital again, even though I've been staying connected with Vlad, and he's been updating me about everything that's been happening.

The cops have taken over Jimenez's compound and have confiscated the illegal weapons. Adrian's been hailed a hero for his capture of Jimenez, even though he'd been killed by Valentino. The entire episode has been covered up to look like a mob squabble between the Lastra family and Jimenez, and no one else has been mentioned in the official report.

On the other hand, the Gallaghers have placed a bid for power for the remnants of Jimenez's empire, with Ortega and some other smaller cartels trying to assert their own independence. The entire situation is messy, in Vlad's words. It doesn't help that the Marchesi have made camp in New York as well, trying to build up their power as part of one of the five families again.

Enzo eventually makes it out alive and is released from the ICU. With his health still precarious, he hasn't yet involved himself in the political games afoot.

I'm lost in my thoughts when the monitor beeps suddenly. I jerk my head towards Adrian, panicking at the idea that this might be the end. After so many days with no response, the doctors have told me that the chances of him ever waking up are dwindling.

"Doctor?" I yell, opening the door to the salon. I see some nurses hurrying towards me, followed by a doctor. They all push me in the back, telling me to give them space to work on the patient.

Adrian... My lower lip tremble, my eyes mist. Is this the end?

I can't even see what they're doing, as they all surround his bed.

"Hi, I'm Dr. Evans, your attending physician. Can you tell me your name?" The doctor ask a question.

"I... Theodore... Hastings." I hear Adrian's voice answering. He's... awake? I can't even control myself as I step towards him.

"Do you remember what happened?" the doctor asks.

"No."

"You were shot in the head. You've been in a coma for the last two weeks. What's the last thing you remember?"

Even though the doctor and the nurses are still around him, I manage to find the right angle to see his face.

"I was at a meeting with the mayor... we were discussing..." He stops and frowns. "I don't remember."

"That's perfectly normal. Don't worry. You've suffered major trauma to your brain. It's completely normal to feel confused and for some memories to feel fuzzy," the doctor assures Adrian, before finally spotting me.

"Mrs. Hastings. As you can see, he's still confused. But him waking up is good news. Far better than we would have expected. We will continue to run some tests to make sure everything is in order," the doctor explains to me, and I see Adrian look even more confused at the mention of my name.

"Theo," I take a step towards him and say, using his official name since there are still people around.

He regards me for a second, tilting his head to the side.

"Who are you?" he finally asks. My eyes widen at his question.

"Doctor?" I ask, panicked. He doesn't remember me?

Dr. Evans is about to leave the room when he hears the exchange. He comes back to Adrian's side and asks him again.

"Mr. Hastings, what's today's date?"

"You said I was in a coma for two weeks? Then it should be... September 20th?" He looks hopeful.

"And the year?"

"2010."

"Mr. Hastings, I need you to be calm. It's 2020. It seems that you don't remember the past ten years."

The doctor looks at me and shakes his head, motioning me to step outside.

"You said he was only confused," I say when we're outside the salon.

"Memory loss can happen. His injury was to his temporal lobe, and as such, amnesia is not uncommon."

"When will he remember?"

"I couldn't say. It could be tomorrow, in two months, or..."

"Never," I finish his sentence. He grimaces at me but nods.

"I'm sorry," he says before leaving me.

I slump against the wall, all my fears materializing. He's alive... and yet he doesn't know me. Seven years of memories made together... just gone.

What if he never remembers me?

What if...

But wouldn't that be better for him? Not remembering? He wouldn't know of his friend's betrayal... he wouldn't know his real parentage... and he wouldn't know me.

But what good has it done to him, knowing me? All I've done is lie to him and hurt him, all in the name of my selfish obsession.

Wouldn't he be better without all of this?

There's also the matter of my own father, not that I'd like to claim him as such, killing his parents. Would he even be able to look at me without remembering that glaring detail?

I admit I've been contemplating this since I'd first seen him lying helpless in his hospital bed.

I've had two long weeks to think about our life together. Fourteen days in which I've realized just how much I've depended on Adrian for *my* happiness.

He's been mine, and so that makes *me* happy.

But being mine comes with repercussions... countless dangers.

One decision, and I can give him a brand-new life. A life where he doesn't live for revenge. A life he can enjoy.

Without me.

Maybe this is a sign. A sign that I should finally let go.

My feet slide to the floor as a hand goes over my mouth to cover my sobs.

A lifetime without my Adrian. Can I do it? Probably not, but for him, I will try.

He deserves to be happy.

I have seven years' worth of memories to last me a lifetime.

And he has a clean slate.

Once my mind is made up, I know what I have to do. And I have to do it fast before I lose my resolve.

After all the nurses leave, I head inside, putting on my best smile.

"Who are you?" he asks again when he sees me. I expect it, but I still freeze when I see the suspicion in his eyes.

"A friend," I lie.

Here it goes, the beginning of the end.

"A friend?" he repeats, studying me closely.

"A friend from work," I amend.

"Then... do you know what happened to me?"

"You were caught in the crossfire with a dangerous cartel. But the good news is that you're a hero now. Jimenez is dead because of you, and the FBI's managed to confiscate millions worth of illegal weapons."

"Jimenez?" I can see his mind working. Assuming he remembers everything from before 2010, then he still remembers his crusade against Jimenez.

"Yes, he was the leader of the cartel," I add.

"And I caught him?"

"Yes." I don't give him more details. He doesn't need to know.

This is a good thing. He won't only stop his quest for revenge now, but he'll also *not* remember Marcel's betrayal or the fact that Jimenez is his biological father. He won't have to experience that heartbreak again.

We talk a little more, and I give him vague information, enough to help him build a narrative. As our time draws to a close, I rise from my chair and tell him goodbye.

"Will you come again?" he asks as I'm about to leave.

"Probably not." I give him a rueful smile, and he seems disappointed.

On the spur of the moment, I drop my head and give him a kiss on the forehead.

"Be well, Theo," I whisper.

I head to the apartment and empty it of my stuff. I contact a moving company and send everything to my spare apartment. I also decide to take Mally with me.

It takes me two full days to erase every trace of Bianca Ashby from Theodore Hastings' life. After I'm done, I contact Vlad and ask for a favor.

"Are you sure you want to do this?" Vlad asks a couple of days later, as we near the aircraft.

I nod, looking at the horizon that signifies my new future.

"You asked me once if what I feel towards Adrian is love. I guess it wasn't at that point... but I've learned since. Before, I loved Adrian because he was *mine*. He was my toy, and that made *me* happy. But I never once stopped to ask myself if it made *him* happy, too. Later, I saw how my presence in his life affected him. I hurt him, but I never recognized just how much. It wasn't until I saw the light in his eyes die when he learned of Marcel's betrayal or that Jimenez was his biological father. I was so incensed on his behalf that only later did I realize I'd done the exact same to him. I'd lied and manipulated him, and I'd betrayed his trust.

"Yes, I loved him, and I wanted him more than anything, but it was toxic. I know that now. Just how I know that I love him enough to give him a chance at true happiness. Without Jimenez, without the mob... without me." I clench my hand on my carry-on. "I'm not normal, nor will I ever be. He deserves someone better. He deserves to be happy."

"What about you?" Somehow, a tear makes its way down my cheek at his question.

"I'll survive. I always do. I'll just do what I do best—kill."

"I'll miss you, B." Vlad turns to me and takes me in his arms.

"We'll be in touch... boss." I smile and pat his back.

"I hear Moscow is nice this time of the year," he says wistfully.

"You can always visit."

"I can... can't I..." We stand in silence for a moment before taking my first step into the plane, leaving Vlad behind.

"Thank you, Vlad. For everything."

53

ADRIAN

I wake up to a throbbing pain in my temple.

Again.

The doctor's assured me it's normal and it should go away soon. I'd gotten the gist of how I got shot, even though it all seems foreign to me when I try to remember it. Of course, the most unbelievable thing is that Jimenez is dead...

The man I'd been after my whole life is dead. And I'd helped do it. I'm still waiting for that sense of relief to come, but it doesn't.

My stay in the hospital has been rather lonely, if I can use that word. I'd had people from work come by and wish me a healthy recovery, but they'd been rather reserved, especially when they'd heard about my memory loss. But that's not why I've felt this aching emptiness...

Somehow, I can't stop thinking about that woman... The one who'd been there when I'd first woken up. It's been three days now, and she's all I can see when I close my eyes.

Her plump lips... The way she'd looked at me.

I have to wonder if we were involved before in some capacity. She seemed disappointed when I didn't recognize her. Although... maybe my brain didn't recognize her, but my body sure did. I'd almost asked the doctor if being constantly hard was a side effect of my brain injury. Otherwise, I can't explain this. I just have to picture her face and...

I sigh.

It's happened again.

Making sure there's no one around, I slip my hand into my blue hospital pants and grab my cock, moving my hand from base to tip and picturing her pouty mouth. A groan escapes my lips as I increase my movements, focusing on that soft kiss she'd laid on my forehead.

I recall her breath on my skin... My own breathing picks up.

I swipe the moisture seeping from the head of my cock and use it as lubricant, imagining it's her mouth swallowing me whole. One pump...two pumps and I gasp, coming all over my stomach. My vision goes white as I ride the wave of pleasure.

Bianca...

Her name is Bianca.

Small snippets burst inside my head.

"Fuck!" I groan aloud, moving out of my bed and towards the bathroom.

I try to clean myself up. Recurring flashes of pain make me stumble, and I grab onto the sink to stabilize myself.

I take a deep breath.

Bianca...

More images appear.

Our wedding. Us at home, making love. Her betrayal. She lied to me...

Shocked, I back into the wall and collapse on the floor, gasping for air.

I remember...

Seconds pass by and the images trickle into my mind unbidden.

It's like a flash. One moment I'm doubting everything about my life, the next, I'm able to see everything with astounding certainty.

I remember...*everything*.

Including Marcel double crossing me and Jimenez revealing he was my father.

I blink twice, somehow burying that in the back of my mind, focusing on only one thing.

Bianca...

Where is she?

With great difficulty, I get up and ring one of the nurses, asking her to bring me my cell phone. She's reluctant at first, but eventually complies. She hands me my phone and leaves.

I immediately dial Bianca's number, but it doesn't go through, saying that the number's been disconnected.

What?

Did something happen to her? Knowing Bianca, there's absolutely no way she'd leave me here on my own.So where is she?

Then I remember something else.

Jimenez saying he poisoned her. Jimenez dying, and with him dying any information regarding an antidote.

No, that's not possible. How much time has passed?

I frown, thinking back to what the doctor told me. A couple of weeks? Maybe more? What if...

No, no. I shake my head vigorously at the thought. I refuse to believe something might have happened to her.

But then why did she lie to me? Why did she say she was just a coworker, and then left me?

I'm almost hyperventilating, my thoughts straying into dangerous territory. I don't even want to think that she might have left me to...

Die.

No, she's all right. She has to be. Maybe she's only giving me some space.

Yes, that must be it. Although it's unusually thoughtful and nice of her—and entirely antithetic to the Bianca I know—that must be it.

Just to confirm what I already know to be true, I call the only person who'd know where she is.

Vlad.

He'll just confirm my suspicions. She's probably at home with Mally.

"Hastings..." Vlad's voice is dripping with amusement as he answers.

"Where is she?" My tone is harsher than I would have liked.

"My, but you recovered faster than I would have expected. If only B knew." He chuckles, and I grit my teeth. It's not going to be easy to get anything from him, is it?

"Tell me, where is she?" I repeat.

"How much do you remember?"

"Enough."

"Interesting... I'll be there soon." He says and hangs up.

What?

I don't even get to be mad because the doctor comes in with his army of nurses and they start asking me questions, taking my vitals and doing all sorts of things. I'm only halfway listening to what they are saying, too preoccupied with Bianca's whereabouts.

They leave and I retrieve my phone and start calling Vlad again. And again.

"Chill, Hastings, will you?" Vlad is in the doorway, holding up his phone and dangling it around as it rings.

He rolls his eyes at me and comes closer.

"You look almost human," he says, scrutinizing my bandage. I don't want to question what he means by that, so I just go straight to the point.

"Where is she?"

Vlad's expression is no longer bright. He leans back and regards me in a serious manner.

"She left you," he simply states and I frown. "Who would have thought she had it in her, right?" His mouth curls up in an attempt to smile, but it's not quite there.

"What do you mean?" I ask.

He moves again, and starts to pace around the room. I'd forgotten about Vlad and his inability to stay still.

"She thought you'd never remember, so she decided to spare you the unpleasant details of Jimenez's death. That fool." He shakes his head. "She's too impulsive for her own good. I don't know how she equated you not remembering immediately after an obvious brain injury, to you permanently not remembering... But I digress. You know Bianca. Once she gets something in that brain of hers, granted, coke-free now, there's no stopping her."

"So she just up and left? And you didn't stop her?"

"Why would I? I have to say, though, I'm impressed by her noble—admittedly stupid—actions. Who would have thought her capable of that, right?" He muses, and I'm getting impatient.

"So where is she?"

"She's in Moscow. I sent her to work for an acquaintance."

"So... She's fine?" I hesitate, trying to steel myself for the answer.

"Of course. Turns out Jimenez was bluffing."

I sigh in relief.

"So what are you going to do now?" Vlad asks as he settles in front of my bed.

"Go after her. After my doctor clears me..." I add reluctantly add.

"Hmm... You might want to reconsider."

"What do you mean?"

"Word's out on the streets about Jimenez's heir. You'll be targeted. Many people are trying to consolidate power right now, and you're just the thorn they can't wait to get rid of," he chuckles.

I frown.

"So what do you propose I do? Fake my own death?" I add rather ironically. But the look Vlad gives me tells me he doesn't think so.

"Indeed. You do just that. Might work."

"You're kidding."

"Nope. In fact, I should have thought of that. Yes..." He nods, more to himself. "That might be your best bet. Otherwise, you'll have who knows how many cartels after you, and possibly the Irish too."

I'm stunned. I hadn't had the time to think about the repercussions of Jimenez's death, or the fact that we were related. But Vlad does make sense... Chances are, the moment I'm out the hospital I'll be a hunted man, regardless of my position in NYPD, or maybe even because of it.

"I guess you're right," I admit, and Vlad hufs.

"Of course I'm right. I'm always right."

His hand goes to the pocket of his blazer and he removes a pack of gum, popping some into his mouth. Why do I feel like I've seen this exact scene too many times before?

"I'll even help you," he says while chewing.

"Gee, thanks." I add dryly.

Vlad turns to leave.

"Although... One more thing." He turns slightly. "Cut Marcello some slack... Don't shut him out until you've heard his side of the story."

I raise a brow at him.

"Really? That's what you have to say? When you've known all along who he was?"

"My relationship with Marcello is complicated at best. But he isn't like me. And I know he valued your friendship."

"How? By betraying me?"

Vlad pauses a little, his eyes narrowing a little.

"Things are rarely as they seem Hastings. Just...listen to him. If anyone deserves a second chance, it's Marcello." He shakes his head. "He's a wretched being, that man. Even for my standards."

"That's assuming he will even try to explain why he did." I grunt.

"He might. It really isn't my place to say anything but..." He takes a deep breath. "The things Marcel has lived... It's a wonder he is who he is today."

"Fine..." I grumble, not wanting to delve deeper into this.

Vlad gives me a mock salute and leaves.

It's only been hours since I've recovered my memories, so I can't say I've had the time to ponder the reasons behind Marcel's betrayal.

Marcello, I correct myself.

I shake my head at the thought. He didn't just betray me. He wasn't even who I thought he was.

Marcello Lastra. The son of a mobster. A mobster himself for all I knew.

I let out a sarcastic laugh.

Why does this seem so familiar?

It feels like only a while ago I went through the same thing with Bianca.

They'd both hidden who they really were and lied to me. And yet, I'd forgiven Bianca...

But she didn't betray you, my inner voice tells me.

Yeah, there is a slight difference between Bianca's treachery and Marcel's. Bianca had never meant me harm. In fact, she'd done everything in her power to protect me, even when it meant putting herself in dangerous situations.

Marcel... He knew. He knew everything, damn it!

He knew how hard I'd searched for JImenez and how much I'd wanted to make him pay for what I thought he had done to my parents. And yet, he'd so easily sold me to his brother.

What had Valentino Lastra said? That Marcel owed him a debt?

Was that debt more important than our friendship?

I remember the early days of our acquaintance, and how we'd eventually bonded over the fact that we were both extremely private people as well as mildly taciturn - Marcel more so than me. In the years that I'd known him, he'd started to become more open, even though some things simply stuck.

Like his phobia of touch.

That brings me to a halt.

Why had I never wondered? Why had I never asked?

The more I think about it, the more ashamed I am at myself for being such a lousy friend.

He hadn't told me and I hadn't pried. But maybe I should have?

I'd often thought about how private Marcel was about certain things, like his personal life, or day to day activities. If it wasn't work-related, or more so, Jimenez related, we rarely saw each other.

Had I been blind this whole time? Blind to what was happening to him when no one was watching?

I remember his face when his brother had revealed every-thing. He'd been shameful and remorseful.

It might be that...

I shake my head, now more confused than ever.

In one regard, though, Vlad is right. I'll listen to him, if he does in fact want to tell me, and then I'll think about it.

The following day, the doctor comes for another check-up and given that I've now remembered everything, he tells me I can get discharged in a couple of days.

Vlad, though, has proven to be even more unpredictable, as he's started forwarding me messages from Bianca, about her settling in and mundane stuff about her life in Russia.

I have to say. Those are probably the highlight of my day, and I've started looking forward to each and every one of them.

I miss her.

I didn't think it was possible to miss someone so much.

But I know there are some things I have to take care of before joining her. With the first item on the list being faking my death.

It's my last day at the hospital when someone knocks lightly at the door. I'd been packing up everything and was already looking forward to some not so bland food - considering I'd been eating mostly porridge.

"Come in," I say, and my eyebrows go up when I see who it is.

Marcel.

His face is blank as he comes inside the room and closes the door.

"I see you've spoken to Vlad?" I ask, observing him closely.

He shrugs, and he grabs the chair by the door and places it in front of me.

"What are you doing here, Marcel?" I ask, seeing that he's not inclined to start the conversation.

"I'm not here to ask for forgiveness." He finally starts, lifting his eyes to look at me.

"Then why are you here?"

"I thought you deserve to know why I did what I did. I won't excuse my behavior in any way... But I want you to know why I *had* to help my brother." He takes a deep breath. "It's something that I haven't told anyone before, and you may end up hating me even more after." He laughs nervously.

"So tell me." I prompt him. I honestly doubt there's anything that could make me see what had happened with different eyes, but I'm willing to listen to him.

"I guess I should start with who my father was..."

***

I was wrong. The entire time Marcel told me his story I sat there listening, not even moving a finger.

It had all been...too much.

At some point I had to wonder if he was describing a horror movie. Surely there weren't any people like that in the world. And yet, the more he talked, the more I had to calm myself, not show any reaction.

It was his story... and I could see it affected him reliving it like this.

Then he finally mentioned how his phobia of touch had developed. How he'd made the mistake of showing weakness. And then everything had spiraled so out of control he'd had to make multiple deals with the devil in order to keep everyone he loved safe.

When he was finished, I could only stare at him.

"So now you know... I never wanted to betray you. Hell, you were probably my only genuine friend. But I had to. I owed it to my brother. And what he did to me..." He shakes his head.

"I'm sorry." That's all that comes out of my mouth. What else can I say, really?

"I understand if you won't forgive me. But I wanted you to have some closure. And more than anything, I wanted to let you know that I do value you as a friend."

He stands up to leave.

"I'm sorry." He says once more, before closing the door behind him.

I don't know how to react to what he just dumped on me. How does someone even process that?

But I suppose there will be time for that later.

For now, I must plan how to get my wife back.

54

BIANCA

I'm carefully cleaning my gun when my phone rings. I spare a glance and see that it's a message from Vlad.

I've told him that I don't want to know what's happening in New York, but he's continued to send me links to different articles relating to the ongoing mafia war. It's not surprising that with tensions rising high, the situation has gotten out of control, and hysteria has hit the streets. For all my reluctance to keep up with the times, I always cave in and check the articles.

It's my damn curiosity.

At least Vlad has kept to himself any news of Adrian.

I can't say it's been easy so far. I think about him at least once every hour. But day by day, the pain of being separated from him has become more bearable.

The moment I'd landed in Moscow, I'd gone to the apartment Vlad had helped set up for me. I'd then spent a couple of days just walking around, familiarizing myself with the new city.

Vlad had put me in contact with the Andropov family, one of Russia's most prominent crime families, and had recommended me for my skills. I'd gone for a meeting with their Pakhan, and we'd found ourselves establishing a comfortable partnership.

Of course, as any suspicious Russian leader, he'd tested me first, and it hadn't been entirely pleasant.

He'd sent me on an endurance mission to assassinate a renowned political figure. It had taken me two weeks to complete the task, but he'd been more than impressed with my results. He'd offered me an exclusivity contract on the spot. He'd initially wanted five years. I'd talked him down to one. I don't want to just settle. The world is my oyster at this point, right?

Whenever my thoughts stray to Adrian, I just try to find something else to take my mind off him. One of the things I've started obsessing over have been tattoos.

Andropov has a few talented artists, and one of them has managed to turn to life my disjointed ideas into a wonderful tale. I've gotten an entire sleeve on my left hand, spreading further onto my back. The tattooist has warned me against getting too many at once, but I've needed the pain to keep going. He's eventually relented after a few threats.

Starting from my hand, a bow spreads across my knuckles, with an arrow sticking out and extending towards my middle finger. Upwards on my arm are different scenes that depict the myth of Hero and Leander. I'd thought it entirely too appropriate since I could see my story with Adrian in them.

Both had been on opposite sides, never to be together naturally. But their love had tricked fate, and they'd enjoyed beautiful moments together as Hero swam towards Leander, guided by her torch. But like all love stories, it ended tragically when the light went out, and Hero was swept away by the waves. And so, I'd failed to protect Adrian, and he'd been swept away from me by his memory loss.

In the original tale, Leander joins Hero in death. The finale of the rendition on my back is still a work in progress... yet I already know how it'll turn out.

I sigh and open the message. Another article. Great. Wonder who died now... Shaking my head, I put the phone down. I try to go back and continue cleaning my guns, but the curiosity is killing me. I eventually relent and open it. When I see the article's title, my eyes go wide, and I drop the phone.

NYPD Chief Commissioner Theodore Hastings was found dead, aged 34.

I blink once. Twice. I take the phone again and read, dread accumulating in the pit of my stomach.

NYPD Chief Commissioner Theodore Hastings was found dead, sources say. The hero who put an end to Jimenez's reign of terror had been suffering from a head injury that led to complications. NYPD and the mayor's office have refused to comment on the issue.

The more I read, the more I feel like I'm losing my mind. It can't be right.

I try dialing Vlad, but he's not answering.

It can't be right.

I google Theodore Hastings, and few other news sources come up with the same information.

Dead.

Head injury complications.

It *is* true.

I can't process this...

For what feels like forever, I sit on my apartment floor, staring at the walls. Flashes of Adrian inundate my mind. It's slow at first, like a fissure in a dam. But slowly, I'm flooded to the brim, and I can't help it, but my non-existent emotions spill over.

"No!" I yell, throwing my phone at the wall. I grab whatever's closest to me and throw it as well, smashing it to pieces. I repeat the action with everything in my path until my apartment is a pile of broken things, just like me.

Unable to stand there one more minute, I grab my coat and head to Andropov's club.

I can't deal with this. It's too much... feeling.

The moment I get to the club, I make a beeline for the bar and order an entire bottle of vodka. The bartender doesn't even bat an eye as he slides it in front of me, together with a shot glass.

I pour the first shot and down it. And then a second. And then a third. At some point, I lose count.

One of the Pakhan's brothers Nikolai spots me and makes his way towards me.

"Artemis." His eyes go to the Vodka bottle, and he frowns. "Rough night?"

"You could say," I slur my words.

"Come dance." He tugs on my hands and brings me to the dance floor. I don't know what I'm doing, my limbs just moving about. I thought that alcohol would help dull the pain. It doesn't.

"Make it stop!" I yell, my hands going to my ears. "Please, make everything stop."

Nikolai tilts his head and studies me, slowly withdrawing his wallet and fishing something out of it. It looks like a small tablet.

"Want this?" I try to squint my eyes to see what he's showing me, but it's kind of blurry at this point.

"What is it?"

"LSD."

"Will it numb the pain?"

"It may." He doesn't need to say anything else. I snatch it from his hand and put it in my mouth.

We keep dancing for a little longer, and I start feeling off. I can't even feel my limbs anymore.

I need to go home.

I don't know how I leave the club, how I walk home, or how I even know where home is. I have very few moments of awareness.

I just know that at some point, I'm back home. I fall on my bed, my eyes open. I see this blue lace covering the walls. I'm so intrigued by it that I trace the intricate design from one end of the wall to the other. My finger draws the form in the air, and I smile at the silliness of it. If only Adrian were alive.

As I trace a lace thread, I suddenly stop when I feel something soft on my fingertip. I frown. I push once. So soft. I push again. And again. Until something grabs my finger.

"B?" The hallucinations have started as I raise my eyes to look into Adrian's face. His beautiful, angelic face. He must be with the angels now, no? Maybe I'm communicating with him in heaven. My mouth drops open in awe at the realization.

"Adrian... is an angel.

"You're an angel," I tell him, my hands going to his face, trying to feel him for the last time, even if it's under psychedelic influence.

"You have wings." I point to the white, almost immaterial contour on his back.

"B? What's wrong with you?" His voice is worried as he furrows his brows.

"I'm talking with an angel," I keep on saying.

I jump on him and hug him to my chest, mumbling, "My angel."

That's the last thing I remember.

I stretch a little and groan aloud. What is this hangover? I swear I've never felt so ill from alcohol in my life. But then I suddenly remember Nikolai's tablet.

Shit... And then more memories come flooding. And with them come the tears.

Fuck! Fuck! Fuck!

My hands clench around the sheets on the bed, and I try to take a deep breath. When I do, I scrunch my nose, smelling food. Food? I don't have any food in my apartment.

My eyes snap open, and I jump out of bed. What if someone had come inside while I was out of it? I take the gun I always have hidden under my pillow and go towards the kitchen. Inside, I spot something that makes me simply drop my weapon.

Am I still hallucinating?

Adrian is in *my* kitchen, wearing an apron and making pancakes.

"There you are." He turns and gives me a smile. Mally circles his legs, elegantly licking her paws and purring against him.

I'm in motion before I can even think about it, jumping on him and hugging him.

"You're not dead?" I ask, peppering kisses on his face.

"No," he says, amused. "*Theodore Hastings* is dead. Adrian Barnett is very much alive." It takes me a solid minute to process what he's saying. But when understanding dawns on me, I push him off, and grabbing the fluffy pancakes off the table, I throw them at him.

"You made me believe you were dead, asshole?" I demand, and he crosses his arms.

"And you made me believe you were *just* a friend from work." He arches an eyebrow at me.

Okay, yeah, I did do that.

"When did you remember?"

"Not too long after you left," he admits, and I get even angrier.

"And you waited until now to show up?"

"See here, Miss, you were the one who left *me*," he says indignantly.

"Only because I thought you might never remember, and I wanted you to *never* remember certain things." I try to defend myself. I also have to add, "I do the only *not* selfish thing in my life, and you throw it in my face?"

Adrian chuckles. "Well, I think I like you better when you're selfish."

"Asshole," I mutter under my breath, but I can't help a little smile.

We sit, and he manages to salvage some pancakes.

"How did you remember?"

"A few hours after you left, I started getting flashes of memories. I needed some time to come to terms with what had happened."

"Especially with Jimenez and Marcel... I thought you were also trying to give me space. But when you failed to show up, day after day, I looked for you. Vlad was very forthcoming, for once."

"That traitor."

"I would have come sooner, but I needed some time to set up everything for Theodore Hastings' death. I was supposed to get here before you saw the news, but my flight had severe delays," he recounts.

"So now, you're just Adrian Barnett?"

"Yep, and all yours." He flutters his eyelashes at me the same way I used to do to him. "I'm unemployed now, though, so you'll have to support both of us. Think you can manage with a house-husband?"

"For you, I'll make an exception," I tease. "Besides, we need to stay here for a year until my contract ends."

"And then?"

"Wherever life takes us."

55

BIANCA

"How long have you been planning this for?" I ask Adrian as we step into a sumptuous ballroom. The orchestra is playing by the side, a beautiful rendition of Blue Danube.

There is no one else inside the room.

In the middle, there is a round table with two chairs waiting for us.

"A month?" He tips his lips up in a mischievous smile. "I've been counting down the days until your contract ran out—and until we got out of Russia." He feigns a shudder.

He's not the biggest fan of Russia, mostly because he's sick of hearing *Amerikanski*, followed by an interjection every time he interacted with a Russian. Oh, and the random American brands thrown at him.

The moment my contract ended, two days ago, he announced that he'd booked tickets for a vacation in Venice. I'd been surprised by his choice of location, but when he'd spun some romantic tales about gondolas and carnival masks and some other things I forget, I was convinced. Mostly about the romance aspect. I don't care about weird ass masks and boys on boats. I can drive my boat, thank you very much.

430

Adrian leads me to the table, pulling the chair for me like a gentleman—my gentleman. As he rounds the table to take his own seat, I let my eyes feast on him. He's wearing a blue velvet suit that complements his olive tone perfectly and accentuates his hazel eyes.

He's handsome—too handsome. Good thing there's no woman in that orchestra to see him since I would have had to escort her out—perhaps give her some drugs to wipe her memory. Actually, what if there are gay men in the orchestra and they're eating him up just as I am, imagining all sorts of lewd scenarios and undressing him with their eyes?

I snap my gaze towards the orchestra.

"All of you. Out."

The notes falter before the music stops a second later.

Adrian's eyes widen in shock and I can tell he's about to make some excuses for me. But I won't have it.

Only I am allowed to have lustful thoughts about my husband. No one else. And yes, he is my husband again, so I have legal claim over him once more.

"Don't make me repeat myself," I say, pulling on my dress to reveal the guns strapped to my thigh. This might be a fancy ballroom, but danger has a way of following me everywhere.

They finally rise from their seats and scurry out of the room.

"B..."

"Now." I smile and sit down. "Where were we?"

"Why did you do that?" He frowns. "Do you know how hard it was to find an all-gay orchestra so I wouldn't think about murdering them the entire night for staring at you?"

I blink. Then narrow my eyes.

I was right. We spent moments in here and they ogled him.

Unacceptable.

"And because of that, they could ogle you. Now I fixed it. You are welcome." I nod at him.

He frowns.

"Welcome? He raises a brow.

"That I am the only one who will ogle you now." I wink at him. "And I forgive you."

He frowns again.

"You forgive me. For?"

Why is he so slow tonight? Never mind, I'll forgive him for that, too.

"For the oversight. It seems we had the same idea about no ogling."

His lips slowly tip up until he gives me such a radiant smile I find myself audibly sighing.

I've been doing this a lot lately. Sighing. But I guess I have had a lot of things to sigh about. Adrian wasn't kidding about the romanticism of Venice. But that is odd too since I've never been a romantic before.

Perhaps it's the fact that I no longer have the stress of my job.

Yes, that must be it. It's also making me more murderous toward everyone who looks at Adrian, and that must be because I'm not killing enough people.

Makes sense.

A waiter comes to our table with a bottle of champagne and fills our glasses before starting us on appetizers.

I take a sip of the champagne and I immediately notice something off.

"This is non-alcoholic," I say. "Why?"

"Well—"

"I hope you're not worried about me. I haven't touched a single substance in over a year. A little alcohol won't do anything to me."

"It's not that. Actually—"

"I'm really fine, Adrian. I haven't even felt the compulsion to take anything. You don't need to worry about me," I continue.

He sighs, but his lips are curled up in a smile.

"You've been feeling a little tired lately, no?"

I frown. Where is he going with this?

"A little more than usual, but maybe it's that time of the month." I shrug. Though I haven't gotten my period yet. In fact... I don't remember the last time I did.

"You haven't gotten your period in almost three months, B," he comments.

I blink.

"You've kept track?"

"I *always* keep track."

"But why?"

"I suppose you can imagine why." He smiles.

"But that's impossible. I'm on birth control."

"Are you?" He raises a brow as he takes a sip of his champagne.

I stare at him as I try to make sense of his words.

"Yes, I am. You know I am." I pause. "There must be another explanation for this."

"Another explanation?"

"I'm not pregnant," I state. "I can't be pregnant. I'm on birth control," I repeat like a broken record.

"But what if you *might* be?"

"What are you trying to say?"

"You mentioned a while back that you were ready to start trying once your contract was over."

"Which is now. Today."

"Yes. That is correct."

"What are you *not* telling me, Adrian?" I narrow my eyes at him.

"I might have done something to your birth control?" He says innocently before he takes another sip to hide his grin.

"Y-you..." I stare at him. "*You* might have had something to do with my birth control? You?"

"It takes time to become fertile after you stop taking it." He shrugs.

I stare at him some more, somehow unable to believe what I'm hearing.

Adrian, *my* Adrian, messed with my birth control? This sweet man? The same Adrian who's always been nothing but gentle and cautious?

"Are you mad?" He asks after a moment.

"Mad? I'm fuming!" I tell him.

He appears stricken at my words.

"You... are?"

"You're telling me you messed with my birth control *on purpose* and that now I am pregnant?"

"Well, yes."

"You got me pregnant on purpose?"

"Yes."

"God damn it, Adrian!" I burst out.

"Now, B—"

"I can't believe it took you this long to get on my level. Really, I didn't think you'd *ever* do it."

"W-what?" He blinks in confusion.

I roll my eyes.

"Let's face it, if the roles were reversed, I would have knocked you up the first chance I got," I tell him matter-of-factly.

"You would have what?" He croaks.

"I would have put a baby in your belly the first time we slept together. Just to make sure you're mine. God, I can't believe it took you this long to do it. Man..." I shake my head as I wipe the moisture away from my eyes. "Well, better later than never. I'm proud of you."

"So just for the record. You are *not* mad?"

"I'm mad you waited this long to do it. Haven't I given you enough signs?"

"You...have?"

I shake my head. Men.

"Well, I am glad you finally decided to use a little trickery. Though is it really trickery if I wanted you to do it?" I muse aloud.

"You're strange." He chuckles.

"Says the man who messed with my birth control."

"Yeah, well, your brand of strangeness is contagious. Consider me infected."

"That is good." I nod. "But fair warning. I get the naming rights for my offspring."

"*Our* offspring," he corrects.

"You're lucky I love you. I don't usually like to share."

"I know." He smiles. "I am glad you've decided to share *our* offspring with me."

"It's going to be a *very* superior offspring, too. Why, with my good looks and your intellect, and of course, *my* brand of trickery, since yours is a little underdeveloped, it will be the best offspring ever!"

"Right. I'm happy you're taking the news in stride."

"It's going to be a girl," I state. "And she's going to be beautiful and smart and she's going to break a *lot* of hearts."

"I'm not sure I want her breaking hearts," he murmurs.

"So you'd rather have others break her heart?"

"Of course not. Can there be *no* breaking of hearts?"

"No. She's mine. Of course she'll break hearts. It's like imprinted in her DNA."

"And what hearts did you break, B?" His tone becomes serious.

"Oh, all types. You know..."

"No, I don't think I do. Who are we talking about here?"

"I don't know, all the heterosexual men who see me?"

His eyes darken.

"But then they see I am taken and wholeheartedly in love with my husband?"

He's still not smiling.

"And of course their hearts break because I am so unavailable I need to invent a new word to quantify my level of unavailability. So you see, our daughter will inherit that."

"And if it's a boy?"

"Doesn't matter." I wave my hand. "Same breaking of hearts."

"You have it all planned out," he mentioned, amused. His gaze is filled with love as he reaches across the table to grab my hand.

"Of course. In fact, it all works out. Think about it. Our kid will be breaking the hearts. You can break their legs if it's a male—I know you don't hit females. And I can break everything else. See? It's perfect!"

"Your logic is flawless as always, B," he murmurs seductively.

"I'm glad you think so. I've given it a lot of thought." I nod.

It was entirely unexpected to realize I might want to have a child. From the beginning, my fear stemmed from the fact that I wasn't sure whether I would be able to love my child as it deserved. But as I've thought about it more and more, I realized that there is no way I won't be able to love that child. It will be mine.

It will spend nine months in my body, it will feed through me, and it will have half my DNA. Of course, it helps that the other half is that of Adrian, the only other person in the world I can say I love.

"I have another surprise for you," Adrian mentions.

He removes an envelope from under the table and slides it toward me.

I take it and open it to see that it's a picture of a house, with an address underneath it.

"What's this?"

"That is our new country house in Scotland," he explains.

I narrow my eyes at him.

"This isn't a house, babe. It's a freaking mansion."

"Well. I might have gone a little overboard. It has twelve bedrooms. And a large basement that you can turn into a training ground. And expansive grounds so we can perhaps get Mally a companion—or more."

"This must have cost a fortune, though. Where did you get the money?"

"About that..." he trails off and scratches the back of his head. "Before Theodore Hastings died I liquidated all of the assets Jimenez left in his name. Vlad helped me move the funds around to different offshore accounts. I only recently got access to them since I wanted to make sure I covered my tracks first."

"You liquidated Jimenez's assets?" I repeat.

"Only the ones in my name."

"And how much are we talking about?"

"I've even set up a trust fund for our child and—"

"Adrian, how much?"

He smiles sheepishly.

"A couple hundred million."

I gawk at him.

"A couple hundred..."

"Well, almost three hundred with the interest."

I blink.

"You're telling me you're rich?"

He nods guilty.

"I'm sorry you won't be my sugar mamma anymore. It was nice while it lasted though."

We've been mostly living off my paycheck since he had nothing to his new name. I didn't mind it of course, even though things might have been a bit tighter than I am used to. But this?

He's a freaking multimillionaire!

"I really liked being your sugar mamma though," I grumble. "Though I suppose I can be your sugar baby now."

"Sugar baby?" He chuckles.

"Yup. I am waiting to be spoiled. I am almost a decade younger than you anyway. This works perfectly. Just so you know. I have a very thorough wish list, which I will send you. There are a few weapons in there that might be hard to procure, but I trust you."

"Why doesn't it surprise me that your wishlist is comprised of guns?"

"You bought a mansion with a large basement so I can do my target practice," I counter. "Great decision with the location, by the way. I do love a remote location so no one can bother us."

"I'm happy you approve. I thought you might like it."

I wave my hand at him.

"Enough of the house talk. Let's get back to the part where you're rich now."

"And?" He asks with a wicked gleam in his eyes as he leans back into his seat.

"Well, I suppose I should start practicing my sugar baby role then," I murmur as I get under the table and lay my head on his lap.

he watches me through hooded eyes, a smirk playing on his lips.

"Let's assess those skills then," he drawls as I unzip his pants and nuzzle my cheek against his erection before taking him inside my mouth.

I think I pass with flying colors.

EPILOGUE - BIANCA

EIGHTEEN YEARS LATER

"Slow down, B, you're going to kill both of us!" Adrain grits out as he holds tightly onto his seat.

I don't reply, merely focusing on the road and pushing on the gas pedal.

Thirty more minutes and we'll get there.

"B! You're not thinking straight!"

"I'll tell you who's not thinking straight. That Agosti little shit. How dare he enroll at the same university as Diana?"

"It's a university. Anyone is free to enroll." He rolls his eyes at me.

"Not *him*. Not after I told him I would put a bullet through his head if he came near her again."

"B, he's a good boy."

"He's *not* a boy, Adrian. He's a man. A twenty-two year old man who has designs on our daughter. I am not letting this slide."

"Diana is eighteen. She can date whoever she wants."

I glare at him.

"What?" I screech at him. "Instead of pulling out a shotgun you're encouraging this?" I ask in outrage.

"You know I'm not Enzo's biggest fan. But Luca is different.

He's always been the quiet and studious type. I don't see him trying to take advantage of Diana." He sighs.

"That's because you're too blind to see. It's clear as day and night that he's been harboring a crush on her for *years*. *Before* she was eighteen."

"And he's stayed away from her."

"Because I pulled a gun on him every single time I caught him near her. But he must have a death wish if he enrolled at the same university. There are *thousands* of universities in the world. Why did he have to enroll at Cambridge, too? Tell me you don't think this is a little *too* much of a coincidence."

"B," he groans. "So what are you going to do? March into the university and shoot him? Don't think I didn't see the artillery you packed in the trunk."

"Maybe," I grumble.

"You know. You might just ask Diana what she wants. She's old enough to decide for herself."

"No, no." I shake my head. "I don't care what she wants. No man is good enough for her. Especially that Agosti little shit."

"B, you're overreacting."

"No. I am not. I knew I shouldn't have let her go to university so far away from us. I should have kept her close," I mumble under my breath.

"You wouldn't have been able to stop her from living her life. You've already made sure that she never dated while she was at home. She needs to experience life like a normal teenager, not one who can assemble a gun in less than a minute."

"If only she'd use that gun to shoot any prick who tries to get close to her..."

"Bianca," Adrian groans.

"You're her father. You should be more strict with her. How come you're so lax about this? *You* should have been the one to drive over there and threaten the living shit out of that Agosti prick."

Adrian closes his eyes and takes a deep breath.

"Diana already has you breathing down her neck. She doesn't need another overbearing parent."

"Adrian! I am *not* overbearing."

"Oh, dear, I think you are way past overbearing. You might get both of us arrested if you keep this up."

"As long as I stop that little shit from going near my daughter."

He shakes his head at me.

I press on the gas pedal, moving faster towards Cambridge. I may be breaking a few speed limits, but my daughter is more important than a few tickets. Adrian can pay them, as usual.

When we finally reach the university, I drive around until I find Diana's building. I'll check on her first and then I'll go coerce someone from the registrar to give me all the information they have on Agosti. Yes. That is a good plan.

Parking near the entrance, I get out and open the trunk, grabbing a couple of guns and strapping them to my thigh.

Adrian comes behind me and wraps his coat around my shoulders.

"People will see," he whispers.

"See, this is why I love you," I murmur as I turn to give him a quick kiss on the lips. "You might disagree with my choices, but you're always supporting them."

"Don't remind me." He rolls his eyes, but a smile creeps on his face.

Now armed, I grab his hand and pull him toward the building.

When Diana told me she'd found a place, I, of course, found out everything about the location and made duplicates of all her keys. I haven't yet gotten to the point of installing cameras, but now that Agosti is sniffing around her again, I might have to.

We get past the doorman and we go to the elevator.

"I don't know what you think you're going to find, B. They likely haven't spoken in ages. I doubt she even knows he's studying here, too."

"You're far too optimistic, babe. Even if Diana doesn't know *now*, she will know soon enough. I have no doubt Agosti will try something."

"I truly don't understand what you have against that kid."

I suddenly turn to him and stare him in the eye.

"I don't like the way he looks at her."

"And that is?"

I take a deep breath.

"The way I used to look at you before you knew me. Intense. Calculating. He's waiting for the right moment, I know it. And he won't stop."

Adrian blinks. Then he releases a string of curses.

"Then I suppose we must make sure he understands she's off limits."

"I'm glad we're in agreement." I nod.

The elevator pings and we reach Diana's floor.

I march down the hallway with Adrian following behind. But as I get closer to her apartment, the worst of my fears start to materialize.

"Shhh," I whisper.

We both lean to listen at the door.

Moaning.

I hear moaning.

Both Adrian and I turn to look at each other, and for the first time, we're on the same page. He reaches for my thigh and grabs one of my pistols.

I unlock the door and we both burst inside, guns out.

She's on the floor, on her belly.

Naked.

A man is on top of her, pulling on her hair while he's fucking her from behind.

He has a buzzcut, three ear piercings and an eyebrow one. His entire body is covered in tattoos. But there's no mistaking the signature Agosti green eyes. He certainly doesn't look like the *quiet* and *studious* boy Adrian was talking about.

Oh sweet Jesus and mother of God, this is *not* what I wanted to see today.

"Diana!" Adrian thunders.

Both Diana and Luca startle. She wiggles from underneath him and puts her body in front of him to protect him.

Adrian squeezes his eyes shut.

"For fuck's sake, Diana! Put something on." He grits out.

Her eyes are wide with shock as she looks between her father and me.

Luca is the one to cover her with a sheet, all the while holding her tight.

"Luca, run!" She calls out.

He doesn't move.

"No, no. There's nowhere to run," I snicker.

At the same time, Luca grumbles, "I'm not going anywhere. I'm not afraid of them."

With how much smaller Diana is than him, I have quite the aim, so I don't think twice about pulling the trigger. But since I don't want to risk injuring my darling girl, I only get him in the shoulder.

"Mom! What the hell is wrong with you!" Diana cries out. "Luca, you need to run. Now. She *will* kill you."

"I will kill you first, damn it!" Adrian says, and though he's not the best shot, he fires the gun into his other shoulder.

Luca groans in pain. Diana's eyes are full of tears as she pleads with him to run away. He reluctantly agrees, and once more, Diana places himself in front of him to protect him.

Too bad there's nowhere to run. We're standing in the doorway.

Blood pours from his wounds, and I can see the signs of pain in his face. They move toward the back of the apartment. He leans in to whisper something in her ear, after which she nods.

I'm waiting for her to move again to get a better aim.

I can't say I've been left speechless too many times in my life. But this time might be one of them.

That crazy ass man doesn't try to run past us. No, he dives out the window.

On the sixth floor.

What the...

Adrian and I rush to the window to look for any signs of him, but there's none. No body on the pavement, nothing.

We can the surrounding area without luck.

Diana's put on a robe. His blood is still splattered all over her blonde hair and across her skin.

"You guys are insane, you know that? You could have hurt someone."

"You, young lady, are grounded!" I tell her firmly.

She shrugs.

"You don't seem too worried about your boyfriend," Adrian interjects.

"Why should I? He's fine. Though he could have done without those two bullet holes."

"What?" I gawk at her. Adrian too, is frozen in place, as speechless as I am.

"I'm late for class," she says as she heads into the other room to put on a pair of shorts and a shirt. "You can make yourselves comfortable in the spare bedroom. I'll be home later in the afternoon."

"Diana, we just shot your boyfriend. Twice," Adrian adds drily. "I thought we'd get some more... I don't know...tears?"

"He's not my boyfriend," she mentions with a roll of her eyes.

We both frown.

She's almost out the door when she waves a sparkly ring at us.

"He's my husband."

Oh, no, she didn't. That little....

"Will you, or should I make her a widow?" Adrian asks.

I nod at him, proud. There he is, finally asking the right questions.

THE END

For more dark romance check out **The Cute Psycho**, featuring Bianca's best friend Vlad!

MORE BY VERONICA LANCET

Morally Ambiguous Duet

The Cute Psycho

His Hell Girl

Standalones

Fairydale

Frivolous

Morally Corrupt

Marlowe & Minnie Trilogy

Mayhem & Minnie

Myths & Madness

Malice & Mischief

War of Sins Series

The Taste of Revenge

The Foiled Plan

The Counterfeit Lover

The Sins of Noelle

The Moral Dilemma